One Woman ... Two Months ...

Four Marriages

A rollicking romance with the craziest cast imaginable, from a one-legged man to a raucous rooster. Follow this eclectic ensemble to Hawaii, where Angelique, widowed on her wedding day, hopes to escape to paradise on her ill-fated honeymoon, only to be shadowed by almost everyone in the wedding party, most of whom want something from her: a share of her dead husband's money. Angelique slowly realizes the man she married wasn't the man she thought he was.

It's when Squeegie, her surprise 8-year-old stepdaughter, shows up at the resort with a senile grandmother in tow that Angelique has to face a devastating realization: Not only was her precious Lucas taken from her, but his fortune might belong to someone else, also.

The only person in the wedding party who seems to understand Angelique's plight is Houston. Angelique finds his shoulders broad enough to carry her grief, and he is attractive, too. The problem is, Houston is in a relationship with another man.

Or is he?

Nothing is as Angelique thinks it is, but one thing is certain. Love is waiting for her on her tropical island. The real question is, will she open her eyes before love boards a plane to disappear into the blue skies forever?

A Small Contingency In Paradise

Farley Dunn

THREE SKILLET

A SMALL CONTINGENCY IN PARADISE, Dunn, Farley L

First Edition

 THREE SKILLET

www.ThreeSkilletPublishing.com

Cover design by Farley L Dunn
Cover photograph by Diane E Dunn

v.3

ISBN 978-1-943189-09-0

CHAPTER 1

THE DAY HAD COME together perfectly, and nothing could mar Angelique Donetti's happiness.

The organist's flawlessly played notes resonated throughout the stone walls of the cathedral, her Uncle Barry was waiting to walk her down the aisle, and Lucas! Her charming fiancé Lucas Abercrombie was finally here to stay, his myriad business trips concluded just in time for their wedding vows to commence.

Even the blizzard from the previous day had the city more beautiful than it had ever looked before.

"Mumsy," Angelique whispered. "I feel Daddy watching over me. He's helped make this day so perfect in every way."

She stood in front of a floor-length mirror, beautiful in white, with a veil covering her dark hair. Her mother was at her shoulder.

"Je vous aime." Pinky Donetti, Angelique's mother, gave her beautiful daughter a kiss. "I do so love you, my sweets. This is a perfect day. Yours."

Angelique giggled. "Je vous aime? Shouldn't you say Je t'aime?"

"Sweetie, the Paris runways are on the other side of the world. It's the love that matters." Pinky pursed her lips as she adjusted the veil in her daughter's hair and draped it down her shoulders. "I still love my Emilio, but you should be glad for his insurance policy, my dear. Pinky, he always said to me, I want my Angelique to have the best. All this is your father around you, sweetheart. He can't be here, but his love is."

"Oh, Mummy!" Angelique hugged her mother's slender frame. "Sometimes I miss him so much, but today I just feel how much I loved him."

Her mother gently touched her arms and looked into her eyes. "Love him, daughter, not loved. As long as we remember him, he's still inside our hearts. Now, there's another man waiting outside, and he's not just in our hearts, is he?" She winked. "Be strong for the crowd out there. You were just a girl, but I've seen you walk the runways, and you have it in you. Your Uncle Barry and I will be your best cheering section." She reached under the veil and brushed the tips of her fingers along her daughter's cheek.

Angelique took a tissue from the table at her side, and she dabbed her eyes. Looking at her reflection in the mirror, she pulled a strand of hair from her cheek, then she touched her finger to her tongue to moisten it and dabbed at the corner of her mouth.

"No, you don't, girl." Her mother frowned in reproof, the expression barely making a crinkle in the perfection of her face. "I walked in front of those tungsten lights too many years to tolerate that. That lipstick might claim to be waterproof, but you keep that tongue off." Then she smiled and drew in a deep breath, letting it out in a slow release. "You are so beautiful, my wonderful daughter. No one would guess you're now twenty-nine. That Lucas Abercrombie could do worse." She sniffled and looked away.

"Tears, Mum? Don't forget that we're already legal." Angelique turned and placed her hand just under Pinky's chin.

"I remember, that silly trip to the courthouse just before Christmas, and it still breaks my heart that the justice of the peace saw you married before I did." Pinky dabbed at the corner of one eye with a tissue. "I can't believe I wasn't there with you. Oh, my little baby."

"It was tying up the trust fund, remember, for the movie Lucas is underwriting this summer. It was just a formality. Oh, Mumsy! This is my real day, and you've made it so special."

Pinky wriggled her fingers at her and reached for another tissue. She dabbed at her other eye, then she laughed, the shift in her features coming across as bright and charming.

"I just saw one of your old commercials on the television the other day. You remember the one where you were on the swing, and all the butterflies landed on your arms?" Pinky placed her hands under the veil to rest them at the base of her daughter's neck, once more stroking her fingers against the skin there. "After seeing that, I pulled out some of your old catwalk shots, and I laughed at the skinny fourteen-year-old with all those crazy hairstyles they made you wear."

Angelique smiled. "You've worn some strange get-ups, too. Remember that pink bubble-dress that everyone could see through?"

"Dear, your mum hasn't been on the runway in years. I really don't remember, anymore. Besides, today is about you. You have six bridesmaids all ready to charm your audience today, and I saw one or two of the groomsmen, too. Your Lucas knows how to pick the handsome ones."

"Fraternity chums, Mum. That's what's kept Lucas away so much the past year, that and his business interests. He's had to fly out to sort the latest wedding details." Over and over, but she didn't bring that up.

He'd been gone a lot, though, and it had bothered her. She'd met the best man, Houston Richemont, at his place right on the beach in L.A. However, as soon as she and Lucas had arrived, her fiancé had been summoned to San Francisco, leaving Houston to entertain her. Then, another man had demanded Houston's attention, and he'd disappeared, too. Left alone much of the weekend, seeing Lucas and their host only intermittently, she'd walked the beach for hours, wishing she'd never gone. Then, she'd been whisked back home in a wild whirlwind, hardly given the chance to interact with her wonderful fiancé.

"Fraternity chums, you say." Pinky smiled as she worked in a hairpin to secure the veil. "I should have been so lucky to be in the sorority next door."

Angelique frowned. "There's one I don't know, though. The fourth groomsman isn't from the fraternity. He's a last-minute replacement. Something about Lucas' friend going to Rio for Carnival. Ricky Rinaldo. I haven't met Ricky, yet. Mum, who would abandon a friend's wedding to run off to Brazil?"

She quipped, "Someone who really loves a party?" Then she laughed. "I'm so sorry. I've seen the replacement. I think you might have caught a glimpse of him yesterday here at the church. Rather rugged, but quite handsome in a craggy sort of way." Her eyes twinkled conspiratorially. "I've worked with a few men like that my day. Quite the attractor for a certain type of women."

"Not for me. I've got a man." Angelique held up her hand, moving her finger so her engagement ring caught the light.

"Still," Pinky smiled. "You have friends out there who don't. And he is handsome. Gator, I think. Yes, I clearly heard the minister ask if Gator Gallagher was here, and I saw the new man wave and call back in acknowledgement." She leaned in and whispered conspiratorially to her daughter, "Needed a bit of a shave at the groomsmen's special rehearsal early this morning, if I do say so."

"Early rehearsal?"

"The minister insisted he practice at least once, thank goodness."

Both women paused as they heard the organ music in the old building's walls shift in tempo

"The time, Mummy?" Angelique felt her voice tremble. As much as she adored Lucas, she felt as if she would soon be marrying someone she barely knew.

Her mother patted her on the shoulder and whispered words of encouragement to her. "Jitters, dear daughter. Every bride has them. I experienced my share. Today is perfect, one you'll remember for the rest of your life. Let's go enjoy it."

Angelique smiled, but that didn't stop the sudden dance of butterflies that filled her stomach. She remembered the feel of them on her arms—real ones, not computer generated illusions—and she liked them better on the outside than on the inside. But her mother was correct. Today was absolutely perfect, and she couldn't be happier.

Anyway, Lucas wouldn't be a stranger much longer. Another hour, and he would be all hers, forever and ever, until death did they part.

"Mum." She lifted her veil and gave her mother a kiss. "Let's go knock their socks off."

Her mother beamed. "It's just another walk down the runway, isn't it? Only this time, there's a prize at the end, and he's tall, handsome, and very charming. He's certainly charmed me." Pinky leaned in, sleek and polished in her haute couture, and her gleaming lips just brushed her daughter's cheek. "Now, let me say a prayer that you'll be as happy as I've always wanted you to be."

As her mother prayed, Angelique was chilled. She realized Lucas had also charmed her, but had he ever given her more? Oh, he had said he loved her, and many times, too. Surely his affection hadn't all been charm.

She shook her head to clear those thoughts away. Lucas loved her, there was a crowd of people out there to cheer them on, and tonight she would be Mrs. Lucas Abercrombie. Pinky was right. Pre-wedding jitters, that was all. After all, today had come together perfectly, and nothing could mar her happiness.

"UNCLE, AM I MAKING a mistake?" Angelique stood at his side. She remembered a comment she had overheard Lucas make to Houston before running off to San Francisco. *When I pull this off, they can't keep the trust fund from me.* Now it seemed odd. She didn't know what made her recall it.

Uncle Barry wrapped his arm through his niece's, and his round face smiled. "Sweet Pea, you're doing fine. Just hold your head high, and the whole crowd will cheer for you. Remember, this is the finest fashion show in the world, and you're the star." He lifted her veil to kiss her cheek. "Lucas is a lucky man. If I were thirty years younger—"

"And not my uncle." She grinned. She had heard this before.

"—and not your uncle, I'd be standing up there waiting for some old fogey to bring my vision of a bride down that aisle to me. If his heart doesn't do double time, then he's not the man we all hope he is." He winked.

"He is, Uncle. He's the man all of you hope he is. I know." Hoped, anyway. He would be. She loved him, and that was all she needed.

He frowned. "He hasn't, you know, I mean, you two haven't . . ."

She laughed, and as the auditorium doors began to open, she whispered, "He's been too much of a gentleman, Uncle. Just kiss. That's all we've done." He'd been gone so much there hadn't been much of an opportunity, even if she had been so inclined. During that trip to California, even during the nights he'd often been away from the house until nearly sunup. No, there'd been no opportunity, even though she'd not minded waiting.

She was giddy about tonight, though. They'd be in New York for the rest of the week at The St. Regis, and then they were off to Maui for six weeks. It was only recently he had told her his reason for waiting a week after the ceremony to go to Maui. He'd given an open invitation for his groomsmen to fly down on his meal ticket, and would Angelique like to ask her bridesmaids? He'd rented the entire floor at one of the resorts on the island, and there was room for all of them.

That was very generous, she'd told him, and she'd put aside her misgivings about having a crowd along. It would be a nice treat for the wedding party, although she knew most of her attendants would be back at work once the festivities were done. However, she'd assured him she would encourage them to tag along.

Stepping under the grand, vaulted ceiling as the wedding march reverberated throughout the structure, the rustle of people as they stood vied for control of the room. Then all was still except for the pulsing throb of the organ. Rose petals greeted Angelique's feet as whispered words assailed her ears.

"So pretty!" That was from a woman.

"Hubba!" A man, obviously.

She smiled at the masculine voice, taking the compliment as it was intended. There were many more, but they blended into the background, fading as she approached the front with her treasured uncle on her arm.

As the minister questioned her uncle about giving the bride, she let her eyes glance at her attendants, remembering Lucas' offer of six weeks in Maui. Trina Ridley was married with two children already. Angelique's twin cousins, Sara and Clara Riverton, were both at Yale. Tishawna Burton had to fly back to Nashville before dark. Her band was in the middle of a recording session. That left only Beckie Black and Heather Gray, and neither one had committed. They had been wild as Maine nor'easters back in college, though. With a sigh of relief, Angelique was pleased to see their hair was no longer its usual vibrant neon glow.

As her uncle called out his response to the minister's question, she glanced at the groomsmen. She actually had no idea who might be making the trip to Hawaii from Lucas' friends. Every one of them, for all she knew. None of his friends were married, unless that Gator Gallagher character was. She picked him out immediately. Now she remembered seeing him for a moment the previous day. He was rough, just like her mother had said, and he had needed a shave. However, that stubbled chin had added an alluring appeal to his craggy face. His jaw was smoothly clean now, though, and she was grateful for that.

Then there was Houston Richemont with his provocative humor and his dark good looks. A race car driver, she'd learned during the visit to L.A. At his side, Jerrold Ritchey was in commercials. He looked like the grown-up version of a boy she'd acted with in a deodorant ad. His given name was even the same. She remembered because there had been a Geritol commercial filming next door, and the name had struck her as amusingly similar.

Treavor Daley at his side was a jock, Olympic swimming. He had that look. Bobby and Robby Lanier were Lucas' twin friends. They didn't do anything except shop as far as she knew.

They had an antiques place on Long Island and perhaps did a bit of decorating in the Hamptons.

Then there was Lucas standing before her, and she knew it was worth all the time he had been gone during the past year, the weeks he had spent with his friends from the old frat house making arrangements for them to be present today. They would be together forever now, bonded in holy matrimony, until death, and so on.

As she stepped before the minister, that was all she wanted, to be with Lucas for the rest of his life. *Till death do we part.* She smiled when the vows reached those words.

She meant it, too; and with all her heart, she was certain Lucas felt exactly the same way.

THE RECEPTION LINE WAS long, and Angelique was glad to see it at least half complete. The church had been packed, and everyone had decided to join them afterward. After a hug from her Great-Aunt Lucy, she held her hand out to the next person in line, a slender and shimmering . . . woman? only to have Lucas brush her aside.

"Cheeky! I hoped you'd come." His face lit up—really lit up—for the first time since the receiving line had started.

Angelique glanced at her husband's smile. She was glad to see it, too. After the ceremony, he'd seemed rather distracted, as if an onerous duty had been completed, and he could finally shift his attention elsewhere.

"Surely you didn't bring Squeegie." Lucas' smile fell away. When Cheeky shook her head, he brightened once again.

Before Angelique could introduce herself to their guest, Lucas laughed and wrapped his arms around the oddly dressed, slender shoulders—she was beginning to think she might be a man—and hugged her/him far longer than seemed appropriate. However, this could be a friend whom he hadn't seen in a very long time, so she was patient, even though the receiving line was still very long. When they released each other was when she was especially surprised. Lucas' eyes were red.

"Lucas," she smiled. "Introduce me to your friend."

His voice was broken with emotion when he spoke. "Cheeky, this is Angelique, my wife. Angelique, Cheeky Zimmerman." Then he looked away, sniffling.

"I'm very pleased to meet you, Cheeky." Glancing at Lucas, she was puzzled, but she remembered her own twisted emotions from earlier. He could be having a few of his own. "Cheeky, Lucas mentioned someone named . . . Squeegie?"

The slender woman/man tore his eyes from Lucas for the first time to glance at her. "Our . . . I mean, my daughter. Lucas . . . knows her." She/he smiled, but it crumbled quickly. "She had . . . um . . . school and couldn't come."

She watched this . . . man? . . . and tried not to smile too broadly. His long, blonde hair was swept back at the temples, and he . . . or she . . . moved with a silkiness that was suggestive of a female impersonator. His suit, a shimmering gold lamé shot through with red threads over cream silk trousers, was of good quality, although he seemed ill-at-ease wearing it. His hands never stopped fluttering at his chest.

"Your . . . spouse . . . must be very sweet to keep her so that you could come. That is very kind of him, er, her." She grimaced at her slip.

His eyes flicked from Lucas' face to hers just for a moment, and his hands flew open. "No, no. There is no spouse . . . not anymore. My . . . significant other has abandoned me for a woman." His eyes narrowed for a moment at Lucas. "Poor Squeegie is with her granny."

"Granny?" Lucas stepped forward as if pulled by a hidden and very taut string. "Cheeky, you didn't leave my . . . our . . . er, your daughter with Granny Swell. Tell me not."

Cheeky puffed up then, and he put his hand on his hip, looking away, apparently irritated. His voice took a new, rather petulant tone. "You want her, friend, I'll send her to you. I still need the loft kept up, though. I have to paint. In fact, I'd go to Rio in a heartbeat if I didn't have your . . . um, my daughter to watch over . . . and that Granny Swell." He made a pouty face. "Then I'd be with Ricky. He's already there, you know. He told me I could come if I didn't have Granny Swell. He only wants Squeegie."

Angelique was now confused—and concerned—about the possessives these two men were bantering about when claiming this daughter. Lucas had never mentioned a child, and surely this man, this Cheeky, was not a woman impersonating a man, not at hers and Lucas' wedding.

Before she could ask any questions, Lucas interjected forcefully, "Rio? With Ricky? You wouldn't dare take my Squeegie there!"

"Try me, buster! Two can play at this game. All I have to do is figure out something to do with that Granny Swell." Cheeky grinned maliciously and began to walk off.

Lucas hissed after him, taking a step forward, "You know why I had to do this." The departing man simply wriggled his fingers at him over his shoulder.

Grabbing her husband's arm to pull him back beside her, Angelique whispered to him, "Lucas, I don't know what's going on, but it can wait, can't it? This is our reception, and the line's backed up. That awful man's gone, now. He *is* a man, I take it."

With a snort, he stepped back into line, clearly perturbed by the odd man-woman. "Yes, he's a man, after a manner of speaking."

Angelique put a smile on her face to greet those who pressed down the line, and she nudged Lucas to do the same. In between guests, she whispered, "Bad blood?" When he didn't respond, she insisted, "Lucas? What's going on?"

"I did something very cruel to him, but it was necessary. He can't forgive me, even though I promised to make it up to him." He forced a smile as an older woman came up to him. "Auntie Rubie."

"Luke, I'm so proud of you." Her voice was raspy, and she spoke much louder than necessary. "You finally grew up and got you a girl." Then she leaned in to Angelique. "You keep him on the straight and narrow, girl. Get it? Straight and narrow." Leaning further in to give her an unexpected kiss on the cheek, the old woman chuckled and waddled away.

"Lucas?" The line was finally thinning, and it was Angelique's opportunity to question the old woman's odd greeting.

He sighed. "She's never gotten my name right, even when I was a kid."

"That's not what I meant. Got you a girl? Straight and narrow? This day was perfect, my dream wedding day, Lucas. Now, with all these people . . . ."

However, he turned and caught sight of Cheeky. He was on the far side of the room holding a glass of champagne in each hand. Lucas sighed before he took Angelique's arm and gave a tired smile. "Bad seeds. That's all it is. Every family has a few. You're just meeting all mine at once."

"Cheeky? That man seemed rather . . . intimate."

He licked his lips, and his eyes looked everywhere except at his bride's face. "Cheeky has a . . . crush on me, or he used to, anyway. We were very close, and then life changed. He won't accept that, and he won't turn loose. He'll be gone tomorrow."

She smiled, touched by her husband's sudden tender bumbling in the light of this silly crush this other man had once had on him. "To Brazil?"

He closed his eyes for a moment, and when he opened

them, they were red and glistening with moisture. "God, I hope not," he mumbled. Just then a redheaded man with a skinny doppelganger nearly his height stepped up.

"Lucas! You pulled it off. I'm proud of you, man. You've not seen my son since the divorce." Then he turned to Angelique. "What a beautiful bride you are! Too bad Lucas snagged you. By the way, the 'hubba' was mine." He laughed at his revelation. "Angelique, meet my son, Buzz. He's thirteen going on twenty, except most of it's in height. Skinny height."

"Dad!" His son groaned. Then he reached a hand to Angelique, his face brightening. "Ever been hang gliding?" He waited with an expectant smile.

Angelique glanced at Lucas, who seemed very preoccupied, and then back at the red-haired duo in front of her. "Hang gliding?"

The father piped up, glancing at his son and back to her. "Just go sometime, before this bozo you've married leaves you a stranded society matron. By the way, Lucas seems to have zoned out, so I'll introduce myself. I'm Riley. We met briefly in L.A., but you obviously don't remember. I monopolized Houston's time that weekend. Family issues. My wife—ex-wife, now—said I loved him more than her, and it was true." He laughed, glancing between Lucas and Angelique. "What can I say? I left my wife for another man."

His son grinned. "For Uncle Houston, you mean. Besides, Mom left us."

Riley slapped his son on the shoulder. "You can call him Uncle all you want, but you know Houston is really your second father."

"I know," the boy laughed. "Dad One, and Dad Two."

Riley whispered to Angelique, "Houston and I are both raising this boy, have been ever since he was a baby. I'm better off without the wife, not to impugn your new marriage."

19

Lucas growled, "Move on, Riley. Tell Houston Cheeky's here—and he left Squeegie with Granny Swell."

"Granny Swell?" It seemed Riley knew exactly who Lucas meant. "Has anyone called up there to check on her?"

Buzz's face brightened. "I'll do it, Dad One. I'll call to check. I'll tell Uncle Houston, too." He turned in that quick way overly mature thirteen-year-olds move, calling to the other side of the room, "Dad Two! Houston, come in! It's Buzz calling. Acknowledge!"

His father slapped him on the shoulder. "Just go over there, Buzz. You're not an astronaut."

"And Dad Two's not a city? C'mon, Dad One." The boy laughed and ran towards his Uncle Houston.

Angelique smiled brightly, her head starting to spin. Was everyone in Lucas' circle, both family and friends, a bad seed? Did he have any good seeds growing around him? Now all she needed to do was meet Gator to find that he had one leg, because an alligator had chewed it off.

However, she had to admit her family wasn't perfect, either. Neither were her friends. Her mother had been a runway model, and everyone knew how bad their lives were. Her father was dead, and her closest relatives other than her mother and her uncle were her two cousins at Yale—on academic scholarships, for goodness sakes—and one great aunt. Her best friend had two kids who drove Angelique crazy, and Beckie and Heather—why, Angelique wasn't sure she even knew them anymore. Her half of the family was every bit as crazy as Lucas'.

That's what had him disgruntled, rolling his eyes, and acting distant to her, she was sure. What they really needed was a week alone together. Then everything would be fine. They could really get to know each other, and they would find that with all the distractions of life out of the way, they were perfect for each other, indeed, just as she had known they were all along.

CHAPTER 2

ANGELIQUE turned at a touch, and there was her mother, red-eyed. She pulled her into a quick hug. "I love you, Mum."

"You'll always be my baby. You know that." Pinky brushed her daughter's face, and she kissed her on the cheek. "You have your father's cheekbones. Have I ever told you that?"

Angelique pressed her mother's hand to her face as she smiled. "Only a hundred times, Mummy, and I love it each time. How else am I like him?"

Pinky brushed the softness of her daughter's face with the backs of her fingers as the sounds of the wedding party swirled around them. "Baby, everything you do is just like him. He loved you so much, and when he left, he was still here all because I had you. I want you to have a good life, sweetie, just like we had." She looked away, her eyes red with emotion.

"Mum, I'm not going away forever. I'll be in town this week, still, and then it's just Maui for six weeks."

"You'll understand, someday. It's not how far you go. It's

the turning loose that's hard. Quickly, now. Everyone's lined up. It's cold outside, so you be sure to bundle up. It might be warm in that limousine, but the run to it will give you frostbite. Baby, your mother loves you, and you make that Lucas treat you right."

She laughed. "I will, Mumsy. You know that. Lucas and I haven't had much time together the past year, but things will change now. Till death, you know. Richer and poorer, and all those promises we made." She held up her ring and flashed the diamond. "I definitely like the richer part."

Her mother pushed on her daughter's shoulder. "Go, Angelique. Throw your bouquet to a lucky girl, and enjoy your new husband. Love you, sweetie."

Angelique grabbed her mother's hand and squeezed it with a laugh, and she ran to her bridesmaids and the coat they were holding open for her.

"Thank you, all, for being here for me. I would tell you that you can shorten your dresses and wear them again, but I know better. Trina, give your two little ones a hug for me, and give Paul a hug for yourself. He doesn't need one from me." A ripple of laughter ran through the group. "Sara and Clara, make your scholarships pay off with a couple of 4.0 averages, and Tishawna, I want to hear you on the radio soon. Good luck."

She turned to the last two and gave them a special hug. "Beckie and Heather, I hope you can arrange to come to Maui. If you can't stay the entire time, at least for a week or two. Lucas has everything covered, and the rooms will sit empty if you're not there. Try, please?"

"We will, just for you," they responded as one.

The six friends wrapped Angelique snugly in their arms, and Trina handed her the bouquet. "Tishawna needs it," she whispered. "We're standing back to let her catch it. Aim well, girl." She laughed a low and luxurious burble as she backed away.

"Let me get Lucas." Angelique held up one finger and laughed as she moved his direction.

Lucas was surrounded by his buddies, and Angelique was surprised to see one man with his arms wrapped around her husband. As she tapped Lucas' shoulder and he turned, she noticed Cheeky's lips brush her man's face. She felt a shiver run down her spine, and she knew she'd be glad to be away from this crowd. Maybe Cheeky would go to Rio for Carnival after all, and maybe he'd stay. She was glad Lucas didn't have a crush on him.

"Let's go, Lucas. The limo is waiting, and I'm ready to throw the bouquet." Leaning in closer, she slipped her hand inside his coat, feeling the welcome warmth of his skin bleeding through his shirt. "I want you all to myself for a change."

He smiled, but it faded quickly. "These are my very best friends, Angelique. I was just saying farewell." Then he brightened, his change in demeanor sudden and obvious, as he put his arm around her. "You know you're married to a very rich man. Well, six months from that day at the Justice of the Peace, but technically we've fulfilled the terms of the trust fund." He laughed brightly. "How exciting is that?"

"I don't care about the trust fund, Lucas. I care about you. You spend it all." And she didn't care, really. She'd married him for love.

As they walked towards the door, he whispered in her ear, "Start caring. They wrapped great-grandmother's cash in rules and regulations, just hoping I'd never get access. I proved them wrong. I've beaten them."

"Lucas! Why do you say that?"

"Now that we've had the religious ceremony, even if I die, the trustees can't regain control of the money." He chuckled, and it sounded vengeful.

She looked at him. "How horrible! I don't want to even think about that."

"You'd better." They stopped at the door, and he looked at her with a smirk.

"Why, Lucas?" She didn't like this line of talk, not on her wedding day.

"It would all go to you, and they know it. Just stick with me, Angelique. I'll make sure you're taken care of. Trust me. I'll make all this worth your while."

She didn't really understand what he was telling her, but it didn't matter. She had her column with *Fisherman's World* that forced her to publish under a male pseudonym. Heaven forbid a woman who didn't fish should publish in a man's outdoor magazine. Yes, it was okay that Lucas' trust fund had rules, and it was fine if she never saw any of the money. It was Lucas she loved, and she would take him even if he had no money.

"Throw it, Angelique!"

The cry roused, and she laughed, immediately swept into the spirit of the moment. The crowd waiting at the door had pulled on coats and scarves in anticipation. Hats were doffed by the men, with fur-rimmed collars warming the women, and laughter and catcalls good-naturedly filtered into the air.

"Who wants to get married next?" She laughed again when all the fingers pointed to Tishawna. "Get ready! Here it comes!"

She turned and flipped it over her shoulder to resounding cheers, and looking, she let out a screech of excitement to see it resting in Tishawna's hands. Running to her, she threw her hands around her friend and kissed her on the cheek.

"I hope someday you have as wonderful a day as I've had today. It's worth it. Take a chance on love. You won't regret it one moment."

Turning, she ran to the door, and grabbing Lucas' hand, she waved to the crowd. "I love you all," she called as loudly as she could. Then, as birdseed showered them, she pulled close to him, and the doors were flung wide.

It was bitterly cold outside, and a black limousine idled at the bottom of the steps. The wind was blustery, and dry snow from the previous day's storm whipped across the heavy, wet layer from the week before. It was beautiful, even if the buzzing of cable stays and lighting standards on the tops of nearby buildings occasionally shrieked to bone-jarring intensities. From time to time, the high-pitched sound of metal against metal squealed in protest, decrying the strain of two feet of snow on rooftop water tanks and storage structures. The streets had been plowed, though, and nothing had dirtied the snow. The rooflines were beautifully mounded with the heavy, wet froth, and a water tower on the building across the street looked like a giant snowman.

It was a wonderland.

With the wedding guests pushing them out the door, the music inside swelled into the street, and Angelique and Lucas ran to the car. As they approached, a liveried driver stepped out and deftly opened the door for them. Laughing, she fell on Lucas as they tumbled inside. As the car pulled slowly forward, he began to remove his coat, and she looked out the window to see her mother step from the door and wave. As she did, Pinky's slender hand reached to her face to wipe away tears.

"Lucas, stop the car. I must give my mother one last hug. Please." She turned to him and placed her hand on his chest once again, slipping it just inside his shirt. Feeling the warmth of his skin a second time, this time with nothing between her hand and his flesh, made her stomach tremble with desire, and she knew this man would be the light of her life. He could do nothing wrong. The very feel of his skin was perfection to her.

"Driver," he called. "Pull over, if you don't mind. My wife needs to exit the car for a moment."

"Thank you, Lucas. I'll be right back." She leaned to kiss him, and as she did, she ran her hand along the side of his neck, barely able to contain her longing for him. Pulling away, she felt the blast of cold as the driver opened the door. "I love you, Lucas."

He smiled at her sentiment. "Ditto, Angelique. Hurry. It's freezing with the door open."

As she stepped from the car, a terrific blast of wind surged through the city streets, whipping the snow violently, and causing the driver to stumble and nearly lose his footing. The cable stays overhead hummed with the force of the gale, and Angelique had to brace herself against the car door. A screech of metal far overhead preceded a series of gunshot-like popping sounds. Looking up, she could see nothing untoward, and she smiled at the driver as he closed the door behind her.

"Hurry back, miss. It's cold out here. You don't want to get chilled."

She held up her hand to show him her glittering diamond ring. "It's missus, now." Laughing, she ran across the street and up the steps toward her mother.

Pinky threw her hands around her daughter. "Sweetie, your husband. He needs you."

"Mummy, you were crying, and I couldn't resist." She brushed her mother's face with her hands. "One last hug before we go."

Then, before they could wrap their arms around each other, a metallic scream rent the day in two. In a slow motion cascade of snow, the water tower on the building opposite the cathedral tilted its burden of white frosting sideways, dumping it into the street directly onto the limousine. The driver took several quick steps backwards, brushing his coat off as yet another screech ripped the frigid air. Everyone looked up to the horrific vision of the water tower tilting, its movement barely perceptible, then leaning farther and farther, drawn downward by invisible fingers of gravity.

When Angelique realized it wasn't going to stop, she screamed and made as if to run toward the car. Before she reached the first step, the falling tower had hit the roof of the limousine, crushing the vehicle, while splitting the tumbled behemoth down the side, bleeding chunks of ice and water into the street.

The world stood frozen in silence except for Angelique's repeated screams. She collapsed on the steps, as several of the men in the wedding party crowded around the car to see if they could do anything.

When Pinky threw her arms around her daughter, Angelique fell against her, mumbling through her tears, "Oh, my precious Lucas! Till death do we part."

CHAPTER 3

ANGELIQUE RAN HER HANDS across the surface of Lucas' bronze urn. "I don't care about the money. I never did, never knew how much there was, really. I have a job, you know."

It had been five days, and she still could not believe this was her Lucas inside this container.

"The lawyers care," her Uncle Barry insisted. "Apparently, so does this Cheeky character. He, she, it, or whatever that person is seems to think he deserves some of what Lucas had. Do you have any idea what the connection is?" With a meaty hand, he reached to an open candy bowl for a toffee, and as he sat back in his chair and unwrapped it, he glanced at his sister with a scowl. "So, Pinky? Anything?"

"They were friends," Angelique shot out with more force than she might have intended under other circumstances. "They were friends with an old history, that's all."

With the monthly payments to Cheeky and the furnished

but unoccupied lofts that Lucas had maintained—the lawyers had revealed that and much more to her—she had seen vivid writing on the wall in the intimacy she had so casually brushed aside at the reception. She couldn't bear to think of it, though, and she would have no one impugn Lucas' character. She was still deeply in love with him, and especially in death, she wanted everyone else to believe in him just as she had . . . or rather did, she corrected herself with a twinge of guilt.

"Dear, Lucas isn't going anywhere. Come away from the urn." Pinky put her arm around her daughter's shoulder. She glanced at Barry and closed her eyes a moment before continuing. "Maui. Are you still going? You should, you know. Take your cousins. Beckie and Heather, too. You've been out of touch with those two for entirely too long. This is a good chance to get reacquainted. Go." She motioned with her hand to her brother for him to join in her encouragements.

"Yes, Maui." He stood and walked across the room. "The sea air, Angelique. Warmth. You need this, to be out of New York."

"People, Uncle Barry." Tears filled Angelique's eyes at the very thought of all the invitees who might be there. "I can't bear to be around people. I can't be cheerful and full of life. All I can do is wish each day to go away. I have no energy for anything else. Not even prayer." She had done that for days, prayed, and it hadn't helped.

"You let me worry about the prayers, and remember, these are not just people, sweetie." Pinky rubbed her daughter's arm. "These are your family and friends. They won't expect you to be full of life. They'll be good for you."

"Oh, Mum, it's not Beckie and Heather, or the twins. It's all the other people who'd be there. Am I supposed to hide away in the resort on our floor, never going outdoors? I can do that here."

Barry smiled, and new animation crept into his delivery. "I have very good news. The resort called to confirm yesterday. When I explained the situation, they generously offered you their mini-villas just up the coast from the main resort. Of course, they said the villas are much more expensive than the rooms Lucas had reserved, and they could only offer you eight in exchange. They did say two are suites with two bedrooms each, and while that's not quite the sixteen rooms you currently have in the resort proper, if you could make do, they'll be glad to set it up. It's very private, they say."

Angelique walked to the window and pulled the drapes aside. Hawaii. Maui. That was originally to have been hers and Lucas' time together, six weeks of bliss without his business interests or friends. She'd been disappointed when he told her about inviting the rest of the wedding party, but he was always so generous. How could she criticize him for what she considered a redeeming quality? So, she'd set that aside and known they'd still have plenty of private time. Now she was being asked to share even the time that was to have been hers and Lucas' alone, and to not even have her husband there with her.

She glanced at her mother. "Can I take Lucas with me? The urn, I mean? Will the airline let me fly with him?"

Her mother laughed nervously and cut her eyes to her brother. "Barry?"

"No, dear Angelique. Lucas must stay behind. I'm sorry."

Angelique turned back to the window and looked out at the remains of the snow that had toppled the water tower onto her limousine and the man she had married.

"Will you come visit him, Uncle Barry?"

He chuckled. "Every day. I'll dust him, too."

Her reply revealed a small portion of the unfairness she felt at her loss. "He doesn't need dusted, Uncle. However, if I do this, you must leave the heat on. Lucas must be warm. Will you leave the heat on every day?"

With a kiss to her temple, he patted his niece on the shoulder. "Dear, you can afford to pay to run the heat as much as you want. You are a very rich woman, now."

Tears began to run down her face once again. "I don't want to be rich, Uncle. I want Lucas." She did, too, but she also wanted him without Cheeky, all those fraternity brothers, and most certainly without that race car driver who seemed to be involved with a married man—well, a divorced one, now—and who had a son taller than she was.

"I know, baby." Pinky put her arms around both Barry and her daughter.

"Do I have to take Lucas' friends?"

"He did invite them," she pointed out. "However, without Lucas, they may decide to bail out."

Angelique carefully brushed accumulating moisture from the window glass. Then, with tentative bravado, she whispered, "I'm not certain what I want to do. Not yet, anyway, but I know I want to be away from the snow. Uncle, see who might go with me, and I'll decide then." She whipped around to face her mother and uncle, forcing herself to be bright and hopeful. "You two must go. Say you will. You are the ones I want with me."

Pinky brushed her daughter's face. "This is your trip, my sweets. Barry and I cannot resolve this for you. Stay here in New York if you must have us, but I feel you'd be better off if you went. Spend time with people your own age. Do this, no matter who goes."

They all turned as the door to the apartment burst open. In tumbled a scrambling madhouse of sacks and boxes. Angelique glanced at Pinky, who gave a wide-eyed shrug. Then, in the midst of the disarray appeared one pink head of hair and one yellow.

With wide eyes, Beckie and Heather looked at the three somber faces standing in front of the window. "Please tell us Hawaii is still on! We just put our hair back to its natural color, and all these swimsuits! Don't force us to take them back." They rushed over to grab Angelique's arms and pull her toward the bedroom. "We have one for you to try on, Angie, and we won't even tell you what all we found out about Lucas, or that shemale, Cheeky, if you don't want to know."

$\mathcal{A}$S THE VOICES FADED behind a quickly closing door, Pinky turned to wink at her brother. "Good idea, Barry. Getting those girls to help out was an astounding solution."

"Charm, Pinky. I have it, and you know it." Then he took her arm and held up a plastic card. "Dinner, sister? I have a rich niece who generously offered me this debit card. I guess now I'll have it for at least six more weeks. How does Bella Luna sound?"

"Deliciously expensive and far away. May I order wine?" She laughed, fluttering her fingers at her throat.

"Only the best, my sweet sister. Besides, your daughter has some packing to do. We can take as long as we like."

As they were closing the door to the apartment, they heard Angelique screech, "No! I will not wear hot pink!" Pinky and Barry laughed and let the door click shut behind them, confident that Angelique would be nicely distracted during the time they were gone.

Stepping into the silent street, Barry held a hand up and was gratified to see a car pull to a stop. He looked at Pinky. "Shall we, Sister?"

She laughed, tucking her hair behind one ear. "Of course, Brother."

Only the car's taillights were left to wink around a corner, and the street was silent once again.

TREAVOR DALEY, OLYMPIC competitor, leaped with abandon from the diving board and flayed the water in a tangle of flying limbs.

Jerrold Ritchey, aspiring actor, cringed.

When Treavor came to the top, he swam easily to the side to grin at his companion, calling out with a laugh, "That was a crazy landing! Get you wet, Jer?" When his friend snorted and shot him an insulting hand gesture, he laughed. "Get over it, Jer. You can't bring Lucas back. Besides, he only had eyes for Cheeky. You know that. You and Lucas were never going to be a thing. The only reason he spent time with you was for your screen creds."

"Stop it, Treavor. You were jealous even back in the frat house. You know how much I cared about Lucas. If he hadn't needed to fulfill the terms of that trust fund, he'd still be here today. I told you he was planning to underwrite me into a starring role on the big screen. I was going to be the next Tom Cruise." He paused, looking at the back of his nails, his eyes red, and his lips pursed. After a moment, he looked up brightly. "Well, perhaps Leonardo, or maybe even that guy from that werewolf movie."

"Idiot. That was a vampire movie. The guy just played a werewolf. How are you ever planning to make it big if you don't even know what Hollywood's about?"

Jerrold snorted, "I've been in Hollywood. Have you forgotten? I did that deodorant commercial."

"And a whole string of parts as uncredited extras." Treavor splashed water his direction, laughing. "I guess it's the dare of a straight player that challenges my libido. I was always attracted to Houston."

Jerrold laughed, and he threw himself back on his lounge chair. "Look at who's the idiot. Houston was never interested in any of us, not even Lucas. Not like that. He liked us because he enjoyed spending time with us, that's all." He laughed again, kicking his foot playfully at the man floating before him. "Even so, I guess I should have seen you had eyes for the only straight man in the house. No-o, I was always chasing you, just hoping that someday—"

Treavor tossed a handful of water at him and pushed away into the pool. "The trip to Maui is still on. I talked to Houston. He's still planning on going, and so are Robby and Bobby. I'm rooming with Houston, by the way, so don't you dare try to butt in."

"At least I don't have to imagine Lucas being in bed with that woman." Jerrold leaned his head back and closed his eyes, letting out a snort. "That was what hurt, you know. I could take him being with Cheeky, but not with a woman."

"You know he had to do it. He would have lost access to the trust fund if he hadn't married."

Jerrold waved the comment away, and then he sat up. "Room with me. I promise I'll stay on my side of the room. Just room with me, and I'll go. Please?"

Treavor snorted and sank beneath the water. When he came up, he was next to the diving board. He pulled himself out of the pool and stepped to the board. He called from his perch, "You'll go if we share, will you? Certain?" A grin tickled the corners of his mouth.

"Good as gold." Jerrold put his hand up in a two-fingered salute, switched to three, and then back to two. "Scout's honor, if you room with me."

"Cannonball!" Treavor sprang from the board and landed as close to Jerrold as he could. This jump his aim was better, and the water in the pool drenched his friend. When he came to the surface, the only thing he saw of Jerrold was a set of wet footprints leading to the exit door.

"GATOR, tell me about your name." Houston swirled the ginger ale in his tumbler before setting it on the counter.

Gator laughed. "My name? It's an old story from grade school." His drink was stronger than Houston's, and he took a sip before setting it down. "Nothing to do with the four-legged monster."

"So," Houston insisted, "I'm interested, and I've got time. By the way, how did you know Lucas? I can't place you in the old frat house."

"I wasn't. The minister and I went to divinity school together, until I dropped out." He laughed. "He told me the wedding party was getting six weeks in Maui, and it was one groomsman short. Was I interested? Well, I'm not stupid. Everything in the northern hemisphere's closed this time of year, so maybe I can climb Kilauea. It's not quite Everest, but if it's free, then I'm there."

"You're a mountain climber?" That interested Houston, as a man who liked adrenalin-laced sports.

He chuckled and picked up his drink. "I like to think so, even if I'm one leg short."

"One leg short, huh?" Houston laughed. "When I went into racing, an old girlfriend used to tell me I was one lobe short. So I guess that makes us even." He offered a hand to shake.

"Racing? As in horse?" Gator grabbed the proffered limb and gave it a single pump.

"Formula 1. Bahrain in March. Then Australia, Malaysia, China, and so on."

"Not Monaco? That's where I think of when someone mentions Formula 1."

"There, too. This year I think they've moved Monaco to late May, so yeah, it fits somewhere in the lineup. But first, I'm flying directly to Bahrain from Maui—after my six-week layover there, of course. You might want to come along. I'm pretty certain you'll find some mountains you can climb along the way."

"Maybe," and Gator grinned, his eyes focused on his drink. "All that distance between those mountains." He turned to Houston. "Choppers. That's my thing."

"Bikes?" Houston pictured extended chrome forks and fat, black tires.

"No. Helicopters." He chuckled. "She's pretty, you know."

Houston lifted an eyebrow.

"Her mother, too. I like fashion models. I understand her mother was quite famous in her day. You think the bride, you know, might hook up with one of the other guys?"

"Angelique?" Houston snorted. "You don't know the group, I guess. If you're going to be in Maui with us, I think you better think about rooming alone. They're all good men, and I couldn't ask for better friends, but they're, well, a bit open-minded."

"You think, we?" Gator motioned between them, obviously asking about rooming assignments.

Houston shook his head. "Sorry. My brother might come down. Of course he'll be with me. Otherwise, I'd be glad for the company."

"Your brother? Was he at the wedding?" Gator took a sip of his drink, then another longer one, setting the empty tumbler on the counter when he finished.

Houston laughed. "You must have seen him and his red-headed son. They look just alike." When Gator nodded that he had, Houston went on, "I'm hoping he can manage a week or two on the island before he's off again. His son will be staying with me. The kid wants to hang glide off your mountain—"

"My mountain?" The skeptical response cut Houston off.

"That one in Hawaii. Kill-a-way."

37

Gator laughed. "It's a volcano, Kilauea. I don't know how good it is for hang gliding, though."

Houston took a sip of his ginger ale, frowning. "That's not what I said? Kill-a-way? Anyway, about your name. I've got two days before I have to sit in a plane for twelve hours to the middle of the Pacific, so I've got time to listen, if you want to tell me the story."

Gator grinned and shook his head. "I haven't had to tell this in years, and it's almost embarrassing that it's not better." He took a big swig of his drink and motioned to the bartender for a refill.

"I like embarrassing stories," Houston encouraged. "Go ahead. It'll give us something to laugh about when we get to the island. Also, if you want, when you get finished, I'll tell you of the race in Singapore where I climbed out of my Formula 1 racer, and my pants stayed behind. I sure wish I hadn't worn red underwear that day."

Gator looked at him, and his eyes crinkled when he asked, "Your pants stayed behind?" Already his consonants had begun to slur.

"Let's just say it started in the middle of the night, and a very pretty girl was involved. When I woke up the next morning, my team was putting my helmet on my head, and the race was about to start."

Gator was laughing by the time the story was finished, and he could barely start his own. "I was a kid, and I'd never use a gate, just climb over the fence. My folks would always ask if I'd please use the gate . . . or was I just planning to climb the fence? Well, that slowly morphed to Gator. See? Gate or fence? Embarrassingly mundane."

Houston stood and smiled. "Okay, Gate-or-Fence, with that, I'm heading off to my room. Enjoy the rest of the evening."

Gator nodded once. When he nodded the second time, his

forehead hit the bar, and he was out. Houston chuckled and patted him on the shoulder.

As Houston walked away, it was Angelique he was thinking about. She had seemed awfully distraught for someone miraculously released from a marriage of convenience. Surely, Lucas must have told her something; she couldn't be the only one who didn't know.

There was one other thing. No one knew if Lucas made out a will before he died. His friends had depended on the man's generous handouts. As for the missing Ricky? He had once berated Lucas about his irresponsibility with his daughter, and the rift had driven them apart.

It was also late, and Gator was passed out at the bar. It was time for bed, and Houston knew right where his was. After all, the key to his room was in his pocket, right where it belonged.

CHAPTER 4

"HONEY PIE, PUT THE RED paint down. Daddy Cheeky needs to create today." Cheeky kept his voice bright, but his next words bled his anxiety. "I think I may need to actually sell one of these to pay the rent."

"Tell the paintings that, Daddy Cheeky. They need to know."

Cheeky pushed his blond hair from his temples, and he sighed dramatically into the room. Raising one hand, he called out into the canvas-filled studio, "Paintings, sell yourselves! The rent is due, and Daddy Cheeky and Squeegie need to eat. I command you!"

The little girl's hands clapped, and she shrieked her approval. "How funny, Daddy Cheeky!" She reached to Granny Swell to pat her pallid hands together. "Clap, Granny! Clap!"

"Clap?" The old woman's crinkled eyes brightened, although her voice was strained with age. "There's a party? Am I the guest of honor? Do I get a present?"

"Yes!" Squeegie cried. She took hold of a small canvas, and she handed it to the old woman. "It's your birthday, Granny Swell. Be happy!"

Cheeky lunged for the painting. "Not that one, girl! I just finished it. It's not dry."

However, before he could get to it, Granny had wiped her hand across it, smearing the oils. Then, laughing, she tried to lick the canvas, and instead, she decorated her hair and face with the brightly colored paints.

Squeegie cheered at the gaily hued results.

When Cheeky dropped to the floor in frustration and despair, putting his hands to his face, Squeegie came and put her arms around him.

"Daddy Cheeky, we have money. Daddy Lucas sent you a check just before you went to his wedding. I saw it, remember? You let me draw your name on the back."

He pushed her away petulantly. "It's the last one. Can't you see that? Daddy Lucas can't send us another one. We'll starve!"

"Why can't he? Daddy Lucas always has money." She reached inside her pocket and pulled out a small mouse. It struggled, squeaking numerous times.

"What's that?" Cheeky shrieked at the squirming creature, causing Granny to clutch the painting to her chest in alarm. "Drop it before it bites you!"

"Drop it? I just found it, and I love it very much. I'll feed it cheese every day for the rest of its life. Just like Granny Swell." She leaned her head forward and kissed the animal on the tip of its nose.

"Cheese?" Granny's voice brightened. "This doesn't taste good. I want cheese." A trembling hand lifted the canvas from her chest and held it out to Squeegie.

"Granny, you smeared it." The girl looked at the old woman reprovingly, forgetting her cheers from moments before. "You

41

made two white spots on it. You rubbed the paint all the way off."

Cheeky knitted his brow. "Let me see, girl. White spots?" He took the painting and turned it one way, and then the other. After a moment, he smiled, and he felt a rush of enthusiasm. "Wonderful! This is wonderful, Granny Swell." He stood and held out the canvas. "Squeegie, I shall call this masterpiece Mother's Milk. I must phone the gallery now. They've been pressuring me to finish something for months. Sell, I will tell them. They must sell it today. It is absolutely divine."

Granny giggled. "Please, Squeegie. I would like milk with my cheese. Thank you, dear."

Her adopted granddaughter laughed and hugged the old woman. "I love you, Granny. I'm so glad I found you under that bridge. I'll get you cheese."

"And milk?" The broken voice quavered with hope.

"And milk."

As he went in search of the phone, Cheeky called out, "What a genius idea! Once I sell this, Rio, here I come!" He stopped and called very loudly, looking around and letting his eyes search the ceiling. "Ricky! Wait on me, dear. I don't have Lucas, anymore. You're all I have to live for." He searched the ceiling a moment more, then he sniffled and wiped his eyes as he walked out the door, fingering the small glass vial he now carried everywhere in his pocket.

"DADDY CHEEKY WANTS to go to Rio." Squeegie smiled at the mouse. "Do you want to go to Rio?"

"Rio?" Granny sat up straight. She looked around as if she could see the fabled city on the bay right there beside her. "I always wanted to go to Rio. Samba, samba." She tried very diligently, although unsuccessfully, to snap her fingers.

"Granny Swell," Squeegie leaned to kiss her on her painted

nose, "I don't think he means to take us."

Her hands melted to her chest. "No? What will we do, Squeegie?"

"Live under a bridge!" The girl lifted her stray mouse high over her head and twirled around, bumping several canvasses and knocking one over. "That's right, little mouse, we'll live under a bridge." Then she brought it down to peer directly into its eyes. "You've been there before, and you survived just fine, didn't you? So did Granny. We'll be all right, even if Daddy Cheeky only loves us for Daddy Lucas' money."

When she slipped the mouse back into her pocket, she dragged one hand over her eyes, and she turned away so Granny Swell didn't have to see.

"OH, MUM. YOU KNOW Sara and Clara can't just leave school to gallivant off to the islands for six weeks. That scholarship at Yale is too important to them. Beckie and Heather will keep me in fine company." Angelique dropped her wad of tissues in the trash. "Besides, I'll have four of Lucas' friends with me. Maybe I can hook up with one of them, catch one on the rebound, so to speak. You've always said I'm quite beautiful. Surely one of them will want me."

"Angelique!" Her mother's rebuke was sharp. "That is so crude. At least that blond-headed man won't be there. I understand he went back to 'Frisco the day after the services. The audacity of that man, begging for some of your husband's ashes, and money, too. You should have never given him that vial."

"He wouldn't let me alone." She dropped into a chair, closing her eyes at the reminder of the intimacy she had witnessed between Lucas and Cheeky. "I just wanted him gone, Mumsy. He was begging, you remember."

"Well, dear, you are packed, and your Uncle Barry and I are very glad to see you're willing to take this trip in spite of all your troubles. A fresh place and friendly faces will do you well. You didn't take those swimsuits out again? You'll swim while you are there."

A deep breath and an even deeper sigh preceded Angelique's answer. "Mummy, those are not swimsuits. The best they can be called are stringsuits. They're more string than suit."

Pinky laughed. "I've been on the runway in less, my poor, depressed daughter. Besides, your villas are very private. The resort has said so. Now stand. The snow is gone, but it's still very chilly outside. You'll want your jacket on."

A beeping horn outside caught their attention, and glancing through the sheers, a yellow-painted cab could be seen maneuvering to the curb. The trunk popped open, and a man in a dark sports cap climbed out to wait.

"Go! Go!" Pinky cried. "I've got your extra case." Then, as they reached the car and the driver loaded the items into the back, she lovingly placed her China doll-perfect hands on either side of her daughter's face. "Sweetie, I cannot believe this has happened to you. I wanted you to be so happy, and you would have, too. Your life would have been perfect. Now you'll have to find that happiness all over again. You can do this, Angelique. Grieve, God, yes! Go down there and cry until your eyes burn. Then, please, for your mother, put on those stringsuits Beckie and Heather brought you, and frolic in the sun. I love you, my little sweet flower." She threw her arms around her daughter.

"I love you, too, Mummy. I don't know if I can frolic, but I'll give it my best." Then she laughed. "Beckie and Heather will probably have me hang gliding the first day. Will that do for a frolic?"

Her mother kissed her on the forehead. "Parasailing, girl. It's Hawaii." A chuckle accompanied the words. "Even if you

44

can hang glide there, you'll want to stick to parasailing. Trust me."

"Mum." Angelique brushed her mother's face with a smile. "You've become modern. You know parasailing."

"Go. We've said our prayers, and now you must go." Pinky pushed her daughter into the cab with a bright smile. "Maui awaits."

THE ISLAND DID, TOO, along with two girlfriends sporting neon-colored hair, a Formula 1 race car driver, a mountain climber, an Olympic hopeful, and one actor who had starred in a commercial with Angelique many years ago. Oh, a redheaded brother and his son would also be there, but that wouldn't surprise her too much. After all, the man had left his wife for the Formula 1 driver, and the boy called them both Dad.

The real surprise would be Cheeky, accompanied by a senile, homeless grandmother, and an eight-year-old girl. Also, no trip to Hawaii would be complete without a rooster. Yes, a Maui rooster would be there, too, and that would ice the cake.

"WHERE CAN SHE BE?" Jerrold listened to the sound of yet another departing jet as his paper ticket worried the pocket in his jacket. He was nervous about the upcoming trip, and he'd insisted on a printed version. All he could think about now was what might be in Lucas' will. If Angelique didn't show, then what was the point?

"Look. There she is." Treavor had on thin cotton chinos in spite of the cold New York January sparkling just outside. He crossed his legs and let one foot bounce in the air. His ankles were bare, and he wore tri-color boaters on his feet. "I wonder if she brought a copy of the will."

Jerrold patted his arm, causing his companion to frown. "I don't care if she has a copy. I just want to know if I'm in it."

"Don't touch the arm, Jer. You know better. People might see." He closed his eyes and gritted his teeth.

"I'm in the same boat, you might remember. It's hard when all the world has to think we're walking the straight and narrow. Houston over there is lucky with those race cars. How macho would that make someone?"

Treavor laughed and stood. "I might decide to get married someday. I could have a son—or a daughter. Think of it, me with a baby."

Jerrold kicked Treavor's shin with his foot. "You could not do that, and you know it. You're being ridiculous."

"Lucas did." Treavor narrowed his eyes at him. "That wild-child Squeegie. She's his."

"Surrogate mother, stupid. That's probably why she's like she is. Don't take a chance. Just room with me like you promised, okay? Please, Treavor?" Then he kicked his friend's leg once again with a sly grin.

"I thought, maybe with Houston—" It was a clear tease.

"Riley's rooming with Houston."

"Riley! He wasn't in the wedding party. Why would he be going?"

"Maui, stupid! His son, too. Besides, Houston's his brother. I'd room with Houston if he were my brother."

Treavor took a deep breath and let it out slowly. "The happy trio." Then he looked at his seatmate with a grin of undisguised anticipation. "I heard that Riley got divorced. Do you think, maybe—" There was one more quick jab to his leg. "What was that for, Jer?" He grimaced as he reached to rub his shin.

"You know better. Give it up, Treavor. You're with me this trip."

About that time, a whistle interrupted their discussion. When they turned, two very pretty women on the far side of the lounge area winked at them and motioned with their fingers. One touched her palm to her lips and blew the men a kiss.

Treavor turned to Jerrold and grinned. "Nice. I might just do that, get married after all. Come with me?" He jerked his head toward the women.

Jerrold sank farther into his seat. "Not a chance."

"Your loss," Treavor quipped. He straightened his collar and stepped away.

"You have a flight in one hour." The warning words shot after the departing man.

"Right, right," he called back.

Jerrold turned to a hand on his shoulder, and Houston sat beside him.

"Always picking up women, huh?" He laughed. "Treavor's always been the ladies' man."

"That's not who he likes, though. You know that, Houston." Jerrold leaned forward in his seat and rubbed his hands together, refusing to look at the Formula 1 driver.

Houston guffawed at his remark. "Still? I thought I was just a college fling."

"You didn't ever . . . did you?" He turned and caught the man's crystal blue eyes, locking his gaze there in disbelief. "Treavor keeps talking like you might—"

Houston's hand slapped the other man's shoulder hard, and Jerrold winced. "You know better, man. You guys are my friends, and I love you like brothers. However, I'm a skirt man. Just like any good family, I don't sleep with my brothers. Hanging out's good enough for me."

"Treavor wants to room with you in Maui. Did he tell you that?"

"No." He smiled. "I expected it, though. I wouldn't mind, either, except Riley is coming—"

"So Treavor said."

47

"—and he's bringing his boy. God, I love that boy."

"Dad Two, right?"

Houston grinned and slapped him on the shoulder again, more gently this time. "Treavor's good, you know." He pointed to where the man, tall, good-looking, and toned, was sandwiched between the two women from earlier. They were laughing, obviously enjoying his charm very much. Occasionally Treavor looked to see if he could catch Jerrold's eyes.

"At what?" He waved at his friend's grin.

"Timing. He can vamp it up with those two women, sign an autograph if they recognize him, and he can run away to board his flight, the perfect straight man. Those women are certainly convinced."

"He wants to get married."

"Like Lucas?" Houston raised his eyebrows. "Marriage can be very dangerous. Lucas found that out. I hope Treavor knows what he's doing."

Jerrold ran a hand through his hair. "I think he wants a kid."

"Tell him to adopt. In fact, we'll be there together for six weeks. I'll tell him myself . . . oh, I see Riley. Catch you on the plane, Jerrold. By the way, I'm looking forward to all of us being together again. This'll be like old times." Then he paused. "Except for Lucas, that is." His body was suddenly jarred with the impact of a red-haired boy crashing into him.

"Uncle Houston—Dad Two, I mean—I've missed you!" The tall boy looked like a slender, wiry man on the outside, but his actions said all kid inside. "I brought my harness."

Jerrold raised his eyebrows. "Harness?"

"Oh, hello, Uncle Jerrold."

"Uncle?"

Houston laughed. "Live with it, Jerrold. You haven't seen much of the kid, but he knows all of you by Uncle. Tell him about the harness, Buzz."

"Hang gliding. That's what I want to do, maybe wind-surfing, if I can. Can I, Dad Two? Please? Dad One says it's okay with him if you don't mind."

"My opinion counts? Why's your father letting me have a say?" Houston grinned, glancing at Jerrold and winking.

"In two weeks Dad has to be in South Africa for a conference."

"On what? He didn't say anything to me." Teasing, again.

"Nanoscale spin-wave buses as a mechanism for logic and data something or the other."

Houston groaned. "That's computer talk, right?"

"Yeah," the boy grinned. "Tiny computers, like you can't even see them. Hang gliders are better. Can I? Windsurf?"

"Let's go talk to your dad. See you, Jerrold." Houston turned to wave.

"Windsurfing, Uncle Jay." Buzz shot him a thumbs-up. "You don't want to miss it."

As they walked away, Jerrold mumbled to himself, "Uncle Jay? Uncle Jay?" Another hand slapped him on the shoulder, and he looked up.

"Uncle Jay?" Treavor dropped into the seat next to him. "The kid called you that?"

Jerrold slapped him beside the knee, and he made sure it was hard. "Don't you tell me not to touch, either. You deserved that. The kid also said we're both going windsurfing with him, Uncle Tee." He shot him a look of satisfaction. However, he was disappointed when the swimmer's face lit up.

"Uncle Tee? That's rich! I love it. And windsurfing? I always wanted to do that. Boy, I love that kid."

"You are a goof. So, what happened to your marriage prospects?"

"Already married." He grinned. "It was perfect. I can enjoy their company, and they don't expect anything more. Usually, anyway." He was interrupted by two brightly coiffed women talking very loudly as they surged into the lounge amidst a wave of unknown people arriving to board the flight. "Are those Angelique's friends?" Treavor pointed.

The women's arrival seemed to be the signal for everyone to gather together to enjoin their fellow passengers. Searching the crowded terminal, pink-haired Beckie called out in a high-pitched squeal, "Angelique? Is that you? Did you pack those string bikinis? We brought you some extras just in case. Do you want to see?"

In the crowd, an arm waved.

Beckie poked Heather, and her yellow-haired friend reached in Beckie's purse to thrust a dangling, vivid green wad of cloth and string into the air. Beckie called, "Do you like it, Angie?"

"I have a purple one just like it." Heather's lower-pitched voice purred, smooth and sultry next to Beckie's, but the excitement was the same. Then Heather shifted the green cloth, and a silver flask flashed into view. "Party!"

Together, they harmonized, "We're going to Hawaii!"

The remnants of the honeymoon party following the pair through the door included the mostly unknown and roguishly craggy Gator Gallagher. It was quickly agreed by the men that this might be quite a plane ride, indeed; they had twelve hours yet to fly, and that didn't include a California layover along the way.

CHAPTER 5

$\mathcal{A}$NGELIQUE RECLINED IN the airliner's expansive leather seat, while the real party went on several rows ahead. They were in the upper tier of the aircraft, with a lounge and a private bar. It seemed Lucas had booked this entire section of the cabin for the wedding party.

Pity it was half empty.

"Being in this section of the plane does give you special privileges, you know. The First Class of First Class."

She looked up to see the flight attendant sit on the arm of the empty seat just in front of her, and the trimly uniformed woman glanced around at the merrymaking.

"It all belongs to your party. Your drinks are included, also."

"Just ginger ale for me," Angelique murmured. "I'm not in a rush, though." The attendant was being so pleasant that it seemed a shame not to request something.

After a moment, the attendant ventured to observe, "You

seem very blue. Is something wrong?"

A yellow-haired Heather leaned in and giggled an answer to that question. "Her husband got killed by a frozen water tower. We're on the way to the honeymoon." Then her eyes widened, and she put her hand over her mouth. "Oh, that wasn't funny at all. I don't know why I'm laughing. I think I need another drink." She giggled again and wandered off down the aisle.

"That really happened?" When Angelique nodded, the attendant put her hand to her chin, leaving the tips of her fingers covering her mouth. "I'm so sorry about your husband." She reached out to touch Angelique's hand in sympathy, then with the polish of much practice at her job, she attempted to divert the conversation to a pleasanter topic. "The happy couple? The ones that got married, who are they?" Her eyes roved the merrymakers. Looking to Angelique, only seeing her distress grow more pronounced, she laughed. "Not you, surely."

Angelique nodded, her eyes burning once again, and she looked away. "On the day of the wedding."

"How horrible!" The attendant slid into the seat next to her. "When?"

"A week ago. His name was Lucas."

"Lucas?" The attendant frowned. Then her eyes opened wide. "Frequent flier Lucas? Abercrombie? Oh, my word!" She stood and turned away for a moment before looking back to her. "Killed by a water tower? He flew with us all the time."

Angelique nodded, surprised this woman knew him. "We were leaving the reception the day after last week's blizzard. He was in the limousine waiting for me, and the tower just fell off the building across the street and onto the car."

"How horrible! Did anyone see it happen?" The woman touched her fingers to her mouth again.

Angelique nodded, her eyes once more growing gritty. She rubbed along the bottom of one, not wishing to cry, not here in front of this woman.

"Not you? Don't tell me you actually had to see that."

Tears began to flow down Angelique's cheeks. From that point on, the overwhelming feeling of sorrow was unstoppable.

"You poor baby. Funny, I never thought of him as the marrying type." She looked at Angelique, handing her a tissue from a packet that seemed to come out of nowhere. "Don't get me wrong, Lucas was a charmer. Everyone loved him. And he never tried to hit on any of the female attendants. That was a relief. So many good-looking men do." She paused, and her eyes widened. "Although, now that I think of it, he did have one trip when his hotel was overbooked, and he had to stay the weekend with Frederick." She smiled. "Poor, poor Frederick."

"Who's Frederick?" Lucas had never mentioned a Frederick.

The attendant winked at her, somehow relieved. "Frederick's on our San Francisco run, and he's as sweet as they come, even if he is a bit, you know. Now it's clear all his fancy bragging the next week was just bravado. Ha!" She winked again. "Lucas was too the marrying type, no matter what Frederick said."

Angelique remembered Cheeky. This didn't seem amusing to her.

"You must be really special to have snagged Lucas. I so hate to hear this news." A hand waved for the flight attendant's attention several rows up. "Oh, there, I have someone to attend to. Will you be okay by yourself a bit? I'll bring your ginger ale in a moment. Will that be all right?"

Angelique nodded. "Certainly. Your waving hand needs you." She pointed to the man whose face once more needed a shave. He was stubbly again, and it seemed to be permanent this time.

The attendant touched her arm. "Thank you, dear. I'll be

right back with that drink." She smiled and walked off.

Angelique closed her eyes, and after a moment, she felt a cold glass against her forehead.

"For you," a deep voice intoned melodramatically. "To assuage your grief."

"What?" She looked up to see Houston standing over her. "The stewardess, um, flight attendant—" Flustered, her words escaped her.

"She wanted to bring this to you. I snatched it away. I've hardly spoken to you since the, um, incident, and I happened to notice you're the only sober member of this party, excluding the boy. He's thirteen and can't drink, or I suppose he'd be soused, too."

"Your son." She sat up, forcing a smile, glad for his company. This man was very good looking, even though he was clearly taken. It didn't matter, anyway. Men like him didn't bother with women, and even if he did, Lucas had just died. The stress of that alone was all she could handle, no matter how lonely she felt.

Company, though, she could use.

"In a manner of speaking," he responded, his voice pleasant and warm. "On this trip, anyway. Still, I'm proud to claim him. He's a good kid, even if he is a bit tall for his age. Maybe we can turn him into a basketball player. However, all he seems interested in are motorcycles and hang gliding. Well, windsurfing, too, now that we're on the way to Maui." He gently touched the arm of her seat, his hand not quite against hers. His gesture seemed casual and very unintentional. "This was thoughtful of Lucas to do this, by the way. It's great of you to carry out this last wish for all his friends to be together."

"Lucas was always so generous." She whispered her response as she looked at the seatback in front of her, uncomfortably aware of how soothing this man's voice sounded.

"Do you mind if I ask you a personal question? I won't if you'd rather not."

"Personal?" She looked at him. He even smelled good, and that seemed rather unfair in the light of being the only one on the flight who had bothered to speak more than a few words to her, other than the attendant. "Sure, go ahead. I can always refuse to answer."

He smiled. "You can at that. Actually, the question isn't mine. Some of the others, though, have some concerns." He lowered his voice, although no one seemed to be listening. "It's none of their business, really, but it might ease their minds. There's a rumor that you and Lucas had a civil ceremony previously."

She nodded. It wasn't something she saw any reason to hide. "Lucas insisted. He said there were legal issues he needed to get the lawyers on, transferring assets or something." She laughed roughly. "He was rather vague about it, hinting the lawyers might interrupt the honeymoon if the actual marriage was during the wedding ceremony. It seems the honeymoon got rather rudely interrupted, anyway."

"It does seem so." He paused for a minute, and then he softly interjected, "You act as if you really cared for Lucas."

Her pent up disappointments and frustrations hissed from her. "Act? You think I'm acting? We were getting married. I loved the man with all my heart, and now he's gone. I have nothing left." Her anger melted away as quickly as it had come, spent in her outburst. "I want him back."

"I spoke out of turn, and I apologize. Do you want me to leave?"

"No, please. Ask your question." Her eyes were on his hand. A fraction of an inch closer, and they'd be touching. She could feel the touch already. Of course she didn't want him to leave.

"Okay, here goes. I'm sure with the civil ceremony several weeks behind you, all the arrangements were in place. The money you were to receive, I mean."

She snorted. "I did okay." She emphasized the word okay, making it clear she didn't feel her husband's death was a fair trade in any way. "I'd rather have Lucas, though. I didn't know he had money when I met him, not real money. I make enough I could have supported us both if it had come down to it. The money was more important to him than it was to me." She remembered his comments at the reception, murmuring, "I think it was very important to Lucas." She continued louder, "The trust fund, you did know about it, didn't you?" He nodded. "I had no idea how much it was worth, really I didn't. He told me a bit about it after the ceremony that day, but even then I had no real concept of the size. Houston, I just miss him." She impulsively grabbed the hand at her side, pulling it to press it to her face. Under other circumstances, she would have never dreamed of such an act. However, this one night, she needed someone to touch, and this man was the only sober one on the airplane.

He was also the only one at her side.

IN THAT TOUCH, HOUSTON froze. Her sudden, unexpected action electrified his body's nerve endings, both in his brain as well as in other places he didn't dare let his thoughts dwell on just at that moment. After all, they were on an airplane with almost a dozen of the wedding party, and this woman was the widow of his very good friend. He was mortified.

However, behind that, something else hovered in his mind. It was highly unlikely this marriage would have ever been consummated. Lucas had known back in college he could get access to all the money on his twenty-first birthday if he had a family by then, and rather than get married, he had made a point to arrange for a surrogate mother.

For his child, Lucas had gone to some high-priced clinic, and in some private back room somewhere, the man had provided his share of the goods that had eventually gone to the surrogate mother. Nine months later, he'd received a call from his lawyers that his daughter was ready.

He'd done that at twenty, conveniently timing it so she'd be ready on his twenty-first birthday, just after graduation from college. However, to his dismay, even with DNA verification, the lawyers had conveniently discovered—after much diligent searching—that it wasn't just a family he needed. He had to be married. By then, he was stuck with the baby, and had farmed the child out to his elderly great-aunt, paying her to assume full legal custody. Had he loved her? Houston certainly thought so, at least after a fashion. He just hadn't been willing to raise her.

However, after the elderly relative's death three years before, Cheeky had "offered" to take the girl for a small "maintenance fee," enough to cover the monthly cost of an art studio, accepting full legal custody as part of the deal, although it was Ricky in Rio who had always loved the girl.

Then, greedy for greater access to his funds, Lucas had put the marriage gambit into motion. He had always liked to play games, but this time he'd played one too many, and the final one he'd lost.

Yet, it seemed this woman had lost something, too, even with all she had apparently gained.

A familiar voice jarred him back onto the airplane.

"Dad Two. Buzz calling Houston. How's the weather down there? Come on, Dad, we want you to tell that joke about the race car and the red underwear. Gator said you already told him earlier." The skinny boy brushed his hand over Houston's hair, rumpling it.

Houston turned and pulled his hand from Angelique's, strongly aware of just how attracted he'd been to her touch. His heart pounded in guilt over that—not desire, he told himself—as she smiled and lifted her hands to wipe her eyes once he backed away. He put his arm around his nephew's shoulders to steady his knees.

When he forced a laugh at the boy's description of the red underwear incident, it came out cracked and dry. "Son, that little thing with the girl and the underwear? Well, it was no joke. That was me, and it really happened." It was a forced admission; however, he would say anything if it took his mind off Angelique.

Buzz turned red, even under his freckles, and he ducked his head. "You mean you really, um, were with her, um, and you spent the night in your race car? You really raced the next day in red underwear?"

Houston pulled his arm up around the boy's neck, and he tucked him in close as they moved up the aisle. "Yes, yes, and yes, and for your information, you're thirteen. You keep your clothes on, young man. I was just showing her the car, it happened to be dark, and well, things happen sometimes."

"Was she pretty?" The boy's face had turned beet red.

Houston chuckled. "Very, Buzz. They didn't come any prettier."

"Even Angelique?" He ribbed his uncle with his elbow. "Gator said you needed to be distracted, so I should ask you about the girl and the red underwear. You think Angelique's pretty?"

"Very," he conceded. "However, that's between you and me."

𝒜NGELIQUE'S head was nestled into the coolness of a gel pillow, the partying having long quieted down. Sleep had taken its time coming, and her dreams had been fitful.

The flight attendant gently shook her arm. "Honey, the

plane's landing. Honey."

"Are we there?" She opened her eyes, only to find glimpses of early morning sky through the windows.

"Just about." She took the empty glass from the drink holder in the armrest. "Honey, I need you to fasten your seatbelt, all right? Try to come awake before we hit the runway. Ricardo up there, that's the pilot, well, he's pretty good, but sometimes he bounces a few times. I don't want you to be surprised." She smiled at her and moved on to the next group of travelers.

Looking out a window, Angelique could see dawn just breaking across the distant line of the ocean. Hawaii. Glancing around the cabin, she saw several of her party rousing, more than one obviously hung over. When Houston caught her eye, he grinned and nodded, flipping his thumb up. She smiled at him, remembering last night's conversation.

The boy was standing, his shirt and jeans rumpled where he'd slept in them. He turned to his father, Dad Two, and said something quick and pointed. Immediately, he burst into a laugh, hitting the back of the headrest in front of him with his hand as he fell into his own seat. Someone with bright pink hair in the seat he hit must have complained, because the boy sat back quickly, causing Houston to laugh.

That pink hair was Beckie's, Angelique knew.

She smiled when the attendant tried to wake the Olympic swimmer, Treavor. He was sprawled across two seats, and in one of the seats curled Jerrold from her deodorant commercial. He had his fingers in the swimmer's hair, and she laughed at that. It was one of the reasons she didn't drink. Strange things happened when too much alcohol entered a person's bloodstream. She hoped he wasn't too embarrassed when he woke.

Gator was chatting blearily with Beckie and Heather, his hands on their knees. Maybe Angelique did still know them pretty well. They didn't seem to have changed too much since college after all, and anyway, she could see the appeal in that man. His rugged good looks were only strengthened by a night of additional stubble.

She looked for Houston's significant other, finding him when the lavatory door opened, and he stepped out. In the odd light of the airplane cabin, she was intensely aware of just how much he and the boy looked alike. It seemed amusing for a child to have two parents and only resemble one. Rather, she corrected herself, how could he look identical to one and be so unlike the other? Then she shook her head, coming fully awake. No boy could really have two fathers and look like both. However, watching the tall, redheaded man exit the restroom made her aware of just how long she'd been sitting in her seat.

She motioned to the attendant. "Miss, do you think I have time to visit the lavatory?"

"It was occupied a moment ago. I can check for you. We have a few minutes, yet." She smiled and began to fold a blanket from one of the empty seats.

"Oh, I'm sure that one just down the aisle is vacant. That redheaded man, Riley, just came out of that one. On the left."

"Mr. Richemont? I haven't seen . . . oh, there he is. Yes." The attendant smiled brightly upon locating him.

"Not Houston, miss. I mean the father of the, er, the other father of the boy, the one that looks like him. He's the one I saw." She shook her head at her description. It had nothing to do with the restroom, anyway, so it didn't really matter.

The attendant laughed. "I understand your confusion. They're both named Richemont. The sign shows it's unoccupied. Hurry, though, dear. The seatbelt light will be on soon."

Snapping her belt loose, Angelique stepped to the lavatory and closed the door behind her. Even having known the situation between Houston and Riley, she'd been very attracted to the man who had come to her side the previous evening. Loneliness, perhaps, the conversation, or whether it had just been the proximity of a man, she didn't know. When Houston had stepped to her, he had felt like a man who enjoyed the company of a woman, but if he and Riley had actually taken the same last name, then there was no doubt of their involvement with each other. They were a family unit—of sorts—and that told her very clearly that even if he was friendly and seemed concerned about her troubles, it was no more than the warm concern of a considerate person, and she could never take it further.

For some odd reason, that made her cry, and she forgot all about the reason she had entered the lavatory. She leaned her head against the door and let the tears run down her face. She was truly alone on this trip to paradise, and at that exact moment, she wished she hadn't come.

"Dear God in Heaven," she prayed in a hushed whisper, her voice crushed and desperate. "I want to be home with Pinky and Uncle Barry. Oh, Mummy, I want you. I don't want to be here."

Then a knock came at the door, and the attendant called to her, "Honey? The sign just came on. Finish up so we can land."

She wiped her face, and she took a deep breath before splashing her hands in the sink and responding brightly, "Just a moment. I'm drying my hands."

"All right, honey." Then there was silence.

She was angry with herself as she exited back to her seat, though. She still needed to go, and now she'd have to wait until after the plane landed. Then, once she was seated, the feeling was even worse. The pilot did bounce the wheels a few times, and each time he did, she let out a little yelp of alarm. From that point on, getting off the airplane and finding a restroom was all she could think about, no matter how badly the previous week had gone. Sometimes, priorities had to come into play, and right then, finding a restroom was one of them.

"Dear God," she prayed in a slightly different vein, her

whisper so quiet she hoped no one else heard. "Just don't let me leak. I'll be nice to both the Richemonts, rather, all three of them, and I'll even frolic with Beckie and Heather on the beach. God, I'll even hang glide with the boy. Just don't let me leak."

Exiting, the others left her alone, perhaps thinking her tears were for Lucas. However, for once they would have been very wrong. The tears that pooled in her eyes as she exited the airplane were for the pressure she felt between her legs.

"Dear God, please," she moaned once again in desperation, moving gingerly into the terminal itself, and then her tears really began to roll.

CHAPTER 6

ANGELIQUE STEPPED INTO the warmth of the Hawaiian sun. At least she'd made it to the restroom, and there had been no accidents along the way. For that, she was grateful.

"Angie, you're ours." Beckie had already found an empty cab, and she pulled her friend into one of the three taking them to the resort. "You know how to be quiet so my head doesn't explode."

"I do, huh? You poor thing." She wasn't exactly filled with sympathy. Still, she knew the puddle jumper from the airport in Honolulu had been hard on all their hangovers, and all they wanted right now was silence.

"Heather," Beckie called. With that word, her face took on a pained expression. By a wave of her hand, she motioned her inside, and then she leaned her head back and closed her eyes. "Dear Father, Jesus, and Mary, I wish I'd had more self-control on that airplane."

Heather, her yellow hair visibly rumpled, fell into the seat beside them, trapping Angelique in the middle, and then she stiffened with a groan. "My head!"

A knock came on the window, and the two hung-over women jumped and grabbed with their hands for some sort of purchase. They found it just between them, and it was Angelique.

"Ouch," she cried. "Beckie! Heather! Let go of me! I'm not a handhold. Good heavens!"

Gator leaned into the opening, grinning. "Aha! I definitely want to ride in this car. May I join you, ladies?"

Angelique snorted. "Well, I have to get unencumbered, first. What about riding with Houston? You two seemed to be chumming up earlier." She put her friends' hands back in their respective owners' laps.

He sighed. "Riley and the boy. The three are riding together. Peas in a pod, so to speak."

She smiled. "I remember. The three Richemonts. They seem to be inseparable."

"You don't know the half of it, I'm afraid." He chuckled. "I was invited to room with Houston, if he was available, but his other half is here, so that cuts me out."

"Oh . . . if he was available." He picked up strange men—if he was available.

"Shh! Angelique! Our heads!" Beckie and Heather chimed in as one.

She frowned at them, continuing, "It's just as well Riley showed. It'll keep the man honest while here on the island. The third car? Who has it? Geritol?" She laughed, embarrassed at her slip. "I'm sorry. There's a story behind that. Jerrold, I mean, and his friend?"

"The swimmer? Yeah, Treavor, I believe. I'll pay for a fourth cab if you want, just for you and me . . . . " He motioned with his hand, pointing to her and then to himself. When she didn't respond, he continued, "More room for the hangovers. You'd really be doing the ladies a favor." He smiled in encouragement.

"Sure, let me climb out. Excuse me, Beckie, Heather. You can have this whole back seat." It was crowded in the cab, and his offer did make sense. They groaned, refusing to do more than simply sink farther into the seats, but once Gator had the door open, his helping hand made it easier.

"Ah," he said, winking. "You'll make for very good company. Look. Our car. The driver is holding it for me." He touched her elbow and motioned with his free hand.

She turned to see a black stretch limousine on the opposite side of the street. When she turned pale, he grabbed her arm to steady her.

"What is it?"

"Gator . . . I can't ride in that. The car Lucas was in . . . . You must understand. I'm so sorry."

"It's the color, isn't it?" He smiled. "Let me see if another color is available."

"No." She put her hand to her forehead and sighed, suddenly very tired, and wishing she hadn't said anything. "I can ride in a black car. I do have to deal with this, although I'd hoped I could put it off for another year—or two or three." She laughed weakly. "It's already been a week, though, and I am having better moments. Not better days, just better moments. I cringe to think what I'd be like if we'd already been on the honeymoon when this happened."

Or, she thought, if she hadn't seen Cheeky kissing on Lucas—and then Lucas hugging him back. Somehow, over the past week, that memory had become a thorn she hadn't been able to get out from under her skin.

Gator beamed with excitement. "Let me tell the guys in the last cab." He slapped the side of the limo, and almost dancing, he made his way with an awkward gait to the last car and back again.

"Now tell me," she quizzed after he returned. "You don't seem to have a hangover. I saw you pretty tipsy last night."

He stepped in after her and closed the door, a grin still on his face. "Hollow leg." He slapped his left knee. "I can drink 'til the cows come home, and I never get hung. Not for long, anyway. Lucky me."

"Lucky you, indeed. You must let me bill the car to the room, or villas, if you want me to be accurate." She leaned her head back and closed her eyes. "This is really wonderful, and the black isn't so bad. Thank you for offering to share."

"You're welcome. However, villas? I was certain I was told that an entire floor in the resort was reserved for the wedding party. That has changed?"

"Villas. We now have mini-villas farther up the coast. I think we have eight."

"Are we choosing our own, or are they assigned?"

"Your choice. My uncle set it up, so I don't dare ask you to trust my numbers, but most have one bedroom, and a couple have two. I think the three Richemonts should get one of the bigger units, otherwise the boy will be forced to toss and turn on a sofa sleeper. For six weeks? I don't think so. That leaves at least eight additional beds. We'll be fine, I think."

"Are you sharing?"

She frowned at the question. "Of course not. I'm here to be alone—or as alone as I can be with the whole wedding party following me down." She waved her hand at him. "Oh, don't mind me. My husband was killed, and now I'm here with his friends. What kind of honeymoon is that? I'll probably be crabby the entire time. Just ignore me."

"Lucas' friends? You've also got those two neon nymphs you were with, and I didn't know Lucas. I hardly think I count as one of his friends."

She opened her eyes and looked at him. "Why did you come, then?" She sighed, exasperated with her continued bumbling. "That sounded horrible. You are most welcome and will continue to be welcome at our little beachfront party. Now, why did you come if you didn't know him?"

"Blame Houston. He told me there was a mountain I could climb. I told him it was a volcano."

"On Maui? I've spent time here before, and I didn't know there was one that was climbable. You can hike all the ones on the island."

"Kilauea."

"That's on the Big Island, Hawaii. I remember enough of the topography to know that. You'll have to fly over. You can hike Kilauea, too, but it's not as picturesque as what you'll find on Maui. You might like that better. Mauna Kea's probably your best bet for steep grade." She paused for a moment, thinking of travel brochures she had once looked over on a previous visit. The name of one place had struck her as especially beautiful. "The Valley of the Kings. Try there."

"The Valley of the Kings?"

"Waipi'o Valley. It's very remote, so plan to take a four-wheel-drive. Bill the room for all your expenses. There's enough of my husband's money to pay for it—my money, I should say. Sorry. Still, bill the room, no matter what it costs."

"I'll do that. Thank you. Do you climb?"

"Only the stairs. All I want to do on this trip is mope, be miserable, and cry at least three times a day. I don't expect to be good company for anyone. Sorry."

She closed her eyes, and let the comfort of the limousine carry her in silence to her destination, grateful for Gator's thoughtful consideration.

"BOBBY! YOU HAVE TO come see!" Robby, one of the Lanier twins, stood on the front lanai of his mini-villa with binoculars to his face, looking at the road winding down the valley. The villas Uncle Barry had traded for were tucked into the side of a hill verdant with tropical greenery. The twins were lodged in Hydrangea Villa. Plantings kept the individual courtyards private, but the Laniers' balcony provided a sweeping view of the roofs of the different buildings and the road leading up to them. "It's a limo with a z-e-n-e. Black, and probably forty feet long. Houston, you think?" Four cars could be seen stirring up a dusty trail, with the black stretch last in line.

Bobby joined him. Both men were of medium height with sandy hair, and had dazzling green eyes that sparkled in aquiline features.

"Gator." Bobby ran a hand through his hair. "I saw him looking at Angelique. He had eyes for her, and what with poor, poor Lucas not even a week dead."

"Oh, B-Bob. You are so not good with numbers. Eight days. I counted each one. One for not making payroll. Two for the electric bill that Lucas would've paid. Three for new inventory we can no longer afford. Four for travel expenses. Do I need to go on? I've been overtaxed with stress for the entire week. Do you think Lucas left us any money?"

"Who knows? You think Angelique's interested? Already? Good God, Lucas just died." The cars were pulling up to a stone courtyard centered with a luxurious fountain.

"She didn't really marry him. She had to know it was all about the money." He patted his brother's cheek. "Grow up and smell the roses."

Pink-haired Beckie emerged from the first car, putting on great, round sunglasses that hid half her face. From the other side of the car, yellow-haired Heather climbed slowly out, her eyes already guarded by slits of jet-black glass. Both paused and looked around, and finally, Heather worked her fingers into her hair. When she drew them out, she let her forehead fall against the top of the cab and stood there in the brilliant, mid-morning sun.

Robby elbowed his brother and grinned.

When a skinny, redheaded boy leaped from the second cab and jumped into the air pumping his fist, his shout of triumph could be heard on the villa's balcony. Houston and Riley emerged more slowly, stretching and yawning. Riley slipped on trendy sunglasses, while his brother pulled out mirrored aviators.

Bobby grinned. "We might see some romance in Paradise after all." He ran his hands over his head as his brother chuckled. "If Treavor and Jerrold get out of that next car, that means Gator and Lucas' ex are already hooked up."

Just about then, Houston caught sight of the two men on the hillside. "Robbo! B-Bob! I didn't know you were here, already. How are the rooms?"

"Not too shabby." They yelled down, waving as the others turned to look up at them. "Angelique and Gator?"

Houston pointed to the limo and grinned. "Behind the tint."

Bobby rolled his eyes. He ribbed his brother. "Cha-cha, little bro. Romance might be happening tonight."

"Little bro, my foot." Robby grabbed his brother around the neck and began to rub his knuckles into the other man's sandy-haired scalp. "I'm the oldest, and you'd better not forget it."

"Get off, Robbo. I just had my hair done. Besides, you might be older, but I'm better looking." He pulled his head away and glared at him.

"Robby to you, B-Bob. Only Houston gets to call me Robbo."

He laughed. "Robbo. Robbo." Then he ducked into the villa

just as his brother lunged for him.

RILEY CALLED TO HOUSTON over the top of the cab, pointing up the hill, "What was that about?"

He shook his head and chuckled. "Live with 'em in a frat house for a few years, and you quit asking. Just let it go, Riley. That's the only way to love 'em."

Buzz called loudly and with excitement, "Hang gliding, anyone? Please? Anyone?" He was looking around, nearly spinning in a circle.

From the next car, Jerrold and Treavor looked at each other in dread, while leaning against the first one, the girls just groaned.

Houston called to him, "Give us time, son. We're not even unpacked. I thought it was windsurfing, though."

Buzz piped up again, "Both, Dad Two. I want to do both." Excitement made his words ring.

"He's your boy, Houston," Riley called with a laugh, reaching into the cab for his bottle of water.

ANGELIQUE STEPPED FROM the limo, slipping her sunglasses to her face. As Riley's words rang out, her eyes found Houston. The picture was a classic scenario from *Fisherman's World*. Tall, handsome man casts fly. Foolish fish lets itself get hooked, except in this case, she was the fish.

She looked away, ashamed. Then, Riley's words sank in. The man's voice calling out to his . . . companion about their shared son was a knife driving deep into her devastated heart, and the words made her feel guilty and low. She had let herself be attracted to this man's significant other, when she had no right.

In spite of her unwelcome surge of guilt, deep down where she dared not look too closely, she knew what Lucas had done, and that she should have no compunctions at snatching up any man who crossed her path. She should be bold and brash, announcing to the world that she would not take life's thrashings without striking back, grabbing what she would, just as Lucas had been so cruelly taken from her.

Then her eyes shifted to the dark-haired man in the mirrored aviators, and she felt her spirits fall. He could never be what she needed him to be, but she was finding it strangely painful that such an amazing man had chosen to live his life with someone of his own gender.

Her eyes felt suddenly tight, and she knew she'd cry if she didn't get away quickly. She fumbled with her purse and for a tissue, hoping she didn't have to use it. She wouldn't, because she was determined not to cry. No one here would see her break.

A new determination rose in her. She would be bright and strong, and there would be no mourning in her, at least not that anyone would see. That man who loved another man would see that she didn't need him, even if he had crystal blue eyes, a musky smell, and the most soothing voice she'd ever heard. She'd cry her eyes out into her pillow every night for her lost Lucas, and she would refuse to think of that Cheeky person kissing her husband's face. Then she'd arise each morning and frolic, frolic, frolic for six whole weeks.

She turned from the crowd and stared out to the brilliant blue sea, refusing to let her eyes return to Houston. She hated auto racing, anyway. It was a stupid sport, and anyone who drove race cars wasn't someone she could love in any case. Hadn't she always said that?

Yet, even in the depths of her pain, she knew she had never said any such thing, and underneath her frustration, she knew how she really felt about that handsome man lying in another man's bed at night. It was unfair, unfair, unfair. That's why she

71

hated all race car drivers, and she would say that to anyone she knew.

Except Houston. She would never tell him that. It might bruise his feelings, and she could never do that, not even if he was the most awful man in the world.

CHAPTER 7

ANGELIQUE LOOKED AROUND her room, not seeing anything except for the crowd that had followed her inside. Only her well-bred manners kept her from telling them all to leave.

"You needn't stay in this villa alone. I could take the second bedroom right over here," Gator gracefully offered. "And it wouldn't be inappropriate. The bedroom doors have locks. I've checked, already."

Houston glanced at Riley and frowned. "We have two empty single villas still, don't we, Riley? Gator is certainly free to take one of those." He continued to ramble, turning to Angelique, "Riley and I appreciate you putting us in the other two bedroom villa. Apricot Villa." He chuckled at the name. "Buzz especially will appreciate the extra bedroom, I'm sure—"

Riley interjected, "He usually has a roll-away when we travel."

"He thinks he's getting too big to bunk with the men,"

Houston threw in, and looked knowingly at his brother.

"I snore," Riley laughed.

"And I'm such a light sleeper, I turn on a light and read for hours at night. Buzz hates to sleep in the room with either of us."

"Especially both of us at the same time. He always begs us to take separate rooms, and we never will. One room's enough to pay for, we tell him. Now, he's finally gotten his wish. He'll worship you, Angelique, the whole time he's here. When he drives you crazy with gratitude, feel free to beat him off with a stick."

She smiled, but she couldn't hold it, and she felt her expression crack. Houston's bantering explanations only reminded her how unavailable he was. Emotionally, she was drained dry as a crusty piece of old bread about to be crumbled and fed to the fishes.

Fishbait.

"Gator," and she turned to face him. "Bird-of-Paradise Villa is to be mine, alone. Please take one of the empty villas. I intend to write some while I'm here. I want to use the extra bedroom for my own purposes. I'm sure you won't mind." She hadn't intended to write, even though she had a laptop and a portable printer in her luggage, but now she guessed she would. Before the wedding, she had written her magazine column ahead for two months, but this would be a great opportunity to get a jumpstart on the next one. "I think I'll rest for a while. If you will excuse me." She flashed a quick smile and turned, finally able to give in to her utter exhaustion.

She walked by Houston on the way to her bedroom, and as she passed him, unable to resist, she casually placed her hand on the bare skin of his arm. "Thank you, Houston." She stepped away without waiting for a reply, closing her bedroom door after her.

HOUSTON STOOD FROZEN in his shoes. He couldn't have moved if the villa had been burning to the ground. It wouldn't have mattered, anyway. With just that touch, he was on fire inside, and he felt his face heat up. He was also mortified. This was Angelique, the widow of his good friend, and all she had done was be polite to him. She had been proper, aboveboard, and was obviously grieving deeply. He had no right to be attracted to her. Yet, that didn't change the electricity he felt.

"Houston, are you all right?" Riley grabbed his brother's shoulder.

"Yeah, Riley. Just having a moment." He shook his head to clear his thoughts. He looked up to see Gator still there. "Well, Gator, let's go get you situated. I suspect our boy's already in his board shorts, ready to hit the beach. How about you get changed and go with us?" He walked toward him and offered a hand to shake. "No hard feelings about the room, all right? The woman's husband just died. She needs some space right now." From me, too, he thought.

"Sure," and he nodded. "I think I'll skip the beach, though. The old leg. I can't get it wet, and I hate to swim in front of others without it."

Riley stepped up behind his brother. "I'd hate to swim without one of my legs, either. You're missing out, though. The boy's a fish in water, almost as fast as he is on a motorcycle." He chuckled. "Thank your lucky stars there are no motorcycles here at the resort. You'd have to run for your life each time you crossed the motor court. I understand there's a pool behind each villa, if that's more to your taste."

Buzz burst in and wrapped his arms around Houston's and Riley's necks. His teenage voice burst forth, "We don't have to share the pool at our villa? That is so cool. Can I skinny dip at night? I've always wanted to do that."

He was, indeed, already in his suit, as Houston had predicted, ready to swim at a moment's notice.

Riley turned with a hoot and grabbed his son's bare torso, digging his knuckles into his ribs. When the boy collapsed into his arms in laughter, he nodded to Houston, and his brother grabbed his legs. Together they carried him out the villa's front door, calling back to the third man with laughter, "Come on, Gator. Buzz wants to skinny dip. We're going to make sure he gets his wish right now. We're going to throw him in our pool, but his shorts are going to the beach with us. He can come get them if he wants them."

Buzz began to struggle, but he was out of luck. As they made their way to their villa, Houston untied the boy's suit, loosening the waistband for easy removal.

The boy wailed, "Don't undo my shorts. I don't want you to take them off with anyone looking."

His father growled to him, "Skinny dip, you said. Be careful what you wish for." Then he called to Houston, his words loud and dramatic, "Off with the boy's shorts!"

BACK IN THE VILLA, ANGELIQUE stood on her pool lanai listening to the antics of the men leaving her rooms. That was what she wanted, or at least a small part of her. The rest of her would be horrified to admit it, but she wanted to be the one in Houston's arms. She wanted that, and yet, when she tried to be sensible, she didn't.

She knew it wasn't to be hers, anyway. Riley got that privilege, even if she was paying the bill.

GATOR STOOD FOR A MOMENT in the villa's living room, and he looked at Angelique's closed door. The porter was gone, already, and Gator had told him to put his things here. Now, he'd have to tote them to another villa without help. He sighed in resignation, and he picked up his bags.

Rubbing his left leg with his free hand, he felt the strap that encircled his thigh. Sometimes he wished his leg was back again, just the way it had been the first time he'd climbed Everest. It wouldn't be, though, ever again, and he might as well get used to it. He stepped forward to find his own villa, keeping his steps even and straight. Sometimes it was hard to walk with a hollow leg, but on the plus side, it was sure great for drinking.

When he thought of that, he began to whistle. These villas often had private bars, and if so, he intended to make the most of his tonight, even if he had to do so alone.

HOUSTON AND HIS VILLA companions were on the beach, and he and Riley were tormenting Buzz mercilessly. He stood on the sand and threw the boy's board shorts high in the air, yelling to Riley to catch them, as the tall, freckled teenager held a towel around his waist with one hand and jumped, grabbing for the shorts with the other. Cries of desperation erupted from the boy, while the men hooted with laughter.

"Hey, Riley! Remember the small boy of just two summers ago who would be so excited at getting in the water that he couldn't be bothered with taking the time to put on a suit? Now he's mortified we won't give him the one flying through the air."

"Dad," Buzz cried, as Riley snatched the flailing shorts just out of his hand, falling back into the surf and swimming out too far for the boy to reach him without soaking his towel. "It was bad enough what you did in the pool. You can't expect me to swim without a suit out here. People will see. Girls. C'mon, Dads." He grabbed the waist of his towel with both hands, bunching it up in frustration.

Riley ducked his head underwater, tossing his hair to the side when he came up. As streams shed in crazy rivulets down his freckled arms, he looked around dramatically. "Like who, Buzz? We're in the middle of the largest ocean in the world, and this is a remote island beach. Frigate birds, maybe? Seagulls? I don't think we'll find monkeys here. Chickens! I saw some on the drive out here. Chickens will see what God gave you and be shocked. Come get the suit, Buzz." He laughed and fell back into the water.

When he came up again, Houston was holding his sides and wiping tears from his eyes. Buzz stood, one hand gripping the waist of his towel, as breakers wound out their lives at his feet. His other arm pointed to a person standing on the shore, a bright sarong wrapped around her slender body. Catching sight of their unexpected audience, Riley immediately tossed the shorts, now wet, to his son, and the man's face turned a brilliant red that rivaled his hair.

He shaded his eyes and called, "I'm sorry, Angelique. You weren't meant to see that. We were teasing with the boy, and we thought it was just our family out here." He glanced at Houston, who was still grinning, and at Buzz trying his best to put on his shorts without removing his towel.

When she didn't immediately respond, he called out, "I don't mean to suggest you aren't welcome. This is your beach. I mean—" he fumbled, "—if you would rather be alone, um, we can lounge around our pool—"

"Riley, I think it's all right," Houston interrupted.

Angelique waved and made as if to return to the compound. "I'm intruding, and I realize it. I, uh, understand about your, um, family situation . . . two fathers and all. I should respect that. You were probably enjoying the privacy that I interrupted." She smiled wanly and paused before stepping away, taking a moment to adjust her sarong.

Houston looked at Riley with a frown. Family situation and interrupted privacy? What was that about?

"Angelique, stay," Houston called. "There's no privacy needed. This is everyone's beach, not ours."

"Please," Riley added. "We'll have more privacy than we need back in the villa tonight. Seriously, if you find yourself in need of company at any time, Buzz would love a little less privacy." He grinned.

"Less privacy?"

"He likes to sleep in. He complains that we keep him awake with our roughhousing." Houston stifled a laugh.

"Roughhousing." She pressed her lips together. "So that's what it's called now."

"Wrestling, to be more specific." He laughed and called to the boy, who was finally tying up the waist of his shorts. "Hey, son! One day you'll get a wrestling buddy of your own, won't you?"

"Dad Two!" The boy flushed red. "Don't say it that way."

Then his father burst from the water and crashed into him, toppling his son onto the sand. They rolled once with Riley winding up on top. He sat across his son's waist, sand-covered, pinning his arms beside him, and splattering him with seawater as it dripped from his hair.

"There, boy," he panted. "That's how I've done it with Dad Two all these years. Then I make him say uncle and tell me I'm the best at this there is. I am, too." He released his son and leaped off him to stand at his side, brushing the sand from his hands onto his Buzz's heaving stomach.

"Uncle—" Buzz cried, rolling to his side and calling to his Uncle Houston for help, but that was all he could get out before his father interrupted with a laugh.

"Yes! That's what Houston says whenever I've got him down. You learn quick, son. Just give up when you wrestle with your old dad!" He pumped his fist into the air, exultant as he stood in the sun, with his hair wet, and sand still plastered across most of his body.

"Dad Two!" Buzz's voice broke as he yelped the words. "Help! Dad One's lost touch with reality." Then the boy jumped from the sand and pushed his father back until they both stumbled into the water.

"You really are welcome here, you know. We're not trying to exclude you. Riley sometimes stumbles over his social graces." Houston stepped to Angelique. She was every bit as beautiful here as she had been during the wedding and on the airplane the previous night. "You must be overwhelmed with all that's happened the past week. Whether you knew about Lucas or not, your world has been turned upside down."

"I suspected, but I didn't really know." She let out a sigh.

He watched her face. He saw something there, although surely not interest in him. Still, he felt something akin to hope flood his body before he could squash it away.

HOUSTON'S ENGAGING VOICE filtered over Angelique's shoulder, unexpectedly close. She thought of all the money she'd inherited. To her, the amount had been an eye-opening surprise. "Lucas only mentioned it the day of the wedding."

She was entirely too aware of this man's alluring aroma. Here on the beach wearing only swim trunks, with his olive skin and that firm torso, she realized she actually felt jealously, and it was aimed against the man swimming with that skinny boy in the sea. How could someone who was parenting a thirteen-year-old, and doing it with another man, arouse her senses so? It was very frustrating to her, especially since she felt she should still be loyal to Lucas. It was that kiss she'd witnessed between Lucas and Cheeky that was turning her to the dark side. She knew that, but it still didn't feel fair—or right—to her.

"So, he did tell you," Houston responded with a chuckle,

sounding relieved.

"Can we talk about something else for now? I only came down from my villa because I realized I didn't want to be alone. My two friends in Golden-Rod Villa, Neon One and Neon Two," she chuckled, "are sleeping off their hangovers."

"Neon One? Neon Two?"

"I got those ridiculous names from you and Riley, you know." And Gator, she remembered, but mostly from Houston and his all-too-intimate companion. She laughed as she began to walk, glad to see him following. "I listen to Buzz when he talks to you. Dad One and Dad Two."

He laughed. "There's a long story behind that."

She paused and looked in his face, aware of how much his blue eyes really did a number on her stomach, and it was nothing like the butterflies that had landed on her arms so many years ago during that deodorant commercial. These butterflies made her knees weak. She chuckled to distract herself. "I know enough. That's not what I want to talk about."

She really had nothing specific to say, however. She just needed the presence of a man; and no matter that she'd just seen this man's lover play-act one of their amorous wrestling positions, he was very much a man, at least if her body had anything to say about it.

"So, what do we talk about?" He smiled and started up again as she began to walk, his footsteps following alongside hers.

"Lucas. The first time you met him." She pictured Riley with his son, and her next words just came out. "Wrestling, the private sort. I want to know about that." She cringed at her lack of tact, but it concerned her dead husband, and she deserved to know.

He chortled. "Oh, no! I don't think you do. The first time we met, I learned Lucas knew more, um, private wrestling positions than I've ever learned, if you get my drift."

"I think I do." She turned her eyes to him in a quick glance. "Like you and Riley?"

"Like me and Riley? No, no. Not at all. Lucas preferred a different sort of wrestling."

"Different, how?"

"I hate to say this, but you did ask. Intimate wrestling."

"Not like you and Riley." With a girl was what she meant, that Lucas had been intimate with a girl when Houston had first met him. That was a long time ago, though, and no concern of hers. It did make her feel a little bit better about Cheeky's kiss, in spite of it all.

"Not like me and Riley at all." He chuckled.

After a moment, she eyed a beached log. "Can we sit for a bit?" Without waiting, she removed her sarong and folded it into a pad on which to sit. She was wearing the green bikini her friend had held up in the airport back at JFK, and while she would deny it, she was aware it suited her well.

From somewhere in the trees, a bird called, and she turned her head to look.

Houston whistled. When she looked at him and frowned, he began to apologize profusely. "I'm so sorry. You can't be in the mood for that type of response, and it was very inappropriate to let myself do that. I just like to compliment a beautiful woman. You are, too, and your choice of swimwear shows it."

She laughed. "I intend to get something more conservative first chance I get. My friends picked this out, and my other three as well."

"No, no," he said. "Keep the green. It suits you immense-ly."

She looked at him, sitting and brushing sand from her foot. "I guess you would know, being what you are and all. All the great women's fashion designers, you know, are like you and

Riley. Have you ever done that? Fashion?"

He laughed. "Fashion? I race cars, Angelique. My fashion sense extends about as far as red underwear, but that's a story for the guys. I hope you never have to hear it."

She picked up a stick half buried in the sand and drew a heart in front of her. She smiled as she asked, "You've designed underwear, then? Does Riley wear your designs?"

"Riley?" Down the beach his brother and nephew were exiting the water. When they moved together, their motions mirrored each other's, father and son. He laughed and shook his head.

"What's funny?" She had written her own name at the top of the heart, and she sat, tapping the stick in the sand beside it.

"Are you going to put Lucas' name in?" His question was so soft as to barely be there.

She touched the sand as if intending to write in a second name, and she paused. "Do you know Cheeky?"

They sat in silence for a time. Softly, the water on the beach pushed against the round grains that scattered down to the waterline, shifting them against one another in a low-pitched hum, and in the distance, Buzz could be heard calling to Riley. A loud splash followed by raucous yelling said he had taken his father down once again.

"We all knew Cheeky." Houston paused. "Why do you ask? Didn't Lucas introduce the two of you?"

"Yes," she sighed. "They had words, too, Lucas and Cheeky. Can you tell me about Squeegie?"

He chuckled. "Squeegie's sweet, but she's a railway engine on steroids. What did he tell you about her?"

"Cheeky mentioned her, that's all. I don't know anything." She knew really and truly nothing, and that worried her. How could Lucas have a daughter? That concerned her almost as much as Cheeky's kiss had.

Houston reached for the stick. "May I?" When she relinquished it, he carefully wrote in his own name and smiled. With surprising vehemence, she placed her hand on the sand and wiped it all away.

"I don't think so, Houston."

He frowned, perplexed. "You don't think so? Am I that bad?"

"Why did you laugh earlier? You know, when I asked if Riley wears your underwear designs." She ran her hands through her hair, closing her eyes tightly. She didn't want him to see she was about to cry. He had written just what she'd wanted to write herself, but it had been a jest for him. She wanted it for real.

With the stick, he drew another heart. "Oh, I just thought of something amusing, but to answer your question, as far as I know, Riley wears none at all." He laughed. "I shouldn't say that. It's just that I never see him in his underwear. I don't want to, either. I love the man with all my heart, but never in his underwear—"

"True for most people," she chuckled with a touch of unexpected humor. She was surprised to find she could be amused about this man being so casually graphic about his personal time with his quote unquote spouse, and it was equally strange that she didn't find it offensive.

"I guess so," he said, rubbing a hand down one bare arm. "Something you'll probably hear from one of the guys if you spend much time around them is that I climbed into bed with Riley the first night he came to live with me." He chuckled. "He claims I was too cute to kick out. I guess that's part of the reason we love each other so much, even after all these years."

That said it all, she thought. He couldn't be much clearer than that. It tore her last hope for love from her heart, and now she really wished she'd stayed in New York.

HOUSTON SAW ANGELIQUE blanch and thought he knew why. He chuckled. "I apologize. Don't take that the way it sounds."

Riley was the older of the two, and the year he was adopted, Houston had worshipped him from the moment they met. The first night Riley actually stayed with his family, Houston was three, and he'd followed his new brother around like a puppy. Then, that night, he'd snuck to Riley's bed and crawled under the covers, snuggling next to the redheaded hero who'd come to live in his home.

"No? I think I got the picture just fine." Her eyes were on the horizon and her mouth was tight.

"Ho, ho. I don't think you do." He looked at the red in her eyes. "I was just a kid, and Riley didn't invite me in, so you can't blame him." He laughed, digging in the sand with his stick, remembering a picture his parents took of them that first night, Riley's hair sticking straight up, and Houston curled under his arm. "It was the middle of the night, and he was dead to the world—"

"Enough of that," she said, standing. "Let's go join your, um," and she faltered before continuing, "Buzz's other father." She shook out her sarong and wrapped it around her waist before she started walking, leaving him to follow her if he wished.

He did, too, but she didn't see what he left in the sand. The heart he had drawn now had two names in it. The first was his own, and the second belonged to someone he was trying very hard not to fall in love with. It would seem that it was already too late for that, though, because love tends to place quicksand where it will, and it doesn't always ask those who fall inside if they're ready. Love just draws them into its embrace in its own good time.

CHAPTER 8

"TREAVOR!" JERROLD knocked at the door to Daffodil Villa. "Treavor! You want to let me in, if you know what's good for you. You should look down on the beach. We need to go down there, now."

The door opened, and Treavor stood panting in his regulation Olympic Speedos, dripping water all over the floor. "I'm doing laps, Jerrold. My pool's so tiny, though, that it feels more like I'm just doing turns. One stroke, turn. One stroke, turn."

"Who cares about your strokes? That Angelique. I think Houston's chasing her. If he catches her, we might lose any chance at Lucas' money."

He frowned. "Are you sure?" His eyes widened, and he took a deep breath. "Okay, right now, I'm going to the beach." He bent down, pulled off his trunks, and handed them, dripping still, to Jerrold. "Hold these. I can't wear my regulation pair in the dirty ocean, you know. Don't move. I'll be right back."

Jerrold called into the open doorway, throwing the wet

Speedos into a corner, "I like you like this, Tee."

"Like what?" He stepped outside, now in a pair of board shorts, with a towel in his hands and tinted swimming goggles around his neck.

"Goggles?" Jerrold grabbed them in one hand.

He shrugged in apology. "I couldn't find any sunglasses." He pushed the man's hand away. "Not a single pair. I don't think I packed any." He prodded his friend, "What do you like about me?"

"Less straight. I like you less straight." He grinned.

"Well," he said, grabbing Jerrold's face by the chin. "Don't expect it to last. Everywhere except inside this villa, I intend to be the straightest Olympic swimmer who's ever swum the English Channel." As he spun and marched toward the beach, Jerrold hustled to follow him.

"But Tee, you've never swum the English Channel. Are you planning to?"

Treavor turned to him, walking backwards as they neared the tree line. "Silly rabbit, it's just an expression." Maniacal laughter trailed him as he resumed his forward stance once again.

"But I'm not a rabbit," Jerrold wailed, as he chased after his friend.

"Houston," Treavor called ahead, ignoring Jerrold. "Haven't you been in the water, yet? Angelique, can I steal him from you?" He ran up and threw one arm around Houston's shoulders. "Remember how you used to come cheer me on at my university swim meets? You always taunted me, yelling out how you could beat me with one hand tied behind your back. How about if we see how well you can back that up? First in, Houston!" He pushed on the man's shoulder and then ran towards the water.

Houston looked at Angelique, shrugging.

She raised her eyebrows and gave him a dry smirk, motioning with her hand that he should go play. "He's your friend," she called to him.

When Treavor ran back towards Houston, his feet flinging the shallow water aside, he grabbed the dark-haired race car driver around the neck. Pulling him toward the water, he teased until he gave in.

Jerrold stood back and watched it all unfold. He knew this was what this vacation was all about. Nothing could be allowed to separate them from Lucas' money.

HOUSTON WOULD RATHER have remained to enjoy Angelique's company, but he admitted to himself that he'd known her for a week. Treavor had been a good friend for a decade, and for that, he figured he needed a good trouncing. The toned, slender man might be an Olympic hopeful, but Houston had a more powerful body, and Treavor was aware of that, or, at least he would be in a few minutes.

Energized with adrenalin from being around a beautiful woman, he also had confidence he could reach amazing levels of performance. He didn't think of it in exactly that way. He just knew he was ready to kick some Olympic backside, and Treavor's was the only one available.

"You go, Houston," Jerrold called brightly to the competing duo with enthusiasm. Then, as if remembering Treavor's need to appear masculine, his voice took on a deeper, brusquer tone. "Thrash him, big man, er, take him down, Houston! Show Treavor your stuff."

He did, too, diving in and racing his friend far out to sea and back again. He swam at his friend's request, but he did it exceptionally well for Angelique. However, when he returned to the shallows and leaped from the water, he brushed his hair from his face, and the elated smile on his face quickly faded.

"Jerrold, where's Angelique?" He shook his arms, shedding water, realizing he hadn't brought a towel and not caring.

Jerrold looked around with a mystified expression on his face. It was Buzz who answered his question.

"Uncle Houston, Dad walked her back to her villa. Come back in the water. I found a Frisbee in a box up in the trees. There's a Nerf football, too. I'll toss you a few."

Before he could answer, Treavor's arm dripped water across his shoulders, and leaning into him with laughter, his panting voice conceded defeat. "You were good there, Houston. I'm getting faster, though. You just give me a few weeks here, and you'd better watch out. After all, I'm still in training." He called to Jerrold, "Right, Jer?"

Houston pushed his arm off his shoulders. "I'm going back up to the compound. Men, don't leave Buzz alone down here. Remember, he's only thirteen." He turned to his nephew and waved. "Come up with these two, Buzz. I don't want you swimming alone." He grinned brightly at him, but as soon as he turned away, he let the smile fall from his face.

Angelique was proving a tough nut to crack, and he was finding himself very intrigued. However, with her unexpected exit from the beach, the fuel was gone out of his tank, and just for a while, he needed to head back to his villa. Food, perhaps. That was what he needed. He was very hungry. He realized he hadn't eaten since early that morning at the airport, and that had only been a quick snack from a vending machine.

As he stepped up the path, a bird somewhere made an exotic sound—different from the one earlier—and it was layered against the gentle whoosh of the sea on the beach. A flicker of a shadow from a lone cloud made him look up, and he brushed the limbs of a small bush. As he did, a compact rust and brown chicken beat its wings, disturbed from its hiding place by his presence, and it scurried to find another.

He watched it scrabble along, his eyes following it until it disappeared. Chickens. Thousands of miles from home, and chickens were what crossed his path.

Rooster WAS WHAT Houston should have noticed. It was a rust and brown bird, a Maui rooster, to be exact, and it considered the compound of villas the wedding party happened to be occupying as its personal home.

There was something else Houston should have thought of, too. Roosters are notoriously territorial, and one will defend its turf against all comers, no matter how much money those comers have paid to vacation in its home territory.

He would learn, though. All the wedding party would.

Angelique OPENED HER door to find a round-faced young man with a smile on his face.

"Good afternoon. How has your arrival at Blue Water Maui been? I certainly hope you've found everything satisfactory. My name is Sven Halvorson, and I'll be your personal concierge for your stay."

"Personal concierge?" She laughed at that. Her uncle had done well. After they moved from the main resort to the villas, she hadn't expected a concierge just for the honeymoon party.

"Fresh flowers will be delivered to your villa daily, and I'm on twenty-four hour call. Is there anything I can do for you at this time, anything I can bring you? We have on-site massage therapists, a full kitchen, and a fully stocked liquor bar at the main resort about ten minutes away. Your villa is all-inclusive, including unlimited high-speed Internet for your mobile devices. Feel free to indulge yourself without worry about the cost. Our goal at Blue Water Maui is to be unobtrusive, yet always available."

"Thank you." On-site massage therapists? Maybe. The bar?

That would be a disaster. She remembered the plane trip down. Internet access would be nice, and she did have her computer.

He smiled, and his round face lit up. "My card." Out of a pocket on the expansive blazer he wore, he flipped out a gold-embossed card with his name and the number at which he could be reached. "Ten minutes," he said. "Anything you want, anytime."

"I'm Angelique." She held out her hand to shake.

"Angelique Abercrombie, and you are here for six weeks." He smiled, and after he shook, he rested his hands across his broad stomach.

She was taken aback, though, his words soaking in. Personal concierge? "You are here for all the villas?" That made more sense to her.

He smiled. "Oh, no. Julia Havershine will have the other two-bedroom. That's Apricot Villa. My dearest friend Christian Cox will service the one-bedrooms as a group." He counted on his fingers as he ran through the names. "I believe Jerrold is in Calla-Lily Villa. A guest by the name of Treavor resides in Daffodil. In Edelweiss, you will find Gator." Sven let a smile escape when he called Gator's name. "Forget-Me-Not Villa is currently unoccupied. Golden-Rod Villa is shared by a couple, Heather and Beckie. I believe Hydrangea Villa is occupied by twin brothers by the names of Robby and Bobby. However, I am yours, alone."

"That was most impressive, Sven." She laughed.

"I brought you something." Considering his broad girth, he moved with speed and grace, and he uncovered a gleaming silver platter he had placed on a sideboard. It was filled with a delectable variety of freshly cut fruit. "For you."

"Thank you, Sven." The aroma hit her, and she breathed in deeply. "I'm very hungry. I hadn't realized that before. I'm sure we'll all eat together later, but maybe a lobster sandwich. That would taste delicious at the moment. Can you do that for me?"

"One lobster sandwich on the way. Please feel free to wash up, and I'll have it waiting on you." He smiled broadly and stepped briskly out the door.

As she turned to the bathroom, a phone rang. Adjusting her sarong, she found the intrusive instrument beside the low couch and picked it up. She wondered if Sven was going to be delayed. If so, she planned to head directly to the fruit platter.

"Yes?"

"Angie, Beckie and I are finally clear-headed. Ooh, what a morning! That cute redhead, Riley, stopped by to check on us, and he said he just dropped you off at your villa. We peeked outside, and we thought we saw food headed your way. Can we come over? We're so hungry."

She looked at the fruit platter, knowing she could never eat all that was on it. "Certainly, Heather. Both of you. I've got fruit here, and a lobster sandwich on order."

"Oh, sweetie! Order two more, and we'll be right there. I'm putting on my sunglasses as we speak. Thanks, Angie. You are the best!"

The line clicked off, and she stood with the phone in her hand. Sven was already gone, but she guessed she could cut the sandwich in thirds. With the fruit, there would surely be enough.

Then she remembered the gold-embossed card she held. Punching in the number, she was pleased to hear Sven's familiar voice instantly pick up.

"Yes, Angelique. What may I do for you?" His voice was pleasantly helpful, as if glad to have her call so quickly with an additional request.

"Um, Sven, could I possibly get three of those sandwiches, and with tea? Sweet, please. And, Sven, maybe some peanut butter cups. I have a friend, oh . . . she's not staying in this villa.

Um, Golden-Rod Villa, I believe you said. May I order for her, also?"

"Of course. Will there be anything else?" He chuckled over the line.

"A one-piece swimsuit?" She smiled. After all, he had asked.

Laughter greeted her request. "You were charming in your green, Angelique. However, I will have a selection for you to choose from when I return, complimentary, of course. Will that be all?"

"For now, Sven." She closed her eyes for a moment, relieved at his reply.

"I'll see you in a few minutes, and I'll look forward to meeting your friends."

When he was gone, she hung up the phone, impressed. When he had said all-inclusive, she guessed he meant it. She stepped to the bedroom to unexpectedly find her suitcase missing. Concerned, she looked around to realize it was in a closet. Picking it up, she could tell it was empty, and then she noticed the clothes hanging above it were her own. Stepping to the dresser, she opened several drawers to find her other things already nestled neatly inside. She smiled, pleased, and decided it was very nice to be waited on as if she were special. After the rough week she'd just lived through, she needed to feel that way for a change, and for the first time, she actually felt she could begin to look forward to her stay here.

Pulling out a lightweight blouse and shorts, she stepped to the bathroom. She touched the rim of the claw-footed tub longingly, and decided on a quick shower. Tossing her suit aside, she flipped on the water and stepped underneath. She saw no soap, but when she dampened the sea sponge hanging from the showerhead and squeezed it, out poured a luxurious bevy of foam bubbles. She closed her eyes and let the aroma waft over her. It was heaven to her senses.

When she was finished and out of the shower, she was glad there was no air conditioning in these villas. The walls didn't quite reach the vaulted, beamed roofline, and that let the sea breezes wash through. With a few pats of a towel so thick it was hard to hold, she was dry. She ran her fingers through her hair and let it fall into a loose mass that could air naturally.

Dressed, she stepped to the living area to a pleasant surprise. The sideboard Sven had placed the fruit platter on earlier had been pulled out, opened up, and draped with a white linen cloth. Gleaming white china graced three settings, the flatware next to each plate shone, and iced tea shimmered in crystal goblets. A stack of commercially wrapped peanut butter cups stood beside each glass. A covered silver platter had been placed in the middle, and behind it all, in his expansive blazer, stood Sven with a cloth draped professionally over an arm he held horizontally at his waist.

"Sven, this is beautiful. I had thought . . . sandwiches . . . they would be in a paper sack. I had no idea." Then she noticed a dozen one-piece suits spread across the sofa. "You brought suits. You are a dear."

"Choose any you wish, on the house. As far as the meal, I can provide paper sacks if you prefer. Would you like me to put all this away?" He made as if ready to do just that at a word from her.

"No, Sven. It's beautiful. Are my friends here?"

He smiled. "I saw two young women in very tropical hair wandering the compound when I arrived. They seemed a bit disoriented. Is that who you mean?"

She chuckled appreciatively. "Tropical hair is very generous. Thank you, and yes. Would you mind pointing them this way? I'm ready to eat. Oh, and Sven, let me get you something for all your trouble. I just have to grab my purse—"

He held up both hands, palms out, with a smile. "Thank you, Angelique, but no. All-inclusive. That means me, too. This is all about your enjoyment. Just seeing the pleasure on your face is enough for me." He moved to the door, then he turned to her. "Ah, the timing is excellent. Your guests have arrived. Welcome!" He stepped aside to allow Beckie and Heather to come through the doorway.

"Oh, my!" Beckie exclaimed. "Angie, this is beautiful. This is so much nicer than our place. I like your little man, here. Did he do all this?" She turned and reached her hand toward the concierge, pointing. "I want one of you."

He smiled. "I'm Sven. I believe you must be Beckie, and your friend is Heather. You're in Golden-Rod Villa. Christian will be your concierge. He will be by today to see if you need anything. Christian will be servicing all the single villas."

Heather pulled her sunglasses from her face. "Christian will be servicing us, you say?" She smiled.

Angelique chided, "Grow up, Heather. You know what he means. Girls, let's sit. I must eat now. Sven's been wonderful, and for the first time in a week, I feel like living again."

"Good," Beckie said. "I was worried about you there. Poor Lucas and all. A little nightlife might be nice. Sven?" She turned to the concierge. "Can you arrange that? A party? I would like some Latin music, something with a beat." She raised her hands above her head and snapped her fingers. "Ooh, la, la!" She laughed.

"Of course, if Angelique wishes it. Now, though, your sandwiches." He uncovered the platter to reveal steaming lobster rolls.

"Oh, my hungry stomach. You said sandwiches, Angie. I'm liking what I see. Lobster rolls, stuffed with lots and lots of lobster."

"Yes, instead of simple sandwiches, the resort's chef

95

thought you might prefer these. However, I can return them for plainer fare, if you wish. Angelique?"

"No, Sven. These are perfect. I want lobster rolls every time." She was pleased to see his smile return.

"Ladies, if everything is satisfactory, I'll leave you to your meal. Enjoy." He bowed, backed out of the villa, and was gone.

They did, too, and Angelique was right about one thing. In spite of all that had happened to her in the past week and a day, she had, indeed, begun to live again.

HOUSTON'S WALK BACK to his villa was less than enthusiastic. He had swum, and hard, his testosterone flooding his system. Then when Angelique was gone—and with Riley—he was left with nothing. Now he wanted into dry clothes and to be left alone for a few minutes.

When he stepped through the door, he found he didn't have much choice.

"Houston!" Robby jumped to his feet. "Your concierge was here. Julia, I think she said her name was. I told her you were happy as a clam, that you would call her if you needed anything. Here's her card." He flipped a silver-embossed card his way, laughing when Houston caught it in mid-air.

"Thanks." Houston held the card without looking at it.

"Did Buzz ever get you in the water? Or was that Treavor I saw down there?" Robby stepped to him, throwing an arm around his bare shoulders. "Bobby and I did see you having a little chat with Lucas', um, widow. What's with her? She seems nice enough, but there's not much news coming out of the war zone."

"Where's Bobby?" Houston didn't care to discuss Angelique, not in the state he was in.

"He and Riley went to check on Gator. I don't remember him, ever. Gator, I mean. What do you know about the man? Is he hoping for some money like the rest of us are? We all cared for Lucas, you know that. It just seems unfair that he let himself be snuffed like that without taking care of us financially. Bobby and I, we counted on his help."

"I know, Robbo." Houston lifted the man's arm from his shoulders and stepped to a chair. It seemed half a dozen others had counted on Lucas' help, too, others who were now grown men and should be self-sufficient and not living off another's meal ticket.

"Well, did she say anything? You're the only one who's really talked to her."

"Not really." He looked away, remembering how she'd said she didn't want the money. She wanted Lucas.

"You did ask her, though? You have to ask her, Houston. Maybe there's something there, and the will said we have to meet some criteria or something. Maybe that's it." He leaned in and threw his arm around Houston's bare shoulders once again. "I mean, we're buds, Houston. You and me, well, and Bobby, too. We're all buds from our frat days, and we have to stick together. We need this money."

Houston chuckled. "I don't. I've never needed any of Lucas' money. I did ask her, though, but I don't think she was focused on that. Lucas' death had her attention."

"Mine, too." Robby let him go and walked to the door, looking out. "You know what I mean about sticking together, though." He looked out to the sea in the distance where one small cloud floated high overhead. "I should start a business right here. It really is beautiful."

Houston stepped to his friend's side and slapped him on the shoulder, amused, while digging his fingers in and making him wince. "You said that about Sag Harbor, and Martha's Vineyard, too. 'Anywhere on Martha's Vineyard,' you said. 'Please, Lucas. I want a shop on Martha's Vineyard.' I was there for that dinner party, remember."

Robby shrugged his hand off, and he groused, "But this is different. Look at the sky. You can't even buy paint that color. Bobby and I could really make it on our own here."

"I love you, Robbo. You're a brother to me. You've got to grow up, though."

"Riley's your brother, you mean. He's the lucky one. You and Lucas. You two were always the best of us, the luckiest, too. You know that."

"Think back a week. I don't know that Lucas was so lucky. Besides, you're good at what you do. You and B-Bob just have to manage the money better."

"We have to have money to be able to manage it. Right now, we're a sinking ship without Lucas. Surely, you can help."

"Get to know her, Robby. Go over to her villa and invite her to a dinner party. You and Bobby do parties like God would want them done. In fact, invite us all to your villa, or do it over here, if you want." He looked at the silver-embossed card he'd caught earlier. "Get this Julia to help. Better yet, let's set up a luau on the beach, a real Hawaiian adventure. You've got six weeks here. Get to be friends with Angelique, and then you can ask her about the money yourself."

Robby sighed as if at the end of a very short, tiresome rope, and he rolled his eyes. "Let's discuss it later. Here comes your nephew, and he's got Treavor and Jerrold with him. How do you three do it?" He turned to Houston, shaking his head in disbelief.

"Do what?" Houston looked at him, reaching with his hands to unstick his damp swim shorts from his body and shaking them to get them to dry faster. "What do we do, Robby?"

"Get people to like you so much. You and Riley, and that Buzz, too. I hear he's convinced both those guys he's with to go windsurfing with him. How come they never do that stuff with me?"

"Do you ever ask them? Think of that." He glanced toward the bedroom. "I'm going in to change, Robbo. Be back in a minute."

"Can I come, too?" He made a move as if to follow.

Houston laughed. "Good try, but no. You have company to entertain." He pointed just as one thirteen-year-old and two grown men came roughhousing through the door. They might as well all have been thirteen, though, by the way they were acting.

"Robby, right?" Treavor slapped him on the shoulder. "We're headed hang gliding tomorrow. Come on and go with us."

"Windsurfing," Buzz corrected.

"Whichever. It'll be fun. Go with us, old sourpuss."

"I'm not a sourpuss," Robby whined. "I just need to be asked."

"Are, too," Jerrold laughed. "Besides, we just did."

Robby let out a grunt as two skinny, freckled arms wrapped his neck from behind, and two skinny legs wrapped around his waist, nearly toppling him over. "Go, Uncle Robbo. I want you there. It'll be more fun if you're with us."

Houston laughed as he closed the bathroom door. Yeah, he was the lucky one. Deep in his heart, he knew that. After all, he had Buzz for a kid, and although the boy belonged to Riley, he also knew that anything that belonged to his brother, he could claim, also.

Well, he'd claim the kid any day, and nothing would ever make him change his mind about that.

"HO, GATOR. THERE'S LIFE outside. You know that." Riley, still in his board shorts, stood next to Bobby, and he called to Gator, sitting with three mini bottles of strong alcohol opened and emptied at his side.

Gator's eyes narrowed. He motioned to the bottles with his hand. "These. They're all Houston's fault, you know." He laughed. "He's your brother, right?"

"Of course," Riley said. "Why?"

"Well," Gator started, sitting up, a vocal burr coming across in his words. "How do two brothers look so different? I mean, he's dark with that olive skin, and you, you can't get any more Irish. How'd you manage that?"

Bobby laughed, stepping next to Riley and resting his arm on the man's shoulder. "They're not real brothers, Gator."

"Bobby, don't you ever say that again. Houston and I are like that." Riley raised his hand and crossed the first two fingers. "No brothers are more real than we are."

Bobby laughed, slapping him on the stomach. "I'm sorry, Riley. I didn't mean it that way. You see, Gator, Houston's parents got stuck with Houston, but they went out and picked Riley. He's adopted. I think his parents got a better deal with Riley than with Houston." He laughed teasingly and patted Riley again, this time on the chest.

"He plays father to my son when I'm out of town." Riley shrugged the arm and hand away.

"You going out again, soon?" Gator grabbed a fourth bottle and attempted to open the lid.

"In a week," he admitted. "I've got a conference about nano technology and electron pulses to control data transfer." He grinned at that.

"God!" Gator leaned his head back. "Geeks will someday rule the world. Are you, um, you know, like him, too?" He looked at Riley for a moment, and in a quick motion shifted his eyes to Bobby and back again.

Riley grinned. "Oh, no. I'm divorced, but not that. I'm just here with my brother."

"Your brother. What's he like?" Gator finally had the bottle open, and he raised it to his lips. He paused before drinking. "I've watched him around Angelique. He doesn't seem very, you know, effeminate. I'd think he'd like the skirted kind."

Bobby cut in, "Houston is yardstick straight, just like Riley, here. What about you, Gator?"

He drew a straight line in the air, and Bobby let a soft curse word escape from his lips.

"Your brother's not going with you?" Gator's question was aimed squarely at Riley, and hope echoed in his voice. "Taking the kid with him?"

"Nah. He's free 'til March. He races then in Bahrain or somewhere. Australia, maybe. He's here for the duration, and with Buzz. Why's that?"

"Competition. That's all, just competition. I can manage, if only I know what I'm against. You gotta know the competition in order to beat it."

Bobby leaned in. "What are you competing for? Can I join?"

Gator pulled out three more small bottles. "You," and he looked directly at Bobby, "wouldn't understand or be interested if I told you. Have a drink with me, men." He looked at Bobby a second time. "Rather, um . . . well, man and, um . . ."

"Let it go, Gator," Riley suggested with a grin.

"You're right. Maybe I should." He laughed and held out the bottles.

Bobby grabbed one. "Brandy! I adore brandy!"

Gator muttered, "Surprise, there."

Riley kicked his shoe and smiled. He did notice the man's foot had an unusual feel when he kicked it, but he didn't pay it much mind. After all, he could be wearing custom shoes, and who knew what they might feel like. He just hoped they all got along. Maui was too pretty a place for infighting, even if he was only to be here for a week.

CATOR DIDN'T SEE IT that way. He wanted Angelique, and he could barely think of anything else.

CHAPTER 9

CHRISTIAN COX ROLLED HIS eyes as he stepped from one of his assigned villas. The sun already beat down on him, he had three villas checked off his list, three more to go, and he had found no one home yet.

Reaching the sidewalk, he froze, his heart palpitating in fear. Directly in his view was the evil, much-feared rooster that haunted this part of the island. Why, oh, why did he listen to that silly Sven, when he could have taken that job at the Hilton in Honolulu? He adored Waikiki, and here, what did he have? That maniacal monster. He must have been out of his mind to do this.

He followed the animal's head-bobbing walk as it stepped into the stone-paved motor court that provided access to all the villas. Inside his tailored jacket, he could feel moisture tickling his backbone. It hadn't seen him yet, thank the island gods.

"Crazy devil rooster, go away," he whispered in a hiss. It wouldn't, though. This was its territory, where the demon fowl had taken up residence, staking its claim to torment poor, poor Christian. Then, with relief flooding his body, he saw the door of one of the villas open and two rather tipsy men, one red-headed and the other of medium build with sandy hair, step into the sunshine. In that moment, they became Christian's open door of opportunity.

"Sirs," he called, rather over-loudly. When they didn't respond, he moved rapidly forward in a rolling, marathon walker's gait. Resort rules said he must never run in the presence of guests, but speed was of paramount importance. After all, that cursed rooster was on the prowl. "Sirs! I must insist you step back into your villa."

As he approached, Riley blinked and said to his companion, "Hey, Bobby! Look here. We have company. Would you like a drink, sir?" He laughed and slapped Bobby on the shoulder. "Oops, B-Bob. Do you think we left any for this good gentleman?"

Bobby put his hand to his mouth as he hiccupped. "That's a question only our good Gator can answer." He giggled.

"Please, sirs!" Christian was overcome by panic by then, and he could feel tears of fear hovering in his eyes. The rooster would be upon them soon, was surely about to attack, and these men didn't understand. "For your own protection, you must listen to me."

Moving with the utmost speed he could muster, he threw his arms around the men and crushed them back into the villa, knocking them down in a frantic tangle of arms and legs. In the process, he came crashing down directly on top of them.

"The door," he cried, scrambling to his feet. He grabbed it with his hand and sent it flying closed. "Oh, Mary, I did it."

"Did what?" The muttered question sputtered from Riley.

Christian pulled a cross from inside his collar and put it to his lips for a moment before slipping it back down his shirt.

Breathing hard, he blinked away unwelcome sweat that made his eyes burn, knowing it for what it was: fear.

"Who the devil is that?" Gator's voice rang from his chair. "Is he bringing me more fortification?" Laughter filtered through in the words.

Christian forced himself to shift into concierge mode, although he would rather have taken his cloth from his blazer pocket to wipe the sweat off his forehead. That was a no-no in the presence of guests. He was to always seem cool and relaxed in the presence of the resort's clientele. He had already blown that out of the water like a torpedo on D-Day, but he could certainly try to repair some of the damage. After all, he had been saving these men's lives.

"Welcome to Blue Water Maui. I am your concierge, Christian Cox." He paused and blinked rapidly several times, catching his breath while his heart continued to pulsate wildly. "I apologize for my untoward introduction, but desperate situations sometimes require desperate measures. I do hope everyone is in fine feather, er, that I haven't run afoul of your good graces. Oh," one hand fluttered unconsciously, "you see, there was a cockerel outside—"

Gator called out in a drunken slur, "Cockerel? Don't you mean a cock? Say what you mean, boy! Did I hear you call yourself a cock?"

"—strutting from the greenery, and it forced me to roost you from your complacency—"

"Roost? Roust, my good man. You rousted my friends from their complacency."

"—to get you to safety." Christian's eyes were wide by that time. He was rambling erratically, but his adrenalin was so high, he couldn't contain it. He'd need to take an extra dose of his medication when he got back to the main resort, or he'd be bouncing off the walls and driving his co-workers crazy all day long. That was something he could do nothing about at this time, though. In an effort to ameliorate the situation, he smiled, even as he realized his expression must be a bit on the frantic side.

"Safety?" Bobby called from the floor. "That was safety?" He was laughing so hard he couldn't get up.

Riley lay beside him, and he pushed on his shoulder. "At least you can't fall down again!"

"Maybe we can fall up? Would that hurt? Whoa, doc, I think I just bruised my shin on the ceiling. Is the resort shrink going to believe that one?" Bobby laid his head back, closed his eyes, and chuckled, sounding winded.

"Christian's your name, you say? You're a concierge?" Gator's voice called from the chair. "Does a good concierge bring me refreshment to replenish my dwindling supply? My throat calls for more."

Attempting to focus in spite of his brush with near death, the concierge spoke slowly and deliberately. "At Blue Water Maui, we strive to be unobtrusive but always available. I'm at your call twenty-four hours a day." He felt in his jacket pocket. "My card." His were embossed with a black border. "I would like to leave one with each of you. How may I be of service?"

Gator called, "Liquor, man! Restock the bar!"

"At once, sir. Will there be anything else?" He tugged the bottom edge of his tailored blazer unconsciously, burning nervous energy.

"A ladder," Riley cackled. "It's a long way up there to where you are."

Christian was able to smile at that. "May I lend you a hand, sir?" He was waved away, and told that his services were no longer necessary, except for restocking the bar.

He did look both ways before exiting the villa. In Christian's eyes, it was wise that he did so. After all, there was a marauding, feathered enemy about, and it could have been waiting just outside the door.

DINNER THAT NIGHT WAS a rousing affair. Julia, Sven, and Christian pulled together to create a luau to surpass the most riveting of events.

In the slowly fading evening light, candles on tall poles were strewn about the beach, a giant pit of coals glowed in the sand, and piled nearby were the fronds that had kept the roasting meat moist and succulent. A sun-browned man played a stringed instrument, and several dancers in grass skirts glistened as they swayed softly to the music. Julia, statuesque, precise, and pragmatic, had informed everyone that the music and story-telling dance would pick up in speed and intensity once the meal was over. The guests should enjoy the soothing pace while they could. If the expected overnight showers should arrive early, things might really liven up; the festivities would need to be transferred inside as quickly as possible.

Beckie and Heather arrived first, their clothing bright and form-fitting. Their hair spilled from the tops of their heads in a chaotic and energetic style. Giggling and removing their sandals once they reached the sand, they chose seats as close to the musical instrument-playing man as possible, winking and waving at him to get his attention. They giggled again when he nodded to them and smiled.

The women had already begun plotting the evening's seating order.

"Good evening, Treavor," Beckie called. The first of their dinner mates had arrived, and he was summarily instructed to sit in a particular location. Jerrold wasn't far behind, trailing his more athletic friend.

"Ladies," Treavor responded, raising his hand to wave. He pointed to two vacant seats. "Here would be better, I think. I have—"

The women already had plans otherwise, and Heather cut him off. "Here. Beside us. We want to know all about you and your latest swimming techniques. It's the Olympics, right? Do you dive or swim?" She gleefully took his arm and pulled him to her side.

"Um, both, sometimes." He glanced up at Jerrold, motioning him to take the open place at his other side. Beckie quickly stepped in.

"Jerrold, I so love the cinema. You must sit here by me. I'm saving this spot for you." She laughed brightly and patted the sand at her side.

She also noticed his eyes as they found the ukulele player and rested there for a moment, just a bit too long to simply be a casual look.

"Do you play?" Her words were bright and charming, glittering against the evening sky.

He jerked his head back to her. "Play? What do you mean?"

She patted his arm and pulled him to the sand. "You know, that man's instrument. The stringed thingie. I saw you looking at it. Do you play?" She giggled. "He might let you hold it later, if you're interested. Are you?"

"I'm an actor. I have a starring role coming up this summer." He shook his head nervously.

"I can sense a shift in topic just as well as the next girl, and no, you don't. What's so fascinating about that man's thingie?" She pointed.

"He does have an interesting instrument, what I can see of it. I've never played that one, before."

"I bet he'd be glad to give you lessons—for a price, of course. I can see if Christian can get you two together later." She smiled, running her fingers down his arm. His skin was moist, giving it a sheen in the fading light.

"Christian is your concierge, too?" He frowned.

"Of course. Angelique and the boys have their own, but we have to share Christian." She laughed, reaching to push a bit of hair back from Jerrold's forehead.

"The boys?"

"Houston and that redheaded pair. You know, Riley and his boy. They have their own concierge, all to themselves." Her lips pouted for a moment, and then she brightened. "At least I'm not paying for all this, so I guess it's all right."

"I guess so." He called down the table, "Jerrold? There's a seat beside me. Move down here."

"Nope!" Heather laughed with a throaty warble. "You're mine, Mr. Olympics. Ah, I see swimmer's muscles underneath that shirt. I like my men long and lean." She snuggled next to him, wrapping her arm in his, making sure he was pressed against her side. "This should tighten up your Speedos."

He flushed.

She smiled at him, batting her eyes. "So, are you a relay man, or do you go it alone?"

He looked at her with a frown. "Um, alone, as in? I mean, are you suggesting, do I . . . uh . . . by myself . . . ."

"Racing, silly!" She lightly slapped his chest with her hand, and then she pressed her palm against his pectoral muscle very slowly. After a long pause, she stroked it gently. "Oh, my. I do like your swimmer's muscles. I bet you do the fifty-yard sprint, the homerun thing, you know, to get these muscles. Does it get lonely racing all alone around the bases?" She purred at him. "I played baseball once. I even got a home run. It was so exciting."

"You did not!" Beckie chided her. "I was on the other team. I clearly remember getting you out on first."

Heather leaned in to whisper, "Silly! I know I've never been further than first base. I'm trying to seem worldly and exotically romantic over here."

Beckie whispered hotly back, "Well, you don't have to lie about it. Just tell him you're a klutz, and would he please help you learn."

Heather brightened. "I never thought of that. Thanks, sweetie." Then she stood, and she called to two additional men coming down the path. "B-Bob! Robbo! Just here! This is so exciting!"

She turned to Treavor. "Move down two, sweetie. We need those two there right between us." He brightened as he moved—until he saw Heather following him.

"Bobby and Robby are sitting between you and Beckie?" His disappointment was plain in his face. "And you have to know," he whispered, "only Houston calls him Robbo."

"Is that so?" She looked at Beckie to see her grinning. Then, when the two men attempted to sit across from them, she walked around to pull them over. "Here, boys. How cute you two look! Now, who's Bobby, and who's Robbo?" At a frown on one of the faces, she laughed. "There you are, you sweet pumpkin. I love that little, slender face. You are adorable. Now, Beckie and I have saved you two seats just between us. We want to learn all about the decorating business. We have an amazing sense of color, and we're certain we would be fabulous with a capital F, if we just knew where to get started. Isn't that right, Beckie?"

She nodded emphatically. "All six of us could go in together. Jerrold could play his instrument—"

"His instrument?" Bobby interrupted and looked at Robby.

"His ukulele," Beckie laughed, grabbing his hand and pulling him to the sand. "He's planning to take lessons from that man over there. He said he likes his instrument. I hope he brings it over later so we can have a look at it. Jerrold said he couldn't see it very well." She leaned in and stroked the man's arm tenderly.

"What's Treavor's part in all this?" Robby looked at his friend with a hint of amusement in his eyes.

"Oh, oh!" Beckie bobbed up and down. "He's going to model our swimsuits. I want to sell antique Speedos. I can go on eBay and buy up all kinds. He can carry around a tray of hors d'oeuvres wearing just my Speedos. Everyone would want him, er, them." She smiled brightly at Heather. "Isn't that right?"

She giggled. "I already do." She grabbed the top of his knee, squeezing it in a quick, hard pulse, causing him to squeak in dismay.

"Um, Heather?" His voice was pitched in a higher range than he normally used. "That's my leg."

"I know." Her words were silky and alluring, unlike the hair atop her head. "I like it."

"So do I," he squeaked again, as he attempted to brush her hand off.

"Well!" She turned to Robby, smiling. "Where are our other five compadres?"

He pointed to where three villa doors could be seen opening at once. "You know," he said, "you might be better off letting us sit over on the other side, and giving our spots to the straight arrows coming down the hill."

All the while, the ukulele played softly in the background, and the hula dancers swayed softly in the pleasant ocean breezes.

Beckie looked down the row at Heather, and she winked. "I don't think so, Robbo."

He gritted his teeth. "Robby, please. Only Houston is allowed to call me that."

Heather laughed softly. "You heard him, Beckie. Only Houston is allowed. Let's give the man his wish." She patted his arm. "Is that better?" She paused to watch the musician skillfully strum his glistening instrument, and then she reached around Bobby's back to poke Robby on the shoulder. "It is better, isn't it, Robbo?"

Bobby just elbowed his brother and laughed. It seemed everyone was getting their just desserts tonight.

𝒜NGELIQUE WAS HAVING the time of her life. When Beckie and Heather had tried to seat her where they wished, she just ignored them, and with two red-haired men on either side of her, that left Houston and Gator to fend for themselves at the ends of the row. As their foods were put on display—Kalua pork, poi, and lomi lomi salmon, as well as other fresh fish, in addition to island chicken, assorted salads, side dishes, and desserts—Riley and Buzz regaled the group with stories of Houston's wilder side.

"Remember, Buzz," Riley leaned over Angelique and pointed to the boy's uncle, "that time when you, Houston, and I were in Acapulco?"

"Oh, oh!" Buzz jumped with excitement at the memory, grinning widely as Houston covered his eyes with a groan. "Everybody, listen to this one. We went there on vacation once, and Dad showed me where this happened. Tell it, Dad One."

Houston interjected, "Riley, won't you ever let this one die? Please, God, deliver me from redheaded devils."

Angelique laughed as Robby and Bobby both leaned in to hear the upcoming tale.

"Tell it, Dad One," the brothers yelled enthusiastically.

Robby elbowed his brother, whispering, "He listens to you, B-Bob. Make him tell the story."

He hissed back, "He listens to Houston. We hardly know him." He motioned to those on either side of him, however, and Robby got what he wanted. With their encouragement, everyone on their side of the roasted pig soon cheered the story on.

"All right! All right!" Riley stood with his arms held out dramatically. "I'll tell this wonderfully embarrassing and very funny story about my best friend and soulmate. You have to understand, though," and he paused, looking dramatically at each person sitting around the luau pit, "that this was no ordinary time. My brother in mayhem, Houston, here," and everyone laughed as Houston groaned audibly once again, just now uncovering his eyes, "was only nineteen at the time. It was spring break, at least for me. For those of you who don't know, Houston was already on the Formula 1 circuit. I still had graduate school to finish."

Angelique watched Riley, the tall, well-built redhead who was Houston's romantic partner, the man he'd chosen to spend his life with. She could see why. Tonight, Riley was brilliantly funny as he worked the crowd, and clearly adored by his son. Then her eyes fell to Houston sitting just on the other side of him. He was younger than his partner. She had known he must be, probably by four or five years, too. If they'd shared a bed from the first day they'd met, as Houston had so candidly revealed to her earlier, then these two men had been involved with one another during Riley's entire marriage.

With embarrassment on Houston's face, as well as good-natured enjoyment on Riley's features, the forbidden story unfolded. Angelique was torn between two emotions. She felt her heart twist inside with an emotional response that drew her toward this dichotomy of a man, a response that told her this was a man she could love and trust. Yet, and she hated the yet, he was in love, enamored with another, and that person was the man next to her, the man who was telling his tale to regale the entire group. The one man who could step into her life, whom she unreasonably wanted to step into her life, and who was sitting at this very meal with her, was as unavailable to her as the moon and the stars.

In her moment of sudden melancholy, she was aware of the party as if it moved around her in a slow motion dance. The musician's skin glistened in the flames of the candles as he strummed his musical instrument, and the dancers swayed slowly to the music, their grass skirts singing a gentle song around their knees. Unobtrusive servers had begun to carve the meat, and food was being ladled onto waiting banana leaves in front of each member of the party, immediately covered once again to keep it fresh until the meal should start. Laughter was on each person's face as his or her attention was directed to the storyteller, and in their small, unconscious movements, leaning in to touch one another's arms, or pressing against each other shoulder-to-shoulder, laughing with the hilarity of Riley's words, their motions let Angelique know why this group of men had stayed together so long. She could tell they cared for one another and enjoyed each other's company. She was also glad she had been allowed to join in, even if it had taken a tragedy to bring it about. She hoped Beckie and Heather felt the same way. Then, with the rising sound of Riley's words weaving their string of imagined calamities about her, his story came into focus once again, and she pushed her private thoughts away.

"We were on the cliffs, you know, where they do the diving? Well . . ." and he turned to his brother, tears of mirth flooding his eyes, as his son chanted for him to continue the story. "Well, there were these girls, probably more my age than Houston's, but were they ever beautiful! They had on these bikinis that covered . . . well, let me rephrase that. They had on these bikinis that didn't cover . . . much of anything." He turned and winked at the crowd as the laughter fell to an anticipatory burble. "Houston was still new to the Formula 1 circuit, you remember, and still green around the gills. However, these girls recognized him, and he . . . well . . . my dear, dear Houston was all hormones in those days."

"The dive, Dad!" Buzz's eyes glistened with boundless anticipation.

"The dive." Riley stood for a moment with his hands on his hips, very dramatic in his stance. "The dive. Well, my dear Buzz," and he pointed to his son, "Dad Two had to be provoked, first. No, provoked is not the word. Encouraged? No. How about aroused into action? Will that do, Buzz?"

His son leaned over, snickering into his hand as he looked at Houston, amusement crinkling his eyes. "Aroused, Dad? Like for a girl?"

Riley reached to his brother and ran his fingers roughly through the man's thick hair, until Houston looked up at him, shaking his head back and forth with a grin on his face.

"Just tell it, Riley," Houston groused good-naturedly, letting a smile break through. "Get it over with, if you must."

Riley laughed. "For me! Houston did it for me! He might lead you to think he did it for the girls, but he did it all for me. Isn't that right, Houston?"

Houston took a deep breath and chuckled audibly. "I did it for the girls, Riley."

"Oh, that's right. I got that wrong again. Houston took his shirt off for the girls. Do it now, Houston. Pull your shirt off for the girls." Riley leaned down and made as if to pull his brother's shirt off his head.

"Do it, Dad One! Pull it off!"

Angelique laughed as Buzz scrambled up, dropping to his knees behind Houston and grabbing his shirt. The man struggled for a moment, and then he gave in, raising his arms as the shirt was pulled over his head.

"Make a muscle, Dad Two. Everyone wants to see." Buzz grabbed for his arm, trying to bend it into a crook.

After a moment he grinned and relented. "Sure, kiddo," he laughed. Standing, he did an overly dramatic imitation of a muscle pose or two before grabbing his shirt and pulling it over his head. "The story, Riley? Is it over?"

"Whoa, bro! You know it's not over." He turned to the crowd. "These girls wanted a picture of little bro, here. At nineteen, I must say, he was quite the looker, and he climbed up on the diving stand without his shirt. 'Take off the pants!' they yelled, and lo and behold if he didn't reach down, unsnap the waistband, and drop them off as the crowd watched."

Angelique covered her eyes as she laughed, and as she leaned back, she bumped Buzz. Looking his way, she whispered, "He was wearing a suit underneath, I hope."

He called out, "Was he wearing a suit under his pants?"

"Was he wearing a suit?" Riley paused and looked around as if searching for the answer in the air around him. Then he grinned. "Not exactly. However, he did have on these bright red boxer shorts—"

"Like at the racetrack?" Buzz grinned.

His father looked at him. "Not like at the racetrack. That's another story, altogether. Hm." He paused. "Maybe we should hear that one, instead."

Houston wailed, "No, Riley. Tell the diving story, please, not the one at the racetrack. Please, big bro."

"Diving? There's a diving story?" Riley grinned maliciously. "Well, there Houston was at the racetrack in his red underwear—"

Houston grabbed his leg and yanked hard, causing the tall man at his side to stumble and topple back into the sand. Laughter roared from around the table.

"Up, up, storyteller." Treavor clapped. "I want to know the end." He motioned to Heather at his side. "Clap with me." Before long, their entire side of the feast was clapping in time, calling to Riley to get up and continue his story. Even somber Gator across the pit had begun to join in.

Angelique grabbed Riley's leg and shook it, her laughter barely letting her speak. "Riley, I have to hear the end of this story. Please get up!"

He propped himself up on his elbows, and he looked at the cheering crowd. When his son scrambled over the sand to put his arms under his shoulders, lifting him up, he finally stood and brushed the sand off his clothes.

"The best is yet to come, charming gentlefolk. Nineteen-year-old Houston stood there in all his red underwear glory to the adoring cheers of a growing crowd. It was when they began to chant for him to jump that it got really wild." The crowd around the luau had gone quiet, anticipating the culminating results brought about on the cliffs of Acapulco. Even the music had come to a stop, and the swaying of the grass skirts could barely be heard. The servers and the concierges seemed transfixed as well.

"Little bro stood there, and he flexed his muscles, hoping to quiet the crowd's roars of adulation. However, they wouldn't be contented until they had their way. They wanted satisfaction, and what tipped the scales was when several of the women ran up and slipped twenty-dollar bills inside the waistband of his shorts."

"They did not," Houston lamented. "There were no twenties."

"Fifties, then," Riley smirked. "The girls left fifties. It was the pretty boys who left the twenties."

"Ha!" Houston snorted. "Get it over with, Riley."

"Anyway, this part really happened. One of the girls, the prettiest one, if I do say so myself, walked out to him, and she ran her hand up his arm and across his chest, giving him a little peck right on the lips. That really happened, didn't it, Houston?"

"Say yes, Dad Two. You know it did!" Buzz jumped in ex-

117

citement.

He nodded, his face flushing once again. "I have to own up to that. That was what convinced me to—"

"No, bro!" Riley interrupted him. "This is my story. You can't just take it over. Anyway, my soulmate, here, got this silly grin on his face. Then, when she told him, 'I know you can do it. This is from me,' in French, nonetheless, and she knelt and slipped a hundred-dollar bill into the pants lying there at his feet, was when he took leave of his senses."

"No," Jerrold cried. "In French? How did she know he'd understand her? He didn't jump, did he?"

"F-1 in Monaco? Houston had picked up a phrase or two. Show them, Houston." Riley held his hand out to his brother as if he were on display.

"S'il vous plaît passer à autre chose." The reply was mumbled.

"Get on with it, if you please?" Riley laughed. "Did they say that to you, also?"

Around the luau, the diners picked up the chant. "Get on with it," they called, clapping and hooting at Riley.

"But, wait. It gets better. A bathing suit is designed to stay on. Boxer shorts are designed to come off. Dear Houston was halfway down when those red shorts fluttered from his ankles and into the sea. He hit the water in nothing but the good looks God gave him on the day he was born. Whew, but did he ever get some cheers on that one! By the time I retrieved his pants, there were probably another two hundred bills stuffed inside."

"Three sixty, all together," Houston clarified. "Tell what happened to it."

Riley chuckled. "There's only one way up the cliffs, and that's to climb."

Beckie chortled, "Without a suit?" She leaned over both Robby and his brother to poke Heather, and she grinned. "They couldn't throw him one down?"

"Another suit would never make it," Gator called out in response. "The wind already blew his shorts away, remember?"

"Oh!" She giggled. "We should have been there, Heather."

"I did make it back up." Houston pushed the story to its end. "I slipped into those pants just as the policia showed up. It seemed the regular divers weren't very happy about a gringo taking their business away."

"The money! Tell them about the money!"

Everyone laughed at the boy's enthusiasm.

"Ah, the money," Riled intoned. "Most of it was inside the pants, and I mean inside. The policia confiscated all they could find in the pockets, but they never could understand why dear Houston here crinkled as he walked all the way to the policia station and back again. It was a funny few days, though, afterward, because—"

"Do not tell this part!" Houston grabbed his brother's leg again. "Riley, I swear—"

"—because the wadded up money inside his pants rubbed him raw, and you can imagine what that means!"

Houston ducked his head, but no one noticed. They were all rolling in the sand, unable to control their laughter. Even the hula dancers had stopped their swaying, and they held their hands over their mouths to hide their smiles.

Over the three hours spent around the pit containing the remains of their roasted pig, the merrymakers had a rousing time, and not even Christian running through the crowd being chased by an orange and brown rooster fouled the pleasure of the group's first evening in Hawaii. If anything, the laughter brought on by the poor man leaping wildly in terror from such a small, feathered creature bonded the eleven people even tighter. Shared events have a way of doing that, and this night, laughter was the thread that tied them together.

To top the merriment off, it didn't rain until the party was over, not one tiny drop. The sand stayed completely dry until everyone was ensconced in their individual villas, sleeping as quietly as island birds in their nests.

CHAPTER 10

HOUSTON WOKE WITH his face pressed into his pillow.

Around him birdsong laced the air. The smells of flowers wafted in on the breezes, with the tropical fragrances entering the villa through the openings above the bedroom walls. Taking a deep breath, he turned his head to the side and luxuriated in the feel of the linen sheets against his skin. This was a morning to be savored.

Opening his eyes, he noticed something he hadn't been aware of the previous evening. A curtain of gauze surrounded his bed. Throwing his sheets back, he sat up and realized something else. There were fresh flowers in the room that hadn't been there the evening before, either. He remembered other flowers, but they'd been yellow, and these were intensely vivid in reds and oranges.

A covered, silver tray on his bedside table with a glass container of bottled water next to it caught his eye. Reaching through the gauze netting, he uncovered the tray and was pleased to find a buttery cinnamon roll inside. Julia, he thought. He realized the concierge had already been in. With a smile, he took a bite and set the rest of it back on the tray for later.

Pushing the netting roughly aside, he stepped to the pool, looked around, and noticed his brother's door opened. Glancing inside, two redheaded bodies sprawled on the bed, with four freckled arms and just as many legs protruding at odd angles from the disheveled bedding. Glimpses of brightly colored boxer shorts peeked from underneath the sheets, and he was amused to see the ones on Buzz were nearly identical to his own red, patterned ones. When Riley said the boy worshipped him, he forgot it extended all the way to his underwear.

Stepping inside to the living room, he was surprised to see the side table pulled out and dressed for breakfast. A card stood on each gleaming white plate. He picked one up and chuckled. It was a miniature breakfast menu with Julia's name and number underneath. He turned when he heard the second bedroom door open.

"Uncle Houston," Buzz called. His hair was askew, and he scratched underneath one arm. "Did you order the rolls?" The boy blinked against the morning light, and he yawned, working his fingers into his hair before rubbing his hand down the back of his neck.

"A wake-up gift from Julia." He smiled. "I got one, too. Did you try yours?"

"Not yet. I just heard sounds, and I wanted to see who it was. Last night was fun." He smiled underneath puffy eyes. "Can I really stay the whole six weeks? I brought my schoolwork. Dad says it's up to you, but he also said five weeks is a long time alone with a thirteen-year-old."

"Come here, boy." Houston held one arm out. "Six weeks," he continued. "You're all mine for six weeks. You've never stayed with me that long, have you?"

"No, sir. There were two and a half weeks one summer when I was little. That's the longest time I remember."

"Ah, yes, in that beach house on Cannon Beach up in Oregon with your parents." Riley and his wife had been trying to work things out then, and he and his nephew had slept in hammocks on the porch the entire time, even getting drenched one night in a sudden, summer shower. It had been freezing, and they had gone in and built a big fire in the fireplace. Riley's wife had eventually left, but Houston felt he'd been a real father to Buzz that night.

Then, breaking the moment, the boy pulled away and pummeled his uncle's arm with his fists. Houston roared and grabbed the boy in his arms.

"So, it's going to be like that! Well, I can quench these fires." He did, too, carrying the frantic, laughing teenager through the bedroom and out to the pool. "I guess someone will have to change shorts, Buzz." He flung the boy into the water, his own feet getting soaked as the splash washed onto the deck.

"Oh, it's just you." Riley stood at the door to his bedroom and yawned.

Houston turned at the sound of his brother's voice. "Your boy wanted a swim, brother." He grinned, knowing the boy had wanted no such thing.

Riley scratched his jaw, yawning again. "Our boy, Houston. On this trip, he's yours as much as mine. I'm going back to bed."

As he turned, Houston felt a hand on his ankle, but by then it was too late. Buzz yanked, and Houston toppled into the pool on top of his nephew. When they came to the surface, Buzz swam up behind him, wrapping his legs around his uncle's waist and his arms around his neck.

"Looks like you're right, Uncle Houston. We both have to change." He snickered into his ear.

Riley walked to the pool and knelt at the edge of the water. Reaching his hand inside, he pulled out a dripping pair of red boxer shorts. He held them out to Houston.

"I keep telling you, Houston. Buy a smaller size." Then, as Houston reached for them, he flipped them across the pool. "Marco Polo." He laughed as his brother twisted out of his nephew's grasp and dove for the offending piece of clothing. He pointed at his son, "You, boy, keep your shorts on. You don't let your uncle set you a bad example."

"I won't, Dad. Promise." He grinned, glancing to see his uncle underwater as he attempted to get into his shorts.

"Love you, son. Let me sleep a while, though." He waved and stepped into the bedroom.

Then the boy's head disappeared underwater, with Houston's hands on his feet. The battle had begun.

𝒜NGELIQUE DIALED THE PHONE with her hands quivering, and as it rang, she could barely keep her eyes from the glass doors to her pool.

"Blue Water Maui. This is Sven. How may I be of service, Angelique?"

"Oh, Sven. Thank goodness you're up. I was so afraid I was calling too early to catch you." She breathed her desperation into the phone. "The luau was so wonderful last night, with you and the other two concierges. I'm sorry I can't remember their names—"

"Julia and Christian."

"Yes, thank you, Sven. You all worked so hard to make our first night enjoyable. I cannot thank you enough."

"It was our pleasure, Angelique."

"You must have been up for hours afterward, though. You should be sleeping in. I really thought I might get voicemail, or at the least the front desk."

"It's never too early for you to contact me, Angelique. This number rings directly to my phone. How may I be of service this morning?"

"There's a chicken, Sven, orange and brown with a black tail. It's outside, and somehow it's gotten into my pool enclosure. I'd like to go for a swim, and each time I open the door, it attacks me. I feel lucky it can't get over the walls and into the villa."

He chuckled. "I know that chicken, or rather, I know of that chicken. It's a Maui rooster."

"You've encountered it? Is it dangerous?"

"To answer your first question, I have not. One of the other concierges has, though. Remember the luau and the crazy rooster from last night? It was very late, and you may have been too tired by then to notice."

She laughed. "Of course! So much was going on, my girlfriends and I thought it was part of the planned events. This is that same animal?"

"Yes. It seems to have developed a dislike for my friend, Christian, and it chases him whenever it sees him. Tell me, Angelique, do you keep your nails polished with bright fingernail polish?"

She looked at her hands. "I don't know about bright, Sven. They're certainly shiny. What difference could that make?"

He laughed. "I'll bring you some polish remover. The rooster sees you as competition. Rather, it sees your polished nails as the fighting weapons of an intruding enemy. I suspect that if we remove the weapons, the rooster will leave you in peace."

"Remove my nails, Sven? Did I just hear you say that?" She laughed, knowing exactly what he was telling her.

He played along. "If you wish, Angelique. However, just removing the polish will probably work fine. Let's take that small step first."

Just then, there was a very loud squawk, and the sounds of wings beat at the glass doors to the pool.

"Sven! All I did was wave my hand at the rooster again, just to tell it to go away!" Her heart beat fast. "What made it go wild?"

"Weapons, Angelique. To the rooster, you just brandished your weapons. Be patient. I'll be right there."

"Thank you, Sven. I appreciate you doing this for me."

SVEN SOFTLY HUNG UP the phone, and he yawned and shifted against his pillow. He wasn't up, but now he guessed he soon would be.

Christian, also bunking in the employees' dorm, rolled his eyes. "It seems to have developed a dislike for my friend, Christian. Well, thank you, Sven." He jumped out of bed and stood in front of the mirror admiring his fingernails. The dark burgundy polish glittered against the milk chocolate of his skin. "Do you think Julia is up, yet? I might go over to the girl's dorm to see if she has more of this dark red color. I think I have a chip." He studied one nail carefully.

Sven rolled out of his bed. "You know Julia's been up since dawn, out there setting up her villa. I bet she already has the breakfast dishes out. She keeps her polish in her footlocker, though. She won't mind if you borrow it." He stepped toward the bathroom. "I'm taking a quick shower. Bring me a bottle of her polish remover. I'll replace it this afternoon."

Christian stepped to the open bathroom door and called to him, "Julia always wears polish. Why doesn't that rooster attack her like it does me?" His lips began to pout.

"Gloves, Christian."

"Gloves? If I wear gloves, then what's the purpose of the polish? Good heavens, I might as well not wear it at all!"

126

HEATHER STOOD OVER the jumble of clothes strewn over her bed, her mosquito netting earlier wrestled aside and bunched up against the wall. She glanced at Beckie still asleep on the other side of the double bedroom they shared. Her netting was pulled around her, and she smiled at the bundle of pink hair tousled around her friend's head. Searching the items she'd pulled out, she reached her freshly manicured fingers to a black camisole bunched up on the foot of her bed.

"Beckie, Beckie," she whispered, well aware the other woman was still asleep. "Why did I ever bring a dressy thing like this to Hawaii?" She shook the camisole out and laced the thin straps onto a hanger, stepping to the closet to drape it among all her swimsuits. "It's just like college all over again. Angelique's beautiful, and you and I, girl, have to be flamboyant and flashy just to get the men to notice us."

Across the room, Beckie turned beneath her sheets, and through the gauziness of the netting, her voluptuous figure could be seen shifting under the crisp linens. Heather was glad the girl was a late sleeper. That meant she could be up, dressed, and out of the way before her friend came alive for the day.

She snatched at several items of clothing, leaving most of what she had dragged from her stash, and with a flounce of yellow-haired excitement, she disappeared into the bathroom and gently shut the door behind her.

With the water running in the tub, she dropped the strings from her sleeping gown over her shoulders. Hunching her back and wriggling her body, she smiled luxuriantly as the shimmery fabric slithered down her torso. She liked doing that. It reminded her she still had her college figure, unlike Miss Buxom Babe asleep out in the other room.

Opening several cabinets, she found where Christian had secreted the bath oils she'd brought for her private use. Pulling

127

out her favorite, Jo Malone, directly from Neiman Marcus, she picked Nectarine Blossom & Honey, adding just a touch of White Jasmine & Mint as she poured them into the filling bath. As the amber oils dispersed throughout the churning water, she inhaled the delicious fragrance. Then, putting the glass tops back on the decanters, she turned the faucet off with a quick snap. Setting one foot into the water, she felt the warmth slide up around her ankle. Sitting on the edge of the tub, she slid underneath the water's surface, keeping only her head exposed; and she closed her eyes to relish the heat emanating through her skin.

"Oh, this is heaven," she murmured, slipping beneath the enveloping liquid. When she could no longer hold her breath, she pressed with her feet to force her head out of the aromatic fluid filling the tub. She luxuriated in the water with her eyes closed, knowing that Beckie had better sleep a very long time. She wasn't getting this bathroom for quite a while.

Over the tops of the truncated bathroom walls, where a slice of tropical blue sky smiled through the beamed roof, the early morning sun filtered in. Along with it, the sounds of the surrounding wilds filling the tropical isle floated in, a peaceful curtain of sound dispersed on the sunbeams. From somewhere in the greenery surrounding the villa came the sounds of a cardinal, or perhaps it was a finch. Heather didn't know her birds all that well, but she could tell wonderful when she heard it.

Then she noticed another, more familiar sound, a man's voice, and he yelled at something to go away. Beating wings thrashed the air. She grinned, safely ensconced within her villa, splashing perfumed water gently across one exposed leg.

Heather sat up when the voice yelled, "You evil rooster! Stay out of that villa. Go back to your home, wherever that is!"

She was startled when something hit the outside wall of her villa. She looked up, freezing in terror to find an orange and black-feathered bird calmly perched on the top of the wall just above her tub, and it had its head twisted to look down just where she lay in her beautifully scented water.

"Go away, bird," she shrieked in sudden panic. "Go!" She raised her hands in the air to shoo it away, but as she brandished her bright red, very shiny nails in the air, the feathered animal seemed to take on a completely different disposition. Rather than continuing to sit quietly, it stood and spread its wings, making itself appear much more formidable than it really was. Then, with a maniacal sound tearing from its tortured throat, the red-crested, territorial bird leaped to attack.

When the rooster swooped down, its wings held wide, it seemed to Heather to dive into her tub in a slow-motion parody of a martial arts kick. When it hit the water, she came out of the bath in a violent geyser of flailing limbs. Her shrieks outdid that of the squawking rooster, and grabbing a towel, she flew from her bathroom, directly into the bedroom, and out the villa's front door, holding the towel in her hand as her only defense against the inquiring eyes of the world.

"There's a chicken in my bathtub!" Her words shattered the silence of the early morning, and once she had released that tension to the skies, she realized her chest might be covered by the towel she still held, but nothing else was. Gasping in dismay, she frantically began to wrap it around herself for protection from prying eyes.

About that time, a medium-height man with a very rotund appearance, one wearing a tailored jacket, appeared just off the stoop of her villa.

"Good morning, miss. Are you all right?" His words came in gasps.

She was flustered, but she was pretty sure the man was Sven, Angelique's concierge from the previous day. However, no matter who he belonged to, he was standing outside her villa, and all she had on was her towel. Her earlier burst of adrenalin twisted to anger.

"Turn around, Sven, my good man!" She snapped one finger in the air and twirled it, taking firm control of this unexpected and very irritating situation. After he complied, his eyes wide at her sudden, commanding tone, she burst out, once again frightened instead of angry. "I was so scared. What's that animal doing in there? Is it a karate chicken?" Then she stamped her foot, frustration making her words curt. "Tell me, man. Do you always herd karate attack chickens into your guests' bathrooms to harass them while they soak in your tubs? Is this a Hawaiian initiation rite? Because, you know, if it is, I can perform a few rites of my own." With that, she grabbed his ear and twisted until he turned and fell to his knees.

"Please, miss. Uncle. I cry uncle. Please. I am just poor Sven, and I only want your stay at Blue Water Maui to be enjoyable. Please do not torture me any longer. It is only a poor Maui rooster."

She released the pressure enough to quiet the pleading, but she raked him harshly with her words. "Why did you chase that thing directly into my bathroom? I heard you, you know. You chased it and chased it, and then when it came to my villa, you threw something at it to make it go over that wall. Why?" Her eyes narrowed, and as her breathing increased, she burned with anger once again at being forced to stand in the tropical morning sun, wrapped only in her Blue Water Maui towel.

"Uncle, please." He grabbed at his ear. "I only chased the rooster from Angelique's pool. It wouldn't leave the compound, and then it attacked me. It thought I had a weapon."

"Weapon?" Her eyes narrowed. "Why did it attack me, then? I had no weapon. I didn't even have any clothes on." She let go of his ear and adjusted her towel to make sure it covered her completely, glancing up at the sun with a squint, only now

130

realizing how bright it was outside. She also didn't have her sunglasses, and that doubled her irritation.

He rubbed his ear, grimacing. "I see your weapons, or at least what the rooster sees as your weapons." His eyes locked on her brightly colored fingernails.

"What?" Her question was short and harsh.

"Did you show your hands to the rooster before it flew into your bathroom? It was sitting quietly on the top of your wall, and then it changed personalities. The rooster doesn't like to share its territory."

"These?" She held up her hands and laughed. "Weapons?"

He pulled at his reddened ear, and he nodded. "Most certainly. The polish. It's very bright, and to a Maui rooster, its nails are the only weapons it has. It sees yours as weapons, also. I've provided polish remover to Angelique. I can arrange for Christian to deliver a bottle to your villa, if you wish."

She laughed and turned to the villa's door. "My nails? You have got to be kidding. This is a special mix by my manicurist." She held one hand next to her yellow hair. "It coordinates with my latest color." She glared at the man as she reached for the doorknob, grasping at it with her hand. "I believe I'll go in now."

"The rooster—" Sven's voice barked out a sudden warning, and he threw out his hand to stop her.

"Rooster? That chicken had better watch out for Heather!" Fully irritated as well as rather embarrassed, she interrupted him heedlessly and pushed the door hard and wide.

"—is still in there!" He ducked, covering his head with his arms.

With a loud squawk and flailing wings, a brown and orange bird with a red crown and long black tail feathers flew past her head, startling her into a squawk of her own. The bird ran, stumbled, and then flew down the walk and across the motor

131

court.

"It tried to attack me again! I had no idea Hawaii was infested with such deadly creatures." She put her hand to her throat, inhaling great draughts of air, her knees weak with the sudden surge of adrenalin through her system. "Do you think it's safe, now?" She peered into the villa and back at Sven.

"The animal is gone," he encouraged her, shifting smoothly back into concierge mode. "You have a roommate?"

She nodded. "Beckie. She was asleep."

"Perhaps you should check on her. She may be frightened. Would you like me to wait for a moment until you know?" He bowed slightly at the waist.

In an emotion-filled voice, she agreed. However, when she walked back into the bedroom to see her friend still sound asleep underneath the cool, linen sheets, an unreasonable irritation shot through her veins, and she stepped immediately to the bathroom, forgetting all about Sven. Her concern was for the wasted bath oils, and, with rising disgust at the chicken that had shared her bath water, she reached inside and pulled the drain. She thought a shower would suffice from then on. She had no desire to share any more of her precious oils with that chicken.

OUTSIDE, SVEN WAITED for a time, whistling softly in the pleasant morning breeze. After a short while, when Heather didn't return, he decided things had calmed down for a bit, and he could head back to the main resort. After all, this was Christian's villa, not his, and Angelique deserved all the attention he could give her. She was paying the bills for the next six weeks. The resort's records showed that. If he was really good, she might even return for a repeat stay. That would be when he would see a financial bonus out of all his work. Blue Water Maui loved repeat guests, and he had an outstanding record for reeling them in. He was determined this time would be no different.

CHAPTER 11

"UNCLE HOUSTON!" BUZZ knocked on the bathroom door, yelling over the sound of running water. He had a big grin on his face. "Julia's here. She's promised to bring me a parasailing harness to try on."

"Julia?" The water went quiet. As in the rest of the villas, all the walls stopped at seven feet, with open air above. Houston's question carried over quite nicely.

"You know, the lady from yesterday?" Buzz turned to her and smiled. "Remember, from last night?"

"Hold on." The water started up for a minute before it went silent once again. The door opened, and a wet arm appeared. With a grunt of surprise, Buzz was pulled inside.

"She's still waiting?" Houston frowned at his nephew. His towel was around his waist, and his hair dripped.

Buzz grinned and nodded.

"Look at me, nephew. See me, my towel, this hair?" Houston ran his hand over his head and shook it off in Buzz's direction. "Did she say it was urgent to talk to me right now? I'm not exactly dressed."

"Not really, and she's not exactly here about parasailing. I just asked her about getting me a harness for that. She said she doesn't think the one I brought will work."

"So, ask her to let you try on one of theirs."

His grin broadened. "Okay." He pulled open the door. "You can come in, now."

"Good morning, Houston. Do you mind? I hope Buzz hasn't put you out any. I did offer to wait in the living room. He insisted I join you wherever you happened to be on your regular morning schedule." She worked to keep a smile from her face.

"He did, did he?" Houston glared at his nephew. "He's such a thoughtful boy."

"I thought so, too. I've not had a chance to formally introduce myself to you personally. You were out when I came by yesterday, and as you know, last evening was quite a busy time. I'm Julia Havershine. Are your towels fine, sir? Soaps? Shampoo?"

Houston sighed, and Buzz grinned; and with an elbow, he nudged his uncle on the arm.

"EVERYTHING IS WONDERFUL." Houston shifted the towel around his waist, feeling awkward dressed in so little in front of someone he'd only met briefly the day before.

"Did you enjoy the cinnamon rolls this morning?" A glint of amusement shadowed her words.

He felt his face warm. "So, you *were* the mystery person."

She smiled. "Blue Water Maui's motto is to be unobtrusive but always available. I am very discrete, I can assure you. Were the rolls satisfactory? The fresh flowers? The color pallet is changed daily to reflect the current season and or the activities planned for the day."

"You came all this way just to ask about our flowers?" He looked to Buzz, who still grinned ear to ear.

"It's my pleasure, sir. After all, I am your concierge. I'm here to make your stay pleasurable, no matter what your requests may be. Is there anything you need this morning?"

"Yes," Buzz jumped in. "Do you have a sailboard, one of those windsurfing things? I want to go behind a boat, like in that Jurassic Park movie. Okay, Dad Two?"

Julia smiled. "Parasailing. I can arrange that, if your father wishes," and she turned to Houston. "Your partner, Riley, I believe, looks more like the boy . . . ." She lifted her eyebrows in question. "It's not Blue Water Maui's policy to question too closely about a guest's domestic arrangements, but I will be working with you for six weeks. I can hardly skirt around the issue that long."

Houston threw an arm around the boy's neck. "I claim him, and since he calls me Dad, I can hardly deny it." He looked at the boy and winked, squeezing his neck. "Sure, let's make him into an airplane. Do we need to contact someone, perhaps go to the Big Island for his adventure?"

"Our adventure, Dad Two. I want Dad One to go, also, if we can convince him. Also, Uncle Tee and Uncle Jay. They both promised they'd go."

"Parasailing? Are you sure, Buzz? I thought they'd committed to windsurfing, or maybe hang gliding."

"That's what's so great. Parasailing is both. Isn't that right, Julia?" He turned to the concierge for confirmation.

She smiled. "After a fashion, you are absolutely correct." She paused and coughed. "Um, Houston, would you be more comfortable if we allowed you to dress, first? Your son and I can step to the bedroom if you wish."

Houston chuckled. "No need. I have practice at this." Tightening his towel, he yanked his shirt from the edge of the tub and slipped it over his head. Then he grabbed for a light-weight pair of chinos, and slipped a pair of orange boxer shorts inside for easy dressing. He worked the pants onto each foot, and drew them under the towel, letting it fall in one smooth motion. When Julia cheered and clapped, congratulating him on a dangerous feat safely pulled off in front of a hotel employee as well as his son, he grinned.

"Quite well done, sir. How old is your boy, anyway? Seventeen?" She winked at Houston.

"See, Dad Two? Seventeen." Buzz grinned.

Houston laughed. "She just thinks you're cute. All puppies are, Buzz." The boy's face fell, and Houston grabbed his neck and squeezed it. "I like puppies, Buzz, cute or not. You'll grow into a dashing woman killer, just not at thirteen. Be patient, son." He turned to Julia. "Did you catch the thirteen? He got his height early. Let's head out to the pool. The morning's too nice to spend it all inside."

On the deck they found the wet boxer shorts from earlier. Buzz ran up and tried to kick them aside, causing Houston to laugh.

"Swimming already this morning?" Julia smiled.

Houston laughed. "Not by choice, either of us. It was sort of spur of the moment. The boy went in—"

Buzz protested, "You threw me!"

"—and then he pulled me in. Needless to say, we had to change, and those didn't make it inside."

Buzz snickered in a way that only teenage boys can. "You couldn't keep yours on. They came off again when you climbed out of the pool, just like they did when I pulled you in."

Houston shot him a frown, shaking his head.

"Oh," she laughed. "I get it. Let's have a seat around the table, if you don't mind."

Houston pulled out three chairs, pointing Buzz to one, and

letting Julia take a second. He pulled up the third beside her. Then he glanced past his nephew through the door Riley had left open when he'd come to chide them earlier. His brother was still asleep on the bed, and typical for Riley, there was more of him uncovered than covered.

"Buzz, Riley's still asleep. The door, could you close it?"

Julia cleared her throat for attention, looking at Houston. "That's necessary only if you feel the need. I'll honor whatever privacy concerns you may have, but actual nudity is the official benchmark for the staff. Many people wear very little here in the privacy of the villas, and as a concierge, I'm required to move in and out regularly. Soon, you won't notice my presence. I'm very good at listening as well as making a discrete visual inspection before entering a room. If your, um, partner is not exposed, please let him have the fresh air."

"Fresh air?" Houston pointed to the roof that was balanced several feet above the tops of the walls.

She chuckled. "Still, the doors provide better circulation than just the elevated roof alone. Your partner will appreciate your consideration."

"Okay, then. Buzz, leave the door." Houston settled in. "Surely you aren't here about flowers and ventilation. What do we have to discuss?"

"You have guests arriving." She brightened her face and smiled.

"We have guests?" Buzz grinned and leaned forward to push on Houston's arm. "Uncle H?"

"I don't know, Buzz." He turned to Julia with a smile. "Did they give you a name?"

"They left me a bit confused on that," she said. "I thought if I talked to you, you might clear things up. If you don't know them, we will certainly exclude these guests from intruding. And no, Buzz, it's not Uncle H, whoever that is."

He grinned, slapping his uncle's arm. "Oh, I know that. He's already here."

She smiled politely at the oblique response. "My conversation was with someone named Cheeky, and I couldn't tell from the conversation if it was a man or a woman. I'm very sorry for that. I thought a man at first, and then from the inflection, I decided it could very well be a female. If you know this person, you may need to clarify the gender for me. Cheeky spoke of someone named Squeegie and Granny Swell. I do hope Squeegie isn't a pet, as Blue Water Maui has strict limitations when it comes to pets. We do have a boarding kennel at the main resort, but pets aren't allowed in our guest rooms."

Houston was distracted by his view of his brother through the door, and while Houston might well need to buy his boxers in a smaller size, Riley could do with something a little less snug. He took it as his opportunity to speak to the concierge privately.

"Excuse me for a moment, Julia. Buzz, your dad's door. Please close it." He nodded his head toward Riley's room, and when the boy stepped away, he turned to Julia. "I know them, and there will be no pets, if you don't consider an over-energized eight-year-old a wild animal. Did Cheeky give any reason for the visit?" He thought of Angelique. She said Lucas told her of his reasons for the marriage, but she also acted very despondent at his death. He wasn't sure just where her emotions stood, and he didn't need Cheeky here to stir things up. Last night was the first time he'd really seen her come alive since the wedding, and he hated to see that meddled with.

"It was a bit unclear, sir." She glanced at Buzz before turning back to Houston. She kept her voice low. "If they are unwelcome, well." She shrugged. "It's your call."

"Buzz," he called as the boy reached the door. "Go fill a glass of water and put it beside Riley's bed. He'll be thirsty when he wakes." He was relieved to see the boy step inside without mentioning the bottled water from earlier. Buzz had been told little about either Cheeky or Squeegie, and Granny Swell was close to a mystery, even to Houston. "Why should it be my call? I'm just here as one of Angelique's guests."

"He specifically asked for you. Houston, he insisted. He needed to contact Houston. I didn't think he meant Texas." She smiled. "He kept saying something about having sold Mother's Milk, and Ricky was waiting for him in Rio. Ricky Martin?"

He guffawed at her choice of celebrities. "Cheeky would love you for that. However, no. This is our own Ricky, no kin to Mr. Martin." He paused, wondering how much to tell. None of it was secret, though, and the more information Julia had, the better prepared she'd be. "Ricky's in Rio for Carnival, although he's the one who wanted Squeegie. That's why this is catching me off guard. If Cheeky were dropping the girl anywhere, that's where I'd expect him to take her." He remembered something he'd seen in a pamphlet in the villa. "Don't you do Carnival on the Big Island?"

"Mardi Gras, but you'll need to be on Oahu. You have general information about that and other seasonal events in the white folder in your villa. It's far too early for the annual festival, but I can get you more details, if you're interested." Julia jotted a note in a folder she carried.

"I'm fine, no. I'm simply trying to put this together. Before moving to Rio, Ricky originally wanted to come to Hawaii. Honolulu, I think, but there wasn't money."

"Yes, Honolulu is where he'd need to be for Mardi Gras. How is Rio cheaper?" Julia smiled.

"When it's free." Houston chuckled. "He got gratis lodgings in Rio in exchange for his Carnival designs." He snorted, shaking his head. "Giant devil heads. His designs, that is. He created these giant heads that go on a float. But I'm rambling, and that's not what you're here to discuss. What about Squeegie and Granny Swell?"

"You're fine. The more I know, the better I can provide for you here at the resort. I got the distinct impression he only bought one-way tickets to here for Squeegie and Granny Swell. I had hoped you might be able to offer me some insight."

He groaned. "I think we've got company that's here to stay."

"There shouldn't be a problem. Your group still has one unoccupied villa. It's one of Christian's six, Forget-Me-Not Villa. I can ask him to prepare it for their arrival."

"Did Cheeky say when he was arriving for his visit?"

"Oh!" Her voice was bright with cheeriness. "Cheeky's not staying. He's only landing long enough to transfer to Rio. He said he intends to leave Squeegie and Granny Swell with you. With your permission, of course. We can be as flexible with this situation as you wish. It's not unusual for our guests to be in and out of their villas during their stay here, often remaining off island for weeks at a time."

Buzz tumbled onto the lanai. "Dad One's up," he said. "I accidentally spilled the water on him."

"Does he need anything, a towel, perhaps?" Julia stood, taking a moment to straighten her chair.

"A new pair of shorts?" Houston laughed at his own joke, glancing at Buzz when the boy snickered. Then he turned to Julia. "I apologize. An inside joke. Please let Christian know to prepare the last villa, and Julia, when do we need to go to the airport to pick up Squeegie and Granny Swell?"

She smiled. "I believe they have already arrived, and my driver is waiting with them now. I will see to everything."

"Thank you." Houston stood to shake her hand. He missed the presence of beautiful women when he spent so much time with the guys from the old fraternity.

"I can let myself out." She shook and headed back towards the door leading into Houston's bedroom. Pushing it open, she shrieked and backed out, leaning against the wall, her face bright red.

"What?" Houston thought of snakes or worse.

She laughed, taking a deep breath. "My fault," she apologized, raising her palm to let him know all was okay. "I didn't look discretely before entering. There's a naked man in there."

"Redheaded?" Houston grinned.

"Freckles, too, I believe." She patted her chest and took a deep breath. "I am so sorry."

Houston stepped to the door and yelled, "Riley, get out of my things."

"My underwear's too tight," his brother called back.

Houston leaned into the opening. "Thank God you finally noticed." When he looked back at Julia, her hand covered her mouth, but her eyes were crinkled with laughter.

Buzz didn't try to contain how he felt. He was holding his sides, and taking a misstep, he fell right into the pool.

That got Houston going, and after Buzz surfaced, all three of them were laughing at Riley, and the poor man didn't know why.

CHAPTER 12

CHRISTIAN STRODE INTO the bedroom of Hydrangea Villa to make the bed, after checking carefully to ensure its occupant was in another room. He was startled to see a sandy-haired man lying there, one he was certain he had just seen step into the bathroom.

Blinking his eyes, he backed into the villa's living area to double-check his Blue Water Maui tablet. Scrolling though the list of mini-villas, he was reminded that two men were assigned to this one. Twins. He breathed a sigh of relief. They'd requested a set of martini supplies, and several of the items had been difficult to procure on such short notice. They were already out at the bar.

He paused as he heard the bathroom door open. He sighed and slipped the tablet back into his pocket. One of his six villas—Forget-Me-Not—was to receive two new guests this afternoon, and to get everything accomplished, he needed to stay moving. He'd hoped to save time by starting here, but not now.

A voice called out, "Bobby, did you bring any lotion? I want to smell masculine today." When there was no answer, the speaker called again, louder, "Bobby! Lotion? Is anyone out there?"

Now Christian couldn't simply leave. He'd need to identify himself so no one became concerned about a stranger having been in the villa. Before he could speak, a groggy answer wafted over the partial walls.

"Lotion? Robby, use what you have."

Christian backed toward the villa's front door. Perhaps he could escape without notice, after all. The fresh flowers were out, and he'd set up the martini supplies. The maid would be around later in the day to take care of the bedding. He grasped the door knob and froze as the conversation started up again.

"All I have is Oriens," the man in the bathroom called. "I don't want to smell like raspberry and praline here on the island. Get up, Bobby. I'm dripping water onto my towel. I can't allow my skin to dry just because you want to sleep."

"Van Cleef and Arpels Oriens?" The second man's groggy voice grew stronger. "You've got to be kidding. Where did you get that? I didn't know anyone carried it except Neiman's, and we haven't been there in months."

"Bergdorf's. I stopped by when we were on Fifth just before Lucas' wedding. You ran to see about that console we ordered for Trump's place while I went in. Come on, Bobby. Hurry. I like to lotion while I'm damp."

"I'm digging. The concierge put everything away, and I can't find anything. Ah, here! I have Vera Wang Princess. Can you use it?" There was a pause. "And how did you have enough money to go to Bergdorf's? I've seen the bill for that console you picked out. I do get updates on my phone, you know."

Christian smiled when he heard the first man wail with despair.

"Forget the bill, Bobby. I cannot wear Vera Wang. I want to smell masculine. Go see if Houston has something. Anything I can wear in mixed company."

"First you want lotion, and now you want cologne. Make up your mind, brother."

"I just want to be a man!"

"Good luck there," the second voice snorted.

"Bobby!" The first voice wailed. "Even Old Spice will do. Anything!"

Christian decided to take mercy on them, and he reached to knock on the door, calling loudly, "This is Christian, your concierge. Good morning. I hope your stay at Blue Water Maui has been satisfactory so far. Is there anything you need?" He paused, waiting for a reply.

"Um, Christian?"

"Yes?" Pulling his tablet out, he glanced at the display to make sure he accurately remembered the names of the people in this mini-villa. "Am I speaking with Robby or Bobby?" He'd also heard them called Robbo and B-Bob, but that might be a bit too familiar this early in their stay at the resort.

"This is Bobby, Christian. Please come in."

He did so to find him in a pair of cotton sleeping pants and a lightweight tee shirt. The drawers were all opened, and items had been pulled out haphazardly.

"It is our wish here at Blue Water Maui for everything to be to your satisfaction." Christian knew what the men wanted, but he couldn't let them know he'd been listening. "Is there anything I can bring you? Fresh towels? Soap? Lotions?"

An expression of relief flooded Bobby's face. "Yes, lotions! Could you, please? Do you know Houston?"

"Ah," he smiled. "The dark-haired man with the redheaded boy, correct? I believe they are in Apricot Villa. How may I help you with Houston? Should I check with him for a parti-

144

cular brand?"

A desperate voice filtered over the seven-foot walls. "Christian? This is Robby, and I'm here in the bathroom. My skin's drying, and I'm getting scaly patches. I have to have lotion, either that or cologne. Houston always has some. Even if he has Polo, bring it over. Just hurry."

Christian called out, "It'll be a minute. Climb back in the tub until I return." He glanced at Bobby, who was grinning, and he continued, "I can arrange a massage, too, if you'd care for one. I'm fully qualified and licensed with the State of Hawaii, as well as with Blue Maui Resort. My services are fully covered as part of your villa's standard amenities for as long as you're here."

A sigh of relief came through the door. "Oh, Christian. You're so wonderful. This is going to be the best week of my life."

Bobby tapped Christian on the shoulder and grinned. "You just hit his sweet spot. Thank you, thank you." He bowed before the concierge, moving his hand in front of him in a series of circles as he did so.

"It is my pleasure, sir." Christian smiled and nodded his head.

HOUSTON STEPPED FROM his villa, a bottle of Ralph Lauren Silver in his hand, to see the tropical greenery interspersed with an abundance of flowering shrubs. Lavish beds of blooms were everywhere, and off down the rise, the line of trees that separated the compound from the ocean undulated in the breeze. The blue of the water stretched into the distance as far as he could see.

He chuckled. It wasn't far enough, apparently, for Angelique's protection. Soon, the peace of the island breezes and the languid warmth of the tropical sun would be torn asunder by an

145

eight-year-old freight train running without brakes.

An orange flicker behind one of the villas drew his eyes, reminding him of the bird that had chased Christian at the luau, and thinking of the dark-skinned man reminded him of the bottle of cologne in his hand.

Looking up the hill, he saw the villa he was headed toward perched high above the rest. Robby and Bobby had arrived first, taking their favorite, and he was glad to let them keep it. The one he, Riley, and Buzz were in was at the bottom of the hill, and that meant fewer steps to climb.

Out of the corner of his eye, he saw Angelique's door open, and she stepped outside. Her hair was wet as it clung to her head, and she looked up, blinking at the sun. Glancing around, she raised her hand to wave.

"Good morning, Houston. Am I safe from the rooster?"

"The rooster? Are we under attack?" He laughed, hefting the bottle of cologne in his hand and deciding it could wait. Angelique's presence called to him.

She turned her hand and waggled her fingers his direction. "See? No polish. I'm no longer the rooster's enemy."

"Hold on," he called. "I suspect I might need an explanation, and the distance seems to be hindering our communication."

Behind him, his villa door opened, and Riley appeared, yawning, his ginger hair jutting crazily. He moved into the sun and slapped Houston's shoulder.

"Morning, Riley." Houston dipped his head. "You're not dressed, you know." His shorts looked like the ones from Houston's drawer.

"Yeah. I'm getting there. I couldn't find you, and I wanted to tell you I was wrong and you were right."

"About what?" He hefted the bottle in his hand and gave Angelique an apologetic shrug.

146

She smiled, waving at him to show she could wait.

Riley yawned again. "Your underwear does fit better than mine. I've traded them out." Then he looked to Angelique and waved, throwing an arm over his brother's shoulder. "He's the best, and I love him," he called to her. "You should get you a man like this."

"Riley, off." Houston shrugged.

However, Riley patted his brother on the cheek before taking his arm off his shoulder, and he winked at him. "Go get her, tiger," he leaned in to whisper.

Houston threw his arm around Riley's neck, and pulling him close, he hissed intently, "Lucas has only been dead a week, brother. Have some dignity."

Riley grinned and pushed his brother away, keeping his voice low. "Like that was ever going anywhere. We all know better. She looks at you, Houston. At least don't act like a cold fish." He gave his shoulder a shove, and then he lifted an arm to wave at Angelique once more. "I'm sharing him with you. Send him home by midnight. I don't want him to turn into a pumpkin."

He slapped him on the back and was gone into the villa.

$\mathcal{A}$NGELIQUE WATCHED THE exchange between the two men, and a flood of unwanted jealously came over her. She'd felt unexpected warmth rush through her when Houston had called that he was coming over to talk with her. Then, his . . . partner . . . had stepped out wearing—if she understood his intimations—Houston's underwear. After that they'd leaned in for a moment of intimacy together, and God forbid, might have even kissed one another right on the cheek, although she hadn't seen that clearly. However, Riley's words had been unmistakable. *I love him.* Now, he'd actually offered her his . . . significant other . . . for the day, as long as he was back by midnight.

What would happen at midnight, Riley? That was what she wanted to ask. Then she pushed that thought from her mind. She knew what would happen at midnight, or rather, she didn't know, because she couldn't imagine what men of those proclivities might do in the privacy of their own homes, but she knew it would never include her.

How could she feel such a strong attraction to a man who obviously could feel no such attraction to her? Over the last few days, he hadn't attempted to disguise his love for Riley, so she couldn't blame her misdirected interest on anyone other than herself. It was fueled by grief-driven folly, she supposed, and she deserved to be hurt if she placed her romantic interests on the man's shoulders. She needed to buck up, be strong, and remember that she was a new widow, even if her doubts about Lucas were becoming more and more firmly entrenched in her mind.

She was now convinced there were only two normal men on this island, Gator and Buzz. She didn't think she felt any attraction to one, and she simply could not be interested in the other, not at thirteen. It was her feelings for Houston she'd have to excise from her heart, and she'd have to do it soon, no matter how it hurt.

She turned to see him already on her front lanai, approaching quickly.

"So, what's this about nail polish and being the rooster's enemy?" He flipped the glass bottle he held into the air and caught it as it came down.

"Glass?" She nodded to the gray-green bottle in his hand. "Might'n you break it like that?"

"Oh, this!" He chuckled, and he looked up at the highest villa. "Bobby . . . no, Robby, I think, needs this. According to Christian, he wants to smell like a man, and the only lotions the resort provides are too feminine for him."

"Too feminine?" With the melodious undercurrents of Houston's voice washing the tropical morning, she remembered how this man—who wasn't as much of a man as she wished—kept doing a number on her heart. Each time she spoke with him, he was wonderfully and carelessly charming in a brand new way, and he seemed to truly enjoy each of Lucas' friends, no matter how oddly they behaved.

Then she chuckled, letting herself be caught up in the absurdity of it all. Of course, he enjoyed them. They must all be, how could she say it, *brothers* . . . somehow, in that oddly intimate way that men like him seemed to find so fascinating.

"I heard that, your laugh." He looked at her with a twinkle in his eye. "You don't seem to think the resort's lotions are feminine? Tell me your opinion. You should know feminine. None of us guys do, that's for sure."

She looked at him, chuckling again. "Somehow that rings false, Houston. However, that wasn't what I laughed about." She stepped to the path. "You'll have to walk with me if you want to talk." She would not overtly encourage this man, one who was already committed to another and would only break her heart. He could follow her or not, and if not, she would surely be better off.

"What, then?" He was close on her heels.

"Did you use this today?" She took the bottle from him. "Silver." She slowed her steps and reached to his temple with her free hand, working her fingers into his hair, and pretending to search for something. "There's no silver anywhere. Why's this called Silver if it's not for silver-haired old men?" She took her hand away, and she was horrified at her racing pulse. Reaching to him had been stupid, and she knew she was stoking a churning whirlpool of emotions that she wouldn't be able to extricate herself from later.

He laughed. "I never thought of it that way. Silver. That puts this cologne in a whole new light. Just don't tell Buzz that. He loves this, and he wouldn't ever wear it again." He retrieved the bottle. "Now, to return to my question: What was the laugh for? I've not forgotten you haven't answered, yet. Oh, and where are we going?"

"Two questions," she teased. In spite of his insistence on answers, he didn't seem to mind much that he had no idea of her destination. She looked at him and smirked. "You asked me two questions. How generous do you think I am? You ask one, and before I can even answer, you throw another at me. Do I get any lifelines? 'Yes, Heather, do you know why I laughed? Oh, and Beckie, do you have my destination in your GPS coordinates?'" She looked away and paused before turning back to him. "How do your . . . brothers . . . stand you, Houston, being so pushy and demanding all the time?"

She smiled at him, but she knew why she was rambling. It was the sensations pouring through her bloodstream, the butterflies in her stomach that were terrorizing her. She was here, and he was next to her on this path, and she desperately wanted him to touch her. He wouldn't, though. She knew that, and she also knew that she was frightened by the very possibility he could do exactly that with just a small movement of his arm.

Dear God, she prayed. What have I gotten myself into?

It wasn't God who answered her, though.

"THERE'S ONLY ONE, Angelique."

Houston grinned. The sound of her voice made his heart race, and he was happy just to listen to her speak. When she'd reached for his temple, he'd thought she intended to pull his head to hers to kiss him. He would have let her, too, even after what he'd just told Riley. He might have hated himself afterward, and then he might not. However, he certainly would have been willing to take the chance. Then she'd pulled her hand away and made a joke. Now she was teasing, and he was enjoying even that.

"One what?" She came to the end of the stone motor court, and she paused as she turned into the path to the beach.

"Brother. I only have one. Riley."

As she paused to step over a fallen bloom, he brushed close to her, and the smell of her skin caught in his nostrils, making his knees go weak. He so wanted to touch her, to feel the texture of her skin. They were approaching the beach, and covered by the canopy of green, no one from the compound would see them. He could simply grab her, and in the twisting of her body in his arms, her towel would fall to her feet. She would be in her swimsuit, and he would hold her in a passionate embrace with his lips pressed against hers.

Then, her next words broke the spell he was under, as she retorted to his response with an unexpected slicing parry.

"OH, SO THAT'S WHAT they're called, now. Political correctness, I presume. Brothers." Angelique had earlier used the term for lack of a better word. Now Houston was throwing it back at her in a very specific way. She felt strangely hurt. "None of Lucas' other friends have been your brothers, I suppose. Just Riley. Is that how it is?"

She stopped and turned to face him, her earlier attraction melted away in this man's blatant reminder of his romantic attraction for the tall, redheaded man who shared his villa. Even as she spat her frustration at him, she felt low for doing so, and her eyes brimmed with moisture.

HOUSTON COULD SEE the tears. However, he didn't understand her slicing response.

"I've only ever had one brother, Angelique. Riley. Robby

and Bobby, even Jerrold and Treavor, are my friends, though more Lucas' than mine. We were all in the same frat house in college, frat brothers, I guess you could say, but you already know that. However, only Riley has ever been my real brother."

She barked a short laugh, and she smiled, but it kept twisting itself away, and she was flushed. "At least you're faithful. I know a lot of married men who can't do that, even though your faithfulness didn't help Riley's wife." She turned, wiping her face with her hands.

"Faithful? I'm not married. Besides, what does being faithful have to do with Riley's wife? He was never unfaithful to her, not unless you infer that by virtue of being my brother, our relationship made him unfaithful in some way."

Houston took a deep breath, the moment hitting closer to home than he had thought possible. Riley's wife had accused him of exactly that, of being so close to Houston that at times it felt like he was being unfaithful to her—with his own brother, for crying out loud!

He had no idea how Angelique could know that, though.

"FORGIVE ME, HOUSTON." She sniffled, but she refused to look at him again. Being near him confused her, and she couldn't control her madly fluctuating emotions. "I guess from your viewpoint, having another man as your brother isn't being unfaithful even when it breaks up a marriage. So, I guess you have been faithful to Riley, even if his marriage went on the rocks because of you." She stopped talking, mortified at herself. Remorse made her stomach churn, and she tried to repair the damage she'd done. "It's really none of my business, and I shouldn't have said anything."

She pulled the top of her towel loose and readjusted it before tucking it back in once again. Now, she truly felt the fool, and she wished she hadn't stepped from her villa.

THIS PROVED ONE THING to Houston. With Angelique's husband dead only a week, she needed plenty of space. Her emotional welfare had to come first.

"Angelique," he whispered to the back of her head, "I love Riley more than life itself, and yes, that was apparently part of the problem between him and his wife. However, I couldn't help that she wasn't able to live with that. I never thought I would ever come between another man and his wife, and I never intended to with Riley."

That first day Riley had shown up to live with his family, he had been tall, eight to Houston's three, and Houston had worshipped the ground he had walked on. In his small boy's eyes, there had been no greater person than his new, freshly alive older brother.

"I always felt like the lucky one that Riley came into my life. No, I wasn't fortunate enough for him to be born into my family, a ready-made brother, even though I would have loved for him to be part of my life that way. God didn't see that in his plans for me. The brother I have in Riley is even better. I have loved . . . no, I have worshipped that man since the day he stepped foot into my home, and not even his wife could tear us apart, although God knows she tried. I'm sorry, Angelique. If it's unacceptable to care about someone that much, then I don't care if other people approve or not."

She turned with red eyes, and she looked him in the face. "How do you do this? You make it sound as if Riley is lucky to have found you. I can't even force myself to hate you for tearing a man's marriage apart. Did he love his wife, or only just you?" Then she turned and put her hand over her face. "Good God, this is none of my business. Please ignore my question, Houston. Can we just back this day up about half an hour? Then I won't bother coming out of my villa, and everything will be all right."

Houston REACHED AND touched her shoulder, and the connection was liquid fire running through her. In that moment, Angelique couldn't bear his touch to be against her or to be taken away. She was being pulled two directions, and either led to a pit of despair. The moment of bliss and torment was skewed into a holding pattern when Houston spoke, his words like velvet in her ears.

"Angelique, Riley loved his wife immensely, and he fought to save his marriage. She wanted something he didn't have to offer."

"Buzz is his, though." Her words were sharp once again, her emotions once more out from under her control. "Riley can't deny that, not with that red hair and those freckles. He offered it at least once." She cringed at her words, wishing she could shut up.

"Yes, that, at least once, Angelique. I'm certain of that." He chuckled.

She turned to him, shrugging his hand away, and her face was hot with embarrassment and fury, both at herself and this man beside her. "Don't you ever get angry? I'm being ugly and spiteful, and all you do is say charming things back. Yell at me, tell me all this is none of my business, and insist that I go away. Something. Anything." She raised her arms and shook them in frustration, putting her opened palms to her temples, trying uselessly to quiet the longing for him that was tearing her apart.

In an instant, he grabbed her upraised arms, and he said with a quiet intensity, "I don't want you to go away. I don't understand everything you said to me, but I most certainly am not angry with you. You're grieving, and you need someone to stand beside you. I'm here, you know. We all are. Give us a chance, Angelique. Give me a chance."

154

With those words, she fell against him, wrapping her arms around his torso, and letting her face press against his chest, bleeding her rugged tears of frustration onto his shirt. From the time they were on the airplane, she had wanted to hold him like this. Now, he was in her arms. It wasn't quite what she would ask for, but what she wanted from him, he was incapable of giving.

When she felt his arms wrap around her, she accepted that any port in the time of storm was better than no port at all. For just this moment, with no one watching, he made a pretty good harbor for her battered ship, and she wasn't sorry to be held in his arms.

AFTER HER SOBS SUBSIDED, Houston spoke softly into her hair, surprising himself by noticing that it had mostly dried by this time. "So, what is this about nail polish and being the rooster's enemy?"

She pulled her arms up between them and slowly let light filter between their bodies. After a pause, she looked at him and back to her hands. She chuckled before wiping the remaining moisture from under her eyes.

"The chicken . . . that rooster from last night had somehow gotten in my pool enclosure this morning." She turned from him, and she laughed, holding her hands up and waggling her fingers in the air once again. "Sven, that's my concierge—"

"I know Sven."

She glanced at him as if to question how.

"Go on," he continued. "About Sven?" He could barely keep from laughing.

"My concierge told me the rooster saw brightly painted nails as the weapons of a potential enemy. Each time I waved my hands—for the rooster to go away, you see—it attempted to attack me. I was trapped in my villa, and Sven had to come rescue me. He's the best concierge ever, and I think I might fall in love with him." She looked directly at Houston with an overly bright expression on her face. "If he will have me, I think I might come to live in Hawaii and enjoy a very pampered life." She held her hands up again to look at her nails. "Just with no polish. I'll miss the polish, but some things just can't be helped, can they?"

He had a full-blown grin on his face by then. This woman was toying with him. First, she had berated him, then she'd fallen against him to expel her frustrations and grief. Now, she teased him, and he would walk the wild side if he wasn't enjoying every moment of it.

CHAPTER 13

BOBBY SAT ON THE VILLA'S low, cotton-covered couch, flipping through a brochure for local real estate. His nonchalance was intentional, as he was pointedly ignoring his brother.

"Brother, where is that cologne of Houston's?" Robby stepped from the bathroom with just a towel around his waist. "I can't get dressed, not until I have a manly smell on."

"Just go without. You don't need the lotion, or the cologne to cover the smell." He looked up. "It's the minerals in the water back home that bother you. Here, the water is soft and easy on your skin."

"Too late," his brother wailed. "I've already lathered up with the resort's house special, Lavender Surprise. I can't go all day smelling like lavender."

"You like it enough to import the real thing directly from England, just to put out in the shop." He laughed, but when he saw his brother's eyes redden, he gave in. "All right, Robbo. I'll go to Houston's villa and see what I can scrounge up. Who knows? Maybe they're all at the beach, and we're the only sane people on the island. Keep that towel snugged up to protect that manly image." He snickered as he stepped to the door, calling out, "You wouldn't want them to find out the truth."

As he pulled the door to behind him, he heard the sound of a shoe hitting the opposite side. A voice filtered through the wooden barrier, one distraught and angry at the same time. "I hate you, Bobby. I've always hated you."

Bobby opened the door just a crack, calling through, "I love you too, Robbo." He yanked the door closed just as the second shoe hit in about the same place as the first. He yelled through the closed door this time. "At least being pitcher on the high school baseball team served some purpose. Your aim's still good."

When he turned around, though, he was immediately distracted from his intended destination. Towards the sea, a flash of white deep within the greenery drew his eyes. He opened the door, and underneath his brother's withering glare, he grabbed the binoculars from a small table. Putting them to his eyes, sure enough, through the trees, he could make out two people arm-in-arm, and he'd be an antique horsehair cushion if it wasn't Houston and Angelique.

"Robby, you have to come look." He turned and held out the glasses.

Sulking, and with a pouty face, Robby shook his head. "I don't want to. You've insulted me."

"Are you sure? It's Houston. He's with someone down in the trees."

Robby frowned. "Our Houston? With whom?" He patted the towel at his waist to make sure it was tight, and walked to the door, taking the glasses from his brother. "Let me look." Stepping into the sun, he held the glasses up and looked toward the beach. "Where?"

158

Bobby pushed down on the far end of the glasses. "Look for white. Tell me who you see."

"Angelique!" Robby's voice broke in despair. "Why, it is that Angelique girl. She wasn't in love with Lucas after all. She's down there in Houston's arms, just vamping it up." He turned and handed the glasses back to his brother. "I don't think I want Houston's cologne, after all. Bobby, can you possibly go see Gator? I bet you he has something nice and manly. I don't think I'd mind smelling like him. Please, Bobby?" He adjusted the towel at his waist and leaned his head back in the sun. "I just might soak up a few rays while I wait."

Bobby grabbed the back of his brother's neck and squeezed. "You might just soak up some sunburn, too, dear brother. This is Hawaii, and you're about as close to the equator as you've ever been."

"I'm so pasty, though." He rubbed his hand down his arm, and then he patted his abdomen. "I think my six pack looks a bit like white wine. It needs a little color."

"Wait until it looks like a good burgundy. Then you'll wish you'd never seen the sun. Go inside, Robby. I'll be right back."

He snorted. "Oh, all right. Send Gator back with the cologne, if he's not busy. I sure could use some pleasant company for a change. I've had about all of you I can take."

Bobby laughed as he headed across the motor court to the next-to-the-last villa. He and his brother were a pair of twin see-saws, just trying to balance their lives with the world around them. Some days they were up, and other days they were down, but it all balanced out in the end. He hoped that was true of this trip to this island paradise. If not, he and his brother would soon be to their last spool of thread, and that was if they were careful and sewed every stitch by hand from here on out.

He hated to even think about that.

CHAPTER 14

"YOU HAD A FRONT DOOR, Angelique. Why were you trapped?"

"Front door?" She froze as if just realizing that. "I could have . . . really! I wanted to go for an early swim in my pool. I didn't consider borrowing someone else's pool, and it honestly never occurred to me that I wasn't the one trapped. That chicken was. I did have other options, didn't I, Houston?" She looked around at the tropical greenery, and reaching to one shrub, she pulled a branch gently toward her to take a strong whiff of a red and yellow bloom. "Tell me about Lucas. I really loved him, and for a year we planned the most elaborate wedding. However, in the past week, I've realized I don't guess I really knew him." She laughed, stepping forward once again toward the beach. "Obviously, if that man Cheeky is any indication, I had no idea who I was crawling into bed with, and I mean that literally. No offense." She turned her head and nodded it Houston's direction.

"None taken, at least not on my part. Lucas was a charmer, but he was also all about his money. I've got more news for you, if you're interested in hearing it. It might not be especially good news, but it is going to show up here at the resort in half an hour or so."

"Just tell me. I can't banter any longer. I need things spelled out plain and simple. Lucas didn't spell things out, and look where I am now." She took a deep breath as they came out to the beach.

The view was beautiful. The blue sky draped down to brush an even deeper blue ocean, and the sun glimmered off the surface of the water. In the distance, the white sails of a yacht could be seen plying the waters. Even the flowering bushes that fronted the beach provided a colorful frame for this slice of paradise.

To the side was the location where the luau had taken place, but the resort personnel had already removed the detritus of their escapade, leaving the beach pristine. It was obvious it had indeed rained during the night, smoothing the roughened remains of the party, and giving the sand a mottled texture.

The sea against the shore whispered in the morning light, and it beckoned seductively, although they'd been cautioned about swimming too far out. The surf would pick up later in the day, and for safety, novice swimmers should wear preservation devices. Julia would provide them for anyone who requested them. This was Blue Water Maui, after all. No request was too mundane.

"Are you sure you're ready?" Houston took a deep breath. He hated to spoil all this beauty with his news, but it was unfair not to tell her now.

Angelique turned to him and looked him in the eyes. "Surely your news can't make my morning any worse than it's been already. Then, I want to go for a swim."

161

He smiled, glad for a temporary diversion. "You must be a whitewater fan."

"Why?" She loosened her towel but hesitated before removing it.

He pushed his hand through his hair, looking up and down the beach. "I'm not sure exactly, but in spite of your rooster adventures this morning, I assume you did swim in your pool, what with your wet hair and towel. Now, here you are ready to jump in the ocean." He glanced at her with laughter in his eyes. "Whitewater? Get it? The ocean?" He let a chuckle escape.

"To answer your questions, yes and yes. However, thinking of that animal having been in my pool enclosure made it feel claustrophobic when I finally got in the water. I decided I needed wider vistas. You can't get any wider than this. Now, what's the bad news, and then I intend to swim. You can stay and watch—although I know you have no real interest—or not. Your choice. You won't offend me either way."

He looked at her with a twinkle. He did, too, have an interest, but he'd let that slide. He also suspected that her morning could get much worse, especially if, from the beginning, she truly hadn't known about Lucas.

"Angelique," and he cleared his throat, continuing, "We have two more people showing up today."

"All right. We have an empty villa, since several people have doubled up. I also have an extra bedroom in mine. There's room for two extra people. So?"

"Well," and he lifted an arm to rub the back of his neck, hesitating a moment before continuing. "You mentioned Cheeky earlier." He looked at her to see if she understood what he meant.

"Cheeky?" Her eyes narrowed, and her voice became terse. "And?"

"Well, Cheeky's brought someone to the island. They're on

162

the way here."

She took a deep breath and held it for a long time. Then she released it, and she stood with her eyes closed for a moment. "I take back what I said earlier. My morning can get worse. That man is staying here?"

"No." He navigated cautiously. This was a very precipitous spot in this revelation, and things could grow slippery, if he wasn't careful. "You asked me about Squeegie yesterday. I never really answered your question. Lucas cared about all of us in our frat house back in college. He really did, but he had this enormous trust fund he couldn't get at until he was twenty-one, and then only if he had a family."

"I know about the trust fund. I've met with the lawyers. What about Squeegie? Was Lucas married before?"

He took a deep breath. "No, not married. Surrogate."

She frowned. "Surrogate? Spell it out for me, Houston. Surrogate, how?" She tucked her towel firmly back in. "Just spit it out. I'm a big girl. I can take it, I think."

"Squeegie's eight and Lucas' biological daughter. A great-aunt raised her for years. She was a good woman, good for Squeegie, anyway."

"The child just wasn't good for Lucas."

"It was a big disappointment for him when a child didn't satisfy the legal strictures of the trust fund, and, yes, sadly enough, he was willing to let her go to anyone who would take her. The aunt was childless and excited to have the opportunity."

"Did he love her?"

"Squeegie? After a fashion, I think. She just didn't fit into his plans."

"So, the money, the trust fund, should be hers? The lawyers said nothing about a child or sharing the funds."

"No, Lucas was generous, but the trust fund was his alone.

The great-aunt adopted the child, even left money to Squeegie, although no one—Squeegie, especially—can get to it until she's eighteen, twenty-five, and forty. Not even Cheeky, and that's why Lucas was supporting all of them." He pursed his lips. "It sounds rather complicated to hear it all in one big rush like this."

"Granny Swell? I'm not even trying to follow all this, Houston, especially the eighteen, twenty-five, and forty. I can't, not in my current emotional state. Just tell me the bones. What's happening today? Lay it on the line. I need to know how to brace myself. You said Cheeky was bringing two other people, yet only two new guests are arriving. If he's not staying here, then where is he staying?"

"Rio." He paused to let that soak in.

"Rio de Janeiro? Brazil?" She looked at him hard.

He laughed. "Carnival. He's always dreamed of working there. Besides, Ricky's already in Rio."

"I've heard of Ricky and Carnival. At the reception, Lucas and Cheeky argued about it. How does that affect me?"

"Cheeky's going to Brazil, to Rio, but he's not taking Squeegie or Granny Swell. They're on the island and on the way here."

"Who told you all this, and when?"

"Julia, my concierge, came by this morning. I had to give her permission to allow them to come stay. Otherwise, what would they do? They were already at the airport."

"Granny Swell, surely she could—"

He barked out a laugh. "I don't know Granny Swell except in a general sense, but I understand part of it. She was a home-less person Squeegie rescued. After Lucas' great-aunt died, the girl was desperate for another grandmother. She found this one under a bridge one day and brought her back to the art studio. The poor woman isn't all there, if you get what I mean. Squeegie seems to love her, though."

He watched the color fade from Angelique's face, and he wished he could take back everything he'd said. However, it wouldn't change the facts, and he hoped she was strong enough to take it.

*A*NGELIQUE ABRUPTLY SAT in the sand, digging her feet into its warmth. She reached with one hand and flicked loose grains toward the water, creating a splattering of minute ripples before the sea pulled back out and another wave took its place. A small fish broke the surface, only to find the ripples hadn't been food after all, and it was quickly gone.

A bird cried out, as if it wished for the fish to return.

"This should be in my column. My readers would love it." She laughed to push away the burning frustration in her eyes. She turned to catch Houston watching her before looking back to sea. "She'll be staying here with Beckie, Heather, and all your friends."

"It looks that way."

She closed her eyes against the sun. "Lucas' friends, I should say. Oh, and Riley and Buzz. She'll be staying with them, too. Freight train. You called Squeegie a 'railway engine on steroids,' if I remember correctly. Can I just lock myself in my villa and never come out? Can I, Houston?"

He knelt beside her. "That might not be a bad idea. I could ward off all comers, and you could vegetate in peace and tranquility. I could even arrange to serve you rooster stew one night, and then you'd never have to worry about your morning swims ever again."

She grabbed a handful of sand and threw it at him before putting her fingers into her hair, gingerly resting her elbows on her knees.

"Hey," he cried. "What was that for?"

"For what you just said." His words had charmed her once more, saying just what she had needed to hear. She wanted this man, needed him, and yet he could never be hers.

"What? I just said—"

"Never mind. I'm being overly sensitive." She pulled her hands through her hair and waved his explanation away. She blinked her eyes to keep the tears at bay. "Riley is lucky, you know."

He laughed. "Please explain where that sentiment came from. Riley, lucky?"

"He has you." And I don't, but she couldn't say that aloud.

He leaned over to kiss her on the forehead. "Thank you, Angelique. I'll take that as a vote of approval. Now, I think we need to head back. We have company coming." He offered to take her hand. "Let me help."

She took his outstretched palm, but it wasn't for the help he offered, not to stand, anyway. She wanted to hold his hand, even if just for that brief moment as he helped her to her feet. She knew she should fight her attraction to this unavailable man, but she also knew that she was caught in a whirlpool, it had already swallowed her whole, and all she could do was let it carry her where it would.

BOBBY KNOCKED LOUDLY on Gator's door. "Gator? It's Bobby, and I need to see you."

"Hey, B-Bob! Come on in." The voice sounded as if it came from the far side of the villa.

"I'm here for my brother, Robby. He has something he'd like to borrow, if you don't mind." He pushed the door open and could see through to the pool lanai. Ripples in the water sparkled in the sun, telling him Gator was swimming. Some-one's leg protruded from a towel on a partially visible chase lounge. "How's the water?"

166

"Fine." Gator swam into view, pulling up to the coping and brushing his wet hair from his forehead. "What can I do for you, or for Robby, that is?"

The leg, though. Not Gator's. Treavor? Jerrold?

"I'm sorry, um, Gator." Bobby stumbled over his words, disconcerted that he hadn't seen this coming. "I didn't realize you had company. I wouldn't have come over without asking, except for Robby. He needs to borrow some cologne. He wondered . . . wanted you to bring him some, rather, may I borrow a bottle? You know, Halston or Giorgio for Men. It doesn't matter what." He glanced around for anything that might tell him which of his friends was lounging at Gator's pool, but he could see nothing except what the rugged outdoorsman might have strewn about the space. "I didn't mean to interrupt your social visit."

Gator smiled. "Hey, it was getting lonely down here, and I certainly don't consider your request an interruption. Besides, I hardly think it's possible to interrupt a visit until it's underway. I tell you what. I don't have any of the types you mentioned, but I do have Old Spice. If your brother wants to borrow that, it's there in the bathroom. I'll come by and pick it up later this morning."

"Robby really wanted to know if you'd bring it up yourself." He pursed his lips in concentration, watching the sun slash across Gator's wet face. "I can wait, if you'd like me to. We can walk up together. I had Christian bring me martini makings, and we can enjoy one together, if you want." He dearly wanted to step to the lanai to see who was out there, but he hesitated. If he was certain this was Treavor or Jerrold—or even Houston—he'd barge right out there, and find out who the mystery man was. However, he didn't know Gator well enough to impose on his hospitality that much.

Gator laughed and ducked his head. "Thanks for the offer."

167

Then he glanced at the chaise lounge. "I'm having a little trouble with one of the straps on my leg. It might take me a while to fix the buckle, so I'll head up later. If I go, my companion over there on the lounge goes, also." He laughed again. "As far as the martini, I prefer a little more direct injection."

Companion? Direct injection? Bobby took a deep breath.

Gator threw water at him. "It's the white bottle by the bathroom sink. You don't have to take it if you think he'd rather not use it. I won't be offended. If it's gone when I get out of the pool, I'll stop by your place later to retrieve it." He dropped into the water and was gone out of sight.

Bobby watched the leg on the chaise for a moment, but it never moved. Then, guiltily, he stepped to the bathroom and grabbed the bottle from the counter. Exiting, he glanced back once more, to find the leg still there, and he saw Gator swim past in the shifting pool water. He hurriedly left the villa, but his curiosity was piqued.

Then, as he headed up the path to his own villa, he looked back at the roof of the unit he'd just come from. Trouble with one of the straps on his leg? That was certainly an odd thing for the man to say. Why would he have straps on his leg? Then he shrugged. Maybe the man carried a hidden whiskey flask, or perhaps it was a money pouch. Maybe, just maybe, he was a diamond smuggler, or an international espionage agent. Double-oh-one. He'd have to tell Robby about this. It was exciting to have a mysterious character in their group.

This might turn out to be a fun vacation, the very best ever, even if Lucas wasn't along to enjoy it.

No MORE HAD ANGELIQUE extricated herself from Houston's grasp, than an urgent voice accosted her.

"Angie! Come up here, if you can get Houston to leave you

alone. I have the most exciting news!" Heather stood on her lanai and waved excitedly at her friend. She laughed as she continued, "It was the most terrible disaster."

"Go on," Houston said, putting his hand on the back of her arm. "She'll cheer you up. You also might let her know about our company. Her other friend, too. I'll deliver my bottle of cologne, and then I'll get with everyone else."

"You don't have to walk all over to do this, you know. There's a phone system in the villas. We have concierges, also. I could get Sven to call and let everyone know about our impending company."

He squeezed her arm gently. "Sometimes sharing face to face is worth the effort." He pressed her arm to him as he said that, and she turned to him. He was grinning, and he winked at her. "Like now."

Her pulse throbbed with his words. If she didn't know better, she'd think he was making a pass at her. However, it was just his charm coming across. For him to make a pass at her would be like a pig trying to fly, except that Houston was no pig—in fact, far from it. He was the most attractive pig, er, man she had ever had the chance to get to know, even more so, if possible, than Lucas had been, and she had certainly been charmed by him.

"Are you sure I shouldn't walk with you?" She enjoyed his company, and she hated to be sent off like a kid sister being teased by a favorite big brother. That's all it could be, though. She'd snapped at him, and he'd taken it on the chin, never wavering from his good-natured affability. Now, he was ready for her to be gone so that he could move on with his day. "I . . . I've enjoyed walking with you."

Heather called down again, and Angelique waved at her to let her know she heard.

"We have six weeks here to get to know each other. For

now, I really need to get this delivered." He held up the bottle. "My friend Robby needs it desperately." He grinned. "Very desperately, I'm sure. Give your friend up there some of your time. That's what friends are for." He took off, and he spun on his heels to face her, walking backwards, grinning. "I'll see you again, Angelique. Count on it." Then, facing forward once again, he was gone in a run.

"Angie!" Heather came tripping down from her villa. "Did I just see romance going on? Is my sad Angie gone for a little while?" She wrapped her arm around her shoulder. "I know somewhere inside you must still be mourning after that terrible, terrible accident in New York, but at least you seem to be making progress. I'd be so sad if you were bogged down for months and months." She smiled and kissed her on the cheek. "After all, you have to admit, although you didn't stay married long, there is another way to look at the facts. What happened to Lucas was sort of like a sudden and very handy annulment where you still got really rich."

Angelique frowned. "Heather! That's crude."

She laughed. "I'm so sorry, Angie. You know me. I'm honest to a fault. If you want me to be sweet, I'll try, but I'm not very good at it."

Angelique sighed. She remembered that about her friend from years before. She could be wild and run roughshod over people, but there were times her heart of gold also shone through. "That's all right. Can we go up to your villa for a bit? I'm not sure that I knew Lucas as well as I thought I did."

Heather's laughter was low and sultry as she squeezed her friend's shoulder. "Of course, sweetie. Now, I still have my story to tell you. You won't believe it, but I was chased by a rooster. Your little man, Sven, rescued me."

"An orange rooster?"

Heather led her into the villa, turning to laugh. "You know

170

my chicken, then."

She smiled grudgingly. "He was in my pool area this morning. Sven came and chased him away. God bless that man."

"So, I can blame you. You caused my morning bath to be destroyed." One eyebrow lifted in mock dismay. Heather leaned in to whisper, "Beckie slept right through it. She's still asleep, if you want to know." Opening the bedroom door, she pointed to the full-bodied woman with her sheets twisted around her. "Beckie," she called softly. "Wakie, wakie. We have company."

"Let her sleep, Heather." Angelique pulled her away, shutting the door. "She always did like to sleep in, even back in college. Let me tell you my news."

Heather pulled her to a low couch. "Tell me, Angie. Does it have anything to do with Houston? He's the looker, you know. I wouldn't mind rubbing a bit of sunscreen onto that chest one afternoon."

Angelique smiled, chuckling as she imagined Riley doing just that. "Rub all you want, Heather. However, he's already got someone."

"You?" Her friend smiled with a wink.

"I don't think so."

Heather glanced toward the bedroom door. "Not Beckie! She never said a word about getting with him. Besides, Angie, how do you know? Did he tell you?"

"You can't be serious, Heather. You've seen him with Riley." She returned the wink, a secret signal of a shared confidence, the sort that might be found among conspirators. "They're brothers—" stressing the word very strongly, "—although that doesn't have the meaning it used to have when I was growing up."

"So," Heather murmured, turning her eyes dreamily to the ceiling, following the line of blue sky around the edges, "If Beckie got with Riley, and I landed Houston, then we'd be like

171

real sisters, wouldn't we? How nice!"

Angelique laughed, and it was from the heart this time. "Not possible, Heather. Not with Houston and Riley."

Heather frowned. "Not even sisters-in-law?"

"They're not your ordinary brothers. Do you need me to explain further? I'm not sure of all the graphic details, but I'm pretty sure I can paint you a presentably clear picture. Two men sharing one villa? Get it, yet? Anyway, they're in love. Riley said that in front of everyone."

"That he's in love with Houston? He said that?" Her eyes sparkled.

"You want me to slice and dice it exactly, huh? Fine. It seems like Houston's exact words were that he loves Riley more than life itself."

"Well, I've watched them, and I'll choose to believe the best about them. Houston's so dark and deliciously attractive. I can't believe he drives race cars. I've never known a real race car driver before. How scrumptious! Beckie wants Riley. He's so amusing, and that hunky body! You cannot make me believe anything bad about them." Hearing a noise from the door across the room, they both looked up.

"Ah!" Beckie stood at the bedroom door, with a lace kimono wrap draped over her shoulders and tied firmly at the waist. It was very thin, and in the brightness of the morning, it didn't cover much. She yawned and stretched. "So, I want Riley, do I?"

Angelique shook her head in dismay, as Heather cheerily answered, "Girl, did you see him last night at the luau? He's some good-looking man. I can't seem to convince Angie here to nab our best and brightest, so it's up to you and me. She's determined to find fault with them no matter how good-looking they are." She smirked.

Beckie came and sat beside her, patting her arm. "You

172

know we're trying to help you, Angie. We want you to be happy. After all, that thing with Lucas. You are a poor dear—"

"Not so poor," Heather interrupted, rubbing the tips of her fingers together.

Angelique rolled her eyes.

"Anyway, as I was saying before I was interrupted, you lost your chance at love, and we want to match you up with the cutest men on the island. The quicker love blooms in your heart, the sooner the scars will heal. You know that's true, too. My gramsy always said so."

Heather laughed, covering her mouth as she muttered, "That's why Gramsy was married six times."

"All right, girls." Angelique sighed, standing. "Enough. My scars will heal just fine. Now for my news. Lucas' daughter and adopted grandmother will be here today—"

"Daughter?" Two neon voices chimed as one, cutting her off.

"Yes, you heard me. As I said to Heather, apparently I didn't know Lucas as well as I should have. Since the wedding, I've found a few flies in the ointment." She smiled and patted Heather on the arm. "Find me a man who's not already in love with his, ahem, brother, and then we'll talk." She blew them both a kiss and stepped outside into the sunshine.

BECKIE FROWNED AT Heather. "Brother?"

Heather leaned back and crossed her trim legs. She bounced her foot up and down in the air, letting her sandal dangle from her toes. She inspected one nail before replying.

"It seems that Houston and Riley are brothers, and they love each other very much." She raised her eyebrows but kept her eyes on her nails.

Beckie stood and yawned. "Psst! That makes them even sexier. I get the redhead, you said?"

"If you want. I'm so glad we offered them to Angelique first. Now we don't have to feel a bit bad when they like us back." She smiled. "Besides, I love crystal blue eyes. Who would have thought with that dark hair and permanent tan? Ooh, la, la! I always wanted to know how fast a race car goes!"

Beckie just laughed. "You got that from me, you know."

"What?"

"Ooh, la, la." She snapped her fingers with a sashay of her hips. "Anyway, I'm headed to the shower. Do you need in anytime soon?"

Heather just waved her on. "I've had a bath and a shower already."

"Both?"

She laughed. "Don't ask. Please, don't ask. You were lucky you slept through it all."

CHAPTER 15

"OLD SPICE TO THE rescue!" Bobby threw open the bath-room door and held out the bottle of cologne to his brother.

"Old Spice?" Robby was already dressed in silk shorts, sockless boaters, and a brightly colored Hawaiian shirt. "Why would I want that?"

Bobby leaned against the counter. "Because you asked for it? You didn't want to smell feminine, maybe? You had already used the house lotions? I don't know, you tell me, Robbo."

Robby adjusted the top button on his shirt and frowned. "I'm not Robbo to you, brother. Remember that." He turned and walked toward the pool, snapping a newspaper up off a short table. "Christian brought me a paper. He's such a nice boy." He sat in a chair and opened it.

"All right, what are you not telling me?"

He dropped the paper, and a smile appeared on his face. "Houston's already been here, with Ralph Lauren Silver, by the way. That's almost as good as Atelier." He laughed a light little ripple. "You can take that Old Spice right back." He closed his eyes and tilted his head up into the sun.

Bobby snorted, "Can't, fickle brother. Gator's on the way up to get it. He thinks you're using it, too."

"No! Go fend him off. I can't let him think I'm ungrateful."

Bobby let out a laugh. "You are ungrateful, and you know it. He loaned you this, and you don't want to use it."

Robby wailed, "But I can't let him know that!" A knock came from the other side of the villa.

"That's the front door, brother. Do you want to go answer it, or should I?" Bobby grinned.

"Oh, you are so mean. I wish I were here without you." He stood and hurriedly began unbuttoning his shirt. "And I just got ready. Now I'll have to do it all over again, all because you won't help."

"Not quite, brother. What are you doing?" He continued to watch as his sibling slipped his shorts off and laid them neatly folded on the table.

"I have to get rid of Silver." He removed his shirt, only to turn and see Bobby already gone from the room. Moving faster, he called out, "Let me get my suit so I can jump in the pool and wash Houston's smell off. Then you can—"

A cheerful voice coming through the bedroom doorway interrupted him. "This way, Gator. My brother's at the pool. He really wanted to see you when you came up."

With a frantic leap, Robby went into the pool face first, his stomach slapping the glassy surface of the water with a sharp crack. He broke through the water to see the two men watching him.

Gator glanced at Bobby with a puzzled expression. "Did he forget his suit, or does he always swim in his underwear?"

"Well, Robby? Which is it?" Bobby grinned maliciously.

"Whatever I have on. When the mood strikes, you know."

176

Robby smiled broadly. "You're welcome to come in, Gator."

He shook his head. "I just got out of my own pool, so I'm good, I think. Besides, the leg's been giving me trouble. How about if I leave the cologne for later? I can see you're not ready for it, yet."

"Thank you, Gator," Robby cooed.

"Sure, anytime." Gator turned to Bobby. "So, B-Bob. I can call you that, right? I bumped into Houston outside. I hear we're getting company."

"Company?" He motioned to Gator. "Come back inside, and you can tell me about it. I can't imagine who we know in Hawaii who would come to visit us here."

Robby was left with an incredulous expression on his face as the conversation took itself to the living room, leaving him behind. He called out, "Squeegie's coming! Granny Swell, too!"

"How do you know that?" Bobby poked his head through the door.

"Houston told me." He smirked and pushed off towards the far side of the pool.

"Who're Squeegie and Granny Swell?" That was Gator.

Bobby let out a gasp. "No! Squeegie's Angelique's daughter, now. Oh, my word!"

After a moment of silence, Gator inquired, "Is Granny Swell Angelique's mother or her grandmother?"

"Neither." Bobby, again. "She was homeless, and Squeegie adopted her."

Gator laughed loudly. "Does Angelique know she has a daughter?"

Bobby appeared at the lanai door. "Robby, Angelique has a daughter, and she doesn't know. How horrible!"

"How horrible," he said, dropping into the pool as he smiled.

"TREAVOR!" JERROLD BURST into his friend's villa without knocking, calling again, "Treavor! My vacation's ruined!" Listening for a moment, he heard splashing in the pool, and in one slack moment, a voice called, "Stroke, turn." He found his friend swimming laps.

Treavor broke the surface, smiling, only to have his expression change into a frown. "Jerrold, what happened to your skin? Are you allergic to pig?"

"Pig?" Jerrold wailed in frustration. "Am I allergic to pig? I'm streaked orange like this all over. Just look!" With shaking hands, he unbuttoned his shirt and yanked it off, throwing it to a nearby chair. "I can't let anyone see me like this."

"What happened?" Treavor lifted one foot onto the pool coping, and in a sudden thrust, forced himself from the water and to his friend's side. "Allergic reactions can do this sometimes, you know, turn your skin colors. Remember Michael Jackson? He turned white. We did eat that pig last night."

Jerrold thrust his hands into his hair, grabbed, and pulled. "I'm not white, Tee! I'm orange, and with stripes, too. I tried to wash it off, and it's permanent." He pulled up the leg of his shorts. "See, even here, and I did it to myself!"

"You say you did this? How?" If they were in India, he murmured with a grin, Jerrold might be mistaken for a tiger, and hunted for a trophy. He was lucky they were in Hawaii where he could run free. Jerrold threw himself to the pool deck with a sour sound.

"You're getting wet." Treavor fought a smile.

"It doesn't matter if I get wet, because if people see me, they won't care about my wet clothes. They'll be laughing too hard at the stripes on my skin."

"C'mon, tell me, how'd this happen?" Treavor sat beside him and punched on his leg with a fist.

"I burn easily." Jerrold looked at Treavor as if that said it all, and seeing a smile on his friend's face, he slapped him on the leg. "Don't you laugh at me, Tee. I tried to get you to room with me. You could have helped me out, and then I wouldn't look like this now. That makes this your fault, too."

"My fault?" He finally laughed. "You burn easily, and it's my fault you have orange stripes all over your skin? Explain that one to me, and not by accusing me of refusing to share a room with you. I'm right next door, remember. You just walked right in, so it's not as if I'm unavailable to help if you need me."

Jerrold's shoulders drooped in despair. "I know."

"So," Treavor knelt in front of his friend, "how did you do this? The truth."

He began rubbing the fingernails of one hand nervously with his opposite hand, and he murmured very softly, "I got this self-tanner, you see—"

Treavor interrupted, standing and laughing. "Self-tanner! This is self-tanner? Bronzer, you mean. Jer, you poor thing. Do you have any left?"

"You want to wear it, too?"

"No, silly. I think I can smooth it out for you. Is there any more?"

"Back in my villa. Since the trip was for six weeks, I brought a bottle for each week. I have five left. It's all the same, sort of."

"Sort of?" Treavor snorted. "How, sort of?"

"I wanted to get darker each week, so I got six different shades. I couldn't find all the same brand, though. Some said dark, dark. Others said unique auto-darkening. I didn't know the first one would do this, though." He looked hopeful for the first time. "You can really fix this?"

"Maybe. I'll tell you what, let's go see what you used. I suspect you started with the darkest level first." He reached to

Jerrold's hand and pulled him to his feet. "Grab your shirt, and let's head over to your place."

"I couldn't have used the darkest first. I lined them up like a Cape Canaveral launch countdown: six, five, four, and so on, except the numbers were higher." He laughed as he grabbed his shirt and headed with Treavor out the door. "It was more like ninety-six, seventy, fifty, twenty, and like that. I'm using all the highest SPFs first. When I get to the ten bottle, then I'll be perfect. I saw that movie, you know. 10. That's why my last tanner is number ten."

"Ha!" Treavor grabbed his arm and pulled him along. "The numbers aren't like sunscreen. You arranged them opposite from what they should be. Ninety-six should have been used last."

"Who would have thought that?" Jerrold snickered, in a much better mood now that he wasn't facing his dilemma alone. "Thanks, Tee. I wouldn't trade you for anyone."

As he began sorting through the bottles, Treavor murmured, "That's okay, Jer. I wouldn't trade you, either."

"WE DIDN'T HAVE A resort van pick us up at the airport." Jerrold muttered his words, and he elbowed Treavor, frowning. The sound of tires crunched along the crushed shell road in the distance, and a van, emblazoned on the side with a mural of rolling surf and the words Blue Water Maui Resort and Villas, pulled into the motor court and parked next to the softly burbling fountain.

Treavor bantered back with a distracting, "Your color really looks smoother, Jer. I bet no one will even notice your stripes."

The real question hanging between them was the people showing up in the brightly colored van. Neither man had met Granny Swell, but Lucas' girl? Just the thought made them shiver. Off to the side were Robby and Bobby, together with

Gator, standing on the front lanai of the highest villa. Robby's hair was wet as if he'd just climbed from the pool. He and his brother were in similar clothes, and Gator wore what seemed to be his customary chinos beneath a lightweight shirt.

Down in the last occupied villa, next to the one that Granny and Squeegie would take, two wildly coiffed heads emerged from the shade of the overhanging roof. Their clothing was lightweight, freeform, and very delicious to the eye. A breeze caressed the fabric, and underneath, Heather appeared toned and svelte, while Beckie oozed womanly sexuality.

Buzz and Riley had joined Angelique at her villa, and the three were enjoined in an animated conversation. Buzz wore a loose harness that ran over his shoulders, around his waist, and along either side of his crotch. From their hand motions, and Riley repeatedly reaching to readjust some part of the harness, they were discussing his upcoming parasailing.

Houston was nowhere to be seen.

Jerrold looked at Treavor with a smirk. "Are you ready for that?"

Treavor frowned at the question. "For what? Squeegie?"

"Just look up there." He pointed to Buzz. "What do you think he's getting ready to do? Snorkel?"

"I had a dog that wore a leash like that one time. Maybe Riley's afraid the boy will fall into the ocean and drown."

"Hang gliding, or probably parasailing. We promised to go, you know." He looked at the arriving van, grinning. "Uncle Tee."

Treavor's eyes narrowed. "Thank you, Uncle Jay. I didn't promise. You did, and you know it."

"He's Houston's nephew, though. You'll go. It'll be fun."

"Do I have to wear a harness like that?"

"Of course," Jerrold laughed. "Just like that."

"Between my legs?"

181

Jerrold slapped him on the shoulder. "Grow up, Tee. You'll enjoy it."

He sighed. "As long as it's loose, I think I can stand it. I just don't like anything that binds."

Jerrold laughed again and stepped toward the van. "Like your Speedos? Trust me, Tee. They'll strap that harness up so tight, you'll squeal like a girl."

"Jer!" Treavor took off after him. "Can't I just watch? I don't want to squeal like a girl."

Jerrold laughed and waved for his friend to follow, and he didn't bother to look to see if he did.

"SURELY THEY HAVE smaller ones," Angelique reassured Buzz.

"It's the smallest adult size they have. Julia said I have to use one of the resort's harnesses, even though mine fits me better." He tugged at his shoulder strap, pulling it to tighten it more. "Help me, Dad."

Angelique smiled as Riley reached awkwardly to the straps beside the boy's crotch to pull an adjustment ring tight. He didn't act like someone who was comfortably intimate with other men. Far from it, and in that way, he was like Houston very much. There was no femininity to him at all.

"All right, Buzz. Yell if I pinch something." Riley looked up and grinned.

"Dad!" His son flushed red. "Don't say that with her here."

Riley stood, raised his hands, and looked at Angelique, shaking his head in mock despair. "You want to do the honors? I usually take him to movies and play video games. Outdoor stuff like this is Houston's specialty. When he was growing up, I barely learned to change his diapers."

"Dad! Please!"

"Ignore me." Angelique smiled. "Pretend I'm not here."

"Dad One's a geek. He does stuff with me, but he won't want to parasail—"

"Because I'm a geek." Riley rolled his eyes, grinning and shaking his head.

"—or hang glide, either."

"Nothing outdoors, generally." Riley smirked, clearly teasing. He threw one arm around his son and gave him a quick squeeze before turning him loose again.

The boy's face brightened. "I can get Julia to get you a harness, too. Do you want to go up, Angelique?"

She laughed at him, teasing him good-naturedly. "Do you have an off switch?"

The van on the motor court caught her eye, and she asked, "How well do you two know Squeegie and Granny Swell?"

Riley grinned. "Only what little Houston's said to me, and he doesn't know much. From what I hear, Granny Swell doesn't know much either, but the child adores her. I did learn one thing about her, though."

Buzz had heard this, and he grinned. "Tell her, Dad One. Tell her about Mother's Milk."

He laughed and pulled his son to him, giving him another one-armed hug, this time ruffling his hair. "Give me time. I will."

"Mother's Milk?" Angelique had no idea what that meant.

Buzz dived in. "I found it on the Internet this morning on Dad's computer. It's a painting Uncle Cheeky did, and he sold it to the San Francisco Museum of Modern Art. For a lot, too."

Riley winked at her. "I know Cheeky fairly well." He chuckled. "He's an artiste, if you get my drift, and he's very, um, original. Quite respected in the art world. I don't guess you ever got to know him."

"I met him at the reception. You were there, also, remember?"

"Let me tell the rest, Dad." Buzz grinned, his face red with excitement.

"I've got it, Buzz." He squeezed his son's shoulders, and he smiled. "It seems Cheeky had done this painting, and it was still wet. Granny Swell liked it so much, she hugged it to her chest—"

"And all the paint came off in two round circles. Mother's Milk. Get it?" The boy's eyes twinkled as he laughed, and he looked down in embarrassment. "Mother's Milk," he repeated, as he raised his head with a grin on his face. "Dad had to explain it to me, because I didn't get it at first, but then I did, and it was funny."

"He's a bright one." Riley grabbed the boy's jaw in his hand. "Now, let's go meet our unsung artist, even if she won't get any of the money." He motioned with his hand, and they began to move down the walk.

Angelique touched his shoulder, and he turned to her. "It seems to me that if he gave her credit in the write-up, then she'd share in the profits, or she could, if she wanted to fight for it."

He waved his son on, pointing to Treavor and Jerrold. "Go show them your harness, Buzz. Let them know what to expect. Then go help with the van. There'll be luggage."

The boy grinned and took off.

"The staff will take care of that, Riley."

"I know, but he needs to burn some energy. As far as Granny Swell, Cheeky didn't actually give her credit. He just called her a visitor. We all know, though. It could have only been Granny Swell. Even if he'd mentioned her by name, she couldn't fight for it. She's not quite all there in the head, you see." He tapped his temple. "She's also got sticky fingers, so watch your good stuff. She doesn't mean to steal, but if it's pretty, she gravitates to it. Be warned." He grinned, looking off to the events unfolding on the court.

$\mathcal{A}$NGELIQUE FOUND HER thoughts drifting away from Cheeky and Granny Swell. Riley was just as handsome as Houston, although he didn't make her stomach flutter with anticipation at his every move or word. No, he just smelled good, was very charming, and Houston wasn't here. He would never be here for her, could never be here for her. Neither could Riley, but sometimes, she knew, it was the touch of another's skin that a woman needed.

"Take my hand." She forced a smile to her face. "Hold my hand as we walk. Please."

"Absolutely." Clasping his hand around hers, he pulled her to his side, wrapping one arm inside hers. "Anything for a beautiful woman. I can see why Houston likes you so much."

"Likes me? He told you that?" She had her doubts, there.

He laughed. "No, he did not tell me that. I lived with him for years, remember. I know Houston, and he likes you."

"Likes me how?" God, let it be romantically. Please! She knew better, though. He already had Riley. "Likes me how, Riley? As another friend of Lucas'?"

"Widow, Angelique. You're no friend of Lucas'. You're a widow. A very rich widow, if I understand correctly."

"That's how he likes me? As a rich widow of an old friend of his?"

The van in the court had stopped, and after idling for a moment, the driver got out, opened the back, and removed several mismatched suitcases. Then he walked to the opposite side and seemed to be speaking with someone they couldn't see.

"Not exactly." Riley smiled.

"Tell me, and you can ask me to mind my own business if you want, but did Lucas and Houston ever, you know . . . like Houston and you. Were they ever, um, close, really close?"

"Friends, I suppose, but not brothers like Houston and me."

He seemed to find that amusing.

"Not brothers like Houston and you," she murmured. There was that politically correct term again. Brothers. "Did they share, um, sleeping arrangements, like Houston and you?" Dear God, why couldn't she just shut up? Yet, she had to know, and she wasn't sorry for asking.

"Sleeping arrangements? Not in the frat house, I can guarantee you that. I was there a time or two, and they had private rooms. Now, Houston and I might have shared when I visited. Why do you ask?"

"Something Houston said about you and him."

"Houston has a big mouth, sometimes. Know that." He chuckled. "What did he say?"

"Something that's none of my business." She wanted to let it go, but she couldn't, and she spat it out. "Something about sharing a bed on the night you met."

"Ha! He would remember that. The first night I stayed at his house, he climbed in bed with me. I never could kick him out after that." He laughed softly. "I tried a few times, too."

"You and Houston really love each other, don't you? Even when you were married. I've heard about the divorce."

"It wasn't a secret—the divorce, you know. Has Houston told you much about it?" In the courtyard, the driver of the van greeted Buzz, and the boy, ever gregarious, leaned through the open door to speak with the passengers still inside.

"I was in California, remember, with Lucas. It was when the divorce was in progress. We stayed at Houston's place. I was alone most of the time. Lucas was off on errands, and Houston was with you, working you through your divorce. I was so isolated that weekend, I wished I hadn't gone."

"I'm sorry. I didn't know you felt abandoned. I was pretty distraught during that time, myself. You know, Buzz's mother hasn't been back to see him since. The boy was heartsick for a

186

long time, although we'd both seen it coming." He paused, watching the goings-on out on the stone motor court. "I haven't answered your second question, though. Yes, Houston and I really love each other, but I think he might be on the prowl for a new love in his life. He needs more than just me." He grinned at that.

She pulled loose from his arm, shocked at what she heard. She turned and gave him a hard look. "No! He'd leave you for someone else? My God, how callus! What would Buzz think? He seems to adore both of you very much." Then she paused. "You're all right with this, Riley? You don't intend to try to hang on to him?" She turned and murmured. "I would. I'd never let him go."

Just then he put his arm around her and pointed to the van where a wild-haired child was exiting the door, and she latched onto Buzz's harness, pulling herself to his shoulders. "See? There's Squeegie. It's been a while, but that's her, without a doubt." Then he leaned in close. "If Houston finds someone to love, I can't lose him. He's family, and you never lose family. You just make room for one more. That's what love is all about. There's always room for more." He laughed at Buzz and Squeegie, and then he asked her, "Why did you ask me that question about Houston and Lucas?"

She shook her hair and put her fingers in it to push it back from her face. She blinked moisture away as painful emotions roiled inside. Giving a short snort of a laugh, she shared with this man who, in such a short time, had come to feel like a very old, trusted friend.

"I'm coming to see Lucas wasn't who I thought he was. His friends, his lifestyle. The lies I'm now sure he told me. I loved him, and I think he used me. He probably used all his friends, I think, except I don't know how."

"His friends used him, too. Friends do that to each other.

It's only a problem if someone gets hurt."

"Houston, too? He used Lucas?" That made her body go weak. She wanted to believe more of the dark-haired, blue-eyed man who pulled at her emotions so.

He laughed. "Houston? My little bro? No way. He never used Lucas. They were just friends, and friends only."

"Everyone else, though? Treavor, Jerrold, and those twins up there? How about them?"

"Perhaps, but Lucas is gone. It doesn't matter anymore." Then Buzz and Squeegie were there, and it was obvious the boy had run to them for help. Riley laughed and stepped away to corral the mischief.

Angelique couldn't quite agree with him on one thing. It mattered very much if Lucas had been more than just friends with all these people. After all, he had married her, and now she felt like she hadn't married just Lucas; she'd married a half dozen of his friends, too, and they were all on her honeymoon with her—without Lucas. How odd was that?

Then she saw the old woman who must be Granny Swell. Her hair was wilder than the girl's, and heaven forbid, if she didn't seem to be holding an airline pillow and blanket. She was a kleptomaniac, just like Riley had suggested. She looked up into the sky. "Dear God," she whispered. "Can you possibly make this just a little worse every day? How will I survive six weeks of this? I'll go crazy."

Just then a pair of mirrored aviators appeared over her shoulder, and an angry voice spoke harshly into her ear. "So, it's Riley, now, is it? I thought Gator was my nemesis, and suddenly I find he's living under my own roof. I don't give up that easily, Angelique. You need to know that." Then, Houston was gone, heading up the walk back to the compound.

She stood and watched him walk away, not understanding anything. What did Gator have to do with this, and Houston thought she was laying claim to Riley? She glanced at the sky to see a lone cloud, and despair washed over her. Her lips moved as she prayed another prayer to a higher power she hoped was really there. "I didn't mean it, God. It was a tongue-in-cheek joke, that's all. He might not be able to love me, but please don't let him hate me, not for the full six weeks we have together. I at least want him to be my friend."

Then she heard him slam the door to his villa, and she suspected it was too late for that. She had lost him, and how, she wasn't entirely sure.

CHAPTER 16

ANGELIQUE SAT AT A hastily arranged picnic with her erratic menagerie of oddly assembled guests, and she wondered what her life had come to. In the aftermath of the meal, the place settings from the resort's picnic service had been either pushed aside or piled up, and the leftover food was sorted in refuse containers. Her newest two guests monopolized the attention of everyone else.

"I had to let my mouse go, you see." Squeegie was speaking, and her high-pitched voice carried across the lawn. "It had to go back to its bridge, or it couldn't be happy. Granny Swell still loves her bridge. Don't you, Granny Swell?" The little girl smiled at the old woman and patted the side of her lined face.

Granny laughed and clapped her hands. "Can I make another painting, Squeegie? Cheeky said I did so well. I never had mother's milk before." She leaned towards Beckie. "Are you breast-feeding, my dear? You are so full, you know. I was never that full." She reached and touched her on the chest, making a disgusted face and giggling. "Too soft for milk. You'll never paint a picture with those." Then she laughed wildly and picked up a butter knife to begin licking it repeatedly.

"Granny says she likes your dinner service." Squeegie sounded very formal and proper. "She'd like to go to bed soon. She says the ride on the plane was very long, and Daddy Cheeky wasn't very nice to her. She would like to take a nap for a while."

Granny continued to lick her knife, and the entire honeymoon party could only watch in fascinated amazement.

"So," Houston muttered, looking at Angelique and then back to the girl. He'd been distant since his earlier, rather pointed vent. At the same time, he'd been very polite, excessively so. "Your new guests seem to fit right in."

"As in?" She looked at him, unsure what he meant. She'd been attracted to this man, and now he'd changed on her. She knew it had to do with Riley, but she wasn't exactly sure how.

"One person taking over for another." He pinched his lips together, and in that action, she could see he wasn't containing his earlier irritation quite so well after all.

"Granny needs someone to mediate for her." She looked out to sea, her eyes burning with impending disaster and not wanting him to see. "The poor woman would probably be dead if it wasn't for the girl."

"Let's see if she holds her hand." Just then, Squeegie stood and took Granny by the hand to help her stand. Riley also stood to help with the old woman. "Like daughter, like brother." Houston's face was hard. "See? The hand? Of course, the old woman had to give it for it to be taken." His eyes cut to her, and they were ice.

She felt her heart pound with anxiety, but she had a few barbs of her own. She remembered what Riley had said about

Houston finding another love and running away from his responsibilities. After Riley had left his wife, and with that wonderful Buzz for a son, how could he?

She spat at him, "Well, at least the girl doesn't love 'em and leave 'em. Riley told me you were looking for someone else to love. He loves you. He left his wife for you. How can you just run away from him?"

HOUSTON LEANED IN, hissing, "Riley's the one running off. I'm sticking around."

Angelique's eyes narrowed, and her words came out with a bite. "Sure, if that makes you feel better about yourself, Houston, you can tell yourself that. Riley told me, though. Even with all that, he said he'll still love you as much as ever. Do you have any idea what a good man he is?" She twisted away, her anger written in the set of her lips.

Houston muttered, "Do you have any idea what a good man I am?" He glared at his brother off sitting between Buzz and Gator. The man had Gator laughing at his jokes. Houston saw Angelique turn to look at him. In that moment, he hoped somehow for a reconnection. Instead, her eyes narrowed, and she ripped him apart.

"I thought I did, knew what a good man you are, but now I'm not so sure. You need to work this out with Riley before he leaves. I have to admit, in spite of your relationship with him, I was starting to find you very attractive. You don't seem at all . . . well . . . like some of Lucas' friends have turned out to be, and I let that fool me. However, it's clear that appearances can be very deceiving. You can't love me, and I've told myself that. It's just that . . . that . . . ." She turned from him, putting a hand to her face to wipe a tear.

"Angelique," he began, but she held up a finger to stop him.

"He loves you, Houston. He told me so. For Buzz's sake,

make up with him. You don't need to find someone else to love. Your love is right here on this island with you, waiting on you to make things right. A family's what you make of it. I've always believed that. You, Riley, and Buzz are a family, whether you think it's enough for you or not."

She looked away and covered her mouth with her hand. When he touched her shoulder and tried to explain, she held her free hand up with her fingers outspread. "Don't speak to me right now, Houston Richemont. If you let someone else come between you and the man you've professed to love, I'll never speak to you again." She snapped her face around to look at him, and her eyes shimmered with moisture. "He deserves more from you."

She jerked to her feet, calling out, "Gator!" Her voice was bright. "I need you, Gator. You must come with me. There's a watermelon up in my villa, and I wish to bring it down."

Houston could only sit back, stunned. He never expected this, not in a million years.

GATOR SHRUGGED AND stood, awkwardly favoring his left leg, as he begged off from another of Riley's jokes. "Sorry, man. The beautiful siren calls." He grinned.

"You'd better behave." Riley held his hand up for a fist bump. Buzz broke out laughing, and leaping to his feet, he bumped his dad's fist without waiting on Gator.

Gator waved and headed after Angelique. He'd been attracted to her from the beginning, and now she wanted to spend time with him. That was all right. He wasn't one to question a gift horse when he saw it, not that he thought of Angelique as a horse. She seemed more of a skittish colt, the sort that was young, attractive, and very full of life.

Gator liked life, too, especially Angelique's kind, and he wanted this woman in the worst way.

RILEY HANDED THE LAST folded blanket to Christian as Buzz slammed into his dad, his boyish enthusiasm bubbling from every pore.

"All the picnic stuff is cleared, now. Can I get Julia to call the boat?" Buzz wrapped his arms around his father's torso, and they stood almost nose-to-nose. "Please? Uncle Tee will be there. Uncle Jay and Uncle Houston, too."

"Get your harness buckles out of my chest, and I might be able to think about it." He grinned at the boy. "You've asked all those people you mentioned, and everyone else, too?"

"Everyone, Dad." He grinned.

"Angelique and her two friends? You've asked them, and also the twins? Your Uncle Houston would be disappointed for anyone to be left out."

"I'll ask again." The boy's face brightened, and he danced with excitement as he darted away, stopping to call back, "I haven't seen Uncle Houston since the watermelon. Did he tell you where he'd be?"

"I haven't seen him, either, son."

The boy's smile wilted. "Can I still go if Dad Two doesn't?"

Riley gave him a thumbs up. "You let me take care of my brother. You double-check with everyone else, and after that, we'll get Julia to take care of all the arrangements."

With a renewed grin, the boy was off like a shot.

Riley headed towards his villa, pulling his brightly colored, tropical shirt over his head. Whistling, he tucked one sleeve into the waistband of his shorts and let the rest trail behind him, enjoying the sun on his shoulders.

Stepping into the villa, he called for his brother. "Houston? Buzz is ready to parasail. The boy's out rounding everyone up."

When there was no answer, he shrugged and headed to his

bathroom, flipping the water on, and stepping to the drawer where he'd stashed all Houston's boxer shorts. It was empty. Puzzled, he pulled out several more drawers before finding his own stuffed roughly in one.

He carried them to his brother's bedroom and began pulling open Houston's drawers. At one point he paused, amused to hear his shower running on this side of the villa. The sound carried better than he imagined over the truncated walls. He yanked open one final drawer, and sure enough, crammed into the bottom were all the briefs Riley had taken from his brother earlier. Julia, maybe, had done this, he decided. She must have been in, and surely she would have remembered which clothes she had unpacked in which bedroom.

Grabbing the stack, he carried them back to his bathroom and set them on the counter. Then, seeing the steam rising from the shower, he grabbed a towel and stepped under the spray. He was surprised when the water started to cool as soon as he'd soaped up.

When he turned the controls off and stepped out, he perused the stack of briefs until he came to a red pair he especially liked. Grinning, he slipped them on. They fit comfortably, unlike the too tight ones he was more than willing to bequeath to his younger brother.

The door flew open, and Houston thrust his bulk inside. He had a towel around his waist, and he crossed his arms over his chest. His eyes were dark underneath a shock of wet hair.

He glared at the red briefs.

Riley grinned. "Hey, I was looking for you earlier. Thanks for the shorts, brother. I think Julia switched them back. I swapped again, though."

His brother's reply wasn't what he expected.

"So, those *are* mine. You stole them a second time." Houston's blue eyes narrowed, and the emotions in his words lashed out. "Take them off, *brother*. I want my underwear back in my own drawer. You can't steal from me and expect to get away with it. Not my underwear. Not anything, from this point on."

*A*T THE PICNIC, HOUSTON had hoped for something . . . anything more than a verbal lashing from Angelique. She'd soundly rebuffed him, and the hurt had reopened the seething wound of betrayal he'd tried to push aside. There was no longer any question of why he didn't have Angelique; it was because of his brother. His throbbing pulse told him that. If Riley hadn't stepped in the way earlier, he might have had a chance. That morning on their walk, she'd wrapped her arms around him, and that had been at least a start. Now, everything was ruined. Love for a man's brother was one thing. Betrayal was something else, entirely, and his seething anger made this feel too much like the second to him.

"Anything?" Riley frowned. "You offered the underwear. Is there something I'm missing?"

"Don't give me that innocent act. I saw you with Angelique."

"I've stolen her? If you're talking about the picnic, she went with Gator, if you'll remember."

"My underwear. I want them back." Houston snorted his disdain.

"I left you my set. Did you try them?"

"I want mine, *brother*." He held out one hand. "Now. The ones you're wearing."

"All right. The others are in your room." He made to step by Houston, only to be stopped by a hand on his shoulder.

"Don't walk by me." Houston's voice was a growl. "Take off my underwear now, Riley. Don't make me take them off you. I will, you know. I'm younger and quicker than you. I always have been."

196

"What's your problem?" Riley brushed the hand off. "We've had our arguments, sure. But over this? What's wrong with you?"

"Stealing! That's my problem. I won't let you steal anything else from me." Houston threw himself against his brother, forcing him to back up into the living area. "I saw you with her."

"Her? Is this still about Angelique?"

Houston leaned into Riley again, forcing him back another step. "Of course it's about Angelique. You knew I liked her. You even encouraged me to let her know. 'Go get her, tiger,' you said. 'Don't act like a cold fish.' Didn't I move fast enough for you? It's been one day, Riley, and you had her in your arms."

"Houston," Riley tried to explain, "It wasn't what you think—"

Houston wasn't prepared to listen to another word, and he crushed forward against him once again. "I asked you nicely, already, so I guess that means I'm taking them off for you. Now's as good a time as any."

His last push threw Riley off balance, and unable to find anything to brace against, he stumbled several steps backwards and tumbled into a table, knocking over a lamp, and falling onto the couch. With the inertia of his anger carrying him forward, Houston landed on top of him.

"BUZZ! CAREFUL!" ANGELIQUE saw him before the others around her did, but only a fraction of a second before he landed with a jump right in front of her and her friends.

"Julia's about to set up parasailing for everyone on the beach. You have to come, all of you. Please say you will. Please?"

Angelique laughed. "We can't let Buzz down, now, can we,

girls?" When her friends blanched, she put her arm around the boy and pointed to the other two women, calling them out to goad them into doing this. "You two, I know you. You've been wild since the day I met you. Don't you tell me you won't do this."

"Para . . . sailing? Like flying?" Beckie's eyes narrowed.

"Be brave. And I will if you will. Is it a deal? All three of us?" She winked at Buzz.

He broke out in a grin. "You have to convince Dad Two to come, please. I have to tell everyone else. Thanks! I'll see you at the beach!" He leaped, and he was gone.

Beckie laughed good-naturedly. "I guess I'll go up in that sail-thingie, Angie, if I have to. It might even be fun. However, Dad Two." She snickered.

"What's that for?" Angelique knew, and she closed her eyes in dread.

"Well, someone has to go up there and ask him. For Buzz's sake." Beckie snickered again. "Angie? For Buzz's sake?"

"Yeah, Angie. For Buzz's sake."

She opened her eyes to see her friends laughing. Well, she deserved it. However, he hadn't been exactly welcoming to her the last time they'd been together, and she'd thrown ugly barbs at him.

"Well, I guess I could." Beckie pursed her lips, but she winked at Heather. "If Angie won't."

Heather pouted. "I want to be the one to talk to him. He's cute." She pulled the front of her brightly colored top out, fanning it against the heat.

Angelique rolled her eyes and sighed. "This is where I leave you two. I'll find out about the parasailing and work on Houston." What was she promising? He hated her, now. However, the boy had asked, and she didn't want to quash his endearing enthusiasm. She put a smile on her face and pointed to Heather and Beckie. "You two get your mettle up and running. I'll root you on when you're in the air."

"Remember, you have to go, too."

"A promise is a promise." Angelique waved over her shoulder as she walked out the door.

$\mathcal{A}$NGELIQUE TOOK A DEEP breath at the two-bedroom villa occupied by Houston and Riley. She wasn't entirely sure she wanted to knock on that door. However, everyone was depending on her, or at least Beckie and Heather were. Then there was Buzz, and for the boy's sake, she couldn't back out, now. He'd be devastated.

She remembered her earlier words to Houston. She'd been very pointed, telling him exactly how she felt about someone who would abandon a person he loved for no apparent reason. Now, she had to face him, and if he was angry, he might also have some choice words of his own for her. That made her nervous.

Steeling herself, she pulled her hand back to rap on the door when she heard a terrible crashing noise from the other side. Then, something shattered with a brittle, too-bright sound. Involuntarily, she dropped her hand to the doorknob and twisted it open, calling out, "Is everything okay?"

Before her was an overturned table, and just to the side, a broken lamp lay on the floor. The back of the couch was a blank canvas of patterned cotton.

There was no one to be seen.

"Houston? Riley?" After a moment of too-quiet silence, she saw a red-freckled hand appear, grabbing at the couch's seat-back.

When she stepped forward and peered over, two faces looked up at her. One was Houston's, and the other was Riley's.

Her face burned hot with embarrassment as she took in the

scene. The man on bottom was wearing only a baggy pair of red boxer shorts, and the other one—directly on top—was wrapped in just a towel.

She put her hand to her mouth and looked away. "Oh, I'm so sorry. I'll leave immediately."

"Angelique, wait!" There was a loud thump, and she turned her head to see Houston on the floor. He lurched to his feet, one hand holding the towel around his waist in a tight fist. "Don't go. I need to clarify this to you."

Under other circumstances, she might have found the sight funny, an amusing anecdote to be repeated at future gatherings and laughed about again and again. However, this wasn't funny at all. Even so, she suddenly and irrationally giggled.

"Oh, no, Houston. Nothing at all needs clarified. I can see exactly what's happening here, although I'm so sorry I had to step in and see any of it at all. However, you're doing exactly what I demanded you do. You're making up with Riley, and your son will appreciate you for it. This is something it took a real man to do—" a second giggle escaped her lips "—and I'm proud of both of you. Riley, you, too. Don't you let Houston find another person to love. You fight for him. I would if he were mine."

She giggled again, and she could hear the hysteria in it. However, laughing was much, much better than crying, and she'd cry if she couldn't laugh.

She turned away, nervousness giving wings to her words, "It sure is warm in here. Can you tell, or is it just me?" She giggled once more, hating herself for doing so. Things were out of her control, though, giggles included. "But I guess with so few clothes on, you two wouldn't notice. Hot would be a better choice of words, I think. Yes, definitely. Very hot."

"Hot?" That was Riley's voice.

She fanned herself with her hand. "Or, maybe it's just me.

I'll knock next time, you'd better bet your life, maybe cast a lure over the wall, see if I snag anyone home, no matter what I hear through your door."

Oh, lands! Now she was making fishing references, and she didn't even fish! She stepped toward the door, looking up at the ceiling. She'd come here for a reason, and she could no longer think what it was.

"What a day!" She fanned faster, unable to stop talking. "Whew! Your private time won't be interrupted by me ever again. Thank you."

Before the men could say a word, she darted through the door and slammed it behind her.

"SHE TOLD YOU TO pull my underwear off?" Riley glared at Houston, with his eyes narrowed. "That's making up with me? My God, Houston, what's going on here? Earlier I could tell something was wrong, but I have no idea what this is about."

"I don't know about the making up part. That woman has me as confused as you." Houston tucked in his towel and looked at the red underwear his brother still wore. His eyes narrowed, and he growled his next words. "I know this, though. You can't have Angelique, and those red shorts are still mine."

"Whoa. Forget the shorts. You can have them if you'll let me change. What was that about not disturbing our private time? Houston, talk to me!"

"After I have my red shorts back." He fell on his brother, grabbing the shorts by the waistband and ripping them down one side. As he did so, the force of his attack overbalanced the sofa, and it fell over backwards onto the floor, flinging Houston spread-eagled with his hands at Riley's waist, his fingers still clutching the torn underwear.

Just then, Angelique threw the door back open and called

201

out, "I didn't ask about the parasailing, and Buzz said I had to ask." As she spoke, she looked down and caught Riley hanging onto the overturned couch, with Houston's hand holding onto the torn boxer shorts.

"Angelique," Riley cried. A look of horror was on her face. "Wait!" He struggled to get up, grabbing at the torn shorts as he scrambled to his feet.

"It's not like it seems, Angelique," Houston called, jumping to his feet and grasping at the towel to keep it from pulling loose from his waist.

All she said was, "Oh, my God!" Then she turned and slammed the door after her a second time.

CHAPTER 17

"GATOR? ARE YOU in here?" Angelique knocked on the villa door, her eyes still raw with tears. She'd looked but hadn't been able to find him anywhere else. He was the only person on this island she was absolutely sure liked people of the opposite gender, other than herself and her two female friends, and she wasn't completely sure about them, anymore. Well, Buzz, maybe, but he was so full of energy, so enthusiastic about everything, who knew what gender interested him? At thirteen, he probably didn't even know.

She turned and put her back to the door, and she let the tears run down her face. She'd known about Houston and Riley. No one had tried to hide it or tell her otherwise, so she shouldn't be heartbroken. However, the attraction had been so strong that she just knew Houston must feel it, too. Then Riley had told her things, not really told her things, but suggested them, and she had let herself hope.

However, as she had just seen, a tiger cannot change its

stripes, and just because a lion shaves its mane does not make it a lioness. Her analogies didn't really apply, but then they did, too. She had tried to make Houston into a man who could love her, and it had been foolish. Now, look where she was, crying on yet a third man's doorstep.

"Gator!" She turned and leaned against the door, defeated. Certain she couldn't face anyone else at the present, she tried the door, hoping to hide inside. Relieved to find it open, she slipped through, heading to the pool so as not to bother Gator's things. She stepped into the bright sunshine that glared off the rippling water, and reaching her hand to shade her eyes against the piercing light, she was very surprised to be greeted by a laughing voice.

"So, did the watermelon get delivered to my villa this time? If so, it wasn't my fault. Feel free to join me, Angelique, although you'll have to move my leg on the chaise."

"Join you?" She was mortified that she had barged into this man's private villa. It had been forward of her to assume no one was here. It was his right not to answer.

He laughed at her question. "For a visit. I can see you're not suited to swim, but you can keep me company. Just don't move my leg too far away. It's difficult to get to if I have to crawl."

She looked around, still blinking in the brightness. "Your leg? What are you talking about? Pretend I'm really stupid. I feel that way right about now, anyway. Pretending couldn't make it any worse, I don't think." She laughed bitterly. "Now that I think about it, I'm absolutely sure it couldn't get any worse. Go ahead and make my day."

Then she looked up at the sky, and she knew it certainly could get worse, if God had anything to do with it. She'd prayed to him once, already, and matters had certainly gone downhill. The events she'd been forced to view at Houston and Riley's villa were proof of that.

Peering from beneath her hand, she saw Gator swim up to the side of the pool, and he rested his head on his arms as he looked up at her.

"I see you don't know about my leg. I thought you could tell, but then not everyone can. It's not real, my left one, that is. I don't talk about it much. I don't wear shorts, either, although I've had the prosthetic so long, I never really consider it differently than anyone else's leg."

She cleared her throat. "I'm . . . I feel like an idiot right now." Prosthetic leg? He had one of those, and she hadn't been able to tell? That was stupid of her.

"Sorry. I should have said something." He drummed his fingers on the concrete coping, the small splashes each tap made in the water puddled on the deck catching in the light. "I can see this makes you feel awkward."

"No." She paused, certain her distress was written all over her face, and he would call her a liar. "It's not your leg. Well, it is, but it's more. If I've missed that, I just wonder what else I'm not noticing. It seems that no one is what I think they are. Not Lucas, not Houston or Treavor, and now, not even you."

"Your two girlfriends? Are they still the people you thought they were?" There was humor in his words and a grin on his face.

She smiled. "You said I could sit, that I could move this leg?" She reached to touch it, and when he motioned it away with his hand, she picked it up gingerly to set it aside.

"You don't have to be careful. I wear my prosthetics mountain climbing. Well, not that very one, but I could. I have another that's metal with a rock gripper on the end. It's packed in one of my cases. I wouldn't let Christian mess with it." He grinned. "Christian's a hoot. Did you notice he wears fingernail polish? That man's, um, not quite all man, if you get my drift."

She knew what he meant. She'd just seen Houston in the

205

process of pulling Riley's undershorts off. No, that wasn't exactly correct. Houston had been ripping Riley's undershorts away, and Houston had been wearing even less than Riley. She got Gator's drift just fine.

Now, sitting next to his leg, she felt a new compassion for the man she had seen only as an outsider, someone who was ruggedly handsome, but who was more of an intrusion than an addition to the group that had followed her to Hawaii. He had no history with the rest, no real friends to gravitate to, and no real reason for being here, other than for a free vacation. However, he was at her side, he had made his interest in her obvious, and he had suffered in his life. He had also borne it without complaint, at least in the time she'd known him. Perhaps she would go mountain climbing with him. It would at least get her away from the rest of the menagerie she had adopted for the next six weeks here on this island.

She ran her fingers through her hair, and she sighed. "My girlfriends haven't changed." She was relieved to find she could laugh about it. "You're right about that. I know them. It's just everyone else. You, for example. You're not who I thought you were." She smiled, but it was tight, and as she sat watching him, she felt it fade.

He looked at her for a moment without responding, and then he asked, "Do you mind if I get out? You don't have to watch, if you don't want. You can go inside, and I'll join you."

"Would you rather me leave?" She looked at him, then glanced at the leg. She might not have been interested two days ago, but today she wanted to see this if he didn't care.

"I'd rather you felt comfortable enough to stay. It doesn't bother me for people to watch, but sometimes it bothers them. I don't want to force this on people."

"That's very considerate of you, Gator. I'll stay, thank you. Is there anything I can do to help?"

He laughed. "I'm very good at doing this alone. It's part of who I am and has been for a very long time. I appreciate the offer, though. When I'm out of the water, you can hand me the leg. It's not very heavy, just awkward to maneuver when I'm on the ground." Putting his hands palm down on the coping, he heaved himself up and twisted to sit on the side of the pool. Then he pivoted his good leg around to face Angelique. Raising a hand, he motioned for the prosthetic one.

"Oh," she said, surprised at his agility. "You did that so quickly. Here, let me get your leg for you."

Handing it to him, she was fascinated as she watched the terseness of his movements, the economy of motion that had the leg fully attached before she could even remark on his dexterity and skill. Then he shifted, and with that small awkwardness she had seen him present numerous times in the few days she had known him, he stood. Now, towering above her, the leg was forgotten, and he was simply Gator, a roughly hewn man with a stubbled jaw that only made him seem more attractive than ever.

As he sat and dried his swimsuit before pulling on a loose pair of lounging pants, he looked at her and smiled. Then he stood and reached his hand to take hers.

"Shall we go inside? We'll be more comfortable there. You look like you could use a drink." He smiled. "You seem to have had quite a day, and it's barely half over."

Although she would not like a drink, with those words of comfort, she knew she had found her man. He might not make her insides melt, and she felt no butterflies at all, but he was very kind, and he seemed concerned about her. She could use a man like that. She had no use for one who went around pulling other men's shorts off, no matter how many butterflies he might set off in her stomach. No, not even butterflies would change her mind in this, no matter how important they might seem.

$\mathcal{S}$QUEEGIE CROUCHED IN the shadow of a leafy shrub and waited. Seeing a brightly colored bloom nearby, she stretched her neck and placed her nose inside. She inhaled the heady fragrance, and the colors of a very old grandmother figure who had kept her childhood world filled with flowers flashed through her mind. Then, that life had ended, and Cheeky had become her benefactor, allowing her a place, although somewhat neglected, in his world of art. Now, she had been abandoned even by that benign neglect, and all she had left in her life was her adopted grandmother. She'd even given up her precious mouse, and that had almost broken her heart.

Now, however, she had another stray that had come into her life, the rooster, and she had to have it, to provide it a home and love. Hearing the sound of its approaching three-toed feet prancing on the forest floor, she froze, tracking the orange and brown feathers that walked forward, shifted position, then stopped, and finally stepped forward once again.

Her respiration increasing, she waited until just the right moment, and as the feathered animal stepped into her space, her hands darted out. With a squawking flurry of wings, feathers, and smooth skin, the rooster that had tormented guests since the resort had been built was free no longer. It would know love, even if Squeegie had to force it to submit at the dire cost of its freedom.

"$\mathcal{W}$HAT HAPPENED to your harness?" Riley had a hand around a strap on one he didn't recognize. Buzz's previous harness had wrapped between the boy's legs. This one was a life vest with simple bands that did little more than keep it restricted to his chest.

Buzz grinned, kicking sand with his feet. "Julia apologized. She gave me the wrong one. It was packed in one of the parasailing bags, and she didn't know. It never did fit right, anyway."

They were on the beach, and Riley glanced at Houston, wondering whether to acknowledge his presence. The incident of the red boxer shorts was still raw around his waist, and he had the elastic burns to prove it.

"Are you ready, then?" Riley slapped his son's shoulder and looked out across the water at the boat skipping over the waves toward them. Julia stood over a pile of life vests for the other guests, each in an individual bag labeled Blue Water Maui Parasail Club.

"Buzz?" Riley repeated, turning to his son and forcing a grin of encouragement to his face. The boy was pulling at the buckles tightening the straps across his chest.

Before the boy could answer, Houston cleared his throat sharply. He growled, "He's ready, unlike some thieving brothers I know."

"Dad? Is everything okay?" Buzz looked up.

Just then, Beckie and Heather flew onto the beach, their arms full of beach hats, sunglasses, and sun lotions. Heather had a clear bag with two towels inside, which she dropped onto the sand. They giggled when they saw Houston and Riley standing on either side of Buzz.

"Oh, Heather," Beckie cooed in an overloud voice. "Do you think I need more lotion on? I don't want to get a bikini line. Look here on my side. Do you think I have one, already?" She stepped out where she could just catch Riley's eye, and she shifted her hip sideways to show her friend her imagined flaw.

Heather giggled. "I think so, sweetie. You definitely need more lotion." She looked at the men and spoke brightly, "Let me see if I brought any with me. Oh! Right here, you go. I brought some, um, with SPF sunblock. 50, it says. Do you think that will do? I don't know who might put it on for you, though."

Her voice had turned very sultry, clearly inviting one of the men to offer a helping hand.

Houston's eyes glanced from the woman's hip to his brother. "There's your invitation, Riley. At least you wouldn't have to steal this one from me."

"Steal?" Buzz. "Dad One? Dad Two?"

"Never mind, Buzz," Riley said. "It doesn't involve you. Go get life vests for the ladies. Uncle Tee and Uncle Jay will be here shortly. Get some for them, also." He pushed the boy along. Moving a step closer to Houston, he sighed when his brother took a step away.

"Close enough." Houston's jaw tightened.

"I haven't stolen Angelique, Houston." Riley crossed his arms over his chest, not knowing what else to do with his hands. "You already have your underwear back. What else do you want?"

Houston snorted. "The truth. You had her in your arms."

"Brother," Riley tried again, "you've known me for most of your life. Have I ever tried to steal a girl from you? You're my best friend, and you know that."

Houston barked, "Then explain. I'm listening, but you have only one chance."

Heather interrupted, grabbing Houston's arm, and nearly tugging him to the ground. "Oh, I'm so sorry, Houston. It's so hard to walk in this sand, and I must have stumbled. Please forgive me, but if you could help me over to the life jackets, I'd really appreciate it." She giggled. "I have to have one to go up in that airplane thingie."

Riley was startled when Beckie pressed to his side, and a tube of SPF 50 sunscreen appeared in front of his face. She looked at him and blinked her lashes rapidly.

"Please, Riley. I need some of this lotion right here." She twisted sideways and pointed to her bikini strap, just where it crossed over her hip. Then she reached to rub her hand along his bare chest. "Please? It would be the most wonderful thing if you could. If I do it myself, my hands will be all slippery, and I might fall out of the sail thingie. You don't want me to drown, do you?"

As she took one finger and traced it down his sternum, Houston leaned in, "You don't want her to drown, do you, Riley? Remember, one chance is all I'm willing to give you." Then he turned to Heather and laughed. His blue eyes sparkled, and as he stepped away, the sheen of sweat on his shoulders glistened in the brilliant Pacific sun.

Riley watched him go, grabbing Beckie's hand as her finger reached the waistband of his swim trunks. "Far enough," he muttered, taking the tube of lotion from her hand. He looked at it ruefully, and with a twist, removed the lid. He muttered, "Where does this go? I'd definitely hate to see you drown when you fall out of the sail thingie."

He glanced at his brother showing off as he charmed Heather. That one thing alone made him aware of how irritated he must still be.

He was amused to see Houston's childish antics were back-firing, though. Heather apparently saw his interest as a window of opportunity and was determined to initiate physical contact at the slightest provocation. She was all over him.

"Exploding F-1 engines," Riley heard his brother mutter, as he reached a hand to Heather, catching her as she intentionally slipped once more in the sand. "This is all I need, Formula 1 exploding car engines in female disguise!"

Riley began to laugh. When Beckie asked him what it was all about, he just requested her to shift her position so he could lather her other side, please, and then she would be safe from the mean ole sun.

Then he cracked open the sunscreen once more.

"BOBBY?" ROBBY called to his brother. "Hey, come look. This could be fun."

Out across the water, the first parasail lifted off the back of the high-powered boat, and neon-colored hair could be seen whipping in the wind. The sail lifted higher and higher, and across the water, the shrieking excitement of a high-pitched female voice drifted to them, intense in its exhilaration.

"Bobby! Are you coming? Now, brother!" Robby laughed when his brother appeared. He was dressed in bright orange trunks and tiny little sunglasses. "Whoa, B-Bob! What's this? You look so cool." He reached for the glasses, only to have Bobby jerk away.

"Hands off, Robby." He pushed his brother from him. "My eyes burn easily. I need to keep these on."

"You're such a sissy." He pointed to the water. "See? That might actually be fun. Even the girls are doing it. You want to go down and give it a try?"

"We're out of money, remember?" He sighed and turned his back to the scene. "Lucas, and all that. He's paid his last bill for us."

Robby laughed. "Not this time. There's no charge for this. All we have to do is go down there and join in; I spoke with Christian earlier. You want to?" He grabbed his brother's arm to turn him around, and he pointed. "There, it's Jerrold and Treavor heading down. Oh, you have to look at Jer."

Bobby looked, squinting, his attention finally piqued. "That's Jerrold? He seemed rather pasty to me the last time I saw him." He lifted his glasses for a closer look. "His skin's sort of . . . out of focus, if you ask me."

"Let's go see, B-Bob! Come on, say you will. For me? To see Jer's new tan?" He grinned and pulled on his brother's arm.

"I would, but you're not dressed. They'll be through by the

time you change and we get there."

"Oh, no, they won't." He grinned as he reached to the waist of his shorts and unsnapped the clasp. With a smooth motion, he unzipped the fly and dropped the offending item of clothing to the deck of the lanai. Then he grabbed his shirt and snatched it over his head. He was left wearing brightly flowered yellow and red trunks tied with an apple green cord. "See? I come with power windows, overdrive, and new seat covers." He slapped the backside of his trunks, grimacing at the unexpected sting.

Bobby groaned. "Do you come with sun visors, too?"

He knelt to the ground to rummage through his shorts, finally standing with a prize in his hand. "Yep! Fully tinted against solar intrusion. From Christian, and one hundred percent just like yours." He slipped them on his face. "Ready?"

"Well," Bobby conceded. "I guess I'll have to go down now, but I can't promise I'll get up there to fly."

"Good enough." His brother smiled. If he got Bobby to the beach, and if Houston and Riley went up, his twin would be as good as there, too.

BECKIE WAS THE FIRST to scream as the rooster came flying past.

Heather let out a yell next.

Attached to the rooster was an eight-year-old girl running full out with the animal's legs held in her hands. As it passed, Beckie tried to jump out of the way, and she flew backwards into the sand.

"Are you all right?" Riley knelt to brush sand from her arm. "It's just Squeegie. And that rooster, of course. I don't think it will actually hurt you." He grinned. "Squeegie might." He looked around and frowned, his eyes searching the area.

"What is it?" She clung to his arm, rubbing her hand up and down his skin. "I'm fine, really, if that's what you're worried about." When he didn't respond, she pressed him, "Is something else the matter?"

"Granny Swell. I don't see her here, and if that girl is running free, then who's keeping up with the old woman?"

She laughed. "She was going for a nap, earlier. I think I saw Christian heading that direction. He'll let us know if there's a problem." Across the sand, she saw Heather step to Julia for help out of her harness.

"Maybe." He continued to look.

She pattered on, "I've been expecting to see Angelique. She promised if we showed up and boarded that flying contraption, she'd ride it, too. Heather and I went up, and now I can't find Angie anywhere." She rubbed her hand down Riley's arm once again and smiled. "It's her turn just as soon as Buzz gets down, and I can't let her wimp out on this."

Riley jumped when a hand grabbed his shoulder, squeezing hard, and he turned to see Houston's face peering down the beach. "What?" His free hand grabbed the waistband of his swim trunks.

"Angelique's not here." Houston shaded his eyes, looking to the boat where Buzz was yelling in delight at being up on the parasail. Then he turned to scan what he could see of the villas in the compound. "Where's she at, Riley?"

"How would I know? Beckie was just asking the same thing." He shrugged his brother's hand off and continued in a cautious voice, "Maybe she's with Granny Swell. We just saw Squeegie. She's running around here somewhere holding that rooster, the one that's been chasing everyone." When he saw Houston's jaw tighten, Riley disentangled himself from Beckie and stood. "You want me to help you search?"

"No, it's all right. I can look by myself. I appreciate the offer, though." His eyes finally caught his brother's, and he shifted them away again. "Buzz is about to come down, and he's excited. You cheer for him when he does. I'm headed to look for Angelique." He took a deep breath and pulled off his life vest, dropping it at his feet. "Tell him I'll go up another day. He'll be disappointed, but . . . you understand."

"Sure. You'll find her. She's got to be around somewhere. Hey," and he grabbed his brother's shoulder, stepping close to him. "I'm sorry about earlier. I should have thought . . . I mean, I know I take you for granted, and I shouldn't. You're my brother. I don't want anything to come between us."

Houston looked in his face for a long moment, and then he turned away, his eyes red. "We'll talk, Riley. Later, though. Angelique should be here, and she's not. She seemed upset back at the villa. I—" and he paused for a moment, almost as if searching for the right word, "I just need to find her to make sure she's all right." He grimaced painfully, and there was roughness in his movements.

Riley slapped him on the shoulder as he walked away, letting him go.

Then, Beckie squealed, and something hit Riley in the back of the legs. Looking around, he overbalanced and fell right onto Beckie. As they scrambled to untangle limbs, they looked to see Squeegie running away from them, once again chasing the rooster. Heather was pointing to them, and just beyond her, Jerrold and Treavor were holding their sides with laughter.

It was Bobby who got them all going for a second wind. Just as he and his brother arrived at the beach, that Maui rooster headed his direction. As the animal reached him, he turned and began to run, his bright orange trunks flashing in the sun.

Somehow, in a twist of irony, Bobby was soon chasing the frightened animal, and as he was too scared to pay attention, he passed it right up on his way back to his villa.

Squeegie finally did catch that rooster, though. She was right on Bobby's heels, and as he outpaced the orange-feathered monstrosity, she fell onto it in a fit of grasping arms.

That rooster had no choice. It was going to be loved, even if doing so smothered it right to death.

CHAPTER 18

THE OCEAN STRETCHED into the distance, but it was over a thousand feet down. Straight down, causing Angelique's stomach to turn. Heights had never been her forte.

"See? I told you a helicopter was the way to go." Gator unbuckled his seatbelt and reached to help her with hers. "The Valley of the Kings, just like you suggested."

"Just like I suggested?" She glanced down as she climbed out. They were on the upper edge of a green cliff, and she could see the ocean thrashing the base far below. The wind howled.

"You know Hawaii, right? You told me so in the limo yesterday." He grinned. "You mentioned Waipi'o Valley specifically."

She laughed, holding to the helicopter. "Knowing Hawaii and Waipi'o Valley doesn't mean I've ever been up here." Her stomach continued to churn. "My goodness, Gator. You mean you actually climb stuff like this all the way from the bottom?" She leaned out to look down again, and she felt her stomach flip one more time.

"Well, today we're not climbing. We're only going down." He leaned into the helicopter and called to the pilot, "Roy, you did say this is the best place to rappel?" Their pilot, Roy Kaimana, the owner of the helicopter and the small tour company it comprised, nodded in the affirmative, raising his hand and forming an okay sign.

"How will I see you while you're on the way down?" She tried to peek again, but it was making her dizzy. "Will the helicopter fly alongside so I can watch?"

He laughed. "We, Angelique. I'd like you to go with me—"

"Gator!" She heard the fear in her voice. She felt it in her stomach. "Go down this? How could I?" She hadn't realized he intended her to accompany him, and she looked longingly inside the helicopter at her recently vacated seat.

He took her hand. "You can't fall. The figure eight and the carabiners Roy'll hook you up with are exceedingly safe. In fact, at your size, you may have difficulty actually going down." He turned to the pilot. "Could I get you to unload our harnesses and the ropes? Oh, and my other leg?"

"Our harnesses?" Angelique felt her face go numb. Gator had planned everything. "Gator, I'm certain you didn't ask me about this." She looked up at the man unloading rappelling equipment beside the helicopter, silently pleading with him for an excuse not to do this.

"But I did. I said I wanted to go to the Big Island to climb, and you said you wanted to join me. I believe you said as long as anything I planned was off the island of Maui, you'd do whatever I wanted. I didn't think you had any climbing experience, and rappelling is something even a novice can do successfully. I admit, it's pretty far down, but Roy says there's a wide ledge right before the bottom, and he can pick us up there."

She looked at him, chewing her bottom lip. "I agreed to

this, huh? Well then, I guess I'd better suit up." She laughed nervously. She didn't want to. She could just see the headlines. Young Widow, Heiress to Trust Fund, Dies on Her Honeymoon. It would also say it was through her own stupidity. She was certain of that.

"Miss Angelique, let me help you."

She turned to see Roy holding a metal-and-nylon-tape harness out to her.

"If you will step into this, I will adjust it to fit you. Mr. Gator is correct. This is very safe. You cannot fall." He smiled at her. "Please?" Then he whispered to her, "If you do not go, I do not get paid. Please. For my family."

Guilt trip, she thought, her eyes narrowing for an instant. Then she smiled. In less than two weeks, she had gotten married, her husband had been killed, she had come on her honeymoon with all his funny buddies, and she had somehow adopted a kleptomaniac grandmother. To top it off, there was an eight-year-old daughter in the mix. Now she was going rappelling off a cliff? Perhaps death wasn't such a bad option. She grabbed the harness and stepped into it.

Roy smiled. "The other way, please. The two loops go in the front. I will use them to hook you up when you go over the side."

"Over the side," she murmured, looking that way, and then closing her eyes to settle her nerves. Slowly, she slipped the harness off and reversed it. "I don't want to go over the side. All I can imagine is falling straight to the bottom."

"Then we must get the harness tight." He called louder, "Isn't that right, Mr. Gator?"

Gator was strapping on his own harness, and Angelique was impressed to see he had already exchanged his realistic prosthetic for one that was no more than a jointed metal pole with a rubber tip on the end. For climbing, he had said earlier, custom built to his specifications.

He grinned. "Yes, Roy. I don't want my Angelique to wind up at the bottom before she wants to get there."

She glanced at him. His Angelique? She wasn't sure she liked the sound of that. However, right then, she was at his mercy, and it was her own fault. At least he wasn't ripping the underwear off the helicopter pilot, and she breathed a sigh of relief for that.

The rope being tied off to a large boulder made her feel slightly better, but the end Roy threw off the side of the cliff was very long, and she didn't see how it wouldn't become tangled. Then, he snapped a figure eight onto her harness and threaded the rope through. Standing beside her, he put one of her hands on the rope in front of her just where it threaded through the figure eight, and had her hold the rope that draped behind her back with her other hand. Before letting her step backwards off the cliff, he had her squeeze and release the hand at her back several times.

"That is the important hand, Miss Angelique. You must always open and close that hand. Open it, and you move. Close it, and you stop. If you do not remember to open it, you will not go down. I hate to come down after you. Do you understand?" When she nodded, he pulled a pair of gloves out of his pocket. "I put these on you. No blisters, see? Let Roy take care of you. Do not worry." He smiled and worked the cotton gloves over her hands.

"Do I really have to do this?" She glanced at his face to see him smile encouragingly at her.

Gator's voice called over to her, "You look good, Angelique! You'll do fine. I'll see you at the bottom."

She glanced over to see he had already prepped his equipment all on his own, and he was hooked in and ready to go. He seemed immensely pleased with himself, perhaps too much so for her taste. After all, she was the one scared to death. No, not just scared—that was too mild a word. She was certain she was doomed to death.

Then, shooting her a thumbs up sign, Gator was gone over the edge and out of sight.

As she felt her stomach coming up, Roy leaned in very close to her. "Do not try to stand once you step over the side, Miss Angelique. You must try to lie flat as a pancake. A very skinny pancake." He smiled at his own joke. "In your mind, you are in a hammock," he continued. "No one ever stands in a hammock."

Then, she was over the side, and she felt her heart try to explode inside of her chest.

She hung in open space for a moment, swinging back and forth, and she peered down to see that Gator had managed to slip far enough down the cliff face to no longer be in free fall. His feet were pressed firmly against the side, and he waited for her to join him.

"I'm not going anywhere, Roy." She looked up and called to him, although she couldn't see just where he was, and she frowned at his answer.

"Open the right hand just a little. Let the rope slip, Miss Angelique. Close it if you go too fast." He laughed. "You will not go too fast. You are just a Nawao, an elfin creature. Even if you let go all the way, you will only float to the bottom, a flower petal dancing in the wind."

She tried to open her hand very slowly, her heart beating in fear, hoping to float like a flower petal and not a stone, only to find Roy was correct. Finally, she felt herself move, but only when she opened her hand completely. Even then she had to bounce up and down just to slip several feet. After that, friction on her figure eight would slow her to an eventual stop.

So, it was with that awkward gait that she finally caught up with Gator. She did find it much easier when her feet could touch the cliff face. Then she could brace herself to jar the rope loose, leaning back with her boots on the wall, and letting the rope slip through her hand for a few additional feet. Eventually, she learned to walk backwards down the cliff face at a steady pace, keeping tension on the rope, and her descent became much more graceful.

Gator cheered her on, and as frustrated as she'd been at the top, by the time she reached sea level, she was very glad, indeed, that she had braved this majestic spot on the Big Island. At the bottom, she and Gator hugged one another tightly, filled with adrenalin and laughing. At that point, she knew this place was named appropriately. Waipi'o Valley, the Valley of the Kings. She felt like part of Hawaii's royalty. She'd braved its worst, and she'd come out victorious. Unlike Houston back on Maui, Gator had been at her side to help her through.

"I HAVE TO admit I enjoyed the experience very much." Angelique licked the tip of one finger before gently wiping it on a paper napkin.

"Now you understand why I love to climb." Gator dipped a bit of his pumpkin curry and put it on his tongue. "I love Naung Mai Thai Kitchen, too." He motioned with his hand around the eating establishment. "How is your papaya salad?" His eyes wandered to a neighboring table. "See that? Mango with sticky rice. You'll be in heaven if you eat that."

She smiled. "Shouldn't we get back to the resort? I didn't tell anyone I was leaving."

A shrug revealed his opinion. "Spontaneity." He put his elbows on the table in front of him. "What's the point if your life is so drawn out into little bitty boxes that you can't move without everyone knowing your every muscle twitch? Now, here's what I think. Take this island." He motioned around the room, indicating the place they were visiting. "Hundreds of people, no, thousands, maybe even hundreds of thousands of people come here every year. Some of them drop off the radar, go AWOL, simply . . . disappear to the rest of the world. The remainder all go home." He leaned back in his chair, and he draped one arm over the back. "Now, tell me. Who do you think finds more satisfaction in this place? In their lives? You tell me that." He leaned forward suddenly, tapping the table between them. "I know who, and you do, too."

"That's not real life, though, Gator. You can't expect every one of the people who visit this place to just drop off the radar, disappear into the forest, and leave their lives behind. Really, now!" She laughed at him, and he laughed along, picking up one of the eating utensils and rubbing it absently with his thumb.

"No, you're right, there. Not everyone, but that's what Hawaii is all about, if people will let it be. This is a place—and understand that I don't live here and barely know the place, but I can tell already—this is a place that lets people do just that, drop off the radar, just for a little, safe bit. Like a roller coaster."

She laughed again. "Like a roller coaster? How does that analogy fit?" She chuckled, looking around the room at the other diners.

"No, I'm serious." He leaned toward her and smiled. "Why do people get on roller coasters? To live dangerously? No! No way! They get on to pretend to live dangerously. If there were even the hint they'd never get off alive, even a one in a million chance, that coaster would be vacated in a heartbeat. You know that as well as I do. People who really want to live dangerously wrestle crocodiles, climb mountains, or," and he paused, smiling, "get married."

She placed her hand on his, and she looked him in the face.

223

"Marriage was dangerous for me, at least—or perhaps it was just dangerous for Lucas. I seem to still be alive." She looked away, seeing the table next to theirs emptying, the diners noisily rising to their feet. "However," and she looked back at him, "you mentioned crocodiles. Is that how you lost your leg?"

He laughed, turning his hand to hold hers. "I wish I could be so proud. No, my claim to an exotic missing leg is much more mundane. I was stupid."

"Stupid? Not you, Gator. Surely." She laughed, squeezing the hand she held, enjoying its warmth.

He winked at her. "When I was just out of high school, a dropout, mind you, I'd recently come back from climbing Everest, and I was on a binge with my friends. Well, somehow that weekend, I stepped on a rusty nail and didn't know. By the time my drunk was over, the doctors thought I'd lose the entire lower half of my body. Thank God they were able to contain the infection, reversing the effects to some degree, allowing me to keep everything above the knee. I cursed God for losing my leg for years afterward.

"Now I know I was lucky. He must have been watching over me, because I was so high that weekend, I never knew I was slowly dying. My landlady, an old woman who had no kids, came up to check on me. I'd left the water in the toilet running, and she was concerned about her water bill. She found me burning up on the sofa. It was years before I realized God had sent her to me, and I still send her a Christmas card every year, no matter where I am." He pulled his hand away and leaned his head back to look at the ceiling. After a short time he closed his eyes. "I guess she's still alive. I wouldn't know, though. I never do put a return address on the card, just in case it might be sent back. I don't want to know, you see." He looked forward again and smiled at her. "Quite a story, huh?"

"So, you've never married?" His story had revealed a depth

to him she hadn't imagined existed, and she felt drawn to this unusual man.

He laughed. "Who would want a one-legged drunk who climbs mountains, just so he won't have to overdose to get high?" He grinned. "That's some metaphor for life, I guess. However, the adrenalin rush keeps me off the stuff, or at least most of the time. Out there at the resort, well . . . ." He chuckled and looked at her. "I may just run up your liquor bill. I hope you have plenty of money."

"There's plenty. Don't you worry about that." She was enjoying seeing this new, animated Gator. He was away from everyone else, and he seemed to be more . . . approachable, likeable, even loveable.

He chuckled again, though not with real humor. "Good, because I don't have any money, not to speak of."

"You are a real person, do you know that, Gator?" She watched his face. It was still roughly shaven, and she hadn't seen it any other way except the day of the wedding. She wondered how he kept it so perfectly scraggly. In that intimate moment, he seemed just that, perfect.

"Real, Angelique? I should hope so."

"No," she corrected herself, realizing how her earlier sentence must have sounded. "I didn't mean it like that. It's just that before today, you were the man who had stepped into my wedding to fill an empty penguin suit. Now, you're the man who braved a disaster that would have destroyed many men, and you've come to terms with it. You have an amazing philosophy about life, and rather than drink yourself to death, you've found another way to get high." She chuckled. "I mean that in more ways than one, too. Do you have any flaws, Gator? Any at all?"

She laughed to cover her sudden attraction to this man who had told her part of his life history. There were still no butterflies, but she definitely felt something, and for a lonely widow who had no one else to turn to, anything was better than nothing. She put aside an unwelcome twinge of disquiet, as she remembered telling herself that very same thing with Houston earlier that day, that any port in the time of a storm was better than no port at all. However, at least with Gator, there might actually be the possibility of a relationship developing that was something more than platonic.

Looking into his eyes, she searched for some connection, that opposite side of what she felt growing in her own heart. She had six weeks to build a relationship with this man, and if a relationship was ever going to develop, surely that was enough time.

After several soul-searching minutes, he coughed and looked away. "I've never had a woman ask me that question. I've never been able to see anything but my flaws, and eventually, most women usually seem to feel the same way. Thank you, Angelique. I appreciate you asking."

"You're modest, too." She reached for his hand once again. She spoke intensely and with meaning. "The flaws aren't there, are they, Gator? I think I've found the one man on this island who might be absolutely perfect, and I'm having dinner with him. I'm very glad to have come with you today. I've needed time away from that madhouse I've brought with me, and you've given me that. Thank you from the bottom of my heart."

He looked at her for a minute, a series of conflicting emotions writing themselves across his face. Then he pulled his hand away a second time and stood.

"We need to get back." His voice was strained, and he looked at the empty table next to them. "You are right. We really should let the others know where we've been all day. Your friends will be worried."

She frowned, surprised. "Gator, did I say anything wrong?"

He turned, pulling out his wallet and dropping several old and crumpled bills on the table. "I'm not who you think I am. You said that earlier, and it's still true, I'm afraid." He looked at her and smiled. "Thank you, though. What you said. It meant a lot to me just to hear it. However, we really need to go." He took her hand, and he helped her stand. Pulling her to him, he kissed her on the cheek. "You'll be a great woman for someone. You deserve better than me, though."

She looked at him and smiled, her eyes brimming with tears, and she followed him as he led her into the street. There was no one other than Gator, not back at the villas. No one there carried even the possibility of companionship for her. Didn't he see that? She had six more weeks of spending time with men who would rather spend time with each other. How could she compete with that? How could she survive that? She couldn't. She absolutely couldn't.

However, as he led her to the cab that would return them to their waiting helicopter, she knew she really didn't have much of a choice. She was returning to Houston and Riley, with a boy she had come to adore. Her two best friends—if she could call Beckie and Heather that—also waited on her. There was also a pair of twins, as well as two other men Lucas had claimed as friends, and she certainly couldn't abandon Lucas' little girl and the old woman the youngster cared for, until she at least knew more about them.

In the helicopter, they talked only of the Waipi'o Valley and their escapade down the side of the cliff face. They smiled, and Roy even joined in once or twice. However, the joviality was forced, and when they approached the resort, everyone was ready for the trip to be over. It was time to face real life, and there was no doubt in Angelique's mind that real life over the next few weeks was going to be very messy, indeed.

CHAPTER 19

"RILEY? ANY SIGN OF Angelique?"

Riley turned, laughing at a joke in progress. He had Beckie on one arm and Heather on the other. "No, I haven't seen her for some time."

Off behind the trio, Buzz jumped into the air to catch a Frisbee, and when he missed it, his youthful voice cried out in dismay. Treavor cheered and took off to chase the plastic disc as Jerrold and Robby made disappointed sounds. Bobby was on the sideline with sunglasses on his face. The afternoon had finally livened up as a result of the beautiful tropical weather.

Riley waved at his son with a yell, and he turned back to his brother. "You looked already, though, right? Everywhere?"

Houston took a deep breath and let it out loudly. "Ladies, you're friends with Angelique. Did she say anything to you about where she might have gone?"

Heather spoke up, frowning, "She was supposed to come parasailing with us. Beckie and I got up behind that boat. I could wring that woman's neck. She promised, didn't she, Beckie?"

"Yeah. When you see her, tell her she's in the doghouse. That was a mean way to get us up there." Beckie turned to Riley and stroked his arm. "Except I think we got the best of the deal. Don't you think so, Heather?"

Heather snuggled up to Riley's other arm, but her eyes were on Houston. "Sure, Beckie. Thank you for sharing. Houston?" She smiled suggestively. "Want to join us? We're headed to our pool. Riley said he'd walk us up. You can come, too, and we can all get in." She batted her eyelids.

He looked away without responding, now seriously concerned. He turned at the distant chop of a helicopter approaching.

"Gator!" He spat the word as he remembered the time he'd spent with him that night back in New York. They'd been at a bar, with Gator saying something about liking helicopters. Houston realized he also hadn't seen Gator since the picnic.

Everyone's eyes turned to follow the noisome machine. Instead of flying on by, it seemed to be headed right in their direction.

"Beckie, could that be Angie inside?" Heather lifted her sunglasses to peer into the approaching canopy. She removed them completely off her head, and she turned to Houston. "I can't tell, but is someone else in there with her, too?"

He repeated, his conviction stronger this time, "Gator!" The man had stolen her away instead of joining everyone else in the day's activities. "That has to be Gator with her in that copter. I can't believe I didn't think of that."

"Surely Julia could have told you where they were. Or Christian. He would have known." That was Beckie. "Why did no one ask them?"

Riley countered with, "Sven. He probably planned the trip.

229

However, I'm surprised you didn't ask Julia. You must have asked everyone else."

Houston rubbed his face with his hand. "I did, only I just asked if she had spoken with her. I didn't think to ask if she knew whether Sven's plans involved sending those two off in a helicopter together. I just didn't ask the right question. I feel stupid." He did, too, and he had made his worry public, also.

It rankled. He didn't like it at all.

𝒜S THE HELICOPTER rotors began to whip the greenery around the clearing, Angelique could see her guests in the distance scattered across the lawn. When it finally settled onto the grass, Roy Kaimana climbed out to open the side of the machine. He leaned in and lent a helping hand to her.

As she stepped out, she turned to the interior to speak to Gator, to thank him for her afternoon. It was when she turned around that she was really aware of the gathering crowd, and no one was waving to her in excitement. In fact, it was quite the other way around. Every one of them had a look of puzzled incomprehension on his or her face.

"Gator? Maybe we shouldn't have brought the helicopter all the way back here. No one looks very happy to see us."

He laughed, checking the straps on his leg, preparing to exit the aircraft. He looked up and remarked, "That's the roller coaster ride. We're on the ride, and they're the spectators. Of course they're not happy. We've had the good time. They'll live over it."

She made a face. "I hope so. I really hope so."

However, she really wasn't sure if she believed his assurances. If she went by her heart, she knew she didn't, but she kept those feelings inside. It was time to put on a good face before she braved the crowd. After all, she was the pivotal person here. This was her vacation, her money, and her honeymoon. Everyone was depending on her, and she couldn't let them down.

"SQUEEGIE?"

The water swirled around Granny Swell's feet. The cord from the lamp she carried in her hand trailed in the waves after her. As the rising surf broke around her legs, she attempted to pull her dress out of the water, never quite keeping it dry. From time to time, she gave a sharp, distressed intake of noise, feeling small creatures as they nipped at her ankles. The wind had begun to buffet the shoreline, and the surf continued to increase.

"Squeegie? Granny Swell is lost. Are you here, Squeegie? I can't find my way home. I found a new lamp. Squeegie?"

She continued to slog along in the surf, occasionally turning to look behind her, her old, broken voice masked by the noise of the water.

A note of panic quavered in her words as she spoke to herself, unheard by anyone else. "I need an extension cord, Squeegie. I need a really long cord." Then she stopped and looked all around her, as if truly aware for the first time of just where she was.

"The bridge. I can't see my bridge, Squeegie. Did they move it?" With that question, her expression clouded over, and she began to move forward against the surf once more. Her mouth moved, but the sound barely got past her lips, and her words could only be understood inside her head.

"I have to find a plug. My light's gone out, and I have to find a plug. I can't see, Squeegie. I can't see at all."

"LADIES, THERE'S CHRISTIAN. Let me see if he knows what's going on. The copter's too far away for me to tell."

The concierge had just appeared along a walk, materializing out of a bank of greenery, and Riley disentangled his arm from

Heather's grasp, waving to get his attention.

"Yes, may I help you?" Christian smiled brightly.

"Angelique. Do you know if anyone else went with her?" The pilot had exited, helping Angelique from the craft, but no one else had disembarked. In the darkened interior, not a soul could be seen.

"Gator, I believe." He frowned, and then his expression brightened. "Yes, they went together. Sven drove them to the main resort earlier today. We have a helipad there. However, it seems they chose to disembark here. It's why we maintain this open area. Is there anything else I can do for you?"

"That little old lady." Beckie waggled her fingers for the concierge's attention. "Granny Swell. How's she doing?"

Heather chimed in, "We've seen the little girl out, but her granny has been quite incognito since lunch." She giggled. "Is she locked away safely?"

"Very safely." He held up his opened palm as a sign of re-assurance and nodded confidently. "I just came from the villa where she will be staying. Forget-Me-Not Villa. She was rest-ing nicely. I'll be back to check on her in a few minutes. Please don't worry."

"See, Riley?" Beckie worked her fingers into his, claiming one of his hands as her private domain. "I told you not to worry. Christian'll take care of everything. Besides, that's so cute. I love forget-me-nots. I never would have thought of that for one of the villas. Now, I want to go see what Angie's been up to. I'm going to be real, um," and she glanced up at him, pronounc-ing her word with prickles in her voice, "snicky, if she took off with that Gator man just to keep from flying in that kite thingie." She pulled his arm to force him forward. "Coming with us, Heather?"

"Sure, Beckie." However, with her eyes on Houston as he headed to the helicopter, and not where she was stepping, her foot slipped in a soft pocket in the ground. With a cry of dismay, she grasped Riley's arm for stability.

She was not quick enough, though. Her foot twisted, and she went down, still holding him for support. Riley was caught in the middle, attached on one arm to Beckie, and on the other to Heather.

He cried, "Ladies! I'm sorry, but there's only one of me. I can't go and stay at the same time."

From off to the side, Squeegie came running with the rooster in her arms, heading straight for the helicopter. At the same time, Gator emerged to stand beside Angelique.

Beckie huffed. "That scamp. She did find her a man, and she's been gallivanting off with him. I thought Gator was kinda cute, too. I cannot believe she stole him right out from under us."

Heather rubbed her ankle with a wince. "Beckie, you already have Riley. I don't have anyone. Can't I have him?"

"Beckie has me? Ladies, I thought I had me. I just got free from my ex. I'm not sure I want anyone to have me just yet."

Beckie leaned to him and grabbed his hand once again. "Men are never free for long." She kissed his fingers, then patted them with one of her hands. When she spoke again, her voice was hard. "Right now I'm going to get that Angelique, though. She's a scamp right out of the society pages. I went up in that thingie, and she didn't. Ooh!"

In a flash, she was gone.

Riley sat hard beside Heather, and he ran his fingers through his red hair. "I guess that girl doesn't like to take no for an answer." His eyes followed her as she walked away.

"Not usually." Heather stretched her ankle out where he could see it. "Massage my ankle, Riley. It really hurts. Please?" When he turned to her, she batted her eyes and smiled.

"Give it here."

233

"Right there, Riley. A little lower. Yes, that's it." She smiled.

Dear God. He should have just walked away.

"WHAT'S THE PROBLEM?" Angelique knelt at Squeegie's side. She wished the child wasn't holding the rooster in her arms, but with the tears on her face, she certainly couldn't ask her to let it go.

"I can't find Granny!" Every now and then, a black or orange feather fluttered to the ground. "Please, Miss Angie. Granny's gone to find her bridge."

Angelique looked at Gator as he stepped down from the helicopter, and she frowned. Bridge? She mouthed the word to him.

He shrugged and told her Roy and he would be stepping away to his villa for a little nip. She'd figure it out, he assured her.

She turned to the little distressed face that had run to her, and taking a deep breath, she took the frantic rooster from the girl's grasp.

"Now, what's this about your granny? You say she's gone to find a bridge?" The girl nodded her head, and her eyes swam with tears.

As Angelique struggled with the rooster trying to free itself from her arms, she noticed someone behind the child, and she looked up to find Houston's dark hair and blue eyes. She also noticed his scowl. Surely he wasn't upset with her. All she'd done was spend a few hours with someone who might actually be interested in her, and even that had fizzled out in the end. Only God knew why, though.

Now, everyone had turned out to watch her disembark the helicopter, and this little urchin was crying at her knees. All she needed was for the child to utter those pitiful words, "I want

234

some more, please," and it would be Victorian England all over again.

"What, Houston?" When he didn't answer, she frowned at him. "You have a reason to complain, too? If so, join the line." She pointed to Squeegie, and she shifted the rooster in her arms as best she could, reaching one free hand to the youngster.

"My complaint's not with you," he hissed. When the rooster really began to struggle, he reached to take it. "Where did you go?"

His question irritated her. She was no one's. She could come and go as she pleased. This was her honeymoon, after all, and she was here without the man she'd married. He was dead and on her mantle back at home.

"Why would you care?" She heard her words burst from her, hating them as she said them. "The last time I saw you, you were ripping Riley's underclothes off. You were dressed in nothing, barely covered by the towel draped around you. God in Heaven only knows what the two of you intended to do next. Something I hope Buzz has never seen." She glanced away, once again afraid she might cry. Then she heard Squeegie and looked down to see she was indeed crying at her feet. "You do make a point to keep your proclivities private, I hope. He's just a boy."

"What?" His expression changed from a scowl to puzzlement.

"Don't you 'what' me, Houston Richemont! I liked you, even when I knew I shouldn't, and then you had the nerve to parade your passion for that man in front of me like I should be proud for you." She snorted her derision. It set the rooster off, but she no longer cared. "I have a grandmother to find. You can't even do that, can you, keep track of this little girl's grandmother?" She picked her up. "My word, she's in tears." She hugged the girl, and she glared at him.

"But," he started, struggling with the rooster. "Passion? For Riley? I love him, sure, but there's no passion. You and Gator? Are you . . . a pair, now?"

"As if you should care." She started to walk away, and then she turned and looked directly into his eyes, letting her words slice him. "No passion! That's what makes you so despicable. You're involved with that man, and there's no passion between the two of you." Her next words softened as tears began to flood down her face. "How could I ever have fallen in love with you in the first place?"

"Granny Swell. Can we please go look?" The girl in her arms began to rock in desperation. "Please. She's looking for her bridge."

"Let's go see if we can find her." Angelique's eyes were on Houston, even as her words were for the little girl. "At least someone deserves to feel loved."

Houston started after her as she walked away. "Angelique! Wait. You don't understand."

However, she didn't slow down, and the rooster picked that exact moment to throw every bit of its energy into a desperate bid for escape. He managed to hold on to one leg, but in doing so, he went down, grasping wildly for the feathered creature. Once he had the animal back in his grasp, he lay on the ground looking at the departing woman who had voiced her very cutting opinion of him.

"I do love you, Angelique," he called to her, but she was gone, and his words were for himself, alone.

THE ONLY PROBLEM WAS, by that time, Beckie was standing just behind him, and she heard every word. She turned to Heather, still with her hands on Riley, and then back to Angelique's departing form.

She smiled. With her eavesdropping, she was finally getting

a handle on the problem, and it seemed there was some Cupid work to be done. After all, the end of the honeymoon party's six-week stay wrapped up just about Valentine's Day. What could be more perfect than that? She could stick around to help out in this. Of that, she was sure. Of that, she was absolutely sure.

JERROLD LAY SPRAWLED on his towel. The sea breezes felt wonderful, but the late afternoon sun had wrapped his bare torso, and sweat beaded along his mottled skin. At least he wasn't white wine. He just needed shaken up and evened out. A little time in the sun would do that.

"Did you see all that?" Behind his sunglasses, Jerrold's eyes took in Treavor's toned, athletic stride as he walked up to him. He called, "Who do you think Angelique'll pick? They're both hot for her."

"Jealous." Treavor laughed. He threw himself down on an adjacent towel, and he twisted onto his stomach, crossing his arms under his head. Turning his face toward Jerrold, he closed his eyes and smiled. "You just hope it's Houston."

Jerrold sat up to recline on his elbows and snorted in derision. "You might be right." He paused, feeling the pooled sweat run off his chest. "But then you might not. Why would I care if she chooses Houston? Gator's got plenty of craggy charm. What would be wrong with him?"

"What Beckie heard." Treavor was already immobile as he lay face down, absorbing the sun. Only his lips moved. "Out there at the helicopter, she overheard them. Houston's in love."

Jerrold turned his head, and through his sunglasses, he squinted at Treavor. Small beads of sweat were just beginning to shimmer on his skin. A muscle in his cheek twitched, sending a small droplet of water running down to catch on the side of his nose.

"Houston's in love." He repeated his friend's words, and he saw Treavor smile, the movement slight and then gone. He continued, a note of incredulity in his voice, "Houston's never been in love before, not really. He's had lots and lots of girlfriends, but he's never said he's in love. He actually said that?"

Treavor's lips moved again. "Exactly that. Ask Beckie. She overheard it all."

"Angelique, though? What about her? Is that who he's in love with?"

"Yep, except she doesn't know it. Haven't you been watching them? Even I could see the signs. It just took Beckie for it to really click in place for me."

"I don't know whether this is possible. It seems too much. She spent the day with Gator, you remember."

"You didn't watch their faces, did you?" Treavor's cheek twitched again, and the drop of water fell from his nose to the towel.

"Houston's and Angelique's?"

"No, idiot." Treavor's arm darted out, and the back of his hand smacked against Jerrold's side. "Gator's and Angelique's." He grinned, even though his eyes remained closed.

Jerrold barked his contempt. "I thought you said this was between Houston and Angelique. Why would I watch Gator's face?" He dropped wearily onto the towel and closed his eyes. When he heard his friend shift position, he opened his eyes and glanced at him. He was propped up on his elbows, and sweat coursed down the tips of his hair, forcing them into curls next to his skin. His eyes peered at him, and amusement was on his lips.

"Dense as always, Jer? I watched Gator and Angelique, and that's how I know they're not in love."

"How could you tell?" He pursed his lips. "Tell me, and

don't hold back. You're teasing me, you know. I can tell."

Treavor rubbed his hand hard across Jerrold's shoulder and studied the ends of his fingers. Then he chuckled and fell back to the towel, wiping his hand on the terrycloth beside his face.

"What'd you do that for?" He turned his head to look at his shoulder where the sweat had been wiped away, only to see small beads of moisture already reappearing. "Was something there?"

"That stuff doesn't come off, does it?"

"Stuff?" A frown accompanied the words. "Oh, the tanner. No. I told you that earlier."

"Well," Treavor lifted his head, sounding very pleased, "being in the sun is working wonders. The color already looks smoother. Another few days, and I don't think anyone will be able to tell. They'll think you've lived here all your life." He dropped his head back onto his arms and closed his eyes.

Jerrold smiled, pleased. "What about Angelique and Gator? You haven't said that, though. You know for sure?"

"They're just not, Jer. Trust me. Angelique's in love with Houston, and she just has to figure that out. She will, though."

"How?" He poked Treavor. "How will she figure it out?"

"Six weeks, Jer." His words faded with drowsiness. "Besides, everyone loves Houston." After a few moments, a slight snore filtered up from his opened mouth.

"Especially you, huh, Treavor?" Then he looked across the clearing to see Beckie and Heather fawning over Riley once again. They had no problem with showing their desires and affections. Why should it be so hard for him?

Without warning, Buzz came flying up behind the trio and crashed into his father, showering sand over all three adults. As the father and son tumbled over, Riley wrapped his freckled arms around the boy in a familiar motion that obviously came from years of roughhousing. Twisting to his feet, he lifted the boy high over his head.

The women screamed in mock terror and covered their heads as Riley spun the boy in circle after circle, finally tumbling together with him into the sand right between the two women.

As their laughter rang out, Riley pushed Buzz off and told him to go wash in the ocean. The boy jumped up, and with a burst of motion that could only come from a freshly maturing thirteen-year-old, he ran for the beach, with laughter ringing from his throat all the way.

Jerrold watched him as he disappeared into the greenery, and a splash told everyone the boy had found the water. It was only a moment before he reappeared, his hair in soggy tendrils on his head, and his suit clinging wetly to his body.

"I'm heading up, Dad." Buzz waved, and as he passed the trio, he turned and walked backwards for a moment, still talking. "Don't have too much fun without me." His arm jumped into the air, and he shot his dad a thumbs up sign as he laughed.

As he turned, his two "uncles" on their oversized beach towel caught his attention. He raised his arm and waved, asking if they were having as much fun as he was. Then, seeing Jerrold's waggled fingers, he ran full speed for the villas.

Jerrold knew what his problem was. He obsessed over things too much. He should be more carefree, like Riley's boy, and then he could enjoy life as it came.

He lay down and closed his eyes. The sun washed his bare skin, and he felt the beads of sweat dampening his body. He could be carefree and enjoy life as it came, once he had someone of his own. Until then, he had no choice but to obsess, and that was a cross he simply had to bear.

CHAPTER 20

"BABY, WHERE DO YOU think she might be?" It had taken Angelique and Squeegie several minutes to walk to the villas, and they had kept an eye out for the old grandmother along the way. "You said she's looking for her bridge. Where would she go?" She took one finger and wiped a tear from the girl's eye. "Don't cry. We'll find her. I promise."

Squeegie still had her arms around Angelique's neck, and she buried her face against her shirt. "Great Auntie went away, and then I went to live with Daddy Cheeky. I was sad."

"Cheeky. Rio Cheeky?" She looked around. Surely some-one would know that answer, but she was on her own. Then she murmured, "You wouldn't know about Rio, would you?"

"Rio?" Squeegie raised her head and smiled, brushing her face with a free hand. "I know Rio. That's where Ricky went, and that's why Daddy Cheeky wanted to go. That's why he sold Mother's Milk, even though Granny Swell made it for him. He couldn't take us to Rio, so he left us here." She pulled at one of

Angelique's buttons, and then she looked into her eyes. "Granny would like your buttons. Be careful. She might pull them off." Then she giggled and buried her face in Angelique's shoulder.

"I'll be careful." She rubbed the girl's back, and she whispered to her, "I won't go away. I promise. However, right now, we need to find Granny Swell. I'm putting you down on your feet, but I'm also going to hold your hand. We're walking until we find Granny Swell. Let's start with your villa."

Squeegie held onto Angelique's neck, but she leaned back to where she could see into her face. "My villa?"

"Your rooms. The place where Christian put your things. Remember Christian, the man with the brightly painted fingernails?"

The girl's face brightened. "I remember. He was afraid of the chicken. He said it'd chase him, but it never did. I held really tight to my chicken." Then her face fell. "Granny's not in the villa."

Angelique knelt and placed Squeegie's feet on the ground, helping her to stand. With her hand, she held the child's chin and spoke into her eyes with a smile.

"We have to start somewhere. I read a story somewhere that said if we don't know where to start, then it's always best that we start at the beginning. The beginning is at your villa. So let's look there first." She smiled and stood, taking her hand.

"What was the story? I like you, Miss Angie. I want you for my mommy."

"Something about a wizard and a little girl who was very, very lost." Angelique smiled at her as she answered the girl's question, and after Squeegie turned, she shook her head. "It seems neither of us has much choice in whether I get to be your mummy. You're my daughter for now, whether I'm ready or not."

HOUSTON SAT FOR A TIME and held the rooster in his arms, as the murmur of the sea and the quiet voice of others visiting on the beach wafted his way. His emotions were drained, and for the moment, he didn't know what else to do. He shifted his position just enough to see Buzz giving his father a hard time, and he even laughed aloud when Riley spun the boy above his head before they went crashing to the ground. Then, with a coughing spit, the helicopter that was still parked behind him slowly came to life, its motor burping several times before slicing the air with a steadily increasing beat. As the air brushed the grass around him, he stood, keeping a firm grip on the feathered spitfire that seemed so determined to gain its freedom once again.

"What am I to do with you?" His question was aimed at the rooster, but he looked to see if there was anyone around to give him any aid. What he wanted to do was go after Angelique, to find out just what had happened with Gator, to inquire why she had told herself she shouldn't like him, and what in the world she had meant about passion between him and Riley.

"Rooster, rooster," he pondered. The rooms in the villas had no ceilings to contain the animal, and he couldn't see any of the three concierges outside. To call one of them, he'd need to return to his villa for a phone.

However, when he thought of his villa, he had an idea. If he could get the rooster there, surely he could cage it in one of the closets. They had louvered doors. The animal would have air to breathe, and it couldn't get out. It would be trapped inside until Julia could tell him what to do. Rooster stew? It was a definite possibility. After all, he had promised Angelique just that. He grinned at the memory. It had been in jest, but he had promised.

He grabbed the rooster tightly in his arms, ignoring its pleas for clemency, and with determined, quick steps, he headed to his villa. A quick turnaround was what he intended, then back to find Angelique.

"Hey, Houston. I see you decided to abandon the beach. You have a new friend?"

Houston saw Robby on his balcony, wearing sunglasses and a broad-brimmed floppy hat tied under his chin; and holding a vintage martini glass in his hand. He grinned. He caught the ribbing humor in the greeting.

"You want to keep it for a while? I'll have to have it back later, though. I've promised it to Angelique for dinner." Houston held the rooster up, its legs tightly gripped in one hand.

Robby turned and called into the villa, "Come see this, brother. Houston's giving away chickens." When Bobby appeared, Robby pointed Houston's direction. "See? In pretty, designer colors, too. You want one?"

"What are you planning to do with it, Houston? Pluck it?" Bobby grinned. "I could help." The dramatic grimace he made told otherwise.

Houston laughed. "No, B-Bob. I'm putting it in my closet. It's my new mascot for Bahrain in March. I plan to have a suit and helmet built for it, then it can ride with me."

"No red underwear?" The twins grinned at each other.

Houston felt his neck warm with the memory of the story Riley had threatened to tell at the luau, and he rolled his eyes. "No, guys. No red underwear for the rooster. Those are just for me. Sorry, I've got to go. Angelique needs my help. Granny Swell is missing. Enjoy the afternoon!"

Reaching for the knob, as the rooster made yet another try to escape, he fumbled it open. Houston stumbled into the villa, grasping at the rooster, barely holding to one leg. With one foot, he kicked the door closed again.

"Who's there?" Buzz called out, appearing with a towel, and rubbing his hair. "Uncle Houston, what are you doing with that?"

Buzz's suit was gone, and he wore a pair of brightly colored yellow boxer shorts in its place. He snickered at the rooster, reaching a hand toward the bird, only to have it go into a frenzy of squawking.

"Let me through, Buzz. I have to find a place to put this bird." Houston stepped past, kicking aside several items on the floor.

"Sorry, Uncle Houston. Everything was tumbled over when I got back."

"That's okay. The mess is mine and Riley's. We can sort it out later. Here." He held the rooster out. "Take it." It squawked loudly, its wings flapping wildly, as it tried to escape.

"We're going to keep it here? Won't it get into our stuff?" Buzz tossed his towel over the back of a chair. He didn't offer to take the bird, though. "A chicken? Really, Uncle Houston?" He snickered when it squawked again, flapping its wings valiantly.

"Rooster, actually, boy. And yes. It goes in my closet. If you don't want to take it, please go remove everything out of the closet and put it on the bed. I'm tired of fighting this creature, and anyway, I'm already surprised it hasn't made a mess on me. Chickens do that, you know."

"A mess?" Buzz sniggered, covering his mouth with his hand. "I get it. It goes to the bathroom, and if you're holding it, it goes on you."

"Right-o, kiddo. That's why I want you to hurry. I need this rooster caged as soon as possible. Then, if we can get Julia to come get it, she'll need to bring a basket or something similar to put it in. Can you help me with that?" He nodded his head toward the bedroom as a suggestion.

"I can call her, Uncle Houston. Her number's right by all the phones. I got some extra cards from her just in case I couldn't remember the numbers." He grinned. "I put one by each phone."

"The closet for now?" Houston motioned with his head.

"Sure!" Dancing in his excitement, Buzz chortled. He turned and was gone.

Houston wrestled the rooster to the bedroom to see Buzz standing by the opened closet door, with all his suitcases out by the bed. "My clothes, too, Buzz. I don't want them to smell like rooster."

Just then the rooster made its most desperate attempt to escape, and successful, it flew right at Buzz. Buzz shrieked and fell into the closet, knocking Houston's clothes to the floor in a heap, burying himself underneath. The rooster flew to the only opening it could see, and that was toward the bathroom.

Houston rushed after it, slapping one of Buzz's exposed legs with his hand. "Quick, Buzz! Close all the doors! The bird can't be allowed to escape! We might still trap it inside!"

"I'll try," came his muffled reply. Clothes came flying out of the closet, and he made a mad dash for the bathroom door, pulling it to with gusto.

Houston turned at the noise. "I think that does it." Then, he looked to his nephew, his eyes glowing with anticipation. It seemed a little roughhousing was in order. Calling, "Head's up, Buzz," he threw his arms around the boy and worked his fingertips over him until he began to laugh unbearably and cried for mercy, claiming the sudden need for a bathroom.

"Please, Uncle H. I can't hold it any longer!"

"No!" Houston cried. "I won't let you go. You can't cry for mercy that easily. Suffer!" Then his fingers danced across the boy's ribs once again.

"Please! I'm going to wet my pants. Please!"

Houston made as if to grab Buzz's sides once again, as the boy bolted for the bathroom. As soon as he threw the door back, the rooster flung itself straight through the opening, directly at the man who had so carefully ferried it in his arms to captivity. Houston yelled in surprise, frightening the animal, and in an erratic change of course, it headed right into the emptied closet. Houston leaped after it, slamming the door and trapping it inside.

Buzz stood, shifting side to side on his feet, and he snickered. "It's finally where you wanted it." Then he turned to the bathroom and hobbled inside.

Houston stood in the destroyed room, grinning. Out of breath, he looked at the mess all over the floor. It reminded him of a different sort of mess from earlier. Angelique. Women had never been this complicated before.

"Buzz." Houston banged against the bathroom door to get his nephew's attention. "I'm headed to find Angelique. She's out looking for Granny Swell. She's somehow gotten herself lost."

"Angelique's lost?" Buzz's voice filtered through.

"It's Granny Swell that's lost. Straighten all this up for me, please, Buzz, before Julia gets here. Thank you!" Turning, he threw the bedroom door wide, and with quick strides, he was out the front of the building.

ANGELIQUE LOOKED THROUGH the villa that had been given over to Squeegie and her adopted granny, checking in each closet and under the beds. Frowning, she knelt before the girl as she set her on the sofa.

"Squeegie, honey, I need you to remain here for a moment. I have to call Christian, the man who was watching Granny Swell. Can you give me just a second to do that?" She smiled at the girl, taking her chin in her hand, and gently running her fingers along the soft skin on her face. The poor thing had a certain vagabond look about her, but her skin was the same beautiful color Lucas' had been. "Christian might be able to help. Can you sit right here for me?"

Squeegie grinned. "I can sit still." However, she squirmed as she said the words. Then her smile fell, and her face puckered once more with tears. "Granny Swell needs me."

Angelique wrapped the girl in her arms. "Sweetie, we'll find her. I promise. Just let me make this call, and if Christian doesn't know where she is, then we'll go out to look together."

Thinking of her granny, though, seemed to leave the girl inconsolable, and she began to sob. "Granny needs me," she repeated. "She can't be alone."

"I know, I know." Angelique brushed the wild torrent of hair from the girl's face. Then she stood to locate the phone. Looking around, she was relieved to find Christian's number on a card right beside it. She punched the digits into the machine and was pleased to get a quick answer.

"This is Christian. I hope you are enjoying your stay at Blue Water Maui. How may I help you today?" The voice over the phone was bright and eager.

"Christian, this is Angelique." She turned to see Squeegie stand from the sofa, and she stepped to pat her on the head, pulling her to her side. "Christian, we cannot find Granny Swell. We thought she was here in her villa, but she seems to be gone. You were with her, I understand. Did you take her somewhere?"

It was a moment before the concierge spoke, and his voice shook, breaking at the end. "No. She was resting quietly when I saw her last."

"Did she speak of going anywhere?" Angelique smiled at the girl standing next to her, hoping her expression would reassure the child. "I have her granddaughter here, and she's worried about her missing grandmother."

"Ah. This grandmother is lucky to have such a one to worry

about her." The man's voice grew stronger. "I'll contact Julia and Sven right away. We'll put our thumb on the grandmother's location. After all, this is an island. How far can she go?" He laughed, and his voice took on a reassuring quality. "Is there anything else I can do for you, Angelique?"

She sighed. "I'm taking the girl out to look. She's very distraught. I think we'll head to the beach and walk north. If you could meet us there, it would be appreciated."

"Of course. I'll bring a snack for the girl. Do you think she likes peanut butter crackers?" His voice was bright.

"Thank you, Christian. I'm sure the crackers will be fine. Please bring a towel, too, just in case someone gets wet. Squeegie's getting anxious. I'll meet you at the beach." Then she gently hung up the phone.

"Is Granny all right?" The girl's eyes were big with worry. "Is someone taking care of her?"

Angelique knelt and took the child's small hands in hers, and she looked into her eyes. "I think God's taking care of her. He likes doing that, you know. You want to go with me to find Granny Swell? Then when we do find her, we can give God a rest." She smiled and looked away, dismayed. This wild-eyed urchin knew nothing of a normal family life. How could this child have grown up without a real parent? How could her Lucas have done that?

In that moment, she knew she had known nothing at all about him, nothing that was true, anyway. He had been a sham, and he had done everything just for the money, to get unrestricted access to his trust fund. Perhaps there was justice in the world, after all. Perhaps Lucas had received his. Perhaps she had never really loved him.

She knew she had, though, and his death had allowed grief to tear her apart. Yet, while she would probably always grieve for her memories of how her life with Lucas ought to have

249

been, she could no longer grieve for a man who would birth a child, and then refuse to raise her simply because it was not economically advantageous to do so.

She looked at Squeegie brightly, her eyes stinging with emotions she was determined not to show. "So, what do you say? Shall we go give God a rest? I'm sure he's as tired as you sometimes get when you have to watch Granny Swell all the time. How about that?"

The girl's face brightened. "God needs my help?" She seemed to shift internal gears in the way of an overactive eight-year-old and squealed in excitement. "I want to help God out. That way he can take a nap, just like Granny Swell does. Let's go, Miss Angie!" She grabbed Angelique's arm and tugged her toward the door. However, once she got there, her excitement had already cracked, taking on jagged edges, quickly being re-placed by the sandpaper of rising apprehension.

"What is it, baby?" Angelique put her thumb to Squeegie's eyes to wipe away pooling tears. "We'll find Granny Swell. Christian has promised to get the others to help us look."

"What if God loves Granny Swell as much as I do, and he decides he doesn't want me to take care of her anymore? What if God's lonely like I was, and he needs a friend, a grandmother friend? That's why I took Granny Swell home with me. She needed me, and I needed her. I just took her hand, and we walked together all the way home." The little girl's eyes were red, and tears began to run freely down her little cheeks. "I don't want God to be lonely, but I don't want him to take Gran-ny Swell, either."

Angelique wrapped her hands around the tender little face, and she whispered, "God wouldn't do that to you, baby. If you love someone, God takes care of them."

That hadn't happened with Lucas, though. She had loved him, with all her heart, too, and God hadn't taken care of him.

She sighed as she looked into the girl's eyes. Now that she understood about the man she'd married, she had begun to wonder if God hadn't been taking care of her, instead. How dreadful it would have been to be married, only to find out what she now knew about Lucas.

Squeegie sniffled. "Great Auntie went to be with God. He loved her so much, he came to get her, and she never came back. That's what Cheeky said. I don't want Granny Swell to never come back." A racking series of indrawn breaths shuddered through the girl's chest.

"Oh, baby!" Angelique pulled the little girl to her once more, running her hands through her hair. "Maybe God takes special care of the rest of us, if we let him. He can't take everyone to live with him, so he just takes the most special people, and if we really loved them, he takes care of those of us left behind, instead." Tears flowed down her own face, now, and she sniffled as she pulled away to peer into the girl's reddened eyes. "Let's go see if God's going to let Granny Swell stay with us for a while longer. If so, we'll say a prayer and thank him."

She smiled and brightened her expression by widening her eyes and winking. Then she touched Squeegie's chest with her finger and whispered, "You and me. We'll find her, and then we'll bring her home. That way she'll know you love her the very best of all. How does that sound?"

Squeegie just nodded her head, and she put out her tongue to catch a tear that dripped from beside her nose. "God needs a rest, just so he doesn't get too tired. I understand. I feel that way sometimes, too. I'm ready to go, now." Then, with an indrawn breath, she turned and grabbed Angelique's hand, pulling her forward once more.

CHAPTER 21

GRANNY SWELL'S DRESS tugged around her knees, and the wet fabric weighed her down. The lamp no longer rode high in her grip. It dragged at her side, catching the crests of the waves, its shade long gone. A misstep and a slip earlier had dowsed the poor woman, and the water had rushed into her face. She'd stood coughing for some time, not understanding just why water was in her nose. She did realize it was very hard walking down this busy street, as if she were trudging down a long, muddy road, but it never occurred to her that the mud was the beach, and the difficulty came from the water that swirled around her feet.

Then, she spied her bridge. With glee on her face, she called out, "Squeegie! I found it! I'm home again!" It was just as she remembered it. The bottom of the bridge swept high above her head, and in a mighty arc, it curved away into the sky. Far to the other side, it drooped gently down into the river that snaked through the city. Granny knew she would be among friends once she got there. Old Toothless George and Stinky. Two Fingers Larry. They would build a fire, and there were always garbage cans for finding a meal.

As she drew close to the bridge, she saw no one waiting on her, but that didn't worry her. Sometimes they had to hide from the blue suits, the ones with the flashlights who tried to take their home away, wanting them to go somewhere else, to a room where people fed them and wanted to poke and prod them like they were cattle, like they had diseases. No, she would rather sleep with her friends than in one of those rooms, and she knew without question that her friends would return soon. They always did. In fact, they were probably out looking for her right then.

Sure, that's where they were, and if she just sat down under the bridge and waited, all her friends would return soon. Then she could show them her lamp, and they could help her plug it in. After that, they would have light all night long, and everyone would be warm.

They would be so warm, and it would be because of her.

Houston WAS RUNNING and out of breath by the time he got to where he had left Angelique. Treavor and Jerrold were still lying in the sun, their skin glistening with sweat, and Riley was seated on the grass, attempting to disengage his arms from the grasp of two well-oiled women.

"Riley," he gasped. "Did you see Angelique and Squeegie?"

Beckie reached across Riley and grabbed Heather's arm. "Isn't that just the cutest name? I want to have a little girl someday, and I want to name her that."

Riley made a face at her. "Beckie, no! No one should be punished that way. Give her a normal name, like yours."

Heather cackled, conveniently grabbing Riley's bare leg as

she leaned over to chide her friend. "Normal? Beckie with an 'ie' at the end? It sounds like a dog's name." She hugged Riley's knee as she doubled up with laughter.

Beckie snorted. "Well, at least my name doesn't mean grass. 'Let's go play in the heather!' People do say that, you know. Poop in the heather; that's what dogs do. So, there, poop-name. Dogs go on you."

Heather glared and started to speak, but Houston interrupted with, "Ladies, I have no idea what you're talking about, but may I speak to my brother? It's urgent." He was panting, still, and sweat kept running into his eyes.

"Well!" Heather turned her head.

Beckie just rolled her eyes.

Houston held up a hand with his palm outwards to let Riley know to wait just a moment as he caught his breath. Leaning forward and placing his hands on his knees for support, he slowly gasped out his next words.

"It's Angelique. She's gone with Squeegie to look for Granny Swell. You know how the old woman is. There's nothing going on upstairs, and Angelique has no idea. What if they go chasing her and get hurt? We have to go after them, Riley. You have to help me."

"It's an island, Houston. How can anything happen to them?" Beckie and Heather had his arms tangled with theirs once again, and he attempted to disentangle himself as he spoke.

"Riley?" Houston's voice took on a desperate tone. "Please?"

Taking a deep breath, Riley grasped the waist of his shorts firmly and looked at the women on either side of him. "Ladies," he said brightly. "Want to go on a granny hunt?"

"Good thinking, brother." Houston tapped his temple. "The more we have looking, the better." Motioning for Treavor and

Jerrold to join them, Houston began pointing and giving directions. "Treavor, Jerrold, you two go south." He pointed to the right. "You head down that beach. Look for footprints. Remember, Granny Swell's very old, and her mind's not all there. Be careful when you find her. She may not know where she is. If she's hurt, one of you come back for help."

He looked at the others, only to find Heather glaring at him with her arms crossed.

"If I'm doing this, I'm with them." Heather pointed to Jerrold and Treavor, while pointedly ignoring Beckie. "Some people have been nasty to me, and I could use some better company for a while."

Beckie snorted, "Good! Be careful if you run across any dogs down there. They might just find your name tempting. Hey! Get those two guys to call you Skinny, or something like that. Then the dogs won't know to poop on you." She grinned maliciously.

"Ooh! Come on, men!" Heather started off, and when Jerrold and Treavor just stood there, their eyes wide, she put both hands out and slapped their shoulders, both at the same time. "I'm talking to you two. Now, move!"

JERROLD FELL IN BESIDE Treavor. "She can be mean," he whispered. "Where's the friendly Heather we met at the luau? I liked her better."

"No lie, Jer. Just do whatever she says."

"What was that the other one said about dog poop?"

Heather's voice barked out, "I heard that, men. No more talk about either dog poop or my name. We have a granny to find." She stopped abruptly and turned to them, hands on hips. "You're mine until we find that old woman and that cute little girl. Now, get with the program. Move it!" She turned and strode off angrily.

255

"Yes, ma'am," both men chimed together.

Treavor whispered, "I agree. She wasn't this grouchy earlier. What happened, Jer?"

Jerrold hissed back, "That time of the month, I think. It must be."

"I heard that! All quiet back there!"

That caught their attention, and after that, they were, too. Heather wasn't one to be crossed, something Treavor and Jerrold soon figured out.

BOBBY LAY DOZING ON the sofa with a moist towel over his forehead. After his run from the rooster, his day had been devastated. Now he wanted to spend the afternoon in quiet.

Jerking awake, with one hand, he blindly groped the air. "Robby? Robby, do you have my martini? My nerves are spent, and I keep hearing that crazy rooster. It's what's driven me right off the edge. I may have to hire a psychiatrist to sort me out. Do you think the resort will pay?"

When he got no answer, he opened his eyes and looked around an empty room. Staring up at the ceiling, he traced the exposed beams that made up the open-air ceiling, and he noticed a flicker of light from off the pool.

"Robby?" He sat up. That glittering happened only when someone was swimming, and no other time. If Robby was in the pool, how could he take care of him? He certainly couldn't rest if he were up and getting his own martini, now could he? Couldn't Robby see that?

Swinging his feet to the floor, he stood up abruptly, grabbing his head as his vision swam. He squinted as he stepped to the lanai door, and his face clouded as he looked at his twin gliding across the bottom, his sleek body cutting gracefully underneath the surface of the water.

"Robby," he called. "Look at me, Robby." He waited until

256

his brother emerged, grabbing the coping and brushing the water from his face. Then he continued in a weaker, more fragile voice. "I'm sick, Robby. I've had to walk out here to ask you to make me a martini. I really need one. How can I survive my devastating interaction with that rooster all alone?" He twisted his brows together, hoping for a tortured, hangdog expression.

"You've got to get up, anyway." Robby put his hands flat on the side of the pool and vaulted out of the water, landing on his feet with rivulets of water flooding his body and running back into the pool. "I've been waiting on you, sleepy head. We have to go on a search."

"A search?" He closed his eyes and leaned his head against the doorframe. "I haven't had my martini, yet. You can't make me go on a search, Robby. My head hurts too much, and besides, I'm dizzy. I can't think at all."

"Dizzy, smizzy." He slapped his brother's shoulder as he walked past him into the room. "You were so out of it, you missed the whole show. Buzz," and he turned to his brother to look deeply into his eyes, "was here. You do know Buzz? The redheaded kid? Houston's nephew? Riley's boy?" He grinned.

"Don't be catty," Bobby whispered, attempting to look very emotionally destitute, while hoping for sympathy. "I didn't say I was stupid, just that I couldn't think. You'd feel the same way if that feathered devil had chased you. Play nice, Robby."

Robby leaned in and whispered into his brother's ear, "I'll fix you that martini, but you'd better drink up fast. We have a scavenger hunt to join. Granny Swell's wandered off somewhere, and Angelique's gone to find her. Houston's out looking for Angelique, and I want to be there when he finds her. This is better than a soap opera. I always wanted to be in one, and now's my chance." He backed away, gently patting the side of his brother's face.

"You never did, either," Bobby moaned pitifully. "I never

heard you say you wanted to be in a soap opera. You're just saying that."

Robby laughed over his shoulder. "And if I am? So what? I still intend to go. You know Angelique went on that heli ride with Gator. I think maybe we'll stop and invite him along. Fireworks, Bobby. We might have some January fireworks, yet."

"Fireworks?" He pictured booming noises and lots of bright lights. "My head won't take fireworks just now. Can I please stay home?" He leaned the side of his face against the doorframe, stroking his hands plaintively up and down the woodwork.

"Drink up, brother." Robby took his brother's hand and wrapped it around the base of a chilled martini glass. "These fireworks are emotional ones, not the kind you see in the sky. I hope these are between Houston and Gator. Let's go see who gets the girl."

Bobby moaned. "Gator gets the girl. They rode in the limo together. Did you forget?"

Robby looked at his brother and grinned. "I've been watching their eyes. I don't know what Gator wants. Who knows, maybe even he doesn't know. Houston sure has it bad for Angelique, though. That I can tell. I wouldn't miss this for the world."

Bobby slowly sipped his martini, and as he did so, he felt himself perk up. The alcohol was having exactly the effect he needed. He finally smiled. "What about Riley? Is there any possibility . . . do you think?" He looked pleadingly at his brother. "If Houston moves in with Angelique, then Riley has an empty bedroom."

Robby laughed. "You old romantic, you. Don't even dream about it. Wait until you see those two neon friends of Angelique's with him. I think Riley's already taken."

258

Bobby tossed back the last of his martini, and he shook his head to clear his thoughts. "Once again, I'm the last in line." Straightening his spine, he glared at his brother. "I thought you were changing."

Robby grabbed both sides of his brother's face. "It's the beach, brother. I can wear my suit out there if I want. This is Hawaii!" Then he laughed. "Let's go for the show."

Bobby set the glass down and looked at his brother with a smirk. "There won't be a show without finding Granny Swell. That's where Angelique and Houston will be." His mettle was finally up for this adventure, or it would be with his next martini. He picked the glass up and held it out, hoping for a refill.

"What you really mean is there won't be a show without Gator. Fine, bro. Then let's go ask him if he'll help us look." Noticing the glass, Robby laughed. "You've had enough. We don't want you drunk."

Frowning, Bobby set the glass down and headed for the door. "Sure. Let's go. You say Riley's looking, too?" He glanced at his brother for confirmation.

"I didn't." Robby smirked. "He might be, though. Let's go find out."

That got Bobby on the ball, and out the door they went.

HOUSTON AND HIS HALF of the search party were headed down the beach. He turned just in time to see Buzz leap through the air and land squarely on his dad's back, wrapping his arms around his neck and his legs around his waist. Riley staggered under the onslaught.

"Did you find her, Dad?"

"Hey, Buzz!" Houston called to distract him. "Give your dad a break, and come up here with Beckie and me. He's had all the contact sports he can stand for one day. He needs a little down time."

259

Beckie turned and winked at Riley, but she spoke to Houston. "Only if your brother weren't so cute! I'm a sucker for redheads." She primped her pink hair with her fingertips. "Can't you tell with this hair?"

However, Buzz tore around them, his feet leaving widely spaced dimples along the shore. There was a shell on the beach, and he dropped, picking it up and looking inside. With a sudden snap of his arm, the object flew out to sea.

"I like Angelique. Is she lost now, too?" He leaped into a shallow tidal pool next to a tree branch partially buried in the sand, sending out a small shower of water, before returning to his uncle. "Is she with Granny Swell?"

"She's looking for her." Houston grabbed the boy as he darted by, and he pulled him close to slow him down. "We all are, and we need your sharp eyes."

"Okay." He shrugged the hand off. "Why didn't you go parasailing with us? It was really fun up there." He began walking backwards. "You could see the whole island up there. The ocean stretched all the way to the next island, and there were lots of dolphins and sharks—"

"Sharks," Beckie interjected, her face suddenly pale. "In the ocean? I didn't see any sharks."

"Yeah!" His eyes sparkled. "And I could see all our villas, and a waterfall. There was this huge tree I could see way down the beach, too. It hung way out over the water, like a bridge. You know that one in Utah, the one made out of stone? We went there on vacation one summer." He drew the shape of the bridge in the air in front of him.

Riley called, "Buzz, you might turn around and walk. There's a branch behind you. Watch out—"

Just then the boy's legs found the branch, and in a tumble, he went down. Sand flew everywhere, and he yelled out in surprise.

"Oh, honey, are you all right?" Beckie knelt to run her hand across his forehead. "That was quite a fall. You didn't break your arm or anything, did you?" She brushed sand from his shoulder.

His father reached in and grabbed his arm, pulling him up. "He's fine. Thirteen-year-olds don't break, do they, Houston?" He turned the boy to face the front, and he patted him on the back. "Walk that way, son. You can still tell your story to Dad Two. He listens out of his ears, not his eyes."

"Dad One," he cried out, pointing down the beach. "There! The tree! See? It makes a bridge, like that rock in Utah." He laughed. "See where it lays over into the water? I told you I saw it, didn't I? You should have gone up parasailing, Uncle Houston. You would have loved it. Can I run to it?"

"Run?" Beckie's eyes widened. "Is it safe for him to run alone on the beach? What if something attacks him? He said he saw sharks. There might be alligators or bears. You can't let him simply run off."

Houston called to him, laughing, "Watch for bears, Buzz. If you find anything interesting, let us know." When the boy was gone, he turned to Beckie, the smile on his face fading. "He'll be safe enough. He might even find something."

"Or someone, I hope." Riley peered out to sea. "I'd hate to think the old woman walked into the water and got carried away. I don't see anything, though."

Beckie stopped, her eyes on the sand around her, and she walked to where the sand became a green tangle of exuberant growth. "Hey! Come over here and look at this." At a break in the lush foliage, a trail opened up, and coming directly out of it were two bare footprints. They wavered through the sand, disappearing into the edge of the surf. Following alongside the prints was an erratic design smoothed into the sand. She dropped to one knee and touched the prints with her fingertips, with dread washing over her face. "It looks as if someone walked here not too long ago, and they must have been dragging something. What do you think it was?"

Riley stepped beside her. "Who do you think it was, perhaps you should say. Angelique would've had Squeegie with her." He turned his head to his brother. "They were together, right, Houston, when they went looking?" When his brother nodded, he looked at the tracks again. "Surely Angelique wouldn't carry her all this way. If this is from Angelique, I'd expect a second set of smaller prints. Could Granny Swell have gotten onto the beach here?" He stood and glanced around. "Houston? Do you see anything I'm missing?"

Beckie touched Riley on the shoulder. "Your son. Look. He's on his way back, already, and he seems in a hurry, too. Do you think he found something?" Her voice dropped to a whisper, a note of alarm tingeing her words. "Could it have anything to do with these footprints, do you think?"

It was only a few silent moments before Buzz stood in front of them with his hands on his knees and his breathing labored. "Dad One. Dad Two. She's there, and something's wrong with her." He straightened and pointed down the beach before dropping forward again, his chest heaving. "I tried to get her to stand up and come with me, but she wouldn't. She just kept saying that Two Fingers Larry would be along, and he would build her a fire. She said she wasn't going to let herself be poked for diseases. She's in the water, and she wouldn't move. I didn't know what to do." His face was red. "She's under the tree, Dad." He looked directly at Riley. "What if she drowns?"

"Who?" Riley grabbed his son's arm.

"Angelique?" Houston glanced down the beach but could see nothing out of the ordinary.

Beckie stepped up and grabbed the boy's chin, forcing him to look at her. "It's not Squeegie down there in the water, is it?"

"Just go," and Buzz's arm flew into the air, pointing back down the beach, his adrenalin-fueled desperation stealing his words from him. "She needs help."

"Gotcha. Thanks, Buzz." His father slapped him appreciatively on the arm, and he turned to Houston and Beckie. "Follow me. We've got a life to save."

As the three adults started running, the boy stood tall, and still panting, he called after them in as loud a voice as he could muster, "It's Granny Swell in the water. Please don't let her drown!"

$\mathcal{A}$NGELIQUE PUSHED THE fronds on the path aside, and she listened. She must be very close to the beach by now. She could hear the surf, but she decided the path they had taken was definitely the scenic route. Although the villas were just a short walk from the water, this way had taken her past several streams and one waterfall.

Just down from the villa, she and Squeegie had found a set of footprints. Then, on the trail, she had nearly taken the wrong path several times and had been forced to search for the occasional partial print. That had really slowed her down. She had discovered several surprise paths that branched off the main one, and she'd had to backtrack a number of times.

At least she had Squeegie with her, and the girl had been good to stand at the branches waiting for her to check for any visible footprints in the sand, then sticking by her side when she moved on down the main path. However, the girl was only eight, and her small legs were now tired. Angelique had already faced the fact they soon might have to turn back, no matter what.

To her relief, through a break in the foliage, it seemed she could actually see the end, and the path opened directly onto the shore. It would certainly be easier to follow the footprints in bare sand. Then she heard a voice yell, and it made her heart run cold.

"It's Granny Swell in the water. Please don't let her drown!"

CHAPTER 22

ANGELIQUE BURST ONTO the beach with Squeegie's hand in hers, and just in front of her stood Buzz. His hands were on his hips, and he was inhaling great draughts of air. He turned to look at her, his face red with exertion, before peering back down the beach. That was when she turned to see three people running away from them down the shoreline.

"Miss Angie?"

She looked to her side and swept the girl into her arms. Stepping up to Buzz, she spoke softly to him, "Did they find Granny Swell?" She pressed the girl's head to her shoulder, running her fingers into the child's hair to comfort her as well as to keep her calm. When he nodded, she continued, "Is she all right?"

"I found her." He glanced at her and back down the beach again, and there was pride in his voice. "I ran down there, and she was under that tree, just sitting in the water. She was holding a lamp, too. I ran right back and told the others. That's Dad down there, and Uncle Houston. Beckie, you know, the lady with the pink hair? She's down there, too, so she can help." He grinned with the excitement of it.

"Buzz, will you walk that direction with me?"

In the distance, Houston, Riley, and Beckie were gathered beside a huge tree, one that leaned far into the water. Were they pulling a corpse from the waves? She felt tears of frustration threatening her once again. This tired, desperate girl in her arms, the husband she hadn't even known, the man she had fallen for in spite of all her precautions . . . and now this old woman getting lost here on the beach. Angelique felt caught in a whirlwind, and it was as if she was about to be tossed out, to land who knew where.

"I can help with the little girl, if you'd like. I could carry her, if she'll let me."

Angelique smiled. "Would you, please?" She brushed the girl's hair from her small face, to find she had drifted off. "She's asleep. Be careful not to wake her."

He smiled as he reached for her and lifted her to his shoulder. "She's light!" He seemed very surprised.

"To you, perhaps. To me, it was all I could do to hold her. It looks like they're headed back, now. Please, let's walk that way to see if we can do anything to help."

It was all she could do not to run. Then, as she and Buzz drew closer, it became apparent that the old woman was at least ambulatory, if barely. Both Riley and Houston were at her side, but she was walking with her own unsure steps as she moved down the beach.

Angelique turned to Buzz and put her hand on his arm. "I need to be down there. I can't take the girl with me, though, not if there's even the chance her grandmother is injured. Wait here, please, just in case she wakes. Do you mind?"

"She's not heavy. I can wait here with her."

266

With a smile of gratitude, she was off, released to run to Houston, her feet flying down the beach. As she grew close, Beckie sprinted to meet her and grabbed her arm. Her face was flushed, and she laughed unaccountably.

"She's all right, Angie. Barely, though. She thought she was back in San Francisco under some bridge, and all her old homeless friends were coming to see her." Tears rolled down her face, and she brushed them aside, laughing ecstatically. "She had no idea she was in the water, and the waves were rushing up around her. She had a lamp in her hand, and she wanted us to plug it in for her." She looked away before starting up again. "How could she not know? I feel so ghastly, Angie. I made fun of her earlier. How was I to know she was so bad? She has to have help. If she'd do this, what else will she do when someone isn't watching?"

Angelique gave her friend a hug as the men walked up. Granny Swell teetered unsteadily between them. Angelique caught Riley's eyes, and he gave her a quick smile before he glanced away to look for his son.

Angelique turned to Houston. His blue eyes above his pinched mouth were already on her, and as she looked at him, his brow knitted into relief and need, all mixed together.

"Angelique," he said, warmth and tenderness flooding across in that one word. "I didn't know where you were."

It almost seemed as if his eyes glistened, but Angelique knew that must be her imagination. She so wished he was saying what she needed him to say, that his concern was for her, because he needed her, and not just because she was someone who had married one of his friends, someone who controlled a trust fund that had turned out to be very generous, indeed. She wished he was relieved she was all right because he desired her, that he wanted her as Lucas never would have.

However, she knew better. She had to. His concern was for

the one who controlled his friends' chances at some of Lucas' money. His concern was for an old woman adopted by the daughter Angelique hadn't known Lucas had.

"Houston," she said, stepping closer, putting her hand on his arm simply because she could not stop herself, because she needed to be in contact with his skin. "I appreciate you doing this, coming out to look for Granny Swell. I was cruel to you back at the compound, and you didn't deserve it. What you've done here, rescuing this woman, is proof of that. I don't know why I reacted so strongly back there." She did, too, know. She had fallen in love with this man, and it cut her like a knife to know she couldn't have him. Just to be near him was to feel her body turn over inside, violently, too, and to have her thoughts fracture into a million incoherent shards.

And she didn't hate the feeling at all.

"I'M GLAD YOU CAME." Houston's words were husky with emotion as he watched her face, wanting to say more. He wanted to tell her how unfair it was that she'd loved Lucas, only to find betrayal in the man's actions. He wanted to grab her in his embrace, and he wanted to feel her arms around him. He wanted to tell her he'd be there for her, that she didn't need Gator or any other man. He hoped she could see all that in his eyes.

However, when Riley coughed and whispered Granny Swell's name to him, she looked away, and he knew she'd seen nothing at all. He looked down to find her hand gone, and in that moment, he knew her touch for what it had been, concern for the old, adopted grandmother of the child of her deceased husband. Her words to him had been words of gratitude, not words of hope, and with that realization, blackness surged through his thoughts. All he could think of was getting out of this place, off this island, and away from this torment.

Once they got back to the compound, he intended to pack

his things and leave Hawaii to those who wanted it. Let Riley stay if Buzz could convince him to; let him cancel his confounded conference. After all, he had races to prepare for, cars to tweak, and Bahrain was only two months away. If Riley couldn't cancel, then Buzz could follow his uncle to the desert. The boy had wanted to ride the circuit with him this year, and at least being back on the racetrack would be a distraction.

Right then, he needed all the distraction he could get.

"YOU DID ASK HIM, brother." Bobby paused on the trail for a moment, out of breath. "He didn't want to come." He gasped with exhaustion. His martini was gone, and he had no more fuel to trek to the fireworks show. However, Robby wouldn't let him stop. The man was convinced that even without Gator, the event would be well worth the effort.

Robby grabbed a large frond to steady himself, laughing at his carelessness as his foot slipped on an uneven stone. He looked back at his brother and grinned. "He couldn't, actually. He couldn't have walked if he wanted. I know why he was so drunk, though. It's that Angelique."

Bobby snorted disdainfully. "They went to the Big Island together. Why would he get drunk over her if they've been spending time alone? I mean, seriously, brother. She must have offered him some hope for them to spend the whole day with each other." He grabbed his brother's arm and stopped on the trail again, gasping for air that he just couldn't seem to get enough of. He pointed back the way they came. "You know, Robby. We could have walked straight to the beach. Why are we cutting across this tropical nightmare like this? Up one trail and down another. I'm exhausted."

"Wimp! I saw Angelique and Gator, by the way." He held up the binoculars he carried around his neck and chuckled. "Houston, too."

269

"Saw them?" Bobby tried to take the glasses. They were nearing the top of a small rise, and the thinnest line of beach next to roughening surf was visible just beyond the wall of greenery. "I happen to know we just left that man at his villa. I may be slow, but stuffy old decorating dowagers, I'm not that slow." The words came out brittle with contempt.

Robby slapped his hand away. "Not here. Back when the helicopter came." He held up the glasses once again and grinned. "With these. Oh, you should have seen the sparks fly. It was better than Miami Beach on the Fourth of July."

Bobby's focus had finally slipped completely away. He found the largest stone on the rise they had just topped, and he sat, telling his brother he simply had to rest. He insisted he go get him another martini, but Robby laughed, telling him Gator had consumed enough for everyone in Angelique's party. There were probably none left on the entire island.

However, from where he sat on his perch, the beach was now clearly visible, and the breeze was finally refreshing, especially against the lingering warmth brought about by his exertions on the trail. He held out his hand, and Robby surrendered the binoculars. He uncapped them and held them to his face.

"So, what did you see at the helicopter? You haven't told me, yet." He looked south, first, and he dropped the glasses from his eyes to point down the beach. "I think I see Treavor and Jerrold that direction. One of Angelique's friends is with them." He grinned. "Fancy that! I bet it's a first, those two on the beach with a woman."

"Which one? Heather or Beckie?" Robby reached for the glasses, but this time, Bobby slapped his brother's hand away.

"How would I know?" He put the glasses back to his face and peered through the lenses.

"The hair? What color is it?"

"Um, yellow, I think."

Robby yanked the glasses from his brother's hand. "You think? Come on. It's either pink or yellow." He looked, and sure enough, it was their two friends, along with Heather. Dropping the glasses, he snorted. "No party; no fireworks there. How come Angelique and Houston aren't with them?" He chewed his bottom lip in thought, and he took a deep breath and sighed.

Bobby was quick with an answer, and he made sure his words were sharp and cruel. "Duh! Maybe they haven't found them, yet? They're all still looking for Granny Swell. Could that be why?" He ran his hands through his hair, and then he pulled up his shirttail to wipe sweat from his forehead. "You still haven't told me what you saw earlier at the helicopter."

"Oh!" He snickered, and he coughed, the sound turning into an out-and-out laugh. "I watched Gator and Angelique climb out. They weren't chummy-chummy, not one bit. I don't think Houston noticed." He slapped his brother on the arm. "He thinks he's got competition. That's why he's been in such a funk."

Bobby frowned, attempting to grab the binoculars back. "Hold up your fingers, Robby."

His brother glanced at him with disdain, ignoring his request.

However, Bobby insisted, his words clipped. "Both hands. Do it, Robby!" As an incentive, he popped the bare skin of his brother's thigh with the back of his hand.

"Ouch!" Robby hung the binoculars over his neck, and he held his hands up with the fingers splayed. "Now what?"

"Count. Count your fingers. How many days has it been since Lucas died? He was your friend, too. Have you forgotten him, already?"

Robby dropped his hands and grabbed the binoculars again, but he didn't lift them to his face. "How can you ask that? Of course, I haven't forgotten. It's my shop that's going under without his money. How could I forget?"

"Well, I'm pretty sure Angelique really loved the man. We knew what was going on, but I don't think she had a clue. She loved him, Robby. Do you really think she'd be hot for Houston so soon?" He tapped his forehead. "Reality, brother. Get a grip on it."

Robby laughed. "I see your point. That just means we've got work to do. I want our Houston to be happy." He pulled the binoculars off his neck and tossed them to his brother. "We're in Hawaii. This is paradise, Bobby. We can help out to get a good friend a girl, I think. After all, where else could a fairy tale romance happen, if not in paradise?"

Bobby had the glasses back to his face, and he turned north this time. "Uh, oh, Robby. I'm watching a rescue, and I think your fairy tale just evaporated."

"It hasn't even happened, yet. How can it have evaporated?" He turned the direction his brother was looking. "Let me see." When his brother held out the glasses, he put them to his face.

"See?" Bobby snorted. "There are no happy faces in that crowd."

Sure enough, there were Granny Swell, the two brothers, and Beckie and Angelique, all together. Just down the beach was Riley's son holding Lucas' daughter. Angelique's hand was on Houston's arm, and while Robby couldn't hear what was being said, the misery of disappointment was clearly written on both Houston's and Angelique's faces.

He dropped the glasses and turned to his brother, a new determination written on his face. "Bobby, we've run an antiques business, shopped 'til we've dropped, and even decorated people's homes with stuff they didn't know they wanted. Now, we have a new job."

Bobby looked at him, not understanding. "As in?"

"Dating service! We're going into the matchmaking business: Cupid, and all that stuff. "

"You think we'll make any money?" That had been weighing on his mind ever since the funeral.

"Money?" Robby guffawed. "I don't care about the money. This is for happiness!"

"Happiness?" Then it sank in. "Oh, for Houston. Not for us."

Robby was on a roll. He slapped his brother's shoulder and pulled him to his feet. "For Houston and Angelique. Besides, if they're happy, and if we helped, maybe there'll be a little filthy lucre to come our way." He winked and rubbed the ends of his fingers together. "Get it?"

Bobby grinned. "I get it. If Angelique gets away from Houston, then Lucas' money is gone along with her, too."

Robby patted his face. "You are a smart boy." After a moment, he spoke again, and from the redness around his eyes, it was clear he was talking from emotions that were closer to his heart. "Besides, Bobby. Houston deserves it. I want him to be happy."

"Because you love him, right, Robbo?" Bobby had seen the red eyes.

"Sure, B-Bob, because I love him."

He didn't say any more. Bobby was sure he saw moisture glistening around his brother's eyes. Robby didn't have to say more, and Bobby understood why.

"GOOD EVENING. THIS IS Christian with Blue Water Maui. How may I help you?" His voice was bright and cheery over the phone, and Angelique was relieved.

"Christian, this is Angelique. You missed us on the beach. You must immediately bring us extra towels and a heating pad. Also, if you could call a doctor, it would be helpful." She smiled through the bedroom door at Squeegie sleeping quietly on the sofa. The events had exhausted the girl, and she wasn't feeling much better. At this point, she'd be satisfied to go to her own villa, call Sven for a massage, and hope everyone on this island would leave her in peace for the rest of the evening.

"A heating pad . . . and a doctor?"

"Yes," she said. "Granny Swell, the old woman who came in today, has had an event, and she may need medical help. We've gotten her into dry clothes, but we cannot take a risk on pneumonia." She looked at the people around her, giving a quick smile, as she pointed to the telephone receiver.

"She's been found? I'm so relieved to hear it. How might she need medical help? Did she fall?"

"No, she did not fall." Angelique closed her eyes and held the phone out from her ear. She knew her feelings of rising irritation were mostly from exhaustion, but they were very real, in spite of that.

Seeing her aggravation, Riley took the instrument from her, and he put it to his ear. "Christian, this is Riley, with Houston in the first villa."

She looked to him, only to catch his eyes on her. The mention of his brother's name caught her attention, and envy surged through her. He held the phone out a bit and motioned for her to listen. She could just hear the reply.

"Yes, Riley. You are in Apricot Villa. How may I help you?"

"First, Christian, no more questions. Angelique was perfectly clear. We need three things. Please bring us towels, a heating pad, and a doctor. If you feel you will have trouble with that, please transfer me to Julia. I'm sure she can help me get this done." He winked at her, giving her a smile of reassurance. After he hung up, he stepped to her to whisper, "Sometimes you have to be forceful. We'll get help here one way or the other."

274

"Thank you, Riley. I appreciate you staying and letting Houston take Buzz out for some air. You've all been very helpful, even though all this really has nothing to do with you." She pushed her hair behind her ear. "I mean, you aren't really responsible. I guess I am, now." She put a hand to one side of her face, hearing her voice grow thick with the emotions overwhelming her. "I just didn't expect this when I decided to come down here, doing this silly thing, even though Lucas had died." Her tears were building in her eyes, and she turned away, only to see her two female friends standing on the pool lanai in animated conversation with Treavor and Jerrold. "Look at that. No one else is concerned. I feel as though this is all on me, my responsibility." She tried to smile but couldn't.

"Not so." He took her by the shoulders with a smile. "However, we can't do anything more for Granny Swell until Christian gets our requests here. She's resting quietly, and that's the best we can hope for." His voice was soft and comforting. "I'd like to talk with you for a few minutes. Somewhere more private, if possible."

She reached to the hands on her shoulders, and she placed her palms on them, gaining strength in the touch. This day had turned out to be more than she could endure, and his hands on her shoulders, the feeling of support in that simple touch, meant a lot to her. She was awash in this unfamiliar place, and right now, she wished she had Mumsy and Uncle Barry at her side. She didn't, though. She could call them, she knew, but the problem ran deeper than that. She was adrift, and she needed an anchor. Her mother and uncle couldn't be that for her, not now and in this place. She had to be strong, yet she didn't have that in her at the moment.

"All right, Riley. Let's go talk." She turned to him. "Out front?" The women and their companions had the lanai.

"Sure." He smiled to her and motioned with his hand toward the front door. "That's our best bet. I'd rather not have everyone in this compound overhearing."

Stepping outside into the early evening air, she let the breeze brush her hair from her face. Reaching to pull an errant strand from her nose, she worked it back into the rest, and she closed her eyes in the yellow warmth of the distant sun. She shook her head side to side, hard, letting her hair loosen in the breeze, and then she brushed it away from her face. "This feels so good out here. Just for a moment, Riley, I feel I can actually think. Or not think. Maybe that's better."

"I can see why he's lost his heart to you."

She opened her eyes and turned to see him looking at her. A smile ghosted his lips. He'd said something similar to her about Houston earlier. However, now he could mean only one man. Gator had lost his heart to her? She knew better than to believe those words. She'd spent the day with him, and she'd hoped. However, while she'd enjoyed much of their time together, there had been no emotional connection. She didn't know where he was now, perhaps in his villa self-medicating. She looked out to sea as she laughed, and to her, the sound of it was sour.

"No, Riley. He hasn't lost his heart to me, you can bet on that. That man and I jumped off a mountain today, and after we got to the bottom, he told me how he really felt about me. I guess I should have known, too, but sometimes we're too blind to see. I have been, you know. Blind."

"Is that why he's running away? You don't love him? He talked to me, you know."

"He's leaving? Because of me?" She looked at her arms resting on the lanai balustrade. First she had allowed an old woman to nearly die, now another of her party wanted to run away. She had known Gator would when he told her why he climbed mountains. She hated that it was because of her.

"That's what I hoped you could tell me. I wanted Buzz to

276

stay here while I went to South Africa. It'll be difficult for me to take him along, if I'm forced to. I guess he'll have to stick with Houston, wherever that is."

"Houston." The unexpected shift in the conversation twisted her stomach. The butterflies inside fluttered, even as she tried to quiet them. "His other dad, you mean." She closed her eyes to fight the burning tears building there. It seemed she was doing that a lot lately. However, she didn't understand his statement. Of course Buzz was staying. He would be with Houston. She already knew that.

He chuckled. "If you wish, his other dad. I wish he were staying here, though. I think you're a good woman who got caught up in a mess you didn't deserve. You know, I've not heard one word of complaint from you in all of this, not about anything. You've even stepped up to take responsibility for our two new guests today. You didn't have to, you know. They were Lucas' doing, not yours."

She sighed. "They need someone. What can I do? If everyone abandons everyone else who doesn't fit into their plans, then where's love in the world? Sorry, Riley. They're mine, now. Who else do they have?"

"Like I said, I can see why he's lost his heart to you."

She laughed her sour laugh again. "Sorry, Riley. Gator and I already had this talk back in Hilo. There's no future for us." She patted his arm. "You keep trying, though. Too bad you're not available. You're a good man, and I can see why Houston loves you so." She sighed and couldn't help her next words. "I just wish he would be passionate with you, also."

He laughed. "Oh, Angelique. We're not on the same page at all. I'm sorry I wasn't clearer. Gator's not the one leaving. It's Houston. He told me he was heading up to the villa to pack. Formula 1 and all that." He chuckled. "He says he needs to check on his car and get in some practice time on the track.

277

However, Bahrain—that's his next race—isn't until March. Houston's running, and it looks like he'll be taking Buzz for company."

Her breath froze in her body, and she felt her brain go numb. "Houston's leaving?" She choked on the words. "Why, Riley?" He couldn't leave. She'd hoped that once Riley left . . . oh, she didn't know what she'd hoped, but she didn't want him gone, not out of her life. She looked at him, her eyes burning. "Why?"

He shrugged. "I hoped you could tell me. He's lonely, I think. He needs someone—"

"He has you, Riley. He says he loves you."

He laughed. "He needs more than me. Surely you know that." He looked at her with raised eyebrows. "You've spoken with him. I know you have."

"Yes." She hesitated. Surely Riley knew he was losing Houston. "He told me there was something missing between the two of you, and I encouraged you two to work things out. I guess it's not going well."

He frowned. "Yeah, I never did quite understand that. But whatever you mean, we're better, I think." He smiled. "He thought you and I were hooking up. That's why he was upset with me earlier when you found us wrestling."

"Hooking up? Because I held your arm?" When he nodded, she continued, "I'm not the type to break a family apart."

Then she realized who she was speaking with, that Houston had done that very thing. She softly backpedaled. "I'm sorry that happened to you, Riley, that Houston, um, came between you and your wife, but I, I guess—" She turned away in exasperated confusion, aware she was intruding once more, and then she faced him again. "I guess that's none of my business."

"You were there in California when it was happening, so you have some right, I suppose. It's over, anyway, and Houston and I are together again, at least until he packs and leaves here."

He didn't seem as concerned as Angelique thought he might. "You can't convince him to stay?" She wanted him to, desperately.

"I don't know why he's leaving." The resort's electric cart crunched on the crushed shell drive, the sound smoothing into a hushed whisper as its wheels shifted onto the stone court. Inside was Christian. "I think our help's here. Can we talk more about this later?"

She nodded, unsure of her voice, and she reached to dab at her eyes. This wasn't finished, and yet Houston was still leaving. How could she stay? How could she need a man so much, when he was a man who could never need her? How could her life have turned out so horribly? She couldn't even run away. She had too many other people depending on her.

"Dear God," she prayed, whispering her words softly into the tropical air. "Help me. I don't know how to make any of this better, and I can't make it through like it is."

Then, in resignation, she followed Riley and Christian inside to check on Granny Swell. What else was there for her to do? These people needed her, and for that, she had to appear strong, even if she didn't feel that strength on the inside.

Still, no one else had to know that. All she had to do was smile, and everyone else's world would be just fine.

So, smile, she did.

CHAPTER 23

"BUILT OF FEATHERS and tiny bits of metal, the hand-tied fly is the fisherman's treasure. It has been lovingly caressed, stroked into life, as it were, by the roughened fingertips of men more used to the outdoors than to tender ministrations of affection.

"That is why the fisherman sees such beauty in the glistening line as it sparkles in the summer air, holding his treasured fly in its grasp, leading it directly to the mouth of the fish that is waiting to take its brilliance of feather and twisted cord as its final meal . . ."

Angelique clicked print, and then in a fury of motion, she ripped the paper from the printer. She studied it, her eyes blurring at the black and white text. It was drivel. It was wasteful nonsense, and it embarrassed her to know it had come from her fingertips. She wadded the paper and threw it into the wastebasket. Then, she tapped her keyboard to highlight the entire text, and she hit the delete key. She didn't want what she had written to even be on her computer.

She stood and looked out her villa window. When she held very still, she could hear the call of a bird far away, and then another answering it. Off in the distance, at just the right angle, she could glimpse the water, and in the evening light, it was a deep, almost black-blue. It was peaceful out there, if not so much in her mind.

A knock sounded at her villa's door, and she turned from the window. Stepping into the living room, she twisted the knob to see Sven standing before her, and at his side, little Squeegie held his hand. When the girl saw her, she broke free, darting forward to throw her small arms around the woman who had befriended her.

"Yes, baby?" She knelt, putting her arms around the youngster. "It's good to see you, too." Squeegie looked at her with tears in her face. "What's wrong?"

"Excuse me, Angelique." Sven cleared his throat and tugged the bottom of his jacket into position. "The doctor is finished with Granny Swell, and the child overheard her recommendation. I must apologize for the oversight in allowing the girl to still be in the room." He cleared his throat once again, softer this time, and glanced at his feet meekly. "Dr. Caraway offered to come by later to, ahem, settle up."

Angelique stood, brushing the child's hair with her fingers, not overly worried about the bill, or with what the girl had overheard. She was sure Squeegie had dealt with much worse in her life. She did want to know the prognosis, though.

"What did Dr. Caraway recommend, Sven? I'm not concerned about the money."

He smiled. With her words, his demeanor brightened. "Dr. Caraway was very surprised that Granny Swell did not already reside in a managed care facility. She recommends an immediate placement, and she would like your approval before she leaves for town. Openings rarely come up for the best facilities, but Manoa Senior Care in Honolulu just happens to have a spot available immediately. Dr. Caraway would like to place your grandmother there tonight, if possible."

"My grandmother?" Puzzled, she looked at him, and then down at Squeegie to see the girl looking back up at her.

"The girl says—"

"That Granny Swell is my grandmother." Angelique smiled at her.

"Why, yes!" He seemed surprised to have her finish his sentence. "Dr. Caraway feels it would be for the best. Also, Angelique, I do have to advise you that if you choose not to avail yourself of this option, Blue Water Maui cannot assume further responsibility for damage or personal injury caused by your grandmother. I have a release form with me if you wish for her to remain here on the property." He smiled broadly, as if he were asking something as innocent as what her breakfast choices would be for the next morning.

She knelt in front of the girl. "What do you think, Squeegie? Would Granny Swell be happy if she went to Manoa Senior Care? I'm sure it's very nice." She looked at Sven for confirmation, relieved to see him nod. "We could go visit her there."

"Where's Mono Sea Care? Is it far away?" Squeegie turned her question to Sven and then back to Angelique. "Is it across the ocean? I remember how long it was across the ocean."

Angelique laughed, and she stroked the girl's face. "It's across a very small ocean. If we let Granny Swell go to Manoa Senior Care, we can go see her every day. Do you want to give it a try? It will be very good for Granny Swell, and I think she'll be very happy there."

When Squeegie finally nodded, Angelique stood and questioned Sven. "Do you have that paperwork, also?"

He reached into his blazer pocket, and he pulled out a three-page form, unfolding it in a singular motion. With a smile, he produced a pen and asked if he could step inside. "This one form is all Manoa Senior Care requires. If you will initial on the first two pages and sign the third, then we can get immediate transport for your grandmother arranged."

Angelique pulled a stool from the small bar, and she sat to look over the document. She flipped through all three sheets quickly, unable to focus on the words, and finally closed it.

Looking at Sven, she smiled. "You've been phenomenal, Sven. I don't need to read this. However, time frame. How long can my grandmother stay? Is this permanent or just week-by-week? Also, how do I pay for all this care?" She laughed, and then it faded quickly. "Oh, the money is there. I just didn't come prepared for all this . . . checks, credit cards, debit. What do they take?"

He reassured her. "The contract is only for as long as you need to use the facilities at Manoa Senior Care. We can bill the charges to your account here at Blue Water Maui. I will personally handle it all for you."

She looked at the paperwork, and then in a quick motion, opened the papers and signed them summarily, handing them back to the concierge.

"Thank you, Sven. Now, about Squeegie. Surely, she cannot stay in that villa alone. Has anyone spoken to you about this?"

He cleared his throat. "The child has, Angelique. She seems to be attached to you. It is her desire, that if she cannot be with her grandmother—" and he cleared his throat again "—her great-grandmother, I suppose, she wishes to be with you. You do have an extra bedroom in this villa. I can arrange to see the girl's things brought up to share your villa with you, if you wish."

She looked at the child, who was now sitting on the couch in her living room. She was adorable, but Angelique had also seen her run rampant through the compound. Once this matter with Granny Swell was settled, she suspected the wild part of the child would return, and very swiftly, too. However, the girl needed someone to care for her, and she didn't see anyone else stepping in to take over that responsibility.

"Sure, Sven," she said, moving to the couch to sit beside the girl. She put her arm around the small form, and she pulled her close. "And you, Squeegie, are now mine. Do you have a last name?" She smiled at her brightly.

She snuggled in next to her. "Abercrombie."

Angelique laughed and touched the girl on the nose. "Mine, too. I'm an Abercrombie."

The girl giggled and folded into Angelique's warm embrace. "You could be my real mother, couldn't you?"

Angelique didn't reply. Instead, she hugged the forlorn little girl a bit tighter, knowing that now, instead of one lonely person in this villa, there was now a pair. If she knew her card games at all, a pair beat a single lonely ace any day, so maybe she was better off, in spite of the circumstances. She couldn't be much worse, anyway, not if Houston was leaving.

By the time she heard Sven returning with Squeegie's few possessions, the girl was sound asleep. However, when she tried to extricate herself to help, the concierge just motioned her to stay seated. He was pleased to tell her the grandmother was already gone, whisked to secure environs on the island of Oahu, where she could not sneak away again. He could manage just fine, he told her, what with the few things the girl had. He would turn the bed down, and he would lay out towels in the bathroom. Angelique and the girl should feel free to sleep as late as they wished. He would see they were not disturbed.

She felt herself growing drowsy, listening to Sven hum a

little tune as he worked. It was pleasant, she thought, as if she had a child and a husband, as she had wanted all along. Just before she dozed off, she remembered she and Riley had a conversation to continue. He needed to tell her something. It seemed Houston was leaving, and Riley had to find a way to stop him.

As she dropped deeper into her slumber, the story shifted. In her dreams, Riley came to her villa in the middle of the night, and he whispered through her window. He told her he had a secret no one else knew. He would tell it to her as long as she told no one. He knew a man, he said, a race car driver, who had tired of women who were shallow and vain. He wanted to save himself for a kind-hearted woman who would love him for himself, not the fast cars he drove. He wanted to find a woman who loved others more than herself, and who would overlook his flaws, knowing that underneath was a man who could love her back with all his heart.

He told her this race car driver had come up with a plan, one that would give him the freedom to wait, to postpone his decision for years if need be, until just the right woman walked into his life. He had become Riley's close companion, but in appearance only. Now, that was over. Finally, he had found the right woman, and Angelique needed to know that Houston truly loved her, had fallen for her since the first time he'd seen her many months ago. She'd been taken, though, promised, and only now that she was free could he express his love for her, except he was afraid. He'd pretended so long, he was afraid she would drive him away, not believing in his love for her.

In her dream, she smiled at Riley, and, as will happen in dreams, it was somehow already morning. She told him she knew who he was talking about. It was Houston, wasn't it, and he was in love with her. Riley returned her smile, and she shifted in bed, knowing that the day was going to be perfect. She had found her ideal man, and his life with Riley had only been a sham, so that he could take his time looking for her.

Then a rooster crowed, and her eyes jerked open. It was still dark in the villa, and the sound of the bird was very real. Its call came once again before the compound was quiet.

Stirring, she slipped from beside Squeegie, stepping to the bedroom to find a blanket. She covered the girl, and now quite wide-awake, she stepped to the front door of the villa to walk outside. Air was what she needed, time to be alone, to stand under the stars, to think, or possibly not think. She smiled as she remembered her earlier remark to Riley.

She glanced up at the sky as she stepped outside. The moon hung low in the heavens, sparkling on the surface of the sea, and the sound of the surf haunted the air. Then, out of the corner of her eye, she noticed there was a light on in the villa next to hers. It was the men's double villa—Apricot Villa—and the glow from under the low overhangs told her it was a bedroom that was lighted. She had no idea whose it was, though. Houston's and Riley's? Buzz's? She hadn't been any farther than just past the front door.

Then the rooster crowed again, and she heard something hit inside the other villa, the sound echoing with a hollow concussion. Had something been thrown into a door? When a deep voice cursed, she knew who was having trouble sleeping, for that masculine sound made her blood twist in her veins. It was Houston, and if he was up now, his exit would probably be before the sun broached the horizon. She couldn't let him leave without a word.

She took a chance and yelled, "Rooster problems?" The worst he could do was ignore her. Anyway, he probably couldn't hear what she said, anyway. Paradise was not silent, and it seemed the insects considered the night as their private party time. That and the ocean, and when she listened, it seemed someone else—Gator, probably—had some music going.

She leaned onto the railing around the front lanai. No, Houston probably hadn't heard her. His light would go out, and she would be alone in the dark. In the morning, he would be gone, and she would never know why.

Then, the front door to the villa beside hers opened. Out stepped a dark-haired man wearing thin, cotton sleeping pants, and his torso was bare. Dim light filtered through the door, washing over his body, highlighting a masculine form that made her heart throb. Her breath tight, she watched him reach with his hands and run them up and down his arms. He peered into the darkness. After a moment, he shrugged and turned to go back inside.

"Over here, Houston." She had called him out, so she might as well make herself known. It wasn't like she'd been eavesdropping on him, sneaking around his villa, just hoping for a glimpse of him. Besides, she hadn't even called him by name, just asked about the chicken—or rooster, rather. He could go back in if he didn't want to talk to her. It'd be no skin off her back.

However, that was her pride speaking. She didn't want him to go back inside. She wanted to know why he was leaving. She also wanted more, but she dared not admit just what, even to herself. Not in the dark. Not with this man abandoning both her as well as the man he had professed to love.

Waving to her underneath the light of the moon, he stepped to the edge of his lanai and hopped over the balustrade. Walking through the damp grass, he stepped awkwardly in the dark. Then, he hopped a low row of flowering shrubs to the edge of her lanai, sitting on the balustrade to swing his legs up and over. He walked to her and stood closely in the dark.

"It's cool outside. I'd never have thought this, not in Hawaii." He stood silently for a while, the sound of his breathing clearly audible in the night air, and he looked out to where the moon could be seen shining on the surface of the water. "Pretty night."

"Your last one?"

He looked at her. "Who told you that?"

"Riley. We talked for a bit, earlier. Not long, though." She reached her hand to rub her arm, and she shifted her feet just a bit, so that her fingers would brush against his arm. She was relieved when he didn't move away.

"Stupid Riley. He knows nothing about women. He shouldn't have told you." He tensed his upper body, squeezing his arms against his ribcage.

"He didn't sound so stupid to me." She tried to make her voice bright, although her words sounded hopelessly perky to her. "He sounded like he cares about you."

"He does. He just doesn't know . . . what I need, what I want."

She remembered her dream, and she smiled. That Riley, the one from her dream, knew him pretty well. He had offered Houston to her, and she had been willing to accept.

"What?" He looked at her.

She turned to him, unable to let the smile go. "What what?" Then she giggled. "I'm sorry. That was silly of me. What was your what about?" That was hardly less silly, but it would have to do.

"Your smile. I can see it, even in the dark." He motioned with one arm. "See? The moon lights our way tonight."

"Moons are for lovers." She said it quietly, but apparently not so quietly that her words went overlooked. She was surprised when he responded

"Moons are for walking." He offered his hand. "Walk with me? I don't bite, you know."

"You just pack up and go home when you tire of the company. Is that it?" She kept her hands on her arms.

"Please, Angelique. Let's not talk about me packing just now. The moon, it'll be down soon. This is a magical moment. Either we take it now, or it's gone forever. Walk with me?" He kept his hand extended, and he waited.

She wasn't ready, yet. "You are packed, though. Why?" She could not touch this man, not so blatantly, not when she knew he was leaving.

He kept his hand out, but he shrugged. "As I told Riley, I have Bahrain coming. Then Australia, Malaysia, and China. The list goes on. I have my skills to practice, and there are cars to maintain."

"You didn't have all that before you came here? You could take six weeks, then. What changed?" She felt her eyes burn, although whether in anger or hurt, she wasn't sure. He would be gone in the morning. He wasn't her dream Houston, waiting in disguise for his perfect woman, for her. He was not, and she knew it. She couldn't trust him enough to take his hand.

"The moon, Angelique. Walk with me. Convince me to stay. Please?" He smiled in the softness of the moonlight, charming her, and he rubbed the flat of his stomach absently with his free hand. "Besides, it's cool out here, and I need to move to warm up. Have you ever walked the beach in the moonlight? You don't want to miss that in your stay here on the island."

"I suppose I could," she said, giving in and putting her hand in his. "Not far, though. I have a sleeping girl in my villa. I don't want to leave her for long."

"Lucas' girl," he murmured, as he pulled her arm up under his and wrapped his hand around hers. "You're very warm. Thanks. I thought I might get frostbite standing there in the cold." He pointed with his head. "That-a-way to the beach. Shall we go?"

She walked with him across the stone court. The fountain

was silent at this late hour. Enjoying the moonlight, they were soon under the canopy of greenery that separated the compound from the beach. She paused, and she was glad when Houston waited with her. It did, indeed, seem magical, if just for that one moment.

"We stopped here before." She looked into his face, and all she could see was darkness within the outline of his head. "You held me. In that moment, I thought you loved me."

Houston's voice was soft in reply. "I did, and I did."

"Right." She knew who he loved—or should love, if he was the man he needed to be. She laughed softly, and then stepping forward, they broke through to the beach. "This is so peaceful. The beach should always be like this."

"They wouldn't get many tourists. People like the sun." He chuckled.

"They'd get me. I'd love to spend a week in the dark like this. The moonlight makes the sand glow, and it looks like a thousand fireflies scattered on the waves. How can anything be so beautiful?"

He leaned and whispered into her ear, "Ever written poetry?"

She turned to face him, and his lips brushed across her cheek. She froze with the aroma of his skin in her nostrils, and she breathed deeply, afraid to move. "Poetry?" She wasn't sure he'd heard her word, or even if she'd actually spoken it aloud. Maybe she'd only thought it. She hardly knew.

Then he stepped back and coughed. "Whew! That's enough of that. I wouldn't want to start something you'd hate me for tomorrow." Yet, he stroked her arm. "Let's walk. I need to distract myself. Talk to me, anything."

"I'm a sports writer." It wasn't exactly what she wanted to talk about. She wanted the conversation to cover Houston and staying here; and why didn't you kiss me? The answers he might give made her nervous, though.

"A sports writer?" He laughed. "What sport? Speed cooking?"

She chuckled. "I deserved that. I'm not very much the sports type, am I?"

"Not really. However, I'll bite. What sport?" He picked up a stick to poke in the sand as they walked.

"I shouldn't say." She put her free hand on his arm. "My contract says it's a secret, and I can be fired for breaching the terms. My mother doesn't even know."

"How can she not know? I'm sure she sees you go off to work each day." He sounded amused.

"That I work, yes. What I do, no."

He laughed. "Mud wrestling."

She chuckled at his choice of sports.

"Cock fighting? Wet tee shirt contests?"

She grinned. "I really can't tell. I never should have brought it up, but it does involve feathers and tiny pieces of metal. That's the most you'll get from me, and I'll never tell you even if you get it right. Never, so don't bother guessing."

He chuckled. "Well, I know it's not speed cooking, mud wrestling, cock fighting, or that other one I mentioned." He clicked his tongue against the roof of his mouth. "Um, um . . ."

"Wet tee shirt contests?" She smiled as she offered the sport.

"Yeah, that one. So, that doesn't leave much, does it?"

"Nope, but I won't tell if you guess. I need my job."

They took several steps and stopped, digging their feet into the sand, feeling the sun's warmth from earlier that day still lingering inches below the surface.

He leaned in and whispered to her, "You don't really need that job."

"And you're going to support my copious lifestyle?" She

looked at him, and his face was chocolate silk in the moonlight.

"Copious?"

She laughed. His response was a tease, and she knew it. "Well, perhaps not so copious. Very frugal, in fact, but New York is expensive. It takes a lot."

"You have a lot. Lucas' lot. Unless you spend wildly, you'll never run out." Then he stopped and pointed. "There's our tree."

"Our tree?" She looked but didn't see one. "Where?"

He tapped a beach log with his stick. "You sat right there and drew a heart in the sand. Then you wiped it away. Why?"

She remembered. "That love wasn't for me."

"Whose name should have been there? Lucas'?" He pulled her to the log. "Sit for a while. The tide's out right now, and the sand's dry. It's warm underneath, too. It feels good to my toes."

"Not Lucas'." She leaned to take his stick, and she drew another heart in the moonlight. "I'll put your initials in this one, and you can write in your own love. How about that?" She smiled brightly against the moonlit sky.

He grinned. "I'll have to write in yours next to mine. It's only fair. How would it be for us to walk the beach in the moonlight and write someone else's initials on our heart? Cupid would not approve, you know."

She snorted, recklessness coloring her response. "Cupid's for Valentine's Day, not for Hawaiian beaches." She reached with the stick and wrote in an "H" and an "R" in the sand. "Now it's your turn. You can only write in the initials of the one you love, you know. If you write in anything else, you'll wither into an old and decrepit man." She pushed the stick into his hand, daring him to do as she asked. After all, he had asked her to walk on the beach, and he was running away in the morning. If he took offense, what could it matter? He wouldn't be here to ruin her honeymoon.

He laughed. "Whose rules are these? I've never heard them before. However, I hate to spoil your curse. I will turn into an old and decrepit man someday. I don't have much choice about that. So, I guess I can write in anything I want. Maybe I'll put in your initials."

"Someone you love, Houston. Otherwise, there's no point." If only it could be her . . . but that was an impossible dream. Her emotions made her words terse, and she slapped his shoulder, her eyes suddenly tight. She was all too aware of the touch of his skin, as well as the muscle she felt underneath.

He chuckled. "You don't deserve love? Are you telling me I can't love you? What if I decide to do so, anyway, just to spite you? I might. I've been known to do worse things to spite people."

"Name one terrible thing you've ever done." She wanted to hear this.

"Keep a rooster in my closet?" He grinned, and when he turned to her, she could see his playful expression in the reflection of the moonlight off the water.

"You never did such a thing." She laughed at him, charmed, yet ashamed she couldn't fight him off. He would always charm her, no matter what he did. She wished she could give in to it, trust his charm, but it was for another . . . should be for another. Riley.

"Come back to my villa. I'll show you."

She laughed again. "I never heard such a flimsy excuse for a come-on. You should be ashamed of yourself, Houston Richemont. What would Riley say if he knew there was a rooster in your closet? Dare I even believe you?" She didn't, either. She was charmed, though, and she decided she'd relax and enjoy it for the time being. It did feel good.

He made a dreadful face in response. "I'm pretty sure he doesn't know. Buzz does, though."

"You're willing to blame this on Buzz?" With her foot, she kicked sand on him, smiling as he brushed most of it off.

He whispered conspiratorially, "He helped me put it there."

Then it hit her. She hadn't seen the rooster since giving it to him earlier, and she'd heard its cries coming from his villa. It was what had awakened her and caused her to call to him. She slapped his shoulder again, this time not gently.

"You didn't put that rooster in your closet! Why, Houston! We have to go let it out." She stood. "Now, Houston. Get up. That animal cannot spend the rest of the night in your closet."

He held up his stick. "What about the one I love? Do you want me to turn into a decrepit old man?"

"I don't care about that, now. That rooster's been trapped all day. Come on, or I'm going up there without you and letting it free myself." She put her hands on her hips and glared at him.

HOUSTON STOOD, BUT BEFORE he walked off, he did write the initials of the one he loved in the sand next to his own. The name started with the initials "A" and "A," not "R" and "R" like Angelique thought. However, she was bound to save a rooster, and the initials were truly no longer important to her.

They were to Houston, though, and the initials he wrote in the sand were all he could think about all the way back to the villa.

CHAPTER 24

THE PHONE RANG. ANGELIQUE opened her eyes to the brilliance of a tropical morning assaulting the pool just outside her bedroom door. Her head unaccountably throbbed. At least she'd been allowed to sleep past dawn. When the phone rang a second time, she pushed the mosquito netting aside and reached for the receiver, groaning at the simple movement, one that should have been effortless.

"Good morning," she whispered. "This is Angelique." Her brain was groggy, and apparently her clock was unplugged. She had no idea what time it was.

"How's your head?"

It was Houston. He was leaving today—she remembered that—but how would he know about her head?

"Houston?" Stupid question! Of course it was Houston. She'd known that immediately.

"By any other name, it's still me." He chuckled over the line. "Your head? It was pretty bad last night."

"Last night?" She sat up abruptly, and she groaned again, immediately lying back down. "Oh, my head!"

"Not better, huh? Listen, I can come over, bring you some lunch, and we can work on that head. Pourrais-je?" His casual French asked if he had her permission. "Coffee will help."

"Pourquoi pas?" Without thinking, she automatically answered him in kind. Her reply asked, Why not? Today, though, foreign languages were the least of her concerns.

She let the phone drop into its cradle, and she groaned, that one simple movement almost too much to bear. What had she done last night? Then, she recalled it had something to do with the rooster, and she groaned again, feeling embarrassment flood through her.

"Dear heavens! That rooster!" she whispered. She felt her eyes burn, but she hurt too much to cry. All she could do was lie there and whimper, aware that Houston was coming over.

What had she done? And how did he know?

"Dear, dear heavens!" Her lips moved—barely. She didn't know what else to say. Her head hurt entirely too much for anything else.

"HONOLULU Sailing Company. That's the one." Beckie pointed over Riley's shoulder at the computer screen. "See? You can charter boats, and besides, Honolulu's where Granny Swell is. It's the perfect excuse."

He frowned. "I don't know that Houston will go for this. He was up late last night packing, and I'm surprised he's not already gone. I don't think he'll be tricked into Honolulu." He sat back. "It surprised me this morning when he disappeared to Angelique's villa before I had a chance to speak to him." He chuckled.

"He can't leave yet, Dad." Buzz took his father's laptop, and he typed in a rapid set of keystrokes. "Besides, he doesn't have to go to Honolulu. See? One of the charters is right here on Maui. They can come to our beach to pick us up." The boy grinned with his revelation.

"That's brilliant, Buzz." Riley pursed his lips in concentration, letting his eyes take in the new information on the screen.

"I don't want to go away, yet. Uncle Houston said I have to go with him whenever he leaves."

"You know you can travel to South Africa with me." Riley turned from the screen and chuckled. "That is if you no longer want to join your uncle on the Formula 1 circuit this year. Then, of course, your next chance will be when you're fourteen, and that's awfully old to travel the world with an uncle who drives fast cars and gets beautiful women. Once you get past thirteen, the women lose interest. Take it while you can, Buzz."

"Dad!" He looked around, his neck turning red. "I want to go, still, but Bahrain isn't until March. I want to stay here until then."

"I think the boy's right." Robby leaned in to tap a couple of keys on the computer, bringing up additional information. "Look. Barebones or crewed? Bobby and I have sailed off the Hamptons. Haven't we, Bobby?" He turned to look out the door at his brother sitting next to the pool. "Bobby? Wake up!"

Bobby lifted his glasses and peered inside the villa. "I'm awake. I remember that trip. You ran us aground. We were stuck for hours until the tide came in. Order up the crewed version." He dropped his glasses back to his face and laid his head back.

"Aground?" Riley looked at Robby.

"I forgot about that." He grimaced. "I've heard Gator can sail, but I don't think he'll exactly be the oil that smooths the romantic waters. Let's go with a crew. It'll cost more, though."

Heather stepped into the room with her purse in her hand, and she pulled out $500. "Here. Beckie and I have this much.

Angelique's our good friend, and we want to do this for her." She wiped tears from her eyes. "She deserves this. Anyone else?" She looked around the room.

Bobby called from the lanai, "I stashed away $1500 in my suitcase. I'll give that if you charter a crewed boat."

His brother turned to him. "$1500? You have $1500, and I didn't know? I passed up Godiva Chocolatiers at the airport, all because we had no money. You have $1500?" His eyes narrowed.

Riley pulled at his sleeve. "I can cover it, Robby. I know you're short. Everybody is. Houston's told me how Lucas helped all of you out, and now, no one knows what was in the will, except Angelique, I expect." He looked around the room. "All of you, whatever you want to put in, I'll cover the rest. This is my baby brother, and he's always been there for me. This Cupid thing may fall apart on us, but if we can get them alone on that boat together, they may just figure out that they love each other. It's worth the chance to me, whatever it costs."

Buzz held his hand up for a high five. "Way to go, Dad!"

Bobby called from the lanai, "I already talked to Treavor and Jerrold. They can do four hundred apiece. I don't know about Gator, but I'll ask. I don't expect anything from him, though. I bet he has zip."

The front door to the villa opened. Treavor leaned in. "Lookout One, here. All's quiet on the Angelique front. Did I hear my name?"

Heather blew him a kiss. "You're committed for $400. It's a go. We're doing the sailboat thing."

"Four hundred? Ouch. I'll have to see how much of that Jerrold has."

"Four hundred, I hope. That's each." She winked at him.

"Double ouch." He made a face, and then he shook his head. "Anything for Houston, I guess. I'll warn you when the couple emerges. So far, they're still inside the villa." He turned to look, and then he reached back inside, holding his thumb and forefinger circled into an all clear sign. "Jerrold is at his look-out, and he says we're still good." He withdrew and closed the door.

"All right," Riley said, turning from the computer. "Since the charter company sails Maui as well as Oahu, let's get Julia up here to see if we can all sail to Honolulu to see Granny Swell. Squeegie will be a big help there. Then we'll arrange it so only Houston and Angelique are aboard for the return trip."

Buzz snickered. "All three days of it."

His father leaned back in the chair and grinned at his tall, red-haired son. "All three days of it. That's right, Buzz. You'd better hope they work things out, because that's when I have to leave. You'll be with me in South Africa or with your uncle wherever he is. It's a coin toss right now: Bahrain, South Africa, or staying here in Hawaii." He shrugged.

"Bahrain's in March, Dad," Buzz reminded him again.

"Practice on the track's not." He leaned forward. "Hous-ton'll find someplace, and if it's in Bahrain, then that's where you'll be." The boy's face fell, and Riley winked at Beckie standing just behind him.

She tiptoed forward and kissed Buzz on the cheek. "Your father loves you, you know. You'll still be here with us. Love never fails. I heard that in a song once." She patted his arm in reassurance. "Let's give Angie and your uncle a chance."

"You think so?" Hope was back on the boy's face.

"I know so." She cupped his chin in her hand. "You can count on it."

HOUSTON SET A TRAY by Angelique's bed, and he looked through the gauzy mosquito netting where her head lay on the pillow. She was beautiful, but that wasn't all there was to this woman. Beauty tweaked the senses, but it was also skin deep. Angelique had that beauty, but she also had much, much more. He had admired her since meeting her in California, and that feeling had grown deeper during the events of the past week and a half.

She shifted in the bed, and guiltily, he called to her in a gentle voice, "Angelique. It's lunchtime. I have coffee for you."

She opened her eyes, turning her head to him. "Houston. Did I really make you turn that rooster loose last night?" She smiled, but it faded as quickly as it was on her lips. She put one hand to her face. "Oh, I must look horrible."

"Not horrible. You chased that rooster with me all the way to Gator's villa." He didn't know how much more she remembered, but there had been a lot. Gator had managed to get quite a stock of liquors from Christian, and he was very inebriated when they arrived. He had been so charming in his bumbling exchange, showing Angelique and Houston how to take his prosthetic leg off and put it back on, even showing them how he maneuvered when not wearing it. Soon, he had convinced Angelique to try a sip of one of his concoctions, and the party had gone downhill from there.

Once all three members of the midnight party were thoroughly soused, they had laughed and shared things they normally would have kept to themselves. Angelique was the one most unused to the loosening effects of alcohol, though, and as she laughed and talked her way through drink after drink, knowing this was Houston's last night on the island, she bled things that she never would have said without the alcohol.

"You know I've loved you always, Houston." She giggled and reached to take his hand. Kissing it, she looked into his eyes. "I love blue, you know."

"Thank you, Angelique. You don't have to say that. I am a big boy." He moved to pull his hand back.

300

"No, no." She put her hand on Gator's prosthetic leg, patting it, her eyes glancing to the man's face just for a second. "I tried to love Gator, you must understand." She hiccupped and giggled. "We jumped off a mountain together. However, we didn't fall into love. We missed the X. Get it? We missed the X?" She rocked in her chair and slapped her hand on her knee, making kissing sounds with her mouth. "X marks the spot?" She giggled again.

"She did, too." Gator grinned wryly.

"Kissed you?" Houston's eyes narrowed at the idea.

Gator laughed. "No, she jumped off a mountain. Rappelling. We did that together, but alas, I discovered your girl was too good for me. I refused her advances." He leaned forward to touch Houston's arm in order to make his point. "I was her second choice, you know. You should. Everyone else does."

Angelique looked seriously at Gator with a frown on her face. "Um, Gator. May I have the arm you insist on touching? I think I would like to be the one to hold it. After all," and she looked at Houston and laughed, "he's not your kind of man."

Houston leaned forward and put his elbows on his knees. He was intrigued, and he wanted to know more. He winked at Gator and turned to Angelique with a humorous smirk on his lips.

"What kind of man am I, Angelique?"

She laughed and put her hand to her mouth, keeping her eyes on him. "Gator, do you have another one of those little bottles with that worm in the bottom? I want to drink the worm." She giggled, with her eyes locked on Houston, as she held her hand out. When a container was handed to her, she put it to her lips and chugged it down, never letting her eyes move.

Houston took the empty bottle from her. "Angelique, what kind of man am I?"

She giggled, reaching to tap him on the nose. "Not one that

would love me, although that didn't stop me from falling in love with you." She blinked her eyes rapidly several times, her face turning pale for a moment. "Riley's lucky to have you, although that didn't help Riley's wife."

"Riley's wife. How does that have anything to do with what kind of man I am?"

She leaned to Gator. "You know this man broke up Riley's marriage. They were living together before Riley got married." She hiccupped and giggled. "Riley and Houston, I mean, and Riley's poor wife didn't know."

Houston quickly corrected her statement. "She definitely knew, Angelique. She had to. Riley and I always lived together. Well, not always, but since we were just kids."

She hooted. "That's a new way to say it! I bet you were just kids, too. Anyway, Gator," she said, motioning, "well, this man here, Houston, I mean, he likes the, um, masculine profile. That's why he can't fall in love with me. I'm more your type, except you don't love me at all. I'm just poor, lonely Angelique, off in Hawaii without a man. Poor, poor Angelique."

When Houston started to speak, she held up a hand to quiet him, and then she put her finger to her lips while she burped. "No, no, Houston. You don't get to talk, yet. You're not even passionate with that man you live with. How shameful! How can you live with Riley and not be passionate with him? You terrible, terrible man." She blinked rapidly as she hiccupped again.

"Angelique," he scooted forward towards her, "I didn't understand you before when you talked about this, but it now sounds like you think Riley and I are more than just brothers. I don't know where you got that idea—"

"Brothers!" She jerked away, nearly unbalancing herself, and hooted once again. "Brothers! The new term, the politically correct term, for two men sharing the same household." She winked at him, making the gesture overly obvious. "With brothers like that, who needs women?" She chuckled. "Hold my hand, Houston. I won't try to kiss you. You are safe with me, even if I have fallen in love with you." She brought his hand to her face, and she held it there for a moment.

"Angelique—" he began, not liking what he was hearing. His friends from the fraternity were exactly what she was describing, but that was not him.

"Houston," Gator interrupted. "I think I understand, and I think I can help. She thinks you and your brother are, well, romantically involved." He turned to her to explain, only to see her head wobbling and her eyes fluttering closed.

Then, in a last effort at chiding Houston for his perceived faults, she pointed her finger at him. In slow motion, her body tilted forward, and her face landed with a thud right in his lap.

"Um, Gator." He looked up. "Help? Please?"

Gator leaned his head back and grinned. "Got her right where you want her, I see."

"She's passed out. Help me get her up." Houston grabbed her head, but she was leaning hard into him, and he couldn't stand without letting her fall to the floor.

Gator did help, but he also winked at Houston. "I think you found out more than you wanted to know. She loves you. Did you catch that, or should I wake her to tell you again?"

"She also thinks Riley and I . . . Gator, how could she? With my brother?" He shuddered. "Does she actually think I would do something like that with my nephew in the same house with us? I can't figure out what took her along that path."

"Um," Gator started, a smirk on his face. "She did marry someone who even I have figured out wasn't interested in women. Then, there's those two decorators, the twins. After that, you also have Jerrold and Treavor. I'm pretty sure Jerrold's in love with Treavor, and Treavor's in love with you,

Houston. You do know that?"

Houston nodded as he helped position Angelique onto the couch, picking up her legs to place them on the seat cushion. "Since college. Treavor's always had a thing for me. I don't think anything of it, anymore. He's just a good friend."

"Well, see it from Angelique's eyes. Your brother gets divorced, and he moves in with you. You come to Hawaii, and you two share a villa. Robbo and Bobby share a villa. Jerrold wants to share a villa with Treavor. Cheeky, that was his name, wasn't it, was apparently intimate with her husband. Are you seeing a pattern here?"

"Enough, Gator. I get the picture. I guess I didn't help, either."

"How?" He walked to his stash. "You want another?"

"No, thanks." Houston sat, taking a moment to look at the beautiful woman lying sleeping just across from him. "I told her Riley and I slept together the first night we met. You know, shared a bed."

Gator turned and laughed. "You did what?"

"We did, you know, but I was three and he was eight. He's adopted, you know. He couldn't walk across the room without me at his side."

"I figured out the adopted part. You two look nothing the same. You told her you're brothers, though. Right?"

"Yeah, but you heard her. Somehow she seems to think it's a euphemism for men who are in love with one another." He leaned back and laughed. "Like Riley and me."

"Like Riley and you?" Gator frowned, one eyebrow arched skeptically.

Houston stood up, slapping the arm of the chair as he did so. "I'm kidding, Gator." He turned and ran his fingers through his hair. "She's really thought that, hasn't she? I never guessed. Now it all makes sense, the comments and innuendos. She's been telling me, and I was so enamored of her that I only heard what I wanted to hear." He laughed again, relief flooding through him. "I was ready to run away. I even rushed Julia to get two tickets, one for me, and another for the boy."

"Airline tickets? Must have been expensive on such short notice." Gator hefted one of the small bottles as if considering his options.

"Yeah. First Class was all that was available. Then, this beautiful woman called me from my room tonight, and we walked the beach. I never dreamed she might really love me. I never dreamed, and I was headed off without even talking to her, really talking to her. My God, how stupid that would have been!"

"So, you're staying, then?" Gator picked up a second bottle at his side and flipped it into the air, catching it in one hand as it fell. "Because I'm not."

"No?" He might have a use for one of those tickets after all.

"Beautiful widow, free vacation in Hawaii. That's why I'm here. I told you that back in New York. Now I'm here medicating my sorrows in alcohol, and I need to be climbing mountains. Switzerland sounds good to me. The Swiss Alps, maybe. First Class, you say?" He looked at Houston with one eyebrow raised before he lifted the bottle in a toast, and then he uncapped it and chugged it down.

"Can you help me out before you go?"

"Sure. What do you need?"

He pointed. "She has to get back to her villa and into bed. I have an airline ticket you can use if you do."

Gator grinned. "I hoped you'd say that, but I wouldn't miss this for anything, ticket or no."

CHAPTER 25

"HAS SQUEEGIE GOTTEN UP?" Angelique pressed the cool washcloth to her forehead, and she held out her empty cup for more coffee. "The coffee helps, by the way. Thanks."

Houston grasped her arm gently to steady it as he refilled her cup. "It's past noon. She's been up half the day."

"Half the day?" She jerked up and then sank back to the pillow with a groan. "What did I do to my head last night?"

"Tried to kill it, I think, or at least the brain cell parts." He chuckled. "Gator helped."

"Gator?" She sank farther into the pillow. "Oh, sweet fashion show runways, don't mention that man to me. Somehow it feels right to blame all this on him. I just know it, although I have yet to figure out why."

He laughed. "Because it's true. However, it won't do you any good to blame him. He's long gone. Early this morning."

"Gone?'' She glared as best she could. "He can't be gone. He has no money. The resort paid for all those escapades we did yesterday. Well, I did, I guess, just not yet." She called to the ceiling, "Thanks, Gator!" She closed her eyes and made attempts to sip her coffee. When Houston didn't volunteer any additional information, she prodded him. "All right, I give. How's Gator gone? Hitchhiking?" She chuckled at her joke and then groaned when it made her head throb once again. Reaching up, she pulled the cloth down over her eyes.

"I gave him one of my tickets."

"Tickets?" She pushed the cloth right back up and looked at him. "What sort of tickets?"

"Airline tickets."

"You said one. You have more?" She sat up, wishing her head wouldn't pound at every single movement. "Why do you have tickets?"

"I told you last night. You don't remember?" He smiled.

"Um." She put her hand to her forehead and closed her eyes in an attempt to focus her thoughts. "You were, I think, opening a tee shirt factory? Was it a contest . . . preshrunk, or something with water? Oh, Houston," she moaned. "How can I be expected to remember something I'm not even sure we discussed?"

"Formula 1, Angelique. I actually have to work for a living, unlike someone who's inherited a trust fund." He grinned. "Actually, though, I'd prefer to do what I do for a living rather than have that trust fund. I always told Lucas that very thing whenever he offered me money. The others from the frat house took it, and a lot, too. It hurt them when he was gone."

She looked at him hard. "Hurt them? Be specific, Houston. Are you talking about emotions or finances?" It had been a bit surprising to her that so many of Lucas' friends would choose to spend six weeks with his widow, a virtual stranger, so quickly after his death. She'd put it down to a free vacation to Hawaii, or perhaps to people who had already altered their schedules to accommodate the trip and didn't want to return to work. She hoped they hadn't followed her hoping for handouts.

"I shouldn't have mentioned that. I didn't mean to, but now that I have, some of the others have been pushing me to find out what Lucas set up for them in his will. You don't have to talk about it, though. I'm not interested in his money, and I'll be glad to tell them to mind their own business."

She laid her head back and closed her eyes, holding the coffee cup out to him. "Take this, please. No, I don't really want to talk about it, but I guess I should. You mentioned a will. There was no will. Lucas had nothing as far as I knew, not outside of the trust fund. There was a clause that dictated I was to inherit; otherwise, from what little Lucas told me, the bankers would have gotten to keep it all."

"He would have been furious. He hated that they had control." Houston chuckled. "Pity he didn't have time to talk to you about it more."

"Pity, yeah. To sum it up, it means I have no idea what Lucas would want to do with all the money." She sighed and pursed her lips in thought before continuing. "Thank you for slathering one more layer of responsibility onto my world. Can you give me some good news now?"

He chuckled. "Gator's gone, except I already told you that."

"Using your ticket to the races. Formula 1. Was it Riley who told me the races started in March? Gator's got a long time to wait."

"I don't think he went to Bahrain. It was unrestricted First Class. He could go anywhere."

"Did I pay for it?" She smiled to show she wasn't complaining. It was enough that the coffee was finally working, and the throbbing in her head was now manageable. "Or should I ask if Lucas paid for it? Everyone seems to want a slice of the trust fund. Maybe I should just give it all to them."

"Don't you dare!" His words were sharp. "They need to grow up and learn to live on what they can earn. That's real life. If you do anything for them, make it a one-time gift, a legacy from Lucas, but the money's yours. Only share what you want."

She grimaced. "My brain won't process all that now. You did bring food? I'm starving."

He laughed. "You're better, too. Otherwise, you wouldn't want to eat. Are you ready to face the marauding masses?"

"Do I have to?" She moaned, sinking farther down into the bedding. "I never wanted to be the center of all this mess. I just want to be me." She let her hand fall back to rest on the linens.

"They are all very nice people, Angelique. If you never offer anything, they won't form a war party. You don't have to barricade your windows or anything like that. Just get to know them. You may decide you like them."

"And I may not." This was still too sudden and too difficult for her to deal with properly.

"You're right. You may not like them, but I've watched you, from the very first time I met you back in California. You're a good person, kindhearted, too, and I've seen you put others above yourself. Remember the fun we had at the luau? That's why I still maintain friendships with these people. Yeah, Lucas was always at the center of it all, keeping us pulled together, but I really like these people. They're good and decent, if a little odd. Give them a chance is all I ask."

"A chance, huh?" She remembered her dream. Houston had named all the qualities her dream Riley had said Houston wanted in a woman. Too bad it had only been a dream. "I can do that, give them a chance, I guess."

"For me, right?" He took her hand in his, and he pulled it to his lips to give it a kiss.

Her heart jumped. The feel of his hand taking hers, and his lips on her skin. It was as if he truly cared for her, and not just as the widow of a friend. She felt her eyes start to tear up, and she turned her head away.

It was the words he said to her next, just before he released her hand, that truly stirred her emotions, although she didn't know whether that was good or bad. He leaned down to her and whispered directly into her ear.

"I'm not the man you think I am, Angelique. I stayed in the hope you'll give me a second chance. You might just like me." Then he released her hand.

She lay frozen in time and emotion, and when she looked up, he was gone. However, she found one flaw in what he'd said. She could never just like him. She was already head over heels most definitely deeply in love with him, and it would seem the quicksand had long ago swallowed her all the way down. She couldn't even make herself mind that he would only ever be just a friend. Oh, she had once hoped for more, but she understood the facts of the situation. Still, she couldn't deny the truth that permeated her very being.

Love had her by the hair, and nothing she did would let her break free, even if she could never truly have the man she had come to love.

BECKIE FLUFFED SQUEEGIE'S hair. With a smile, she cupped the girl's small chin in her hand and raised her face to peer into her eyes.

"What do you want to ask Miss Angie?" She wrinkled her nose, bringing a giggle from the child.

"I want to go see Granny Swell."

"Right." Beckie touched her on the end of her nose. "What else, Squeegie? Remember, love and everyone else?"

The girl bounced in her seat, and she giggled. "I love Granny Swell, and she misses me. I know she does. Can everyone else go with me?"

Beckie clapped her hands together and laughed. "You are so perfect! I love you, Squeegie. How can Angie say no?" She turned to call through the opened door, "The bait's on the hook. Let's go reel our mermaid in."

"Ooh! Fishing!" Treavor came through the door first, his Speedos tight across his hips. "I never fished before." He grinned at Jerrold, who also had on trunks, although his were of the board short variety. "Now, let me make sure I have this down right. We're barging right into Angelique's villa and telling her we're testing all the pools out to see which one's the best, right?" He caught a towel Jerrold threw at him.

"We have the party drinks!" Robby and Bobby walked in wearing matching purple and white trunks, and their latest sunglasses were now brilliant pink.

Heather laughed. "My God, where did you ever find those sunglasses? I have to have some just like that. How wonderful!"

Riley motioned them closer. "Remember, Buzz has to go in first. He'll make sure Angelique's decent—and distracted, too." He turned to his son. "Do you have my computer? Remember, Buzz, just show her the high-speed connections, then happen to surf to the charter cruise site. Make it seem unintentional."

The boy rolled his eyes. "Dad, you've already told me three times. I'm not stupid."

"No," and Riley grinned. "You're thirteen, and this is very important. Repeat it back to me."

He groaned. "High speed, surf, cruise. How hard can this be?"

"Hard enough." Riley stood and looked at his cohorts. "I'll be working on Houston. Julia already has the cruise scheduled. Eight A.M. Now, we just have to get Angelique and Houston on board."

Bobby raised his hand for permission to speak. When no one called on him, he waved it back and forth. Heather laughed at his antics.

It was Beckie who stepped in to help him out. "You don't have to wait your turn, Robby—"

"It's Bobby."

She glanced to him, frowning as he interrupted her. She rolled her eyes before continuing. "Whichever. You just start talking. That's all you have to do. We'll stop and listen to you." Then she slowly repeated his name. "Bobby." Her laughter tinkled. "Robby. Bobby. It's hard to tell the two of you apart, you know."

"It shouldn't be. I'm the better looking one." He cut a look to his brother to see if he'd overheard. Robby was in animated conversation with Jerrold and Treavor.

"How can you tell?" She let her laughter ripple again.

"See my face? It's obvious, I should think. Anyway, how will we get back here if only Angelique and Houston board the boat in Honolulu?"

Riley interjected, "Helicopter. I've contacted Roy Kaimana, the man you saw when he delivered Gator and Angelique on the lawn. He says he can ferry us back if we don't mind flying over some of the most dramatic scenery in the entire world. I told him I thought we could handle that." He grinned, looking around at the assembled mischief-makers. "Any more questions?"

Buzz glanced at Bobby and raised his hand with a grin. "Can we throw water balloons from the helicopter? That would be so cool to watch 'em smack into stuff."

"No, son. No water balloons." Riley stood to make his way to his villa. As he wound through the room, though, he shook his head as he heard Buzz telling more of his plans to anyone who would listen.

"The next time we parasail, I'm taking water balloons up. I'm going to drop 'em on everybody. Anyone on the ground had better watch out—"

That was as far as he got before Riley got to him and hit him on the back of the head, causing the others to laugh.

When he realized everyone else was laughing at him, so did Buzz.

"THAT *IS* FAST. WHERE DID you say you got this computer?" Angelique smiled at the redheaded boy beside her, knowing the one she had brought with her was even faster. "Your concierge?"

"It's Dad's, but you could get one if you want. Julia has them if you just ask."

She smiled again, charmed by his enthusiasm. "I'd need to ask Sven. I think I'll be fine without one of the resort's computers, though."

"Look," he said, tapping on the keyboard. A selection of Formula 1 sites popped up. "I bet I can find Uncle Houston here, pictures and everything."

"You mean Dad Two, don't you?"

"Sure, if you want me to call him that. Dad Two. Here he is!" He sat up triumphantly, tilting the monitor back so she could see better. "That's in Monaco. I've been there. Everybody wears diamonds in Monaco." The picture showed Houston standing beside a black car. He was holding his helmet at his side, and a smile was on his face.

Angelique pulled the computer to her. She had no idea there would be pictures of Houston on the Internet. She could have looked him up anytime. "Can you do just a picture search?" She was finally interested, and for this, she was glad to have Buzz demonstrate the resort's high-speed access.

"Sure," and he grinned. "Watch." He danced across several keys, pushing the enter key several times, and a whole series of images formed a grid across the screen.

313

She looked and pointed. "There, is that the one from Monaco?"

"I think." He slid his finger across the mouse pad and tapped. The picture soon filled the screen. "It's the same. Dad flew me there for that race."

"Dad One?"

"Yeah." He sighed, and his body drooped. "I had to take my schoolwork with me, though, and I only went to one party."

She smiled. At thirteen—or younger, as he'd probably been—just to fly to Monaco for an auto race would be enough for most boys. They wouldn't complain about having schoolwork with them. Buzz didn't realize all the advantages his two fathers gave him. That was as it should be, though. Otherwise, he'd grow up spoiled and self-indulgent.

"You're a lucky kid. Do you know that?"

"I am? Why?" He reached and flicked through several screens, finally pulling up one website that showed pictures of a picnic, with rows of linen-covered tables laden with food. The scenery was beautiful. He looked at her and grinned. "There I am. See?" He pointed, and sure enough, he was standing beside Houston holding a plate of food. In his hand was a glass of wine.

"Wine?" She looked at him and chuckled. "How old were you there, eleven?"

"Probably, or twelve. I don't remember. It was Italy, though. In Italy, everyone drinks wine. I think the water's gunky or something. Anyway, it wasn't very good. I got a soda just after this picture was taken. Something that tasted like strawberry, I think."

He scrolled through the website, past detailed descriptions of the goings-on, and he finally located one picture far down the scroll bar. A car was crashing into a concrete retaining wall, and just above it, several people were looking down, watching the car explode. Clicking the picture, it expanded, and he stroked the mouse pad, tapping several times until it expanded once more. Then he pointed to a slender, blonde-haired woman standing next to a man who was clearly Riley. Both were looking down, horrified at the events taking place just beneath where they were positioned.

"That's my mom." He looked at Angelique and grinned. "Pretty, isn't she?"

"Very," she said. "Your dad, there. Riley, right?" Buzz nodded. "I don't see you." She turned to look at him.

"I was in school. They sent me back early for placement exams. That's the trouble with Italy. The races are in September there, or they were that year, anyway. I couldn't stay."

"So, did your parents know the driver of the car? I don't see how he could have survived. That accident is horrific."

He laughed, pointing to the exploding car. "That's Uncle Houston." He glanced at Angelique and amended his reference. "Dad Two, for you. His car was crushed, but he didn't even get scratched."

"My word, Buzz. How could he walk away from that?"

"Good design, Uncle Houston, er, Dad Two says. I think he calls them crumple zones. He jokes that the cars crumple, but he doesn't." Then he flipped down through several more pictures. "Look at this one. This guy got killed. See? It's burning, and you can't see it. Race car fuel burns without a flame. But if you look right here, you can see heat distortion in the air. It makes what's behind it look wavy. He burned to death. He was one of Uncle Houston's good friends, too."

When he asked her if she wanted to see more racing pictures, she quietly told him no. How horrible, to live so close to death! She wondered if that might have been part of the reason for Riley's wife to abandon him, especially if she'd known about the romance between the two men from the very beginning. Perhaps the death was too much for her. Some women were like that. Angelique knew, however, for a man she truly loved, it would make no difference. It would make her love him more each time she held him, aware that it might be her last.

Buzz caught her attention once again with pictures of sailing yachts plying the waters of Hawaii. He flipped through several, and when he clicked on one link, a charter company from Honolulu appeared on the screen.

"That would be cool, wouldn't it?" He looked at her and grinned. "We could ride on one of those to see Granny Swell. Do you think Squeegie would like that?"

She placed her hand on the boy's arm and looked longingly at the picture. The ship was very large, and its white sails were filled with wind. The people on board seemed to be enjoying themselves thoroughly.

"I would love that, Buzz. I'm sure Squeegie would, too. However, it must be very expensive, and besides, I don't know how to sail."

He clicked on a section of the page, and more information pulled up. "See? You can hire a crew and everything. You don't have to know how to sail or anything."

Just then, a loud knock came at the door. When she opened it, in bustled the twins. They were dressed to swim, and their voices were boisterous and loud.

"Angelique! We're so glad you're up and around. We have a contest going, more of a competition, really, to find out which villa has the best pool. We know you won't mind us just barging through, so we're jumping in for a bit. Forget we're here." They swept on through, and as they tossed their towels onto one of the two chaise lounges, they called back, "Treavor and Jerrold will be through in a moment. Don't mind them. If you've forgotten which one's which, Treavor's the one in the tight Speedos." Their voices cackled with laughter.

Angelique looked at Buzz, and he just grinned and shrugged. No more had his shoulders settled down, when the door rattled again, and in walked Beckie and Heather. Chattering cheerfully, the group's movie star hopeful hung on Beckie's arm; and laughing at something someone had said, the Olympic swimmer was on Heather's arm. As they breezed past, the two women placed a quick peck of affection on Angelique's face, and they laughed and waved.

She frowned. "Buzz—" She dropped into her chair next to the computer.

Then in walked little Squeegie. She had tears on her face, and she was alone.

"Miss Angie, I miss my granny." She snuggled next to her and wrapped her arm around the woman's shoulders. "I want to go see her new house. She might not like it as well as her bridge. What if she's sad?" She reached up to wipe tears away. They were to have been crocodile tears, but now that the questions she had been coached on were actually being spoken, the emotions had become very real.

Angelique reached for her. "Oh, baby. I'll take you to see her. I just have to figure out how."

The girl's tears weren't so much that she couldn't follow her script, though. "Can we go on that?" She pointed to the computer screen.

Angelique laughed. "You and me? That's a mighty big boat for two people."

"Everybody can go!" Her face brightened. "Please, Miss Angie? I want everyone to go with us. We can sing and dance in the wind. I'd like that." She began to twirl around next to Angelique, her hands intentionally brushing Angelique's hair as she turned. "I'm going on the big boat. I'm going on the big boat. I'm going on the big boat." Her words made a chanting melody.

317

About that time, the six adults out at the pool walked back into the villa, patting themselves dry with their towels. Each of them chimed in as the insistent declarations began to flow.

"If Squeegie gets to go, you must invite us, Angelique. Oh, is that the boat?" They crowded around the computer screen. "This will be heavenly. Are you excited?" Turning to each other, they began discussions of how much fun it was going to be sailing on a yacht all the way to Honolulu. Then, they exited the villa with the trip still ringing out among them.

Squeegie grabbed Angelique's arm and laid her head on the woman's shoulder. "Please, Miss Angie. I really miss Granny Swell. Please?"

Angelique kissed the top of her head and looked at Buzz, who grinned back. "All right, Buzz. How do we schedule this? I have no idea how all this works."

A knock at the door interrupted her inquiry.

"Good afternoon, Angelique. It's Sven. May I come in?" When she told him he might as well, he stepped through the door and smiled. "I hope you are enjoying your stay at Blue Water Maui. I understand you would like to book a cruise to Honolulu with Honolulu Sailing Company. They do sail right out of Maui, and I can assure you they are of the highest quality. Would you like me to make the arrangements?"

She looked at him and laughed. "Sure, Sven. Make the arrangements."

"Thank you, Angelique. Your cruise will be leaving the shore at approximately eight tomorrow morning. Bring a bathing suit if you wish, but casual boating attire is recommended. Will there be anything else?"

She waved him out with a shake of her head, but she glared at Buzz. "So, was the website an accident? Or was all this planned?"

He looked astonished. "I'm just thirteen. How smart do you

think I am?"

When he grinned again, she relented and smiled back. "Pretty smart, Buzz, but I think I'm already looking forward to this. It might be fun."

Just then a melodious voice wrapped around her. "It will be fun. I see both of us fell for it."

She pivoted to see Houston. "You're going, too?" When he nodded, she knew there was no think involved anymore. She wouldn't miss this cruise for the world, not if Houston would be there, and even his significant other, Riley, was welcome to join them.

CHAPTER 26

"IT'S BEAUTIFUL!" ANGELIQUE and Houston were the first to board the big sailboat, and now they watched the final tender wend its way through the mild surf to disgorge the last of the seafaring vacationers onto the yacht. She waved at Squeegie sitting in the approaching boat with Beckie and Heather. "We haven't even hoisted anchor, and I'm already glad to be here."

"Miss Angie! I get to ride on the big boat! Thank you, thank you!" Squeegie's high-pitched voice rang shrilly over the water.

"I love you, too!" Angelique blew her a kiss. She turned to Houston, smiling. "Oh, well! It's just money. That's what we're here in Hawaii for, to enjoy ourselves, so forget the numbers." She laughed. "I didn't quite believe Sven when he said it was on the house. Someone's paying for this, and I can't figure out who. You, Houston?"

He shook his head negatively. "I live okay, but not this okay. However, I intend to enjoy it while it lasts. Look. The anchor's coming up, and I do believe the sails are unfurling. I imagine we'll soon be on our way. You say they're serving us lunch? On board?"

"That's what Sven said. Lobster. Let's go explore the boat with our other guests. It might be very educational."

"I like educational." He winked at her. "Certain kinds, anyway."

She took a deep breath and tried to remain steady. That certainly seemed to be one more come-on than a man of Houston's ilk ought to be sending her way. However, it still felt good to her, and she let herself imagine he meant it like it sounded. He couldn't, she knew, but she could enjoy it just the same.

Then the wind caught in the sails, and the ship heeled sharply to the side. She gasped and stumbled, and unable to catch herself, she inadvertently fell right into his arms.

$\mathcal{A}$T THE FAR END OF the ship, Beckie leaned in and whispered into the captain's ear, "Very nice maneuvering, Captain Flannery. I was very impressed." An arm reached over his shoulder, and she slipped a fifty into his blazer pocket. "Thank you, thank you."

Her lips pressed against his cheek before she stepped away, and for the rest of the trip, he was nothing but smiles and good cheer, even when Squeegie opened the case she was carrying, and out jumped an orange and brown rooster, one with long black tail feathers.

$\mathcal{T}$REAVOR LAUGHED, SETTING his martini glass on the yacht's teak table as he turned to Robby. "So, she actually wanted her bedroom painted the color of her underwear?"

Robby was red-faced with laughter. "Yes. She reached under her skirt and pulled them right off—"

"And she tossed them right into Robby's lap. You should have seen the expression on his face!" Bobby wiped tears from his eyes. "And you know the best part? Her husband was sitting right next to her."

Riley held his side and tried to keep from falling onto the deck of the boat. "What color were they, Robby?"

"Red!" He couldn't speak another word. All he could do was nod his head as he put his face down on one arm.

$\mathcal{A}$T THE OTHER END of the boat, Beckie sat with Angelique and Squeegie, enjoying the wind as it swept through their hair.

"The guys are having fun, aren't they?" Beckie pursed her lips in an effort to keep a grin off her face.

"Too much, if you ask me." Angelique looked that direction and shook her head. "Who would have thought decorators led such a colorful life?" She pointed to Squeegie. "Tender ears shouldn't be subjected to such ribald humor, though. Just thank goodness that feathered fowl is locked up below. They'd probably turn it into something foul, too."

Heather stepped up behind them. "I bet Squeegie's seen worse in her years with that Cheeky person everyone talks about. Ladies, I have some interesting news. It seems that we'll have a show as we enter the harbor." She smiled. "Houston's been monitoring the radio traffic. Carnival has come to Hawaii a month early."

"Carnival? Like, Ricky Carnival?" Angelique laughed. "I've heard all about that."

Squeegie sat up and laughed brightly. "Ricky? Cheeky went to see Ricky in Rio." As quickly, she drooped. "I miss Cheeky. He let me bring Granny Swell home."

Angelique patted her cheek. "Sweetie, Rio is a long way from Hawaii. This isn't Cheeky."

Heather knelt in front of the girl to explain just what to look for. "We'll go by this mountain thing right by the water. It's actually an old volcano. Do you know what a volcano is?" Squeegie made an exploding sound and threw her hands into the air. Heather laughed. "That's right. It's on the edge of the water, and Houston heard that a party is going on there. It's driving down the road, blocking all the traffic. We'll sail right by." She patted the girl's head and stood up.

Squeegie grabbed Angelique's arm and looked into her face. When she turned to her, the girl smiled and said, "I've got a secret." Then she giggled.

Angelique laughed and glanced up to see Heather smiling at them. She brushed her hand over the girl's hair as she spoke to her. "If you tell, it won't be a secret any longer, will it?"

The girl giggled again and climbed to Angelique's ear anyway, whispering her words for her alone. When she was finished, she announced to everyone around her, "It's still a secret, and it's just between me and Miss Angie."

Angelique was tickled. It was no secret, however. It wasn't even true. There was no way Houston was in love with her. True, she had fallen into his arms at the start of the trip, but he had only helped her to stand again. It was also true he hadn't pushed her away, but he hadn't exactly held her tightly, either, not for that long. She didn't want to disappoint the girl, though, so she nodded in duplicity.

"It's our secret, right, Squeegie?"

"Right, Miss Angie. Just ours." And that seemed to make her very happy, indeed.

"COME SEE THIS! It's a hoot!" Jerrold hung over the side of the boat and pointed to the train of vehicles on Diamond Head Road. Beckie was on one side of him, and Buzz was on the other.

"Dad!" Buzz yelled back at the others. "Look at the old cars, and they're all decorated. They have old trucks and

323

trailers, too." Loud music with a heavy beat drifted across the water. When Riley and Houston came up from below, they looked and laughed.

"What's that in the back of those two trucks?" Houston prodded his brother. "It looks like two giant devils."

Angelique wrapped herself in Houston's arm to steady herself on the moving vessel. "I think they are. Someone said a while back this was early Carnival. I've been to Mardi Gras, and I think they're similar. Is this what they do in Rio? Wear devil costumes?"

"Oh, Rio is much, much more. But, yeah, those heads are just like Rio." Jerrold grinned. He looked to find Treavor. "Tee, look at this. Those are like those designs Ricky drew up that time. Remember back in that restaurant in New Orleans?"

Treavor crowded in. "Whoa! He must have finally sold them. Go, Ricky! May Rio treat you well." He laughed. "Hawaii's better, though."

Bobby stepped up and crossed his arms on the back of Treavor's shoulders, with a martini glass held casually in one hand. He hiccupped once. "I miss Ricky. I'd like to see him again. Wouldn't it be nice if that really were him?"

Treavor shrugged his arms off. "Over there with those designs? Sure. He'd have Cheeky with him, though. Besides, Ricky's in Rio. Everyone knows that. Even Cheeky went down south."

"Cheeky?" Squeegie turned to Treavor. "I want to see Cheeky." It was clear she still had positive memories of him.

"I've never heard of Carnival taking place in Hawaii, not a real one like in Rio." Beckie seemed puzzled. "Have you, Heather?" She looked around for her yellow-haired friend. "Heather?"

Angelique tapped her on the shoulder, whispering, "She's in the head."

324

"In the head?" Beckie repeated the words indignantly. "What does that mean, in the head?"

"Bathroom, Beckie. She's seasick." Angelique poked her this time, and hard. "Be considerate."

"I didn't know. Sorry. Besides, I want to be there." She shrugged and pointed to the crater and the party encircling it.

Robby stepped up. "It does look like Carnival, although with only half a Carnival. Only the devil heads look like the real deal. I like the streamers all over the cars, though. It's festive." He paused and looked very closely. "Are the dancers on those flatbed trailers naked?"

Bobby laughed and handed him the binoculars. He still held his martini glass, although it was empty now. "Not naked. See? I remembered the glasses. Look, brother, or in your ignorance you'll smother."

Robby groaned. "Not rhymes, again. We're in public, B-Bob. Just be normal."

"Like Carnival?" he said. "Normal, like those heads so tall?" He giggled. "I think I had too many martinis. Sorry, Robby." He hiccupped and stepped back to find a place to sit. "I went to Mardi Gras in New Orleans once." He giggled again. "A bunch of onces, in fact." An impish if somewhat sloppy grin appeared on his face. "I guess the giant devils wanted to come out and play, even if they are a month early." He yelled to them across the water as he stood back up, "February, giant devils! That's your time!" Then he put his fingers to his lips and whispered to everyone else, "I think I'll have just one more martini. Excuse me, all." He wandered off towards the bar.

*A*NGELIQUE WAS VERY AWARE Houston hadn't pulled away from her touch. She watched his face as he glanced at Riley, apparently catching some comment she must have missed, and he grinned and turned back to the events on the shore. She looked for affection in the glance between the two men, the love she knew must have been there at some point, the passion of true intimacy, and she couldn't find it. It was obvious these two men knew each other like two sides of a racing venue program, but this day, their looks were only familial, not passionate.

She laid her head against his shoulder, glad to be able to share him for a moment without feeling as if she were driving him away. She might not have his touch tonight or tomorrow, or even ever after, but she had it in her hands at that moment, and she could revel in the present. It was all she could do, but she must take the moments she was given, and not worry about the rest.

When she shifted her face against his sleeve, wiping the moisture of unintended longing from her eyes, he glanced down at her.

"Are you all right?" He touched her cheek gently. "It's just Carnival, or more accurately, perhaps an early Mardi Gras parade." He leaned his head down to whisper, "I don't think they'd actually have real Carnival here in Honolulu, not unless Cheeky's back, and unless those really are Ricky's designs. Fat chance of that." He chuckled. "Get it? Fat chance? Fat Tuesday?" When she didn't laugh, he moved her hair and kissed her forehead. "I made a joke, Angelique. You're supposed to laugh. Mardi Gras starts on Fat Tuesday."

She looked up at him and smiled, but her eyes were raw. "This is all too perfect, and I know it can't last. I'll try to laugh, though, for everyone else." She let out a very fake-sounding chuckle. "See? How was that?"

He slipped his arm around her. "Why can't all this last? Some good things do." He paused for a moment before he went on. "I can last, if you want."

"You already have someone. Riley." As the yacht approached the harbor, she looked to the shore where the parade

326

was moving off into the distance. She lifted a hand to pull a strand of hair from her face, and she felt her fingers touch the place Houston had kissed. A new bout of moisture surged at her eyes, and she sniffled. "I can't replace Riley, and I know that's the way it is. I just want you two to work things out for Buzz's sake."

"Don't you worry about Riley and me." He squeezed her to his side. "We'll be all right. It's you and me I'm more interested in."

As she looked to him to see just what he meant, they heard the boat's engines rumble to life. With a humming whine, the power winches on the sails began eating the billowing fabric, and Pearl Harbor grew around them as they passed the airport where they had arrived just days before.

It's you and me I'm more interested in. Now, what did Houston mean by that? However, the ship was all a bustle, and there was no time to ask.

"GOOD AFTERNOON. WELCOME to Manoa Senior Care. How may I help you?" The pretty, middle-aged woman smiled as she raised her head from her paperwork.

Angelique looked at Squeegie standing at her side, glad the child would finally see her beloved granny. She gave her a pat on the shoulder and looked up. Before she could answer, Houston began to speak.

"Granny Swell." He glanced to Angelique and chuckled. "That's the only name I know her by. She was to have checked in here just a few days ago."

The pretty woman appeared puzzled for a moment, and then she brightened. "Oh, yes!" She reached to a computer, and she tapped several keys. Smiling, she turned to Angelique and Houston. "Granny Swell is out for the day. Is this her grand-daughter?" She winked at Squeegie, causing her to giggle.

327

"Gone?" Angelique was puzzled. "As in away?"

"Oh, of course. We encourage all our residents to spend time with family. I believe Granny Swell is with . . ." She looked at her paperwork, pulling a clipboard from a shelf. "Here, yes, a Cheeky Zimmerman Rinaldo, and one, um, Ricky Rinaldo." She smiled at that. "Ricky reminded me of the singer Ricky Martin. Is he any relation?"

Houston chuckled. "He wishes, or, rather, Cheeky wishes."

"Well," the pretty woman continued, "Ricky and his wife said they wanted to take Granny to see their Mardi Gras preparations. They intend to return her before dark." She set her clipboard aside.

"But they're in Rio, or so we thought." Then it hit Angelique. "They're married?" She put her hand to her mouth, remembering the affection Cheeky had shown Lucas at the wedding reception. It was no shock, anymore, but it was distressing, nonetheless.

"Oh, I assumed so. Mrs. Rinaldo definitely had on a ring, and a quite nice one." She flashed her own. "I notice jewelry, you see."

"Um, Miss—" Houston had a puzzled frown on his face.

"Missus," she smiled. "Chowski. Marielle, if you wish."

"Marielle, the resort we're at recommended you to us, but it's only been a few days. How would Cheeky and Ricky have been able to find Granny here?"

She laughed gently. "Cheeky's name was on all the paperwork as next of kin. When Blue Water contacted us, they explained the situation, that Granny Swell had been left with them. At the airport, the resort's driver took down Cheeky's information before accepting Granny into his care, and of course, the resort shared that with us." She checked her computer screen and looked up at Angelique. "Would you be Angelique Abercrombie?"

"Yes," and she nodded.

"And you must be Squeegie." She looked at the girl. "What a wonderful name! We all love Granny Swell, already. She does like to pick up pretty things, but we are well equipped to handle that. Don't you worry about her one moment. Do you have a number I can reach you at when she returns?" She smiled very helpfully.

"Um," Angelique fumbled. "We're here for the day on a charter boat. Blue Water is on Maui—"

"Of course, and you have no phone on Oahu. Here." Marielle reached under her desk and produced a simple cell phone. "Feel free to carry this for the day. If you can't get back before you must leave, you can drop it in the mail at any location, even off island." She produced a small padded bag and offered it with the phone. "The mailer is preaddressed, and postage is covered. Will there be anything else?"

Squeegie piped up, "Where did Cheeky take Granny Swell?" The girl's eyes were bright, and she had a smile on her face.

"Oh," Marielle said brightly. "If you came from Maui on a charter, you might have seen them out on Diamond Head Road. Your boat would have passed right by. They've joined one of the local Mardi Gras practice runs. Ricky explained he knows people from Rio who've settled here, and it already feels like home. It seems they're staying for the event and planning to open an art house to expand the Hawaiian consciousness, one devoted especially to Fat Tuesday and Mardi Gras. We have quite a devoted Mardi Gras crowd here in Honolulu. We think they'll be very pleased to have Ricky and his wife here."

"Houston, if they didn't have money before, how can they afford this? It must be very expensive." Angelique wasn't sure how they could be charging this to Lucas' trust fund, but what else could it be?

Marielle chipped in brightly, "Cheeky was very talkative. She said that once she sold Mother's Milk, within hours, art houses started snapping up all her other works. She must be very good at what she does. Her diamond was enormous." Marielle held her own up once again. "I notice these things, you know."

Squeegie squealed, her enthusiasm ear-splitting. "Daddy Cheeky's here to stay! I want to go find him. Can we, Miss Angie? Please?"

Marielle froze at Squeegie's reference to Cheeky as a man, and embarrassment swept over her features. "Cheeky isn't female? I'm so sorry. I didn't mean to suggest—"

Houston laughed. "Don't worry, Marielle. Sometimes even we're not sure." He turned to his two companions. "Do you want to try to find the parade? I don't see how we could miss it."

"Please, Miss Angie?" Squeegie jumped up and down, tugging at her arm. "I miss Daddy Cheeky, and I want to see the parade, too."

She smiled and patted the girl on the head. "Certainly, Squeegie. I'm sure the cab driver will know the way. Are you game, Houston?"

He grinned. "Sure, why not? I haven't seen Ricky in months, and I don't remember him looking that much like Ricky Martin. I want to see what he's had done."

"Done?" Angelique gave him a puzzled look.

"Done, Angelique, like hair, nails, and nose. He might have even had cheek implants, who knows?"

She was aghast. "Cheek implants?" She touched the side of one of her buttocks. "Seriously?"

He took her hand and placed it to his face. "These cheeks. Not the ones he sits on."

Angelique felt her face warm, but she wasn't entirely sure if it was from the mistake she'd made or from the touch of Houston's face underneath her hand. Whatever it was, it also made her heart pound, and it was suddenly very warm inside her lightweight clothing. Too warm, in fact, and all she wanted was to be outside.

Of course, she wanted Houston with her, also, but that was a given. She loved him, indescribably and completely, and she always wanted him with her, even if he loved Riley most of all.

CHAPTER 27

"DADDY CHEEKY!" SQUEEGIE jumped up and down when she saw the head of the giant devil come off.

Cheeky looked around as if unable to comprehend just where his name was coming from. Then, he spied the little girl, and with an expression of surprise on his face, he tapped the second red devil, getting its attention. When the second head came off, there stood Ricky.

"It's Squeegie!" Ricky struggled out of his costume. "Hurry, Cheeky! We finally found her!" They handed the remains of their costumes to those around them and climbed animatedly out of the truck. "Squeegie, darling! We're coming!"

The child turned to Angelique and Houston, and she yanked on their arms, pleading, "Can I go? I'll watch for cars. Please? It's Daddy Cheeky!"

With a smile, they released her, and off she went, straight into the arms of the two men. Ricky picked her up, swinging her around, and she laughed and squealed, holding her hands out all the while for Cheeky.

After a time, he pushed his blond mane from his face, and he smiled distractedly, reaching for the child.

From where they watched, Houston and Angelique heard the men ask her if she wanted to see Granny Swell.

"When we went by Granny's new home to find out about you, she said she didn't know where you were. We brought her with us because we thought she might remember, but she never did." Ricky hugged the child. "Oh, I've missed you so much, darling girl!"

"I was with Uncle Houston and Miss Angie. Granny Swell didn't feel well and had to go away. Like you, Daddy Cheeky."

Even Angelique and Houston could see the glistening of tears in his eyes as he finally opened his arms to really hug the child. "Granny's there on the float, honey. Do you want to go see her?"

From his shoulder, Squeegie turned to Ricky. "Can Uncle Ricky go with me?"

Ricky's expression brightened. "Of course, I'll be there. That's why we came back, to be with you."

HOUSTON TOUCHED ANGELIQUE'S arm, chuckling. "Marielle was right. With his new tan and longer hair, our Ricky does resemble that other Ricky when he was younger."

"Do you think they really want her?" She turned to him. "Obviously, she's excited to see Cheeky, even though he did abandon her at the airport. But does he want her? And Ricky. I don't know."

He smiled. "Oh, Ricky wants the child, I can guarantee you, no matter about Cheeky. He wanted her as soon as Lucas sent her off, just after she was born. However, he was always on the down and out, chasing Carnival all over the world. Now that he and Cheeky are together, and with the money Cheeky seems to

333

be raking in, I don't think you have to worry about her care."

"But Cheeky abandoned her."

"Remember, though, he did raise her for several years, and she survived with him just fine. You saw that. She's bright and healthy as a horse, if a little wild. It was only when Lucas, um, well—"

"Died, Houston. The word is died. You can't take it out of the dictionary."

He smiled. "All right. When he died, I think Cheeky felt adrift. I suspect he abandoned Granny Swell, not Lucas' daughter. Squeegie happened to be collateral damage. He really is a good person. Ricky thinks so, anyway. Ricky will see that Cheeky does her right."

"I still don't understand why, if he abandoned the old woman, now they've come back for her."

"I bet part of the reason they're here is that once Cheeky told Ricky about Mother's Milk, he was strongly encouraged to get her back in the family, quid pro quo, so to speak. As a family member, her contributions to Cheeky's works will be unquestioned. As an abandoned, homeless woman, should the story ever get out, well . . . I'm sure he finally got the point."

"What about their legal rights? With Squeegie?"

He reassured her. "Cheeky already has legal custody. When Lucas' great-aunt died, custody was transferred at that time. That's part of what makes this a relief to me. You never had any legal rights to her. If Ricky and Cheeky want her—and she seems to be happy at the moment—she needs to be with them."

They watched the three walk down the road amidst the emptying flatbeds that in a month would be decorated with flowers and fanciful designs, finally coming to one that still contained a little old woman seated on a rocking chair. Even from the distance, they could hear Squeegie squeal in delight.

Finding a bench at the edge of a parking lot, Houston asked

334

Angelique if she wanted to sit. A feathery tree provided welcome shade, and the smell of brightly colored blossoms filled the air.

"So, she never was mine." Angelique shook her hair from her face and smiled ruefully.

"You took her on as if she was, though." She gave him a sharp look, but he laughed. "You would have reared her, too, I think. Look." He pointed with one hand. "I think those four make a real family. It's love that bonds people together, don't you think?" His remark was intentional, and he grinned. "Angelique?"

"Like you and Riley. Remember that, Houston." Then she sighed. "Should we find the others? After all, our chartered yacht is waiting on us back in Pearl Harbor."

"Sure," he said as he turned his head to her. "If we must. Actually, I thought we should abandon our mucky crew and live on the lam here in this international garden city. Surely we could hide for a couple of years."

She slapped his arm. "Right! You and me? You can't allow yourself to be away from that man you love for that long, not if you want to hang on to your family. It's love that bonds people together, remember? Go find out about Squeegie and Granny, and then we have to be on our way." She pushed him that direction. "Go. Our yacht is waiting, and time is money. Go, you lazy race car driver."

He laughed. He was biding his time. This had become a game. She was in love with him; she'd told him so. Now it was just a matter of how long until he revealed that he also loved her. The timing had to be perfect, too, and that's what he waited for.

THE CAB PULLED UP TO Schooner's Restaurant, just where the docks stretched their fingers into the loch.

"Here?" The driver, his skin glistening in the evening's smoldering heat, turned around and pointed to the door. "It looks like there's a party already going on. You part of it?"

"I don't think so," Angelique said. "Is the other cab still behind us?"

"Already unloading," the driver said, with a glance in the mirror. When Houston handed him a hundred, he looked at it. "Change?"

He shook his head and reached for Angelique's hand. "I think you can see the Arizona Memorial across the water, just on the other side of that bridge."

"Really?" She climbed out and looked. "I think you're right. It's so pretty. Look!" She turned and pointed the other direction. "There's our boat. Where is everyone? I thought we were supposed to board for our return trip."

"I thought so, too, but there's Buzz waving from the restaurant door. I guess we should probably head that way." He called to those from the second cab, "Ricky! Cheeky! Bring Squeegie and Granny Swell! I think we're headed inside."

It was a party to end all parties, and the jokes flowed freely. Squeegie and Granny Swell were made much of, and Ricky and Cheeky had to share their story of how they managed to be back in Hawaii and in charge of the upcoming Mardi Gras festivities so soon after Cheeky had dropped Squeegie and Granny Swell off.

All in all, they had a great time, and when it was time to say good-bye to Granny Swell, Angelique fumbled in her bag and pulled out the care center's phone.

"Houston, I almost forgot. Please give this to Ricky or Cheeky to return to the center. I wouldn't want to steal it."

"Or to have to drop it in the mail?" He chuckled.

She smiled. "Just do it, please. I want to hug Squeegie bye. You know, for a time, I actually thought I'd have to raise her. I didn't know if I was ready."

"You would have been fine." He smiled at her self-deprecation. "I'm sure she can come visit you, if you want."

She smiled and chuckled, but she didn't answer. She wasn't sure she was ready for that, either. Two nights had been quite enough of an introduction to unexpected motherhood.

When Squeegie and her two fathers had been waved away, and Granny Swell was on her way back to the Center, it came time to board the boat. Surprisingly, everyone except Houston and Angelique suddenly had things to do in the restaurant that simply could not wait. When the tender came to ferry the first group back to the boat, they were the only two passengers aboard.

"Houston," she began as the small boat moved slowly to the charter yacht. "There are docks here. Why couldn't the boat have pulled up and let us go directly ashore?"

He picked up one of her hands and inspected each of her nails, one at a time. He smiled at her, murmuring, "Does it matter? I'm liking this."

"Liking what?" She was a little perturbed that this obvious detail should be out of order.

"That no one else is around but us."

"My God, Houston, why should that matter? It's Riley you love. Quit trying to make me feel better." She suddenly didn't feel better at all. She felt she had abandoned Squeegie, even though she knew she hadn't.

He smiled and refused to let go of her hand. "Sometimes we need people to make us feel better. That's all."

She sighed and let it go. Then she remembered. "Houston, when we get out there, we have to let that rooster go. It cannot stay trapped in that box all day."

He slipped his arm around her. "We will. I promise. Feel better, yet?" When she nodded in affirmation, he whispered,

"See, it works."

She jabbed him with her elbow, and when he groaned, she chided, "Do you feel better, now?"

He chuckled. "I suppose so."

"Good." She turned away with a smile.

THE SAILBOAT'S MOTORS rumbled to life, and standing at the rail, Angelique looked at Houston, puzzled. It was when the anchor chain winch began to sing that she knew something was wrong.

"Not everyone's here, Houston. Surely you don't think the captain's leaving." She leaned over the side. "That's the anchor coming up."

"Maybe it's taking too long with the small boat, and he's going to the dock. He knows what he's doing. Trust him." He rested both arms on the rail, looking at the lights glowing across the harbor.

However, as they began moving towards the mouth of the harbor, even Houston frowned. With a look of incomprehension, he shrugged and forced a crooked grin at Angelique before he turned to head to the cockpit. He had barely moved when the sail winches started to hum, and great, white sheets of fabric slowly filled the fading sky.

He rushed down the deck, calling to the captain to wait. There were others onshore that hadn't had a chance to board. They had no other way back to the resort.

"Oh, no," and the captain laughed, fingering the extra tips he had collected from each person who had remained on shore, except from the tall redheaded boy, of course. "Only you two are aboard for the next three days. I do hope you enjoy your sail. The crew will be very discreet, and later this evening I would like to get with you to plan your preferred itinerary." Just then the boat heeled over, and he reached to the dash and killed the motor. "A stiff breeze. Just what I hoped for. You go back forward and enjoy your time with your girl, and I'll keep an eye on all this back here." He gave the wheel a quick spin to bring the big boat firmly into the wind, and it kicked forward with a surge of power.

When Houston returned to Angelique, she glared at his version of the captain's words as if he were completely loony.

"I overheard. Why, even a rainbow trout has more sense than that. I'll go talk to him. How will everyone else get home? They came on this boat." She tensed up, and her eyes grew damp. She stood just as the boat shifted, and she stumbled. Plopping on a raised bulkhead, she whispered, "They're depending on me to take care of them. I can't leave them stranded."

"Angelique," Houston said, cupping her chin in his hand, "I think they did this on purpose. They had to have done so, and besides, I know my brother. It would be just like him to do this. He's done worse to me before."

She looked at him, her tears now threatening to fall. Worse? It was too much to expect from her, that she should handle all this. For two weeks she had been bombarded with new and stressful situations, and this one was the most awful of all. Besides, why would Riley set up his own companion with a woman, even if she was head over heels in love with him?

Unable to control her rising frustration, she barked sharply, "Stop calling Riley your brother. I'm tired of that. Say what you mean, Houston. You won't offend me. I know grown men sleep together. Call him your lover. That's what he is, not your brother."

He laughed, causing her to look at him. "You've got me and Riley all wrong. He is my brother, my real brother. He's not my lover." He winked at her. "Although I will admit, under extreme duress, that I do love him very much. I just like him clothed all the time."

She narrowed her eyes at him. "I saw you pulling his underwear off. Your son calls you Dad Two. You can't deny that." She sat up straighter, really angry now that he was intentionally lying to her. "You said you slept together the first night you met, and look at the two of you! There is no way you have one gene that's the same, not one chromosome! Don't you lie to me! I cannot take any more lies!" Her anger finally spent, she sat crumpled, her emotions drained, too tired to even look at him.

He turned her face with his hand and looked her directly in the eyes. "Love doesn't lie, Angelique, and I know I love you. I've loved you from the time Lucas first brought you to California. I couldn't tell you, though. You were his. I pushed my thoughts of you away. Then, when he was gone, I let myself hope that someday there might be something between us. I knew it was love when Riley held you, and I was insane with anger. That's why we were fighting that day you came in our villa. I accused him of trying to take you from me."

She looked at him, not daring to hope. She loved him too, but she didn't yet dare hope. "You can't be brothers. He would look like you, somehow, in some way." Her words were words of desperation, determination that she would not be made a fool a second time. For all she knew, he did want the trust fund, and this was his bid for it. She wished it had never come to her, not if this was the result.

"He can't look like me, not even if he tried. Not like you mean, anyway. I was three when Riley came to live with me, or my family, really. He was eight when he was adopted into my life. I worshipped him from the time I saw him, and for the first year, I crawled in his bed every night." He chuckled. "I told you I shared his bed, not that I slept with him. Those terms have very different connotations."

"His wife, though." She grabbed at straws to prove him

wrong.

"She was jealous of her own son. That's why she left Riley. I was one more layer in a cake she couldn't stomach. Believe me, I'm very much in love with you, and no man is going to come between us."

Just then, the rooster in its container belowdecks let out a bloodcurdling series of calls, and Angelique jumped. "Houston!"

"What?"

"That rooster cannot stay in that container. Tell the captain, we must go back immediately. That animal must be set free." She stood, determined.

He pulled her back down. "To be set free in Honolulu? I don't think so. How about if I ask him to head directly to the resort? We can set the rooster free there." He smiled at her hopefully.

She sighed, and as he was very close, she let herself melt into his arms. That would give her time to think, and it would also allow her heart to settle down. One thought kept rolling through her mind. He did love her. It was all she could think about. Houston did love her and was here at her side.

The island of Oahu drifted behind them as Diamond Head towered into the sky. The distinctive landmark receded into the distance, but there were soon other islands for them to enjoy along the way. The sound of the water being torn asunder as the boat took possession of the seas sent a reassuring reverberation throughout the hull. Even the evening sun as it fought back the cool ocean breezes was a friend to the two people who were finally finding comfort in each other's arms.

IN AN HOUR OR TWO, Houston knew it would be time to tell the captain the rooster needed to be returned to the resort, and then he and Angelique would have to decide where to go next. Maybe to a courthouse for a marriage license? It seemed he'd heard that in Hawaii, there were no blood tests and no waiting time to get married. Was it too soon for that?

He didn't know, but he liked the idea. He liked it a lot.

Epilogue

Buzz snapped the red, heart-shaped balloon onto the helium tank and let the latex swell to unrealistic proportions.

"Stop!" Heather grabbed his arm, and upsetting his hold on the balloon, it shot off into the sky with a whizzing noise that attracted everyone's attention.

"Aunt Heather, I was just trying to help." He reached for another balloon, trying to hide it in his palm as he did so.

"The staff will do this, Buzz. We've all told you that." She frowned at him to get him to leave the helium tank alone.

"I want to, though. I'm good at it, too." He looked at her with pleading in his eyes. He ignored the truth scattered about in the remains of the shattered balloons that littered the grass all around him.

Closer to the shore chairs were set up, and red and white flowers were grouped into an altar. Even Angelique's mother and her Uncle Barry had flown in for the Valentine's Day ceremony.

Cupid would be proud.

"Ah, kiddo. Go ahead. Let's have some fun." Heather gave in, reaching for a balloon to snap it on the nozzle.

Buzz grinned as he turned up the gas.

IT WAS WHEN ROY Kaimana landed his helicopter, and Squeegie, accompanied by her adopted granny and her two fathers, stepped out, that the ceremony was ready to begin. The actual marriage had taken place weeks ago on a sailing yacht, but that one had been for Angelique and Houston alone. This one was for the entire world, and it was taking place on Valentine's Day on a beautiful beach in Hawaii.

Once again, Angelique was escorted by her Uncle Barry, but this time it was only halfway down the grassy, flower-strewn aisle. There they stopped, and blowing Houston a kiss, Angelique lit a special candle and said a prayer for everyone to hear. Her words were to God, but they were to everyone else, too, and they told how grateful she was that he had given her such good friends who had helped her see that Houston loved her, even when she couldn't see it herself. Then a skinny red-head took over as her escort, and Buzz held her arm all the way to the flower altar. Squeegie was there with the ring, and Granny Swell clapped in exultation the entire time.

It was the fourth time for Angelique to say her vows in half that many months, but as she leaned in to kiss her husband in front of God and everybody, she knew one thing for sure. This time everyone would be watching, and they would know it was for real.